DANGEROUS PASSIONS

Steve gazed deeply into Ginny's eyes and asked, "Is friendship all you want from me? I don't think so."

"I honestly don't know *what* I want from you, Steve."

"I know, and it's trouble for both of us."

"Why?"

"I'm not the settling-down kind. Look for a husband in Texas."

"I'm not searching for a husband, Steve, in Texas or here with you."

Steve bent forward and kissed her, pulling her tightly against him. Scorching heat licked over his body. He felt her tremble in his embrace. She was so warm and willing and eager with her responses. He knew it would be wonderful to teach her lovemaking, to experience it with her. But what would happen after she surrendered to him? Would she endanger his mission? Would she blind him to her possible involvement in his case?

The intensity of Steve's kisses and hunger, and that of her own, alarmed Ginny. Strange and powerful longings filled her, and she knew she would relish his fiery caresses as long as she dared . . .

JANELLE TAYLOR

MIDNIGHT SECRETS

ZEBRA BOOKS
KENSINGTON PUBLISHING CORP.

ZEBRA BOOKS

are published by

Kensington Publishing Corp.
475 Park Avenue South
New York, NY 10016

First Hardcover Printing: October 1992
First Paperback Printing: May 1993
Printed in the United States of America

In memory of

Roberta Bender Grossman

my publisher and friend who passed away on
March 13, 1992.
I shall always remember this wonderful lady with
admiration and affection and with gratitude
for "discovering" me in April of 1981.
Everyone who knew Roberta and was
touched by her magic will miss her.

Dedicated to:

Rhonda Snider,
who has been like an adopted daughter to me for years,
and still is

And,
Angelia "Angie" Holloway Hogan,
who also has been like an adopted daughter to me for years,
and still is

And,
Taylor Hogan,
Angie's first child and the Taylor family namesake

Acknowledgment and deep appreciation to the following individuals and staffs for their kind and generous help with research on this novel:

Ms. Darlene Martin, Chamber of Commerce, Jacksboro, TX

Ms. Judy Rayborn, Ft. Richardson State Park, Jacksboro, TX

Staff of Fort Leavenworth Museum in Ft. Leavenworth, KS

Pine Bluff Chamber of Commerce and Tour Center at Lake Village, AK

Chamber of Commerce, Museum, and Library at McAlester, OK

Welcome Centers at Kansas City, MO and Kansas City, KS

Welcome Center and Battlefield Museum at Vicksburg, MS

Museum at Fort Smith, AK

Garden of the Gods Campground at Colorado Springs, CO

People of Cripple Creek, CO (though I decided not to use their site)

Missouri Department of Natural Resources/Division of Parks & Historic Preservation at Jefferson City, MO

Welcome Center of AL

Welcome Centers and Tourist Bureaus of Savannah and Columbus, GA

The marvelous staff of the Augusta/Richmond County Library in Augusta, GA

And,

most of all, thanks to my husband, Michael, who made several long and rushed trips to videotape locations and to collect research materials.

Midnight Secrets

PROLOGUE

March 13, 1867
Savannah, Georgia

"You aren't going to die, Johanna Chapman; I won't let you."

"You heard what the doctor said, Ginny; it's too late."

"I won't let it be too late; I'll find a way to save you. I'll get another doctor to treat you. He'll make you well; you'll see."

"We must face the truth, Ginny; I'm going to die, very soon. There isn't much time. You must listen to me and do what I say."

"You aren't going to die. You mustn't talk. You need to rest to recover. Yesterday was strenuous for you, the move from the ship and the doctor's examination. It can't be your heart; you're only eighteen. He's mistaken."

"He said I have infection all through my body. That's why I have this fever, why I have trouble breathing, and every part of me is failing."

Ginny recalled the physician's grim words about Johanna's condition. "He's wrong about there being nothing we can do to get you well; there must be a medicine for what's wrong with you."

Johanna took a ragged breath and shook her head of matted curls. "He said there isn't. So did the doctor on the ship. There's nothing anyone can do to make me well. I've been ill

13

for weeks and I'm sinking fast. I've accepted my fate, Ginny, and you must do the same."

"In the six years we've known each other, Johanna Chapman, have I ever lied to you?" After the girl shook her head, Ginny said, "You aren't going to die. I'll send for your father; he'll know what to do."

"You can't. I don't want him to see me end up this awful way."

A tearful and frightened Ginny said, "We've come this far, Johanna, all the way from England to America. We can't stop now; we won't. We'll make it to Texas as soon as you've recovered."

"You're ignoring reality, Ginny, and that isn't like you: I'm not going to get well, ever. I may only have a little while left."

Virginia Anne Marston looked at the feeble young woman who had been her best friend, like a sister to her, for years. She couldn't believe this tragedy was happening; she couldn't allow it to happen. Yet, there was nothing she or medicine could do to save Johanna. They needed a miracle and had prayed for one, but her dear friend worsened every hour. With tears in her hazel eyes, she vowed, "No, I won't believe that. I can't."

"You have to go on to Texas and take my place. You must do what I was going to do. If Father's guilty, you have to punish him for me and Mother."

"Don't think or talk about that trouble today. You need rest. You must take the medicine the doctor left for you; it will ease your pain."

"I need a clear head to think; I don't have much time left."

"Don't give up, Johanna, please. Fight this illness."

"I don't have any fight left in me, Ginny. I'm as weak as a baby. I can't even tend or feed myself."

"Let's talk tomorrow when you're stronger."

"I won't be here tomorrow. We have to settle this today."

"At least nap for a while. I'll get you some hot soup. You hardly ate this morning or at the noon meal. You can't get well if you don't try."

"I'm not hungry, and I'm losing this battle fast. I want to spend my last hours talking with you. Don't deny me that much."

Ginny felt as if each word was a knife in her heart. She wanted to be strong and brave for her best friend, but it was hard. "In a year, we'll be discussing the doctor's mistake over hot tea and scones."

"Don't dream, Ginny; it isn't fair to either of us. You must go to Father and pretend to be me. You must punish him."

"What if your father isn't guilty?" She thought of their recent discovery of a hidden compartment in Johanna's mother's trunk filled with letters from Johanna's father. It had also concealed money that had provided payment for their trip from England to America to reunite Johanna with her father and to aid Ginny's search for hers. "Remember the letters we found in your mother's trunk after she . . . passed away?" She watched in anguish as the girl struggled to speak between gasps for air and increasing exhaustion. She mopped beads of feverish perspiration from her friend's face with a cool cloth. She witnessed torment in Johanna's eyes and heard it in her voice.

"If Mother lied about him betraying and discarding us, why didn't Father contact me during all those years? Why didn't he come after me or send for me? Why didn't he fight for me? He abandoned her for another woman; he adopted an orphan boy and let him take my place. He loved and wanted them, Ginny, not us. He must pay for what he did. Mother died in England. *I'll* die returning to confront him. His selfishness destroyed us, Ginny. He must suffer as we have. I can't exact revenge; you must do it for me. Please, I'm begging you. This is my last request, my dying wish. You're my dearest and best friend, my sister in heart and soul. I can't rest until the past is settled. Only you can do that for me."

Ginny fought back tears as she watched the near-breathless girl work hard to get out those bitter words. "I love you, Johanna, but I can't pull off such a ruse. I'd never fool your father and adopted brother."

15

"You know everything about me, Mother, and my past. You know everything revealed in those letters we found. They can't catch you in a lie, you have all the facts. You can become me and you can obtain justice or revenge for us. We even look so much alike that people have always believed we were sisters. You can use our resemblance and all that information to fool them."

"If I failed, they could have me imprisoned for fraud, or even killed if they're as bad as you and your mother believe." Ginny kept talking to let Johanna rest for a while. "Besides, I have to search for my own father in Colorado. I haven't seen him since I was sent away to boarding school in London, six long years ago. I haven't heard from him in over eight months. I miss him and I'm so worried about him. He said someone had murdered his mining partner and was trying to kill him. He told me to keep his whereabouts secret and to remain in England until he settled his troubles and either came for me or sent for me to join him. I'm the only one from home who knows he didn't die in the war as reported."

"Your father must be dead, Ginny. If he were alive, he would have written again. If you go to Colorado unprepared and penniless, you'll be vulnerable, in terrible danger. We're almost out of money, so you don't have any safe way to get there. If you go to Father's ranch and pretend to be me, you can find a way to get money for your search. It will solve your dilemma, too."

"I couldn't steal from Bennett Chapman and escape scot-free."

"If it's necessary, you could; you must. You know you can't return home. Your stepmother and her new Yankee husband have taken control of Green Oaks. Your father has been declared dead. She ordered you never to return to the plantation; she cut off your funds."

"I know, and I hate it that I'll never see my half sister. She was born after I was sent away. My stepmother and her son were always malicious and devious. I can't go there or let them know I'm back. If it hadn't been for your mother's kindness, I

16

couldn't have finished my last year at school. I would have been put out to fend for myself without funds, home, or family and in a strange country." A bitter taste rose in Ginny's throat when she had to speak favorably of Johanna's mother whom she hadn't liked or trusted. Ginny knew Johanna had persuaded her mother to pay her expenses and the woman had done so to keep Johanna distracted and removed from her ill-gotten lifestyle. "When I locate Father, I'll repay the money she loaned to me."

"What's mine is yours, Ginny; it's always been that way between us. I don't need or want your money; I want and need your help, your promise."

Ginny wished her own mother were alive to give advice, but she had died when Ginny was eleven. That death had compelled her lonesome and tormented father into a terrible second marriage.

As if reading her line of thought, Johanna said, "Cleniece took your mother's place and Nandile took mine. Our fathers were foolish men."

"I can't blame Father for marrying again; he was so lost without Mother. But our lives would have been different if he hadn't met and married that greedy, selfish, and conniving woman. He thought I needed a mother and Green Oaks needed a mistress. He believed she would take away his pain. All Cleniece did was make us both miserable. She never liked me or wanted me around and convinced Father to send me away to school. I know he agreed because he wanted me safe and happy while he was off fighting in the war. He didn't trust her; that's why he deposited enough money in a London bank to pay my expenses for five years. He never thought the war would last so long; no one did. I would have been fine if Cleniece had sent my money. You remember Father sent me money directly from Colorado until he vanished. He was angry when he learned she had refused to support me, but he couldn't challenge her without revealing he was still alive. That witch believed I would be stranded across the ocean and be out of her hair for keeps."

Ginny helped Johanna with a drink of water and fluffed her pillows. She kept talking to make the girl stay silent and rest. "I know she and her new husband stole my home and inheritance, but I won't fight them over it. Green Oaks couldn't be the same after they've tainted it. But if they learned Father wasn't killed in the war, that he was captured and sent west as a Galvanized Yankee, and that he'd found a silver mine—they would try to lay claim to part of it. That's partly why Father refuses to contact her. After he sneaked home when the war ended and found her married to that Yankee usurper, a man my half sister believed was her father, he decided it was best to stay dead to them. His new trouble started after he returned to Colorado. How could anyone believe my father could murder a friend and partner for his share of their mine? It's absurd, and I'll help him prove it. I memorized the map he sent to me, then I destroyed it. I know how to find his cabin and I know where the claim map is hidden."

"Knowing the culprit's identity won't protect you from harm, Ginny. It's in the wilderness. Haven't you heard of wild animals and Indians?"

"I realize my plan is dangerous, but if Father is in trouble, I must help him. If he's dead, I have to make certain his killer is punished."

"Just as I have to make certain our family's betrayer and killer is punished."

"I know this man is guilty; we don't know if your father is guilty."

"He's guilty of forcing Mother to escape him all the way to England. She wouldn't run away without a good reason. When he cut off our funds to force her to come back, she still refused. For a wife to go penniless rather than return home to a rich husband does not speak well for my father. He forced Mother to become that earl's mistress to survive."

"She loved the earl, Johanna; she said so."

"The earl didn't love her. If he had, he would have divorced his wife and he wouldn't have cut off my support the moment her body was cold after promising to take care of me. At least he had the decency to return her belongings."

"Those letters we found from your father disturb me, Johanna. They contradict so many of the horrible things your mother told you about him."

"He never said he loved her or wanted her, only me, his possession. He offered to *bribe* her to return, no doubt to avoid a scandal or because he couldn't stand to lose something that belonged to him. I wonder how he explained our departure to everyone?"

"We're judging him on what your mother told you, Johanna. What if she was speaking from hurt and bitterness? What if she was being vindictive? He said she could have freedom and great wealth if she'd come home or if she would send you home: we don't know what that means. He begged for forgiveness and understanding for his past misdeeds, whatever they were, or she believed they were. He can't be all bad, Johanna. He even admitted he was selfish, a coward. He said he'd made mistakes and that he was sorry for them. We know what two of them were—his mistress and adopted son—but we don't know the story behind them." Ginny spoke with conviction, yet, she couldn't help but wonder if that assumption was correct. Bennett Chapman could be a terrible person. His "son" could be the same, as bad and mean as her own stepbrother.

Ginny looked sadly at her dear, sweet, funny, beautiful Johanna. They had been inseparable for years. They gave each other courage, strength, and solace; they were always there for each other during the good and bad times. *Don't take her from me, God.* "You're asking me to deceive your father by impersonating you when you'll be . . ."

"Gone, dead and buried here, under your name, Ginny."

Tears escaped Ginny's eyes and she quickly brushed them away to prevent upsetting Johanna. "Don't say such things; I can't bear them."

"Don't you see? If you're allegedly gone, your stepfamily will leave you alone while you search for your father. If they learn

19

you're here, they might guess why. That could be dangerous and costly for you and your father. Before you go to him, you can settle matters for me."

"What if I can't unravel this mystery? Surely Bennett Chapman isn't going to confess any serious misdeeds. Maybe he didn't do anything wrong, Johanna. There's far more to the story than your mother or those letters revealed."

"If that were true, he would have tried to get me back. He didn't."

"According to your mother," Ginny reminded gently.

"A man with his power and wealth could have defeated my mother with ease. He had ways and means of reclaiming me. He didn't. He was too busy with his *son* to miss me or care what happened to me. He's twenty-five now, seven years older than I am. Father may have *grandchildren* by now. Even if he refused to support or contact Mother, he owed me those things. He won't even know Mother and I are dead until you tell him. That's wrong and cruel. A few short letters in sixteen years don't make up for his offenses. I deserve retribution or a logical explanation. I can't die in peace until you swear you'll get it for me because I know you won't break your word."

Ginny tried to soothe her friend's agony. "You were taken away when you were two years old, so you don't even know him. If he wasn't being honest in those letters, he'll probably pretend he was the victim of your mother's tricks. How will I know if he's lying?"

"You're intelligent; you'll know. You can watch him for clues. After he exposes himself, find a way to hurt him as he hurt us."

"*If* he's guilty. If not, what do I do? He'll be furious when he learns I'm not his daughter. He'll be devastated to discover the bitter truth."

"Not if you remain there as me."

"What do you mean? Live the rest of my life as Johanna Chapman?"

"Why not? My father is rich and powerful. He deserted me

20

as a child; he owes me plenty. You can collect that debt for me. I'm his rightful heir, not his mistress and adopted son. There's no way anyone could ever learn the truth. It's the perfect solution for both of us. If he's guilty, drain him and punish him. If he's not, make peace and make him happy. You'll have a home, safety, all you need, for as long as you need them."

"What about *my* father?"

"You left word at school where you could be reached. If your father is alive and contacts you, then you can tell mine the truth. I'll write a letter explaining how I forced you to do this for me as my last dying wish. Find the truth for me, Ginny, so I can rest in peace."

"Let's not talk about this anymore. Please rest now and take your medicine. I know you're weak, and in pain. I can see it."

"This is the last time we'll have to talk, Ginny; I feel it all over. I can endure a little pain to spend these final hours with you. I don't want to die drugged or in my sleep or with things left unsaid."

Ginny had to relent once more. "How will I get to Texas?"

"You know where the ranch is located."

"You heard what Mr. Avery said: Train rails were cut during the war and haven't been repaired. He said stagecoach travel is worse. We were going to telegraph your father after we docked and ask for money or transportation. If I contact him and he comes here, he might discover the truth. He could send your adopted brother after me. I doubt he will be happy to have a blood heir suddenly appear."

"You were planning to travel all the way to Colorado by yourself anyhow. You'll find a way. Mr. Avery will help. Remember how he took us under his wing on the ship, how he protected us. He's a good and kind man. He helped tend me after I became ill during the voyage; he brought me here, summoned a doctor to treat me, and he and his sister are taking care of us. You know he's heading for Texas. He'll take you along with him."

"But he knows I'm not you, Johanna. He'll wonder why I'm lying."

"We can trust him, Ginny. He'll take you with him; you'll see."

"Take Virginia along with me to where?" Charles Avery asked as he entered the gloomy sickroom.

"Mr. Avery, we desperately need your help."

"No, Johanna, we can't do this. I can't do this," Ginny protested.

Though he was two inches under six feet tall, Charles sat on the edge of the bed to keep from towering over them. "Do what, young ladies?"

"Ginny must pretend to be me and get to my father's ranch in Texas. She's in danger here from her stepfamily. After I'm dead and buried as Ginny Marston she can travel there with you as Johanna Chapman."

Charles patted the sick girl's arm. "That isn't possible, Johanna dear. Only families are allowed on the wagontrain. These people are moral Christians. They wouldn't allow an unmarried young woman to travel west with a single older man, friend or not. And Virginia can't take her own wagon; they're scarce and expensive, so are supplies and mules."

Johanna gazed into his clear blue eyes that mutely apologized for having to disappoint her. At least he hadn't pretended she would recover. "She has to reach Texas, sir. Her father has enemies in Georgia and out West who might want her slain or captured. She must pretend to be me and go to Texas until she can contact him to come for her there. Father and I were going to help her. Now that I'm dying, things have changed."

Charles Avery ran his hand through his graying brown hair. He stood and said, "Let me think for a minute."

As he did so, Ginny helped Johanna with more water to wet her dry throat. They had met the lean, fifty-four-year-old Georgian on the ship from England. They had talked every day, shared activities and amusements, eaten together, and become good and trusted friends. He had protected them from unwanted attention by sailors and other male voyagers. He had helped Ginny with Johanna after she took ill.

"I must get to Texas to my new business before the seller moves and leaves it abandoned. I can use assistance with the wagon and chores. By helping you, I'll be helping myself. She can travel as my daughter. She's the same age and physical type as Anna. The poor girl was in school up North during the war and she died recently on her way home so no one will be the wiser." Both girls looked away to give him privacy as he wiped sudden tears from his eyes. "It will be hard work, Virginia; you'll have to learn to drive a wagon and work along the trail like everyone else. The men are meeting with Steve Carr, our scout and guide, next week for training. I'm to get my wagon ready and join them Wednesday. The group is gathering at the Ogeechee River east of town. Most are heading west for new lives. The war and that so-called Reconstruction Act have ruined things for Southerners. The women begin training as soon as we finish our own, in a week or so."

Johanna grasped Ginny's hand and squeezed it with her remaining strength. "I'm begging you to do this favor for me. We've been like sisters. You know I would do it for you. Please."

"It's a wild scheme, Johanna. I could fail or get into terrible trouble."

"They'll never guess the truth. Only you and Mr. Avery will know it."

"I will not betray your confidences," Charles Avery assured. "I'll do whatever I can to help."

"Thank you, Mr. Avery. Do it, Ginny; for me, for us."

"You win, Johanna: I swear I'll carry out your last request, but only if you take at least a little of your medicine, eat something, and rest."

"That sounds like a fair bargain to me," Charles said. "I'll fetch a tray."

"Thank you, Mr. Avery. Thank you, Ginny."

* * *

Near midnight, Johanna Chapman died with Virginia Marston sitting beside her and holding her hands. She wept while Charles Avery and his elder sister, Martha, tried to comfort her. He said he would handle the burial arrangements and pay for them; he would have the young woman interred under Ginny's name. He told Ginny it would be best if she stayed in Savannah with his sister until he came for her, which would allow her time and privacy to deal with her grief and to prepare for her journey.

Ginny thanked them for their kindness and assistance. A clock chimed midnight. So many dark secrets engulfed her. She had made Johanna a deathbed promise that she must honor. With her final breath, Johanna Chapman had thanked her, then smiled and gone to sleep forever.

CHAPTER 1

Twelve days later, Virginia Anne Marston's hazel eyes scanned the crowded and noisy area where a temporary camp was set up on the western bank of the Ogeechee River. Ginny watched the women gathered in a clearing for their instructions. Many of the fourteen laughed and chatted as if they were close friends. She reminded herself they had been given ample time to get acquainted while living there for a week or more while their husbands received their training.

"Miss Avery!" Steve Carr's sharp tone pierced her distraction. He shook her arm until she looked at him. "I need your attention, as well as your body, here this morning. We have no time to waste."

Ginny's face grew warm and flushed with embarrassment. She hadn't realized their guide had arrived and begun their lesson. "I apologize, sir, and it will not happen again," she told him. His eyes were so dark brown that they appeared as ebony as his shoulder-grazing hair. She pushed other thoughts out of her mind and came to alert, thoroughly unsettled.

"Good. As I was saying, ladies, let's introduce ourselves. You'll be living and working as one big family for a long time, so it's best to get off to a friendly start. Some of you are already acquainted, but some have been shy and kept to yourselves; and we have one new arrival this morning."

Ginny felt all gazes look in her direction for a moment.

"Sometimes you'll work alone or with your family, and other times you'll work as a group. Obedience and cooperation are a must on the trail; you are never to let personal dislikes or disagreements interfere with our purpose for being here. My name is Steve Carr; I'm your guide, scout, leader, and boss—whatever you want to call me. I'm in total control of this trip. If you can't obey me without hesitation, don't come along. If you do come with us and cause trouble along the way, you'll be left on that spot. That might sound cruel, but it's for everyone's protection. Is that clear?"

Ginny watched those dark eyes journey from woman to woman and observe each nod her head in understanding and acceptance.

She wished he hadn't embarrassed her over an innocent mistake, and when his gaze reached hers, she said, "I'll obey your orders, Mr. Carr. My name is Anna Avery. I'm Charles Avery's daughter. My father and I are moving from Savannah to Texas." Ginny noticed how Steve's powerful gaze lingered on her as if trying to penetrate her deceptive veil, or maybe that was just guilt gnawing at her for deluding these people, most of whom seemed nice.

"To get under way as soon as possible, ladies, be on time for training and practice every morning and afternoon. We'll start promptly at nine, give you a two-hour break at noon to tend your children, work until five, and quit for you to get your meals cooked, chores done, and children down for the night. The education you're about to receive will move at a swift pace. It will be hard. You'll be sore and exhausted, especially in the beginning. And some of you will be as fussy as a hungry baby past feeding time. But don't let the hardships and pains get to you. When the training is over, you'll be able to take charge of your team and wagon if anything ever happens to your husband . . . or father," he added with a quick glance at the only unmarried female present. "You'll practice along the way to keep your new skills honed. There'll be times when the men

26

need to rest or to ride ahead to hunt fresh meat or cut firewood, so you'll be in charge of driving the wagon to camp."

Steve looked at each woman to make certain all were paying attention. "Today, we'll learn how to harness and tend your team, how your wagon works, and how to take care of it so it won't break down along the way. You won't always be able to ride, so we'll exercise daily to improve your pace, strength, and stamina. This afternoon, we'll begin with a mile walk."

"Walk a mile? After work?" Mattie Epps complained.

"Yes, and tomorrow we'll do the same. We'll increase the distance every two days by a mile. By the time we're finished, you should be able to walk five miles before riding to rest. With possessions and children and sometimes soft ground, too heavy a load will overburden the mules. If you don't take care of your animals, they won't get you far. Treat them as you would family, or better, in some cases. Your lives may depend on them."

"Why couldn't we use oxen, Mr. Carr?" Ellie queried. "They eat free grass, not high grain; and we could eat them later. Why mules?"

"Mules get five miles a day more than oxen, Mrs. Davis," Steve explained to the stout woman. "Every three days by mule team shortens your journey by a day over oxen. What you spend on grain will be less than what you would have spent on added supplies for yourselves on a longer ride. You can't eat mules, unless you get mighty desperate, but they're easier to manage and harness and they make good plow animals. Besides, outlaws don't steal a tough, stringy mule as quickly and easily as a plump, tasty ox."

As Steve grinned, other women smiled and laughed. *A sense of humor to break the tension,* Ginny decided. He sounded educated and he knew good manners, even if he had been curt to her earlier.

"What all do we have to learn?" Mattie Epps whined.

"Driving the wagon, controlling and maneuvering it, circling up for camp and safety, keeping the right pace and distance, crossing rivers, getting out of mud, repairing and replacing broken wheels, calming teams during storms, and defending yourself—things like that!"

"Defending ourselves? From whom?" Mattie asked.

"From bandits and raiders who still roam the land and prey on people," he explained. "If any of you have special feeding times for babies, let me know so I can set our schedule for walks around them."

Considerate, too, Ginny's impressed mind added. She noticed how he had hurried past his first sentence, perhaps to avoid scaring them.

"Any of you ladies know how to harness and handle a team already?"

Ginny watched three of the fourteen women raise their hands. She was relieved she wasn't the only novice in camp.

"How many can ride a horse?" he asked.

All but four hands lifted, and Virginia Anne Marston was delighted she was a skilled rider. She wondered if she should tell him she couldn't ride western-style but she decided not to do so, as it couldn't be much different from English sidesaddle.

"How many of you can load and fire a weapon?"

Ginny noticed how the leader grinned when everyone raised a hand, but something wasn't right about those smiles and grins. *Forced?* she mused.

"Is anyone carrying a child?" He waited a moment then pressed, "Speak up if it's true. I don't want your life or that of the baby endangered. As I told you, this is going to be a tough pace and hard work." No woman responded so Steve continued. "Do any of you have a physical problem that might affect your training or interfere with chores along the way?"

Lucy Eaves raised her hand. "I have a gimp ankle," she said, "but it rarely gives me any trouble."

Steve glanced at the slightly twisted ankle she revealed by lifting her hem. "Be sure to let me know if it does."

"Yes, sir," Lucy replied with a cheerful smile.

"Any questions or comments before we get started?" Steve's

alert gaze drifted from one woman to the next around the circle enclosing him. He didn't care for this pretense of liking and helping these people, but he would do his job and do it to the best of his ability. As soon as he unmasked the culprit he was searching for, he could turn this group over to the genuine wagontrain leader who was awaiting them near the west Georgia line. "Let's get to how a wagon works and how to take care of it," he began his instructions. "Jeff Eaves, Lucy's husband, has loaned us the use of his wagon for today's lesson. Let's gather there," he told them, pointing to it.

Steve looked at the beauty who kept—annoyingly—snagging his eye and interest. "I don't think you want to train in that fancy dress, Miss Avery," he remarked. To everyone, he said, "It's best to wear your oldest clothes, ladies, not things you don't want ruined. If you own pants, those will be easier for you to move around and work in. Don't worry about looking stylish during lessons or on the trail; we'll all be too tired to notice. Let's move out now," he ordered as if leading a cattle drive to market.

The others headed toward Lucy Eaves's wagon, but Steve blocked the disquieting lady's way and asked, "Why don't you make a quick change? I'd hate to see that pretty dress spoiled; and so will you. If you hurry, you won't hold us up too long." He turned and strolled toward the other women, all of whom observed the scene with interest.

Ginny stared into his retreating back before she rushed to the Avery wagon where her trunks were stored. His two remarks had stung. She searched for something more appropriate than the promenade dress she was wearing. When she had dressed this morning in town, she hadn't considered proper attire for her lessons today. She took out a green skirt and blouse and, after drawing the privacy cord, changed clothes. As she fumbled with buttons in her rush not to "hold them up too long," she fumed, *If that was a compliment about my wardrobe, it came through the back door!* Her mother used to tell her, "Pretty is as pretty does." The same was true of handsome, and the leader certainly wasn't behaving that way. March 24, 1867, was not going to be an easy day, she fretted, if he continued to behave in this critical manner.

When Ginny rejoined the others, Steve looked her over with an expression that seemed to ask, *Are those the oldest and worst clothes you own?* She exchanged smiles with Lucy Eaves and Ellie Davis, ignoring him.

"Now, ladies, we can get started." As he pointed out parts of the wagon and harnesses, he explained their functions and care.

Ginny observed the guide with annoyance, baffled by his mercurial ways. He was on one knee as he motioned to the underpinnings of the wagon and detailed its construction. His voice was like gently rippling water as his inflections altered during his explanation. His expression was unreadable. He performed his task with skill and ease, but she sensed he was thinking about something else. Her gaze drifted over his face where not a scar or flaw was visible. Along his chiseled jawline and above his perfect mouth was the dark stubble of one day's beard growth, instead of ill-kempt, it made him appear mysterious and virile. His soft hair was as black and shiny as a raven's wing beneath the sun. She remembered he was tall, about six feet and three inches. Her eyes swept past his face of strong, rugged, and appealing features to shoulders that evinced their broadness and strength through the dark-blue cotton shirt that pulled snugly over his torso as he moved his arms to point out different areas of the wagon.

Ginny found it odd that two pistols were strapped around his waist in a camp so close to civilization. Stranger to her was the fact that they were secured with thongs to his muscled thighs in the manner she had viewed in photographs of western cowboys and gunslingers. The weapons, the initials S.C. intricately carved into the butts and resting in artistically hand-tooled holsters, looked as much a part of him as his darkly tanned flesh. No doubt they provided an important clue to his character; just as the sheathed knife that was strapped to his left leg with its handle peeking over the edge of well-worn boots should tell her

30

he was a man who would defend himself with prowess. She wondered what this man did when he was not guiding wagon-trains west, and if he were married or had a sweetheart. Surely there was far more to him, she concluded, than met the naked eye. It was unnervingly evident to her that concentration would be the toughest part of her training with a man like this as her teacher.

Steve was accustomed to doing and thinking more than one thing at a time, so he knew the beautiful female was studying him and not listening again. He almost corrected her but found it amusing that such a refined lady would find a rough man like him worth her scrutiny. He would be astonished if she could endure the training period; probably within two days she would be begging her father to remain in civilized Savannah, whining peevishly. Surely Anna had been a spoiled, pampered, and wealthy southern belle before the North had challenged the South; and it didn't appear as if the war had changed those things for her. From his observation during the men's training, Charles Avery had not struck him as a scalawag—those greedy and traitorous Southerners who sided with Northern conquerors. He, for one, would never forget or forgive what certain Yankees had done to him in that Union prison after his capture at Shiloh. *Shu*, he had been a fool to get involved in a war that had nothing to do with him.

This particular mission wasn't to his liking, either. Unmasking the cunning man and the illegal group of his that was reported to be using this wagontrain as a cover for transporting stolen gems to a contact out West wasn't the bad part; duping these fine people was. But he always did as ordered. Somehow and someway, he must locate the sinister shipment and stop it from reaching its destination. He must prevent it from being exchanged for arms and ammunition for the Red Magnolias—a band in the Invisible Empire, the dreaded Ku Klux Klan—to use in their evil schemes. The leader of that group was clever; he knew valuable gems would not leave deep telltale wagon ruts as hauling heavy gold would and that the stones could be secreted many places in a loaded wagon or hidden compartment. It was up to him to find the treasure and to expose the culprits responsible.

To keep his mind off Miss Anna Avery, Steve looked at the gentle redhead, Ruby Amerson, who was trying to take in every word he spoke. A young mother of two babies, one a few months old and the other a little over a year, this training period was not going to be easy for her, he was sure, but she had a determined look in her eyes. He liked and respected that, and there weren't many people who extracted those feelings in him. He would do whatever necessary to get to know these people quickly so he could complete his mission and move on to his next challenge.

A child's piercing squeal had captured Ginny's attention; the guide suddenly appeared before her and said her borrowed name with cutting sharpness. Startled, she jumped and jerked her gaze to his scowling face.

"Miss Avery, you can't learn if you don't listen," he admonished with a tone seemingly meant to make her tremble in dread of punishment.

Unaccustomed to the assumed name, she hadn't responded to it immediately. She didn't like being scolded like an errant child. They exchanged challenging looks for a moment before his chilling gaze cleared her head. "I'm sorry, Mr. Carr, but I heard a child scream. I looked to see if anything was wrong."

"Children yell all the time when they're playing, Miss Avery, and I presume their fathers are tending them as ordered."

"Yes, sir," she responded to end the matter. She was miffed by his tone before the other women, who were watching in silence. Her new assessment of him was of an arrogant, rude, and demanding man.

As if reading her dark thoughts, he asked, "Why don't you help me show how to grease axles? That should keep your mind where it should be."

"I'd be delighted," she conceded as she struggled to conceal her vexation and embarrassment. Ginny noticed that only one female, a dark-haired beauty named Cathy King, seemed to find the situation entertaining.

"You'll need the grease bucket from the back," he told her, as if to let her know he didn't intend to wait on her or the others as a servant.

Ginny made her way through the group of women to the location he had pointed out earlier. Lucy, Ellie, and Ruby sent her encouraging smiles. She lifted the container from a hook and returned to her now-grinning teacher with his irritating smirk of victory. She herself did not smile as she asked, "What now?"

Steve took the bucket with a mixture of tar and animal fat, pulled out the swab, and demonstrated on one axle how to apply it in the right places and amounts. "Now, you try it on the other three."

Ginny did her best to repeat his actions. The other women followed her from wheel to wheel to observe. At the last one, she asked Steve, who had been silent along the way, if she had done the task correctly.

"All right for a beginner; you'll do better with practice. Just make sure you don't get distracted and miss a wheel or a spot. If you do, it's certain trouble." He half turned to tell the others to take a break. "But be back here at two sharp, ladies," he added.

In her annoyed state, Ginny let the swab fall lower and stain her skirt. She didn't understand why he was picking on her, unless something he'd been thinking had put him in a bad mood. When she saw what she'd done, she exhaled in irritation. She commanded herself not to let the contradictory man get to her like this.

"It's probably ruined," Steve observed, "but I warned you to wear old clothes."

"These are my oldest clothes," she retorted in a frosty tone and with a matching glare meant to silence him.

"Then you're damned lucky, Miss Avery. The others aren't

as fortunate as you are. I hope you'll do your best not to create envy in them with your good looks and fine clothes."

That's a curious way to compliment a lady after you've humiliated her. "I'll do my best to behave in all respects, sir," she said, her voice dripping sarcasm. "You don't have to be so rude and mean. 'Never let personal dislikes or disagreements interfere with our purpose for being here,' you said earlier. As our leader, mine included, you could follow your own advice and be nice."

His teeth almost gritted out his reply. "I'm not here to be nice, only to get you and the others out West. If I relax as much as you've done this morning, someone could get hurt or killed. Distractions and weaknesses are dangerous. I'm paid to see that everyone—and that means you, too—arrives safe and alive; and I will, in any way necessary, even if it means being 'rude and mean.' I can't afford to be too friendly with people in my charge. If I am, some get lax, take advantage, or get rebellious. I'm sure a charming lady like you will make plenty of friends without needing me as one. See you later."

As he walked away, Ginny wondered what in the world that chiding was about, or if it even referred to her minor misconduct. She hoped he hadn't chosen her to be his example of what happened when he was disobeyed or angered. She didn't need his verbal abuse, not after what she'd suffered recently.

So what if he does have the responsibility of eighty-four people and the displeasing task of training fifteen women! she fumed. *He chose it, so he could be at least pleasant and polite.*

As her thoughts sank in, Ginny realized the seriousness of his job. Maybe he had to be bossy and demanding to maintain authority, discipline, and cooperation. In the past, she'd had teachers like that, and their tough tactics had, in fact, worked to keep their classes in control.

In all honesty, she had provoked him, however unintentionally. She hadn't paid attention or taken the lessons with the gravity they deserved. Perhaps her conduct had come across as an air of superiority. She didn't think she was any better than anyone here. In fact, that moody guide would be surprised by what she had endured and by what loomed before her.

Ginny absently brushed at the axle-grease stain. It not only smeared but had stuck to her hand. She replaced the bucket and headed to the wagon she would share with Charles Avery, her alleged father. He had returned to town to see someone and wouldn't be back for a few days. That was good, for it gave her privacy, fewer chores, and it meant he wouldn't witness her problems before she could correct them.

She wrapped a handkerchief around her sticky hand and sat inside the wagon to stay out of view while she ate the chicken and biscuits she had brought with her. Other women were busy cooking their food or feeding their families or cleaning up after a cozy meal. She shouldn't feel guilty about not having as many chores as they did, or for having more time to rest between training periods. They were the lucky ones; they knew how to cook outside—how to cook period! She had helped Charles's sister Martha for over a week with household chores, but she had only cooked on a stove and never unattended. She stared at the pots in the wagon as if they were enemies out to get her. As much as possible, she must observe the other women and learn from them, preferably while still camped for the week. She could imagine how her ignorance in those areas would amuse Steve Carr, and no matter what she had to do to conceal her inexperience from him, she would do just that.

Ginny changed her skirt and headed to the river with soap to remove the grease from the stained one and from her hand. She knelt on a large, flat rock to work on her smelly fingers. The combination of animal fat and tar was stubborn and resisted her strongest efforts to remove it; and instead of coming off, it spread to clean areas to make a worse mess. What should—

"Use this," Steve offered over her shoulder.

Ginny jumped in surprise. "You move as quietly as a feather falling. What is it?" she asked, looking at the metal cup he was holding.

"Kerosene; it'll cut the grease. Just don't get near a flame until it's scrubbed off or you'll light up the area like a roaring wildfire. Better put cream on afterward; both of those mixtures are harsh on soft hands."

She accepted the cup of strong-smelling flammable liquid and thanked him, wondering how he knew where she was and what she was doing, and why he was being nice suddenly. She rubbed it over her hands, grateful it removed the tar. As instructed, she thoroughly scrubbed them with soap afterward.

Steve had concluded he was being too tough on Anna Avery if he was to get close enough to learn anything from her—if she and her father *were* his target, that was. Clearly she wasn't acquainted with household chores or she'd know lamp oil took off tar, so he hadn't been wrong about her pampered rearing. As she lifted her skirt to pour kerosene on its blackened area, he warned, "It'll take the color out and weaken the cloth in that area." Her response made him chuckle.

"Better faded and thin than to have a sticky mess. I can't use it again like this." She didn't look at him as she added, "It'll give me something imperfect to wear during lessons, which should please you."

She was surprised that Steve didn't comment on her last remark, but he didn't leave, either. She felt his potent gaze on her as she labored on the stain. She warmed and trembled, despite the friction between them. When her task was finished and she saw the truth of his warning, she washed and returned his cup. Holding up the garment, she murmured, "Ruined, but better. Thanks for the help."

"You're welcome, Miss Avery."

As she prepared her items to leave, she looked at him and asked, "I'm not late for class, am I? You didn't come to scold me?"

"No, you have half an hour left. Have you eaten?"

She returned to gathering her things. "Dirty hand and all." When he chuckled, she glanced at him and clarified his apparent amusement, "I wrapped it in a handkerchief so I wouldn't get tar on my food."

"I didn't see you build a fire or cook."

"I ate leftovers."

"From town, because your father ate with James and Mary Wiggins yesterday before he went to fetch you."

"I stayed in town with . . . my aunt, Father's sister, until you were ready for the women."

"A last farewell, eh? More comfortable there?"

"I wouldn't know; I've never lived or traveled on the road before for a comparison. Father insisted I stay there while you men were busy."

"It must have given him a good opportunity to make friends. The way these families are spread out across Georgia and the Carolinas, no one seemed to know any of the others until they came here. Your father must have gotten to know them by eating with a different one each night."

Ginny wondered what was behind his inquisitiveness. Wasn't, she mused, this curious behavior for a man who gave her the impression he was normally a loner and not much of a talker?

Steve watched a curious array of emotions drift across her flawless face. She had expressive green-brown eyes with tawny flecks. Her hair was light brown with golden streaks. She looked around five-and-a-half-feet tall, and was perfectly weighted to that height to be sleek and shapely. He had to admit that she possessed one of the warmest and nicest smiles he had ever seen on anyone. Her voice was pleasing and cultured; she was an educated woman, a refined lady. Steve frowned as his heart pained him with bitter resentment. "Did you hear me, Miss Avery?"

She caught the sudden edge to his voice. "Yes, every word. I didn't know you wanted a response. My father is a very genial and social man. Since he was here alone, it was natural for him to make friends with the others. I hope there isn't anything wrong with them inviting him to dinner."

He had to put distance between them. "Of course not."

"Then to which remark did you want me to reply?"

"I was just making conversation and thought you'd shut me out again."

"I'm not much of a talker, Mr. Carr. If you'll excuse me, I have important things on my mind."

Me and what I'm saying aren't important to a lady like you? "When we take our stroll this afternoon, best cover that head with a big hat. On the trail, you should keep your arms and face protected. You don't want the sun to change that soft, tawny skin to a bright and painful red or to a wrinkled brown, do you?"

She dared not look at him. "I'll follow your advice, thank you."

"We'd better get back to camp."

"I'm going now, sir. I'll put away my things and join you promptly."

"Miss Avery . . .?"

She halted her departure and turned. He hadn't moved. "Yes?"

"Stay attentive this afternoon, and from now on. I don't enjoy scolding you like a child or shaming you before the others. It breeds hard feelings."

Ginny's smile vanished. From the mellow way he'd spoken her name and his friendly words, she'd expected an apology. "Yes, Mr. Carr, it does breed ill will and could create tension in camp. I promise, from now on, I won't concentrate on anything except my lessons. I don't enjoy being humiliated for minor and unintentional mistakes."

"Even *minor* mistakes can get you killed."

"I'm positive you'll teach me and the others how to prevent any."

"I'm glad you have confidence in me, Miss Avery."

"If you weren't qualified, Mr. Carr, you wouldn't have been hired. If you'll excuse me, I have to rush or I'll be in trouble again with the boss."

"Do your best today and I'll say a good word about you to him," he jested as she prepared to leave. She halted a moment

38

but didn't turn or reply. He watched her skirttail sway as she hurried along the path to escape him.

Ginny spread the wet skirt out to dry. *Tact is what you're missing, Steve Carr. Obviously you don't have many occasions to use it.*

She speculated on the leader. He was different from all the men she had ever met, the gentlemen and the rogues. Steve Carr was a blend of both, and he seemed to let whichever facet he wished to reveal surface at his choosing. Maybe he used that trait to keep people off balance or at a distance. Or perhaps he was playing with her from a perverse sense of pleasure at making a lady squirm.

Ginny reasoned she might be overreacting to him because of the secret she was keeping. Yet, that air of danger-if-crossed made her nervous and wary. She had seen it in his challenging gaze, a reflexive warning not to get too close or too nosey. She presumed he could slay in the flicker of an eye if need be and never worry over his lethal action. She wondered if his manner was a result of the war? Years of protecting his very life? A loss of everything and everyone he loved, so little mattered except himself and his pride?

Think only of work, Ginny. You have no time for romance or games, especially with him. Move quickly or you'll be late and provoke him to another verbal attack. She left the wagon to join the others.

CHAPTER 2

Steve instructed the fifteen women on the feeding and watering of the mules. He showed them how to check hooves for painful and possibly crippling splits and stones. He taught them how to examine ears and teeth for problems and how to handle any they found. As he stroked the animal's forehead, he said, "A mule will bite only if he's provoked or mistreated, so don't do either one. Give them good care and affection and they'll get you where you want to go."

Ginny observed the man's gentle treatment of the creature.

"Mules don't spook easily and can be urged into place without much trouble or strength," Steve told them. He demonstrated how to put on a bridle with bit and blinkers, which the animal didn't seem to mind. He slipped on a collar, then showed them how to join the reins, straps, and bands. He added traces and backed the mule into place. With deft hands, he secured the creature to a rear whiffletree, a crossbar that held the leather contrivance fastened in place to pull the wagon. He hitched five others and put them in position, then coupled the six mules into three pairs by chain connecting two collars which kept them under better control.

A long "tongue" separated the two rows of beasts that were standing obediently awaiting their own instructions. When none came, they stood still, not even braying in impatience.

They just flicked their ears to pick up sounds and swished their tails occasionally to discourage pests.

Steve told the women, "Go to your own wagon and work with your team. Get to know them and let them get to know your touch, scent, and voice. Like your youngsters, mules have different traits and personalities; it's easier to manage them if you keep that in mind. I've sent the men and children to another clearing so you won't have distractions."

Ginny was relieved the guide didn't glance at her after his last word. She gave a soft laugh when the jolly Ellie Davis asked, "Or sneak help?"

"Or sneak help," Steve echoed with a genuine chuckle. "I'll come around to help as needed. If you get into a bind, call me. This is a lot of hook-ups and leather to learn and master in one showing. I want you to hitch 'em, then let me check it, unharness 'em, then do it again. You'll practice each day until it becomes a simple chore."

"What if we can't do it alone?" Mattie Epps whined with a pout.

"We stay camped here until each one of you can do your part. The same goes for every step of the training: you learn to do it all before we leave."

"Some of us already know how," Louise Jackson snapped. "What if others can't ever manage it? We shouldn't be held up because of them. Our supplies will dwindle while we sit and wait. I think you should place a time limit on how long they can detain the rest of us."

Steve was grated by her bossy manner but suggested in a polite tone that those of the women who knew how, work with any who have trouble. "By helping them," he explained, "you help yourself because it'll speed up our departure."

"What if that doesn't work?" Louise persisted.

Steve was compelled to back down on his prior threat, which had been used to intimidate the women into doing their best or risk the outrage of fellow travelers whom they were delaying. "If you can't do any of the lessons because you aren't trying hard

41

enough or just don't want to work, you'll be left behind after a reasonable length of time, say . . . eight days."

"That sounds fair," Louise conceded with a toss of her blond hair.

As the women went in different directions to begin their matching tasks, Ginny perceived that Louise had riled Steve Carr, even though no one else seemed to notice. From her position near him, she saw a sudden tautness enter his body and his jaw tighten. She witnessed the icy stare he bored into the blonde's back as Louise departed with a smug smirk. Ginny was surprised he had changed his decision; that showed he wasn't inflexible.

She was glad she possessed a good visual memory. She separated the contrivances into six piles. On the first mule, she repeated the harnessing process she had observed. She talked softly to him and stroked him as she worked. She prayed he wouldn't bite her or get impatient with her nervous fumblings. She'd read and seen that some animals sensed fear or incompetence and became ornery, threatening, or uncooperative.

So far, so good, she encouraged herself. When he was in gear, she tried to guide him into place at the rear of the tongue. He refused to budge! She pulled on the reins, pleaded with him, and finally berated him in whispers in one ear, "Don't be an obstinate jackass's son." The mule gave her a nonchalant glance. "Why are you giving me a hard time? Don't you want us to finish first? Do you want to get your mistress fussed at again?" The contrary beast looked the other way as if bored with her. "If you don't obey, you lazy moke," she threatened, "no sweet and delicious grain for you tonight. Please," she begged him as a last resort.

"It helps to push on his chest here and nudge his shank with your foot there," Steve advised as he demonstrated. "That tells him to back up."

Ginny saw the animal respond to the correct procedure, then stop when Steve pulled on the reins to cease movement. "How was I to know that?" she pointed out. "It wasn't in the lesson."

"An oversight, Miss Avery, since none of mine were obstinate," he observed as she and the animal obeyed and succeeded. "Next, you—"

Lifting the second set of harnesses, she interrupted, "Don't tell me, Steve. Let me see how much I remember. Correct me if I'm wrong."

He caught the use of his first name. "Continue, Anna."

She ignored his grin of amusement as she completed the task, aware of her slip and his response in kind. He had sneaked up unseen and unheard again while she was prattling like a fool to a mule. She was glad her face had not reddened like a vivid sunset to amuse him again. "Right?"

"Right, but you still have tricky connections to master. I'll check on you again later. If you run into trouble, give me a holler."

When Ginny finished and looked around to signal the scout she was ready to have her work checked, she noticed with relief that several other women were still struggling with their own chores. She motioned him over and eyed his effortless approach on long and lean legs. "Ready, Mr. Carr."

He walked around and examined each arrangement. Over the last mule's back, his gaze met hers as he said, "No mistakes. Unhitch 'em and do it again. Call me when you're finished."

Ginny was miffed that he hadn't added something like, *A good job*. Perhaps he had assumed "No mistakes" was sufficient praise.

Ginny and the others rested and chatted while waiting for the last two women, Mattie Epps and Cathy King, to finish. She knew she looked and smelled a mess: sweaty and dirty, wearing mule-and-leather cologne, and hair tousled. Since the others didn't go to freshen up, she didn't want to appear finicky by doing so. Yet, she hated feeling and being seen in this dishev-

43

eled way, especially by the approaching scout who visually inspected her this time like a harnessed creature who couldn't escape.

Steve's gaze took in the sultry Cathy, a black-haired beauty with a spoiled and flirty streak he didn't like. She didn't want to go on this arduous journey, but her husband Ed had given her no choice, and she did nothing to conceal that fact or her displeasure. Steve hoped she'd cool her hot blood before her wanton behavior caused problems for him, as he had more than enough to deal with. It was obvious to him she was late on purpose to snare his attention. Mattie had pulled the same sluggard ruse but for a different reason, with hopes he would cancel the rest of her lesson today—which he hadn't. He wouldn't slack off on any of the women's training for any reason, as he'd agreed to take on this role. "Take a quick break, ladies, for water and . . . whatever needs tending before we take our walk. One mile today. Be ready to move out in ten minutes." He left to take a breather of his own.

"Walk? Exercise?" Mattie complained to Ellie. "I'm ready to drop on the ground and sleep for a year! Haven't we done enough today? We still have chores before bedtime."

"We can't balk, Mattie, or we're in trouble. We agreed to obey him."

"But I just finished, Ellie. I'm tired. You all got to rest a while."

"Because we learned and worked faster," Louise boasted.

"That was hard, and you already knew how to do it. I'll *never* have to do it. Joel will tend that chore on the trail while I tend my own. It isn't ladylike to get filthy and smelly like this; I despise doing men's labors."

"If Joel gets hurt or killed, Mattie, what then?"

In a peevish tone, she spat, "Don't be foolish, Lucy; he won't. But if he does, I'll worry about learning it then."

Louise glared at the group's whiner. "We'll all have our hands full, so learn to carry your own load now or don't go."

"That's hateful, Louise Jackson!"

"It's the truth, Mattie Epps, so stop complaining and do it. If you use only half as much energy doing your lesson as you do whining about *not* doing it, you could be finished real quick and simple."

As the two peevish women glared at each other, Lucy Eaves said, "I'm taking my break before we leave. Anyone else?" she invited.

"Me," Ginny answered, worried over Mattie and Louise's sharp words and sorry attitudes. If she were lucky, she could avoid both women on the trail, as she didn't care for dissension. Elude Cathy, too, she added, as she'd seen the married woman steal improper looks at Steve. She followed Lucy into the trees as she wondered how this lovely woman could walk miles each day on a "gimp" foot.

They trekked half a mile from camp and turned to head back the same way, their pistol-wearing leader out front and prodding them onward. He didn't slow his steady pace to aid the fatigued ones or halt to wait for intentional stragglers. Trying to get finished and rest before taking charge of active children and cooking the evening meal, hardly anyone noticed the greenery and colorful wildflowers of early spring.

Ginny did, but dared not slack off to admire them. She tried to keep as close as possible to the pace Steve set, but a stitch in her side slowed her at the end. The speed and distance he demanded on a first outing was surely unlike a leisurely Sunday stroll! No one wasted energy talking or by trying to match the steps of others for companionship or conversation.

As she entered the edge of camp alone, Steve said, "You look to be in good shape, Miss Avery, but that doesn't mean you can walk all day for a month or more unless you pick up your pace and increase your stamina. I hope you can improve tomorrow. It's hard for me to amble."

"I hope I do everything right from here on, Mr. Carr, so you'll get off my back, especially when I'm doing my best." She

45

left him staring after her, feeling better after her curt retort. She hadn't seen him halt any of the other women to scold their speed. She didn't like being complimented then rebuked. His inconsistent behavior rubbed her nerves raw.

She hated to imagine what demands the future held for her. She glanced back to see him retracing the path to escort the tardy women home, one of whom was the flirtatious Cathy King . . . She gathered her clothes and needed items and headed to the private area the guide had designated for bathing. She passed and spoke to others who were preparing fires or meals, visiting with husbands and children, and doing various other evening chores.

She took a bath and dried herself, then tended a feminine chore that came every month with the cloth pads Martha Avery had helped her make. She buried the used one, covered the disturbed area with a rock, and donned clean clothes. She felt better after removing the grime of today's activities. She dreaded to attack the task ahead—campfire cooking—but she had to eat. As she returned to camp, Ellie Davis solved that problem for her.

The stout and jolly female halted Ginny and asked, "Anna, dear, why don't you join us for supper tonight? No need in you cooking and eating alone. We have plenty and we can get to know each other better that way."

"That's kind of you, Ellie; I'll be delighted, but only if I can help."

"Everything will be ready by the time you put away your things."

"Then you must let me do the dishes afterward."

"That's fine. Hurry before the young'uns start yelling for their food."

Ginny stored her things and returned to the Davis campsite. She smiled as Ellie's husband and their four children were introduced to her and she to them. She took the place on a bench by a table that Ellie motioned to. She bowed her head and closed her eyes as Stuart blessed the food and asked for safety on the trail ahead. Afterward, everyone was quiet, except to ask for the items they wished to be passed along. She realized the children had been taught to be still and silent while eating, so she did the same.

The dishes were done. The well-mannered children, ranging in age from eight to fourteen, were on pallets beneath the wagon. Women gathered in small groups to chat or to listen to music played on a fiddle by Ruby Amerson's husband. The perky redhead was not with him, as she was tending her two babies. She saw Steve summon the men for a short meeting on the far side of the encampment and wondered why.

To prevent disturbing the Davis children, who were trying to go to sleep beneath the wagon, Ellie suggested the two women go and sit on a quilt near a tree to rest and chat. After they were settled, she coaxed, "Tell me about yourself, Anna."

Ginny hated to deceive the sweet woman but she had to keep up her deception. It was the only way for her to reach her first destination, so she must lie with reluctance and a foul taste in her mouth.

Before Ginny began, Lucy and Ruby joined them. They chatted a while about the day's events before Ellie entreated "Anna" to relate her story.

The woman stout of heart and body said, "We shared stories last week, but—since you weren't here—we'll repeat the best parts for you later."

"Wait for me," Mary urged as she advanced in a hurry to join the group. Her damp sandy hair ringed her face with short, bouncy curls. "The boys were so full of energy I couldn't get them to settle down."

"We should have waited for you, Mary dear," Ellie said, "or come to help you finish up. Four kids are a handful; I know mine are."

"After being with their fathers all day, they get rowdy and

restless. I was almost too tired to tuck them in and kiss them good night."

Lucy smiled as she brushed her long dark-blond hair before replaiting it into its thick braid. "That walk wore us all out. I think we have a slave driver for a guide," she jested.

Ruby giggled and whispered, "But he's a fine one to look at all day."

Ellie teased in a matching low tone, "You best not look too long and hard or George will hop on both of you with a brush broom."

In an exaggerated drawl, Ruby said, "It's this fiery red hair I was named for, girls; it flames me up from head to toe when I least expect it. Of course, with two babies to tend and sleeping in the open, it doesn't do me much good to tempt any man to mischief, even my beloved George."

The five women laughed at Ruby's jests and comical expression. Ginny enjoyed the warmth and rapport in the small group, and relaxed.

Ellie warned with a playful grin, "Don't let that King woman see you cast an eye on our Mr. Carr. You don't want to cat fight with her over him."

"You noticed her boldness, too?"

"We all did, Ruby dear. She's shameless and spoiled. Going to be trouble, mark my words," Ellie predicted with a woeful look.

Lucy lowered her brush. "I hope not. Mr. Carr is a nice man, just a little cocky. I like him and appreciate his help."

Ruby and Mary agreed. Ellie winked at Ginny, who didn't voice her opinion of their handsome guide. None of the others had mentioned how he picked on her, but Ginny assumed they couldn't help but notice.

"I'm afraid Louise and Mattie are also going to give him trouble. Us, too. The others seem fine. The Daniels woman is a little hateful at times, but she has a right to be bitter over her losses; those Yanks cost her husband not only the use of his leg but their home. We all have our reasons for anger, but all that

48

can't be changed, so we'd better make the best of our new starts out West."

"You're right, Lucy dear." She glanced at the newcomer. "I suppose we shouldn't gossip about the others like this. Anna must think we're awful."

"No, I don't, Ellie. You four have become close friends. I'm glad you're letting me join your group. Thanks for including me in your circle."

The women felt she was being sincere. Ginny glanced from one to the next and smiled at each woman.

"Please go on with your story, Anna," Mary urged.

With a blend of fact and fiction, Ginny told the four genial women, "I was nineteen less than three weeks ago. My mother died when I was a child, so it makes me sad to talk about her. Father bought a ranch in Texas; that's where we'll be living. He owned several stores before the war, but Yankee taxes were eating them alive. Before they could bankrupt and be taken away, he sold them to purchase the ranch and finance this journey. My aunt owns a small boardinghouse in town; she's planning to sell it and join us later. Railroads should be repaired by then which will make an easier trip for her and it will give Father and I time to get settled."

"Was the war hard on you with him off fighting?" Ellie asked.

Ginny used an apologetic tone and expression as she admitted, "No, because I wasn't home. When things looked bad, Father sent me off to boarding school up north, in Pennsylvania. I was only thirteen, so I was scared at first. When war came, Father wouldn't allow me to return home; he thought I'd be safer there. Sherman's destructive march through Georgia proved he was right. He made me stay until school was over or things improved. When he realized that could be a long time or never and this opportunity arose, he came to fetch me by train. We only returned twelve days ago. I stayed in town while the men trained so I could visit with my aunt before departure."

"I bet you're glad to be out of Yankee land."

"I am, Mary. I hated the cold and icy winters and being with people so different from us and so far away from home. Union girls gave Dixie girls a hard time; we had to pretend to be abolitionists to keep peace. It was a coward's way out and we all hated it, but we had no choice. Some of us were tempted to escape school and come home, but we were afraid of being arrested as southern sympathizers. It was a horrible way to live. We knew we couldn't get home through enemy lines and across raging battlefields. We could have been captured and imprisoned or shot as spies. We had to hide our love and support of the South."

"How awful to live like that," Ruby murmured in empathy.

"I would have been terrified."

"Me, too, Mary," Lucy concurred. "I know you're glad to be back."

"I am," Ginny went on, "but I was shocked by the devastation I saw on the way home. I can't believe how bad things still are. I'll be glad to reach Texas. It will be wonderful to be free and proud again."

From behind the women, Steve reminded, "Texas was a Confederate state and it's under military rule like all the others in the South."

Ginny hadn't noticed his approach again, and was unsettled by his curious presence. Why wasn't he with the men? Why lurk around near the women, eavesdropping? "But it's such a big state and it's not as bad there as it is here. The man who sold Father the ranch said so. Did he lie?"

Instead of answering her, he asked, "Where is your father's ranch?"

If he knew the area, she realized, she could be exposed. Instead of saying Waco, she decided to reply that she didn't know. "You'll have to ask Father," she informed him.

As husbands joined wives in the small group, Steve responded, "I will when he returns. I have friends in Texas, so I might drop by to visit one day to see how he's doing. I like your father and enjoy his company."

50

Ginny didn't believe him. No matter his motive, she wouldn't be with Charles Avery, who would guard her true location. During her fabricated revelations, she'd noticed something to use as an evasion. "Why are the men armed in camp, Mr. Carr?" she asked. "Every one has a rifle within reach."

Mary's husband, James Wiggins, responded before the scout could. "Didn't Charles tell you about the gangs of ex-Yanks and freed slaves who are roaming the South like legalized criminals and attacking innocent folk?" After Ginny shook her head, James continued. "I bet most of them are riding under the cover of that Yankee Loyal League. They claim they want to train black people to become citizens but that's a pile of— Pardon me, ladies, but it riles me. They're nothing but a bunch of outlaws with government protection. Their members spy on honest folk, then attack them without just cause. They find ways to levy fines on us, our women are harassed in the streets just to provoke us, churches are entered and services interrupted, and businesses and homes are confiscated."

Lucy's husband added, "They steal, kill, rape, burn, and imprison decent folk. Some get arrested on fake charges and vanish forever."

"You're right, Jeff," James concurred. "Those Loyal League juries and judges and governors will give even a guilty Northern man a pardon or acquittal if he pays them a bribe."

"The black leagues are the worst," George Amerson stated matter-of-factly. "I admit some of them former slaves were mistreated, but they ain't got reason to take out their hatred and revenge on every white person in the South."

Ellie looked at her mate as Stuart gave his opinion. "That new Reconstruction Act isn't going to work. Greedy carpetbaggers and scalawags and those hot-headed Radicals won't let it. That's why President Johnson vetoed it. As long as they won't readmit us to the Union, allow us to be terrorized and cheated, and keep us under their crushing boots, things will never improve down here. That's why we're getting out while we can.

I don't want my children to endure the shame and anguish we've had to."

"What if some of those gangs attack here?" a worried Mary asked.

"Guards will be posted every night," the observant leader answered, "here and on the trail. That's why we circle up to camp, to be close enough to hear anyone who gets into danger. The men have their assignments. Don't worry; I check the area every evening before I turn in."

"But those raiders usually attack folk in the middle of the night."

"Stay calm, Mary love," James told his wife. "We'll be safe."

"I think it's time for everyone to settle down and turn in," Steve advised. "We all have a busy day tomorrow, especially the ladies."

The people said their good nights and went to their wagons.

Steve turned to speak to Avery's daughter to see if he could learn more from her, but she was gone, probably to avoid him. He shrugged and went to where he was camped near a tree with his horse and sat on his bedroll to think. Her tale had been enlightening, he concluded, but totally truthful . . . ? He didn't think so. Yet, there could be reasons besides involvement in the gem-smuggling scheme for her to mislead the others. He wished he could have overheard everything the women said beneath the tree, as females were more open than men and made more frequent slips. He had been giving the men their guard assignments and advising them to give their wives all the encouragement and help they could during the females' difficult training period. He had sneaked up just as Anna Avery began her personal story. When he sighted the husbands approaching, he had revealed himself to keep from getting caught and arousing suspicions in the wrong person.

He had five suspects so far: the embittered Harry Brown; Cathy's husband, Ed King, bankrupted by the Yanks; the half-crippled John Daniels; Louise's husband, Samuel Jackson who seemed deceitfully quiet and nice; and Charles Avery, about whom he was unsure and uneasy. Maybe Anna's father had fetched her from school up North to use her as a diversional cover for his dirty work, if Avery was the culprit he was seeking. The other men appeared to be open, honest, and sincere about their motives for going west and being on this particular wagon-train.

Steve knew he needed more time to study and ultimately expose his target. From years of experience, he knew how to fake a credible act. But with Anna he was at a total loss. She was unlike any woman he had met. She caused strange and annoy-ing stirrings in him, feelings and reactions that had nothing to do with the case at hand. He found himself thinking about her too much. That had to stop or be controlled.

So did unusual and unwanted twinges of compassion and conscience these pioneers evoked in him. He assumed it was because of the sufferings they had endured during and after the war, the bitterness and resentment they felt, the loss of their roots and pride, and a tragic score that hadn't been settled. He understood such troubles only too well . . . He didn't like getting close to people or feeling sorry for them; that created problems, distractions, and weaknesses that could interfere with his work. He must never be blinded, vulnerable, or betrayed again.

Ginny lay on a pallet inside Charles's wagon. She couldn't imagine what the next few months would bring—but she'd find out soon. It had been a difficult, tiring day. She was too edgy to sleep. In a camp filled with people, she felt alone and fright-ened, in spite of the four friends she'd made and many nice acquaintances. She was plagued by her deception but couldn't confess the truth. It would make her sound terrible and get her kicked off the wagontrain, not to mention getting the gentle Charles Avery into trouble for lying about their kinship.

Ginny's turbulent heart filled with grief and loneliness over the death of her best friend. At times, she believed Johanna's ploy would work like a charm; at others, she feared it wouldn't, and wished she hadn't agreed to the scheme. One thing she knew for certain: she would not emotionally and financially hurt Bennett Chapman if he were innocent. But if he were guilty . . . She'd promised! *Please, Johanna, please, God, help me know the right thing to do when the time comes.*

With Johanna gone, Ginny didn't think she could bear it if her father was dead, too. Anxiety over his safety troubled her. Until the time came to head for Colorado, she must keep worries and fears concerning him off her mind and keep her concentration on current factors.

But Johanna's loss was fresh and painful. The finality of it brought renewed anguish and tears. Ginny allowed the flow; it was needed to cleanse and calm her, especially with Steve Carr harassing her.

She couldn't understand why he picked on her. At times, he seemed to look at her with desire and interest; at others, with almost contempt and anger and a curious suspicion. If only he'd be nice for a while . . .

The scout in mind paused beside the Avery wagon during his last rounds of the evening. His keen ears heard the muffled crying inside. He wondered why Anna was weeping . . . Because she was miserable out of her normal surroundings? Afraid of the journey and new start looming before her? Of what she was leaving behind—or who? Fears of failure? Or because he had hurt her feelings several times today?

The twenty-seven-year-old half-Indian guide didn't know why that last doubt entered his mind, unless it was the way she had looked at him at the river and after their walk. For certain he'd put obstacles in his needed path to her; he'd seen her alter her favorable opinion of him since this morning at their first meeting. He could kick himself for getting so defensive about his strong attraction to her that he overreacted and repelled her with foolish behavior. He was untouchable and unchangeable, so he shouldn't worry about her getting to him enough to cause him the problems and pains like those he'd suffered in the past. She seemed, or *had* seemed, interested in him as a man. Shouldn't he try to take advantage of that opening to obtain needed information?

He was surprised by how quickly she had learned her lessons. He could have given her well-deserved praise as he had with others to warm and to open them up to his probings. Why hadn't he? She could be his target as easily as any of the others present, who all seemed genuine so far—all except for the five men who had caused his honed instincts to go on full alert.

Ginny fed and watered the Avery mules as instructed to give them energy for their joint tasks today. The women's lesson began with how to pack a wagon and secure the load for correct balance and for protection of their possessions.

They gathered around Lucy Eaves's wagon for Steve Carr to explain the correct procedure. He told them to pack from front to back, going bottom to top along the way in three layers. Heavy and bulky items—such as stove, plow, trunks of linens, and out-of-season garments, big tools, small furniture, barrels of household goods such as curtains, and bolts of cloth—went on the bottom and were positioned to spread out their weight for stability. Lighter and sturdier possessions—kitchen items, keepsakes, cook and wash pots, churn, homemade toys, and such—came next and were safeguarded by blankets. Fragile belongings and things needed for use during travel—food supplies, dishes, weapons, clothing, and bedding—were loaded atop the high stacks.

Steve showed them how to use leather straps, cloth strips, and lengths of rope to secure the items in place for maximum protection against breakage. Lamps were suspended from hickory bows that formed the top construction of the wagon beneath its billowy covering of hemp canvas that was waterproofed with linseed oil. Other possessions were secured to the outside of the wagon box, often in wooden containers or suspended from hooks or resting on shelves, such as the fresh water barrel, an easy-to-reach weapon by the driver's seat, crates with chickens, sacks with feed, axes for chopping wood, the axle grease bucket, and saw.

"I want each of you to unload your wagon and begin from scratch," Steve told the women. "Let me check it when it's totally empty, then watch you pack and secure everything as I showed you. While I'm assisting you one at a time, the others can be doing chores or resting or visiting with friends."

"Why is this necessary, Mr. Carr?" Mattie questioned irritably. "If we pack everything we need along the way on top, we won't have to bother the other stuff until we reach our destination."

"There will be times, Mrs. Epps, when wagons have to be unloaded and reloaded. If you learn how, it will speed up those delays on the trail."

"I don't understand. For what reasons?" she pressed.

"Some rivers, the Mississippi for one, are too deep and swift to cross in wagons," he clarified. "You'll have to unload and the wheels have to be removed so we can float or ferry the wagon across, then reload after goods are taken over separately. Other times, loads and wheels have to be removed to repair broken parts. If you have belongings you know will overburden your mules and wagons, get rid of them before we depart or you might have to discard them along the trail. It's best to take them into town and sell them rather than lose their value. The ground gets real soft in parts of Mississippi and Louisiana, so heavy loads become a problem."

"I'm not leaving anything else behind!" Harry Brown's wife said.

Steve tried to appease the embittered woman. "That's fine, ma'am, and I hope it doesn't become necessary to discard anything you love along the way."

"It isn't fair," Mattie said, and Mrs. Brown nodded agreement.

"Sorry, ladies, but it's more important that you, your family, and your supplies get there than keepsakes. The mules can carry only so much."

Louise Jackson scowled at the women and almost commanded, "Stop wasting time, ladies, so we can get finished before the day's gone. The orders are clear, so accept them, bad as they might be."

"Don't be hard on them, Louise; this move is difficult."

"It's hard on everyone, Ellie, but it has to be done. Let's get busy."

Steve forced himself not to frown at the bickering females. "Women with babies and small children will begin first so they'll be ready to tend them later. Get your things unloaded and spread out for my inspection. It's best to pair off to help each other with heavy items."

Before each woman could choose her partner, Steve made his own assignments from his own study of them. Ruby and Mary became a team, as both had babies and were friends. Mattie was put with Louise so the blonde could keep the whiner moving and silent. Dependable, kind, and patient Ellie was paired with Lucy to help the woman with the bad foot. Cathy was told to work with Mrs. Brown, as the resentful older woman might keep the spoiled beauty out of his hair. The other six were put together in three teams of twos. That left Anna Avery to herself, and to him . . .

"You don't seem to have as many possessions as the others, Miss Avery, so my help should be all you need."

"The ranch Father purchased is furnished, so we don't need to carry much with us. Whatever else we need, Father said he'd buy there. He felt it would be an easier and more comfortable journey with a light load."

"You don't need to explain, but thank you for doing so," he replied. "You four teams with babies and small children begin your work now. The rest of you, do as you please for about two hours until we finish."

The women parted to go to their areas. Steve realized that none had balked enough to appear worried about what he might find in her wagon, if the wife knew what her husband might be doing on the sly. He realized what he was seeking could be hidden in the area until departure time, could be with the woman's husband today during this task, or could be in town with Charles Avery.

Steve worked with Mary and Ruby, then with the Brown woman and Cathy, then Louise and Mattie to get the mothers with babies and smallest children finished first. He soon grasped the seeming impossibility of locating a clue with this lesson, which flustered and annoyed him. He kept his feelings disguised by a feigned genial manner. He realized he couldn't search every item and container, and the stolen gems—mostly diamonds—he was seeking could be hidden anywhere and by anyone.

Steve knew his mission was dangerous, as several skilled agents had been beaten and slain while trying to solve this case. The Justice Department knew which group was involved, what their future plans included, and that the gems were being smuggled out on this trip. The many robberies to obtain payment for weapons had alerted the government to trouble and given them a trail to follow for a time. Now, it was up to him—a stranger and an experienced wagontrain scout but first-time master—to complete a mission others had died trying to solve. If this lesson didn't expose the culprit delivering the gems, perhaps large river crossings would. Surely an anxious carrier for the Red Magnolias would safeguard the pouch by removing it from its hiding spot during moments of possible endangerment, so he must keep a sharp eye out to catch the villain.

Ruby and Mary learned fast and were dismissed. Mattie and Louise took longer what with one's whining and the other's bossy delays. As hoped, Mrs. Brown prevented Cathy from trying to stay with him too long. When it came their turns, Ellie and Lucy were swift and smart. One of the other three teams cost him extra time and energy with too many goods.

So far, Steve had seen and sensed nothing to arouse suspicions. No woman had objected to him opening any container, barrel, or trunk to ostensibly see if it was packed correctly to prevent damage. He hadn't detected any location where a secret compartment could be obscured when he'd checked every wagon's underpinnings and wooden bed. He had forced himself to make small talk to evoke the women's feelings about the war, their move, and the problems being left behind. Nothing unusual had been learned. The scout dismissed the seven groups to do chores, rest, and serve their families lunch while he finished his final loading and investigative lesson for the morning: Miss Anna Avery.

CHAPTER 3

Ginny was sitting on the tailgate and reading a book of epic poems by John Milton when she heard the guide give orders to the others before heading her way. She watched his approach in dread of how he would behave toward her today. Sleeves rolled to his elbows exposed hard-muscled forearms and darkly bronzed flesh. A section of ebony hair fell over his left temple and almost concealed that brow from view; its back grazed broad shoulders and made an attempt to turn under. He was clean-shaven, which stressed the squareness of a chiseled jawline. A red shirt enhanced his neat appearance and accentuated his tan. His ever-present weapons—two pistols and knife—warned of a physical prowess not to be rashly challenged. He was a fine specimen of manhood, and her heart fluttered in unbidden desire.

"Ready to begin, Miss Avery?" he asked in a mellow tone.

Ginny put the book aside and hopped down to stand before him. Attired in a split-tailed riding skirt, short boots, and shirt, she hoped she was "properly" dressed today to prevent any curt comments from him. She wanted to start off right, so she smiled cheerfully and said in a polite tone, "Yes, sir. Everything's unloaded for your inspection except for the heavy things."

Steve peered into the white-covered interior. "After I examine this stuff, I'll climb inside to check everything else. No need

60

to pull them out. You two are traveling light, so not much to teach you."

Ginny caught an intriguing change in his tone, as if he were implying that was a curious fact. She didn't think the crowded wagon held a "light" load, but apparently for people pulling up roots and moving far away, it was. "I explained that earlier," she reminded with another friendly smile. "I've been at boarding school for six years, so most of my possessions are clothes and keepsakes; they're in those trunks there."

Steve didn't respond to her words but he did notice the practical manner in which she was dressed today. She didn't act the least bit nervous about his scrutiny, and he was glad. He opened and checked the barrels and crates filled with staples: flour, sugar, salt, pepper, rice, tea, cornmeal, coffee, baking soda, dried beans and fruits, tenderizing vinegar, cured ham, dried beef, salted bacon. "What about eggs and milk?" he asked, not noticing those items.

"Father is bringing chickens when he returns, and he made a deal with George Amerson to purchase milk from him along the way."

It looked as if the Averys were going to eat well during their trip, he concluded. He saw dishes and utensils and cooking ware that included a kettle, two skillets—small and large—coffee grinder, coffeepot, two sharp knives, a Dutch oven, and a ladle for the kettle. Avery carried several weapons—pistols and rifles and plenty of ammunition for both. There was bedding: pillows, blankets, quilts, linens, and waterproof cloths for the wet ground, as most people slept outside beneath or beside their wagons unless the weather was bad. Three crates of canned foods, including homemade soup, caught his attention. A few smaller boxes held medicines, liniments, bandages, candles, matches, writing supplies, and a sewing kit. He found no musical instruments or photograph albums. Odd, he mused, for such a civilized family . . . "You seem to have those jars of vegetables wrapped well against breakage. Some places on the trail can give a jolt to body and possession. Make sure you keep them separated with cloth or paper or you'll have a mess on your hands."

She flushed as she admitted part of the truth. "I'm not much of a cook in the open, so my aunt gave those to us to help out along the way."

Steve chuckled at her expression. In a carefully worded and toned reply to avoid offending her, he said, "I doubt fancy boarding schools would consider that chore an important lesson for a fine lady to need."

Ginny noticed the care he took with his answer and was pleased. Perhaps he had decided a truce was best for all of them. He was being courteous and pleasant, and she warmed to him. "I suppose you're right, but it puts me at a disadvantage for this trip. Ellie, Mary, Ruby, and Lucy have offered to teach me what I don't know."

Steve glanced at her to confirm his conduct was relaxing her. "You seem smart and quick, Anna, so it shouldn't be a problem for you."

She was surprised he used her first name and wondered if it was a slip. "Thank you for the compliment, Mr. Carr."

"Think nothing of it. Be back in a minute," he murmured with a smile as he rounded the wagon to check out the jockey box at the front to find tools and extra wagon parts there.

Steve returned to the spot where the woman waited for him and climbed onto the tailgate. He extended his hand and assisted her into the wagon. He hated to release his grasp but had no reason to continue it. Her hands were as soft as a cloud must be; obviously they didn't do much labor.

"Was I supposed to unload that stuff? I didn't know it was there. I was busy when Father packed the wagon, so I didn't think to check it today."

"No problem, just tools and extra parts." He glanced at the extra front and back wheels, axle, and hand-cranked jack that were stored beneath the driver's seat next to the jockey box. "Your father is certainly prepared for any accident along the trail. A smart man, Anna. You two won't have to worry about being stranded with broken parts. Let's see what else we have in here . . . Four trunks. What's inside?"

Ginny motioned to three and said, "Those are mine," then explained of the fourth, "that's Father's."

"Do you care if I peek inside?" he tested for a clue of reluctance.

Ginny knew the guide couldn't discover anything revealing about her, as she'd left her personal possessions stored at Martha Avery's boardinghouse until she sent for them. She didn't think his "peek" was necessary but gave her permission anyhow. She was confident Johanna's hidden letter wouldn't be found. "Certainly not, but I only have clothes and books, nothing fragile. I don't know about Father's trunk." Maybe Steve wanted to learn more about her . . .

Steve opened her trunks and fumbled through stacks of lovely and costly garments, lacy ladies' "unmentionables," books, inexpensive jewelry, hats, shoes, an old doll, and other items. He lifted the doll and looked at it as if admiring its workmanship. His questing fingers detected nothing suspicious concealed inside, and, oddly, he was relieved.

As if in response to an unasked question, Ginny told him, "My mother made it for me when I was a child. I never could part with it. I'll pass it on to my daughter one day."

Steve remembered that her mother was long dead and heard the love in her tone. He felt the same way about his own mother, who was still alive. "It's pretty and well made. I know it must be special to you. My best friend gave me this knife," he disclosed as he raised his left leg and touched it, "and I'd never part with it." Nor with the matching, engraved pistols from his father, worn to remind him daily of the man's treachery.

Ginny accepted the doll and gazed at it for a moment with misty eyes before she replaced it in the trunk with gentleness and care. The keepsake was the remaining link to her lost mother and she loved it dearly. If her belongings were ever threatened, it would be the first thing she would try to save. She straightened the clothes Steve had mussed.

As she worked, the scout observed her. He liked the way her light-brown hair tumbled from its highest peak to her waist in a display of curls that had gilded edges that shone under the sun like golden tips. He could tell it was soft and wished he could bury his fingers in its abundance. Her expressive eyes were a brown-green blend of allure. She had full lips that enticed a man to want to kiss it, and her nose was a perfect size and shape, as were her cheekbones and chin. She was beautiful and desir—

Ginny's gaze fused with Steve's as she turned to ask what was next. She was astonished to see a seductive and softened glow in those dark-brown depths. She stood near him in the enclosed wagon, its position on the edge of camp not allowing others to view them through the front or back openings. She felt her heartbeat quicken and her breathing alter to a swifter and shallower pace. Curious little tremors with bursts of heat attacked her body. She couldn't move or think of what to say; all she could do was return his admiring stare. She didn't even hear the voices of others or noises of animals not far away. She felt aswirl with new and powerful emotions, and captivated by the irresistible guide.

Steve lifted a long strand of hair that had several waves and curls from root to tip. "You're lucky we won't be going through any Indian territory; hot-blooded bucks would risk their lives to take a scalp like yours. Hair this beautiful would be a prized trophy."

Enthralled by the handsome and virile scout, Ginny's voice was strained as she asked, "Why would they want to kill me and scalp me?"

He looked into her wide gaze. "I doubt any warrior would; he'd keep you for himself, as his slave." At that moment, nothing would be more enjoyable than kissing her, unless it was to lay her on the bedding and make wild love to her. *Shu*, she was a powerful temptation, one he had to struggle to overcome. The way she was looking at him, she would at least accept a kiss, he was sure, but that would be reckless. Steve shook his head to clear it of the unacceptable thoughts racing inside it. "During the journey, Miss Avery, it'll be cooler if you braid it like Mrs. Eaves does. That'll keep it out of your way, too; you don't want it getting tangled on something and causing an accident." He turned from her. "Let me check your father's trunk, then we'll get that other stuff reloaded. You'll need time to eat before we begin our driving lessons this afternoon."

The short and magical spell was broken for her, too. She observed him with intrigue as he examined the contents of Charles Avery's trunk. He didn't strike her as a snoop or a thief, but he *was* oddly inquisitive. Perhaps possessions revealed a lot about people to him and he wanted to know his charges well.

Steve used his knees and hands to shove the trunks into the correct positions. "Keep them like that to stabilize your load. Hand me that rope, will you, Anna?"

Ginny obeyed and saw him cut lengths with the large, sharp knife from his left boot. He removed, used, then replaced the blade with fluid motions that said he had done that action many times; she had no doubt he could draw it from its sheath swifter than she could blink. The way he handled the huge weapon told her he was an expert with it. He secured strips around the trunks and tied their ends to the wagon sides to keep the trunks from shifting during movement. She enjoyed watching him work, but wondered why he did the task for her.

After Steve bumped his head on a lantern suspended from a frame bow, he cautioned, "Make sure you keep those empty during travel. You don't want one to fall and spill oil. Besides being a fire hazard, it stinks and can ruin things. Keep your oil container tightly closed, too."

"I will, and thanks for reminding me to check them."

"Let's get the rest of your gear stored." Steve hopped down and handed the items to her as he told her where to place them. He'd learned the Averys had the basic needs and a few extras but, he reasoned, a curiously small load compared to most who were moving west. When everything was inside, he leapt into the wagon again. He eyed her work, smiled, and said, "Good job, Anna. Just remember where and how it all goes when you have to unload along the trail. Any questions?"

"Not that I can think of, Mr. Carr. Thank you for the help."

"You're welcome, Miss Avery. Best eat before our next lesson," he suggested as he hopped to the ground. He assisted her down by a firm and strong grasp around her waist.

"Thank you again, kind sir," she said with a smile.

Steve nodded and left, unsettled by the contact with her. At least, he bragged to himself, she was as disturbed by him as he was by her.

Lucy joined her. "Here's two biscuits with ham, Anna," she offered. "And a glass of milk. It'll save you time. We've all eaten."

"Thank you, Lucy. I'm glad to be finished with one more lesson."

As they sat down for her to eat and drink, Lucy remarked, "Mr. Carr seems nicer to you today. I'm glad. He was a little harsh yesterday."

Ginny lowered the meat-filled biscuit to reply, "I'm sure everyone noticed, and I was embarrassed. I don't know why he picked on me, but he didn't do so today, thank goodness."

Lucy glanced around to make certain no one was within earshot before she whispered, "I think he's taken with you and it makes him uneasy."

"Taken with me? Why would you think that? We're strangers."

Lucy grinned and explained, "All sweethearts start off as strangers, my innocent girl. It's that instant attraction between two people that makes them pursue each other."

"Pursue each other?" Ginny repeated, then felt foolish for echoing the older woman again. "We aren't pursuing each other."

"Not yet," Lucy teased with a sly smile.

"He doesn't even *like* me; that's why he picks on me. He was just being polite today to gain a truce because I scolded him after our walk."

"He's like most men, only being defensive. Love and marriage scare men; they believe they have to resist it with all their mights. Act as if you aren't interested and he'll chase you even more."

"But I'm not interested in him or marriage," Ginny denied the truth.

"Really?" Lucy challenged with a mischievous grin.

"He *is* handsome and appealing, but . . ."

"But *what?* Will your father object to a romance on the trail?"

"No, but I will. I don't think Steve Carr is the kind of man who's interested in settling down, and certainly not with me. Besides, I think he could be dangerous."

"Being a man who can take care of himself doesn't mean he's dangerous. And don't worry about those guns; he is our guard."

"It wouldn't be wise to entice him, Lucy. He's a roaming type. He strikes me clearly as a loner and happy to be one."

"All men are loners until they meet the right woman."

"I don't think I'm the right woman to tame or change Mr. Carr."

"You might be surprised, Anna."

"If we ever got together, I would be shocked."

They shared laughter and the subject was dismissed.

Within a short time, Ruby, Mary, and Ellie joined them. The five women chatted until Steve yelled out, "Ten minutes to go!"

"Teacher's calling and class is waiting, ladies," Ellie jested.

"This is going to be a hard one," Ruby said with a sigh of dread.

"We'll do fine, partner," Mary told her with a wink of confidence.

"We'd better get ready," Lucy suggested.

Steve met with the fifteen women on either side of him at the wagon he had mounted for his demonstration. "As soon as I finish talking, each of you harness your team," he began his instructions. "We'll head westward into the open. These wheels

67

are built to cross rough trails without breaking easily or miring down in soft ground. The front one is smaller to allow sharp turns without gouging into the wagon. The driver sits or walks on the left; don't work the team from the right or you'll confuse them. When we're on roads other wagons and riders are using, keep to the right side to avoid accidents. Most of the time, you and older children will walk to keep the team rested. I have your husbands exercising the children daily to get them into shape for the foot journey. You'll have to take turns resting on the wagon seat or lazy board," he said, pointing to a small seat jutting out from one side.

"I set the pace and you have to keep up. In the event of trouble, signal me with one gunshot if the train gets too far ahead of you. Not more than one, ladies, or you'll spook the animals into bolting. If that happens during a thunderstorm or raid, I'll teach you later this week how to react. Those are your brakes against the back wheels; the lever for them is here," he said as he motioned to it. "Use steady pressure; don't jam it tight. And don't use them unless necessary or you'll ruin them before they're really needed. If you see humps and holes ahead, avoid them. A bad one can break a wheel or an axle; that can get you stranded along the way. Make sure you keep your axles greased and rolling smoothly. That's as much your responsibility as your man's. We'll practice later on hills; they can be tricky if brakes give way. We'll go through everything today then practice daily until you can do this blindfolded. You have to know how to drive, brake, and maneuver your wagon and how to control your team on any terrain and in any weather."

Steve let his gaze drift from woman to woman as he talked to make certain all of them were listening to him and under-standing and to make sure he didn't stare at Anna Avery too long. "I'll show you how to keep the right pace and distance between wagons. We'll do circle-ups tomorrow; they're tricky to learn, too. So is the use of the whip. You want to scare the animals into obedience, but you don't want to harm them. You may get hoarse because you'll do a lot of shouting at them to be heard over the noise of wheels and hooves. Your back and arms will ache at first, but they'll loosen up. It'll help if your husbands give you a good rub at night with some liniment."

Some of the women exchanged smiles of amusement.

"Have your family fed, your chores done, and your wagon loaded and ready to pull out every morning at seven. We rest for an hour in the middle of the day when it's hottest. We camp at six. Bedtime is at nine."

"We'll have that strict a schedule to follow?" Mattie asked with a pout.

"Yes, ma'am, Mrs. Epps; it keeps order. Each day, the lead wagons will be swapped with the last ones; that way, nobody has to eat dust all the time. But if you're late getting started, you fall in at the rear, no matter your assigned position. Understood, ladies?"

Some of the women nodded, some replied verbally, and a couple frowned.

"As I said, signal if you fall too far behind; it isn't safe to become a target for raiders. Don't worry about your milk cows; they'll keep pace with the mules, and so will your horse if you have one."

Ginny felt warmed by the sound of Steve's mellow voice and his nearness. She couldn't forget the sparks between them earlier, and thinking of them made her tingle. He was strong enough to take care of anything and anyone. Too bad she couldn't pursue him as Lucy had teased, as her "strict schedule" wouldn't allow it, and probably his loner attitude wouldn't permit it, either. Still . . .

"When we're in the open, you might have trouble with strong winds swaying your wagons. If it gets too bad, we'll stop to shift loads to that side to help you keep balance. A strong gust can tip a wagon on unlevel ground, especially if the load isn't packed and secured as you were taught. If you're fussy when you're tired and sore, keep to yourself in that condition so you won't pass along that irritation to others. The last two things we'll learn during this week are how to cross rivers and handle stampedes; I'll explain those when the time comes. Any questions?"

Ginny and her friends were relieved when everyone remained silent.

"Good. This is how you handle a whip and reins . . ." Steve began.

After he finished his explanation and answered questions, he sent the women to harness their teams. Only two required assistance. Milk cows and horses were tied to trees to graze, and chickens in small pens were left nearby. Steve showed the women how to make turns to leave their camping spots and how to get in line. When the formation of fifteen wagons was ready, he mounted his horse and rode to the left side of the group so he could be seen by the drivers who sat on that side of their seats. He took a place by the leader, Louise Jackson, as she knew how to handle a team and wagon, and that role swelled her bossy head even more.

"Let's move out!" Steve shouted, and waved his tan hat to those at the rear in case some couldn't hear him. He sat astride a large sorrel and signaled each one at the correct time to pull out to create a safe distance between wagons, which they were to keep unchanged as ordered.

Though little dust was stirred up during their departure in the grassy campground, he could imagine the griping from some when they hit dry-dirt locations on the trail where dust clouds would be as thick as a heavy fog or when mud was ankle-deep and mushy and wheels and hooves would fling it in all directions.

Steve watched Anna Avery click her reins and tongue to get her team moving. He was glad the six mules obeyed so he wouldn't have to ride to her and help. He didn't want the others to think he was giving her special treatment, as jealousy always sparked trouble and ill will.

The Avery mules trudged along as they reached him but kept moving. He noticed how pale and tense Anna looked. He knew that genteel lady must be shaking with panic. As if she wanted to hide those feelings from him, she didn't look his way when she passed him. Too bad he couldn't be driving that wagon and heading out on a long trip with her to spend many a secluded night under a starry—

Steve jerked himself to attention as he almost missed signaling the next woman during his distraction. *Keep your head clear!*

After the last wagon passed him, Steve patted the neck of his reddish-brown horse and murmured, "Let's go, Chuune." He galloped past each wagon to check how each female was doing. He spoke to every one, if only a few words. Again, he traveled from one end to the other as he let them practice their new skills.

The guide rode next to Louise as he told her to make a wide turn and head back toward camp. He stayed in that spot to watch each do the tricky maneuver and gave instructions when needed. He couldn't help but feel pride in himself for the good job he was doing.

He watched the woman in mind make her first turn. She had a little trouble but succeeded. She seemed proud and happy, too; she sent him a quick smile as she passed him this time. He only nodded a response to keep his surge of desire concealed from her and others.

The routine of driving and turning continued for two hours under a late March southern sun that was hot today. Steve removed his hat and used his sleeved forearm to mop the sweat away from his face. He kept his keen eyes sharp for trouble, as the armed camp would need time to respond to any threat he signaled with gunfire. A Henry rifle, a fifteen-shot repeater, rested in a long sheath on his saddle. He was an expert with it and that was no brag, just a many-times-proven fact. Fingertips on his left hand grazed the butt of a Colt-Walker .44 and absently traced the initials carved there. He halted their movement and curled them into a tight ball for a moment as he frowned in the bitterness that never released him from torment.

Ginny was exhausted. There wasn't an inch on her body that didn't protest this abuse. In spite of the wide-brimmed bonnet to shade her face, the bright sun made her squint, made her eyes and head hurt. Her flesh and clothes were damp and her face glistened with perspiration. The thick hair flowing down her back felt like a winter cloak. Tomorrow she would braid it as Steve had advised and hopefully be cooler. She wished she could wear short sleeves, but she knew the sun would bake her arms to a beet red. As for her riding gloves, they were too thin to provide enough protection from the chafing reins that had to be held tighter than a horse's. Steve had warned of the danger of dropping them and losing control of the team. With dragging reins, if the mules bolted, a rider could be bounced off the high seat that lacked a safety grip.

High? her mind scoffed. It was precariously high and rock-hard and scary. Her booted feet used the jockey box below and forward of the seat to brace herself as best she could. She still didn't feel secure, as the jostling of the wagon caused her to lose contact with her prop occasionally. Now that she knew what she was doing, she didn't have to strain to concentrate on the arduous task. She could tell the long ride ahead was going to be monotonous and demanding. Thank goodness she had her four new friends, Mr. Avery, and— *No, you don't have Steve Carr.* At that thought, her concentration vanished.

Steve joined her and shouted, "Pick up your pace, Miss Avery! You're lagging way behind!" As he moved his mount closer, he lowered his voice to a near normal tone. "I know you're tired and bored. Practice staying alert; an accident can happen or you'll get left behind if you're in the rear. The others are in the same condition, but it'll be worse on the trail when this goes on all day, day after day." He galloped off before she could respond.

Ginny scolded herself for breaking her promise not to get distracted. Steve had been justly annoyed with her. She flicked the reins, popped her whip, and shouted to her mules to increase their speed. In her rush, she was bounced about and feared losing her balance and being thrown to the ground; yet she didn't let up until the wagon was in proper position. Then she ordered herself to "alert."

She listened to the jingling of the harnesses, the snapping of traces against mule flesh, the squeaking of the wagon bed and underpinnings as she passed over bumps and dips, the rumbling of broad-rimmed wheels, the steady footfalls of twenty-four hooves, the breathing of her animals, the clinking of chains on the whiffletrees or those that linked two collars together, the shifting of extra wheels and tools beneath her location, and the yells of women giving orders to their teams.

She watched Steve sit tall in his saddle as if he were born and reared in one. She saw him go from wagon to wagon as he gave instructions and encouragement or simply observed. If she didn't get her eyes off him, she would be distracted and in trouble again, so she fastened her gaze to Ruby's wagon.

The one-mile walk later was agony to most of the women, Ginny included. This time, more of them than Mattie Epps groaned in protest, but Ginny kept her feelings to herself. She knew Steve was doing this for their own good, so she accepted the punishing task in silence and obedience.

The exhausted women stayed closely bunched on this trek and all but two returned to camp together. As it was getting late, Ginny watched the scout head out by horse to ride in the two laggers one at a time: Mattie and Cathy. He delivered the whiner to her campsite first, then fetched the dark-haired beauty, who wrapped her arms tightly around his waist.

So much for you get left behind if you can't keep up! Ginny fumed.

"Don't worry," Lucy advised. "She won't steal him from you."

Ginny met her friend's gaze and sighed. "I got into trouble again today; I suppose everyone noticed. My mind just drifted away for a while."

Neither woman saw Steve as he was about to round the Avery wagon, but halted when he overheard Lucy's next words.

"You want him, Anna. Can you leave him behind? Forget him?"

"I have to, Lucy; I don't have any choice in the matter."

"Yes, you do," the woman refuted.

"No, Lucy, I promise I don't. Are you taking a bath before dinner?"

"A cunning change of subject," Lucy teased. "Yes, right now. Jeff is starting supper for me. With my youngest being nine already, my kids don't take as much tending as those of the other women. Let's go remove this sweat and dirt."

Steve scowled. The little southern belle was playing with him, but all women were natural and uncontrollable flirts. He had been right when he guessed she couldn't be interested in a man like him. But she didn't have to mislead him when she had herself a man being left behind!

Ginny ate with Ellie and her family again, and helped do the dishes afterward. The circle of friends was too tired to visit with each other after their arduous day, so they said good night and went to their wagons.

Ginny sat on two piles of bedding with her back supported with pillows so she could read for a while by lanternlight. To allow an air flow for coolness and for the dissipation of lamp smoke, she kept on her clothes and left the ends open and the sides pushed up a few inches.

Her legs ached from the strain of bracing them on the jockey box. The bottoms of her feet hurt from the pressure against the rigid wood. Her body suffered as if every bone in it had been jarred and cracked and every muscle had been bruised and sprained. Her spine panged with torment every time she took a step. The backs of her upperarms, forearms, and wrists throbbed from the pull on them by the reins. Her fingers grumbled and stiffened from keeping her hands clutched tightly around the leather controls for hours and almost refused to hold the book she wanted to read. Her tailbone protested sitting on

74

it, so she shifted her weight to lighten the load on the tender spot. That caused her buttocks to be vexed that another area was appeased at their expense. She wondered if sitting on a pillow would help prevent the painful bumping of vulnerable body against unyielding stone-hard seat. No, she decided, that would take away part of her already insecure balance.

She had shielded her face and arms from the hot ball overhead so fortunately she didn't have a sunburn to add to her misery. Despite the riding gloves she had worn, her hands felt bruised and sensitive; she guessed she would have blisters and blue marks on them by morning. She wished she had thicker gloves like some of the other women and Steve Carr wore as hers were too thin for adequate protection. She hadn't known special ones were needed for handling the team. When Charles Avery visited during the week as promised, Ginny planned, she would ask him to bring her a pair. She also would request several pairs of pants for easier climbing aboard and working on the wagon's high seat.

After today, she understood what Steve had meant about eating dust. Upon return to camp, she had dust in her hair, dust on her clothes, dust on her skin, dust on her eyelashes and in her eyes, and in every hollow it could find to sneak inside! She felt as if her nose was cluttered by it, even though she had used her washcloth to try to clear it of the tiny and sharp debris. She found grains inside her mouth, though she had rinsed it out many times and had eaten the evening meal. It was as if minute particles played hide-and-seek around her teeth and in the crevices of her mouth. The irritant had mingled with her perspiration to form grimy smudges when she mopped at the mess or tried to clear her stinging eyes. Though her bath had been refreshing, a longer one in a sudsy tub of warm water would have been paradise.

They had worked in an area that was an equal mixture of grass and barren ground. It was surrounded mostly by pines and live oaks, both with lacy greenish-gray moss swaying from their branches. She had noticed patches of spring flowers and wished she could have halted to pick a bunch. But that foolish action would have fallen like a stone on the serious guide.

Steve wouldn't have caught her napping at the reins if she hadn't been so lost in thought, so troubled by all her problems. But if she didn't straighten out, she worried, he might tell her "father" she couldn't travel west because she wasn't well trained enough. That would be one way of getting her out of his sight if he felt as threatened by her as she did by him.

Of course Charles Avery would not allow the scout to leave her behind. He had promised to get her to Texas, and he would. Mr. Avery, she believed, was an honest, kind, generous, and dependable gentleman. He was like a sweet and gentle uncle. On the ship and since docking, he had had plenty of opportunities to attempt to take advantage of her if her judgment wasn't accurate. He hadn't and she was certain he wouldn't. The only threats she faced were possible discovery by her stepfamily or her father's enemy, and a possible seductive siege by the irresistible scout. If he—

"Miss Avery . . ." Steve called to her from the end of the wagon.

Ginny lowered the book she wasn't reading and met his gaze.

"We need to have an understanding before this thing between us goes any further. You're trouble, woman, for me, yourself, and for everyone."

Ginny tensed in dread, wincing as she pushed her tortured body to a sitting position. His grave tone and gaze told her she had misunderstood his opening statement; he was there to scold her, not romance her. "What do you mean? I do my share and try hard. I don't complain."

"You're too easily diverted, a daydreamer. You broke your word not to become distracted again. When you do, you distract *me* by having to correct you. When I'm distracted, everyone's life is in peril."

Ginny's eyes misted from her troubles and pains. She knew he was right, and he probably found this disciplinary chore as unpleasant to dole out as it was for her to receive. "I'm sorry,

76

Steve," she murmured. "If you'll be patient and forgiving one more time, I promise to try harder. I swear it."

Steve experienced unfamiliar twinges. He wanted to comfort the girl in her physical and emotional anguish. But how could he when part of her torment was caused by losing the man she loved? Yet, and he couldn't explain or grasp why, he didn't want to be harsh to her tonight. She looked so vulnerable and she hadn't turned a page since she'd opened the book in her hands. She was deeply troubled, an emotion he understood too well. "I'll give you another chance," he declared.

Ginny's eyes brightened with joy. "Thank you, Steve. You won't be sorry. I'll make you proud of me."

"My feelings about you aren't important, Anna; doing a good job is the only thing that counts."

"You're wrong," she refuted too quickly and strongly, then flushed.

"You care what I think?" he queried, eyeing her for signs of deceit and crafty feminine wiles to dupe him.

Her blush deepened as she admitted, "Yes, very much."

"Then prove it by being a perfect student from here on. Agreed?"

"Agreed," she said, and returned his smile.

"If you'll take that liniment from your father's medicine crate and rub it all over, you'll feel much better by morning. Don't press too hard, though, or it'll blister your delicate skin. I'd do it for you, but that isn't part of my job and wouldn't be proper."

Ginny was aroused by the thought of him smearing oily liquid over her body and massaging it in with gentle caresses. She cleared her throat to speak. "You're very kind and thoughtful, and I appreciate it."

Steve leaned against the tailgate and murmured, "I don't hear that said about me very often. Thanks."

"I would think you hear it all the time. You're so smart and . . ." she hesitated.

"Why did you stop? I'm starving for compliments from a lady."

"I don't think it's proper to tell you what I think about you."

"That bad, eh?" he questioned with a husky chuckle.

With boldness, she said, "Not bad at all, only private, too personal."

Steve felt his loins respond to her subtle message and nearness. "A hint like that certainly gives a lonely man something to ponder on his bedroll at night. . . . I'm surprised you aren't married by now."

That unexpected remark took her off guard. "How do you know I'm not heading west to join my fiancé?" she queried.

Steve sealed his gaze to hers. "You would have said something to the others. Don't you women usually brag about snaring a man?"

"No more than you men boast about your conquests of women."

He laughed and teased, "Ah, a quick and sharp wit."

Ginny felt he was impressed, and that pleased her. "I speak only the truth, Mr. Carr, as I see it from observation and experience."

"You're right, Anna."

She couldn't help but challenge, "For a change?"

He grinned instead of replying. "Good night, Miss Avery."

"Steve?" she halted him, feeling overly brave at that moment. She had to know if he was only being nice or if he was interested in her.

He glued his gaze to hers and saw her fidget. "Yes?"

"I don't have a sweetheart waiting in Texas or anyone left behind."

The scout was intrigued. "Why tell me?"

"So you'll know love-pining isn't the root of my problems. Good night." She pulled on the drawstrings of the wagon and closed the back opening, then wiggled forward and did the same with the front one. She watched him stride away as she slid down the canvas on both sides.

Ginny straightened her bed and pillows. She located the liniment and lowered the lantern flame to a soft glow that would cast no provocative shadows on the thick covering. She sat down in the wagon bed and, her privacy guarded by the deep wooden sides, stripped off her garments. She followed Steve's advice; the hopefully soothing preparation pained and stung for a while as she applied it. After replacing the medicine and putting on a nightgown, she doused the light and settled herself into the most comfortable position she could find. She forced her mind to clear so she could get to sleep, knowing tomorrow would be another difficult day.

Steve saw the light go out in the Avery wagon. For the last few minutes, he had been envisioning the scene inside. His hands itched to do the chore for her. He was baffled by her enticing overtures after what he'd heard earlier. Maybe, he reasoned, he had misunderstood the talk with Lucy Eaves. Or maybe Anna had lied to him tonight or to Lucy and the other women earlier. Yet he couldn't surmise a motive for either theory. Perhaps she required a strong hand to seize her interest and to tame her. Maybe if he backed off or acted bossy she would be intrigued and taken off balance. She seemed to weaken more toward him after he was tough with her. He'd have to test that idea tomorrow to see how she responded.

CHAPTER 4

Ginny awoke to the sounds of animals—mules braying, horses neighing, chickens clucking, cows mooing, and birds singing—and to the voices and laughter of people. She smelled breakfasts either being cooked or just finished, especially the wafting scents of coffee and bacon and ham. Her nose wrinkled as she detected a lingering odor of liniment on her body and inside the wagon. Her complaining body protested movement. Before she could rise from bed, Ellie knocked on the tailgate to make sure her friend was awake. Ginny loosened the cord enough to peek outside and say, she was up trying to get going. "Do you ache this morning as much as I do?" she asked Ellie.

The hearty woman didn't want to say she was used to hard work and strenuous exercise, more so than her sophisticated friend. "I'm sore and stiff but faring pretty good. Do you have any liniment you could use?"

"Yes, and I did so before going to bed. Mr. Carr told me it would help lessen the pain, and I'm sure it helped. So will moving around."

Ellie smiled and nodded. "I'll save you some food. Come over when you're dressed. We're about to eat now."

"Thanks, Ellie; you don't know how much your kindness helps me."

The brunette smiled again. "Yes, I do. See you shortly." Ellie wondered if she should tell Anna that her father had paid them to help her while he was in town, then decided she would be doing it anyway, as she liked the fresh and delightful young woman. Besides, it might embarrass Anna to learn her father wasn't certain she could take care of herself alone.

Ginny tightened the drawstring and put aside the rumpled bedding. She washed her face and hands in the basin and changed clothes. Taking another of Steve's suggestions, she brushed and braided her thick hair into one long plait. It still wasn't pulled tight and severely from her face, as the abundance of tresses and the curls from root to tip didn't allow her to do so.

Ginny opened the drawstrings on both ends of the wagon. After rinsing her mouth with the mint-in-water liquid, she tossed out the contents of the basin and water bucket. She emptied the lantern and stored the flammable oil as she had been cautioned to do. She made certain everything was secured for practice today. After lowering the tailgate, she left the wagon and went to the designated area to relieve herself, then joined Ellie Davis and her family.

"Good morning, Stuart," she said, then spoke with the children. "Another lovely day for you all to play while we work our hands raw."

Everyone laughed at the comical expression Ginny made on purpose to go along with her last sentence. "I wish I could sneak off and play dolls or games with you two," she whispered to the girls.

"We'd have fun, Miss Anna; Momma made us some good ones."

"We're going fishing," the two boys told her.

"We'll have 'em scaled and gutted by the time you and Momma get done so you can cook 'em for supper," the oldest boy planned.

"If we have time while we're camped here, you'll have to teach me how to catch and clean fish," Ginny said. "I've been in a ladies' boarding school for years, so I don't know much about living outdoors and off the land."

The elder boy looked smitten with Ginny. Not one to be timid, he offered, "I can teach you, Miss Anna. It'll be fun. I'll even put the worms or crickets on the line for you."

"That's kind of you, a real southern gentleman. But if I don't learn everything, what would I do later when you aren't around to help?"

"Most girls don't like to hold worms and mess with them, but I'll bet you're brave enough to do it."

"I hope so. Maybe we'll have the chance to find out soon."

"You kids get your chores done and let Miss Anna eat," Ellie told the active children. "We have to be ready to do our lessons soon."

The four laughed and teased their mother about doing lessons.

Ellie ruffled her son's hair. "No matter how old you get, children, there's always something new or important to learn."

Ginny concurred, as children often listened to others more than their parents. "Your mother's right; never stop learning or trying new things." She watched the children and Stuart climb inside to collect what they needed for the day in the other clearing while Ellie was gone with their wagon.

"That's good advice, Miss Avery," Steve remarked.

Ginny turned to give him a look that asked, *Do you always sneak up on people?* "Thank you, sir. We'll be ready for work soon."

"Good, 'cause I hate getting started late. You might want to use these today," he said, handing her an extra pair of thick riding gloves. "They're a mite large for you, but they'll do the job until your hands toughen up enough to use those fancy ones you have."

Ginny accepted the scout's offering. She glanced at the gloves, then looked at him. "Thank you, Mr. Carr; that's very thoughtful. I discovered my own pair was too thin yesterday. I was expecting to find my hands covered with blisters this morning, but all I see are red spots and bruises so far."

"Soon you'll be seeing calluses on those delicate hands, but

I don't want pain anywhere on your body to distract you again. The other women are using their husband's extra gloves. A shame your father didn't get you any."

Ginny felt her high spirits lower at his unexpected mood. She wondered if she had scared him or annoyed him with her enticing behavior last night. "When he comes to visit, I'll order the proper kind from town, then return yours. I'll take good care of them."

Steve saw how his alleged motive wiped the cheerful and appreciative smile from her face. He wished he hadn't hurt her feelings, but it seemed necessary if he was going to learn how to deal with her in the most advantageous manner. He nodded, then left the two women.

Ginny frowned and murmured to Ellie, "Why does that man always have to have a hateful excuse for doing something nice for another person?"

"Loners are like that, Anna dear."

"What do you mean?"

"They use a rough air to discourage people from getting too close to them. Most have been deeply hurt in the past, so they keep people at a distance with cold actions in order that they not be vulnerable again."

"You're saying that being mean is a defensive pretense?"

"Yes. If he doesn't let anybody get close, he can't be hurt again."

"But that's foolish and wrong. Being alone and cold hurts him, too."

"Yes, but someone in torment doesn't see it that way."

"Why would a man like Steve Carr be in torment?"

"I don't know. Could be anything. Maybe something from the war. I think he's taken with you and it makes him nervous."

Ginny recalled Lucy saying the same thing and wondered if it could be true. She eyed the scout who was saddling his horse. What if that was—

"You'd better eat before he calls us," Ellie advised. She was acutely aware of the girl's strong interest in their handsome guide.

"You're right; I best hurry. I have mules to tend and harness before he thinks I'm negligent and has something new to chide me about today."

As Steve was walking past her to summon the women, Ginny halted him. "I didn't get to thank you for suggesting the liniment," she said. "It worked, and I feel better this morning."

"Think nothing of it, Miss Avery. I have to keep my ladies in good working condition. Get your team hitched and ready to leave while I tell the others to do the same." He left her staring at his retreating back, as bewildered and ensnared by him as he was by her.

You're a hard man to open up, Steve Carr. I wonder why . . .

Ginny harnessed the team and connected it to the wagon. She climbed aboard the seat and got herself settled and ready to begin practice. She could almost hear her body grumbling already. Her sun bonnet was secured by ties under her chin, and her feet were braced firmly on the jockey box.

She stared at the large gloves he had loaned her, worn over her smaller ones to make them stay in place better. They were new, so no hints of his masculine scent and odor of daily chores clung to them. His hands were large and strong, and she wouldn't mind being caressed by them. She wouldn't mind kissing him and getting to know him. If only he weren't so contradictory, so befuddling, so frustrating! She never knew what mood he was going to be in when he approached her; but maybe he didn't, either. If Ellie and Lucy were right about his fears, that would explain why he was sweet one minute and sour the next.

But her friends could be mistaken. He could be telling her he wanted to teach her but not be chased by her. That shouldn't be a problem, as she didn't have the time to do so. Their paths would separate when this journey ended in a month or so. She couldn't understand why that panged her so deeply; they were strangers, and he was as hateful to her as he was nice to her. So, she pondered, why did she like him?

That was the crux of her dilemma; she liked him, too much, too soon. She hated to think of him being plagued by anguish; she knew how that felt. Perhaps that similarity was what she sensed, what drew her to him, simply the results of a too-tender heart. But if she could soften his hardness and warm his coldness by being a friend, shouldn't she give it her best effort, no matter how he resisted? If—

"Let's pull out, ladies!" Steve yelled, then he signaled them forward one by one at the precise moment to establish correct distance and pace.

Ginny pushed aside her reverie and concentrated only on her task. It did not take her long to realize and delight in discovering that she felt more confident today. Even her balance was better, and her body didn't protest the strain on it as much as it had yesterday. She was more relaxed and in control of herself and the team.

She congratulated herself on her new skills and independence. She had mastered her grief and worries so they wouldn't be evident to others. Most of the travelers were enjoyable, particularly her four new friends. A stimulating and challenging adventure lay before her and she should make the most of it. As for what to do about the mysterious and enchanting scout, she'd decide that later.

Steve galloped his sorrel back and forth along the line of wagons stretched out in the open on flat land. All but a few of the women were doing fine with their training and attitudes. He hoped they would continue to do so when other hard lessons arrived. He was restless with this part of the mission, uneasy in a camp filled with people, and wary of the way Anna Avery got to him. He was accustomed to staying on the move with only himself to worry about and away from crowds. He was torn between wanting to rush their training and depart, and wanting to go slowly and solve the case. If he finished fast, he could get back on his own, out of reach from the beauty's temptation. He could get on to his next task, a personal one he'd delayed to accept this crucial assignment. Pretenses, lies, and cold-blooded murder—he despised them and anyone who committed them, especially against *him*.

It was difficult to act the pleasant and genial scout, and often he failed to carry off that needed ruse, in particular with Anna. But if he didn't win these people's respect, trust, and friendship, he couldn't learn anything useful from them pertaining to the sinister Red Magnolia he had to entrap.

There was no thorough way he could search the wagons for gems, and he'd used his only logical excuse to do a light inspection earlier. He would have to depend on his probing skills and instincts to glean clues. He needed to increase his rapport with the men; he'd do so this afternoon.

Steve slowed at every wagon to speak with the driver: to praise, encourage, or give helpful advice to get in the good graces of each. Most of the women smiled, chatted, and thanked him; only Mattie and Mrs. Brown frowned and merely nodded, but at least they didn't grate on his nerves with whining. Louise told him she thought everyone was trained enough to head out the next day until Steve related the other things they needed to learn. Cathy sent him a seductive look and purred like a kitten as she talked with him; Steve pretended not to notice or be affected.

"Any problems?" he asked Ginny as he rode beside her on the left.

"None that I know of, Mr. Carr. How am I doing?" she asked, keeping her gaze ahead on Mary's wagon.

"Fine. If trouble strikes, signal me." He galloped away, hoping she would wonder why he had spent so little time with her. With luck, she'd seen how much longer he had visited with the others. That should spark her curiosity and worry her, maybe provoke her to work harder to catch his eye and to please him. Most women, he assumed, wanted what they couldn't have, so Anna should be challenged to chase him.

As Steve passed her again, she ignored him. *Shu*, Anna looked appealing today. She had braided her hair as he suggested, then secured the end with a red ribbon. The thick tuft at the bottom swayed against her waist when she moved. She hadn't dared look at him and lose her pace and distance requirement. That caution meant she didn't want to annoy him with another mistake, so his scoldings, no matter their motives, were working. He had to admit she was doing an astonishingly good job. The dark-blue shirt and skirt she was wearing flattered her skin coloring, and her hairstyle highlighted her exquisite face.

Steve signaled the wagons to halt. He rode to each one to tell the women he was ready to begin corral practice. If Anna dreaded it or was vexed with him, it didn't show. He had told them before leaving that it was necessary to circle the wagons at night and sometimes on the trail itself for safety from enemy or raider attacks.

The scout walked his sorrel in a wide circle and the women followed as instructed, or tried to obey. He knew it was a tricky maneuver to guide the team ever rightward by control of the reins while not allowing a front wheel to jam into the wagon. When a team balked or got out of alignment, Steve halted the others to correct it. Sometimes he had to seize the cheekstrap or sidecheck and forcefully guide the team into place. As he did so, he told the woman involved how to better handle the reins to accomplish it from her seat. "Loosen up on your left rein and pull back on the right one to get him heading in that direction. Not too hard or he'll turn his head too sharp and resist your command. He's the leader, so the others will follow him. They have no choice; they're linked together."

Ginny was relieved the "leader" was earmarked, so she knew which one to always put on the front right side. Every time she fed, watered, or worked with her mules, she tried to earn their affection and respect so they would obey her orders without balking. So far so good . . .

It took a while for most of the women to get the procedure

down, and some never stopped having trouble. When Steve halted his ride, the loop he had made was the perfect size for creating a tight ring with the right side of one wagon front almost making contact with the back left side of the wagon before it. Teams were on the exterior of the ring, adjacent to the front neighbor's wagon where they would be unhitched and led inside. That left no opening for attackers to get through their barricade. If defense was needed, he'd told them, men would stand between the jockey box and seat or behind the seat to fire their weapons, using the thick wooden bed as cover.

He shouted for the women to get down and group in the center. "On the trail, we'll leave two wagons' widths open for movement of animals and comings and goings of people for chores," he explained. "The two grain wagons joining us before we leave will drive straight into the remaining space and fill it before we turn in for the night or if trouble strikes. The animals will be corraled inside the circle to protect them from outlaws. You and your families will sleep in or under your wagons, according to weather and preference. You'll do your cooking near your wagon on the outside; keep a low campfire going at night to discourage wild animals and to prevent anyone from sneaking up on us in the dark. Any questions before we practice pulling out and doing this again?"

"If we park like this, how will we get to our things to do our chores?" Louise Jackson asked arrogantly. "What we'll use on the road is packed at the rear, out of reach from the outside. We'd have to carry things out of the circle to work, then haul them back inside. Why can't we park with our backs pointed outward? It seems just as easy and far more practical for chores. That way, the teams would already be inside when we unhitch them."

"That would make things easier for you women," he began, and saw the bossy creature gloat with smugness. "But it isn't safe, and safety is more important than ease with chores. If an attack comes, the men can defend themselves and their families better from the front of the wagon. If you'll notice, the wagon beds are high enough to pass things underneath to keep from having to walk around countless times."

Ginny was glad when Steve's authoritative tone and gaze hushed Louise, who looked miffed at being overruled. She wondered where he would camp, as he didn't have a wagon to put into the tight ring. Inside, she mused, with the animals, as there was enough room for a small campsite? Or outside, where the loner had space and privacy, as he could defend himself against any threat that might come along? Changing her line of thought abruptly, she was amazed by how he could control the color and expression in his eyes: he could make them blank and unreadable, cold and harsh and intimidating, or soft and entreating. He seemed to have masterful prowess in every area of his life and body.

"Any more questions or remarks?" he asked. The women remained silent and alert. "All right, ladies, let's pull out and do this again."

By one o'clock, they had finished the lesson and eaten lunch. Steve announced with a grin, "I'm going to let you rest and do chores for a few hours, ladies, while the men go hunting for fresh meat. I'm sure your children need some attention from you, more than just a quick visit at night before turning in. We'll start shooting lessons when I return later."

Ginny sat on a quilt beneath a shade tree away from the noise of camp. She read while Ruby Amerson's two babies napped nearby on a pallet. She had insisted on tending the children while their mother washed clothes at the river. She liked the perky redhead and knew Ruby could use the help. She didn't know much about babies, but, as long as they slept, she was sure she wouldn't have a problem. Ruby had showed her how to diaper them if it became necessary, but there was no feeding scheduled.

Ginny stopped reading a while to ponder the mysterious and appealing Steve Carr. He had avoided her today, perhaps to prevent temptation or to conceal his interest from the others and from her. He could be afraid he'd make an embarrassing error if he became ensnared by thoughts of her, and unaccustomed fear must be something he despised. Maybe the self-protective scout didn't know how to deal with or woo a woman who caught his eye. Or know how to apologize for harshness, warranted or not. Maybe he tried to do it by being nice and helpful afterward. Or perhaps he thought she was only being friendly and he could never win a woman so different from his own self. Should she show him otherwise? But why, when their paths would separate soon? She must not risk hurting herself when Steve Carr was unattainable and unchangeable.

Ginny gazed at the sleeping siblings, infant and toddler. They were precious bundles of joy with fine strawberry-blond hair and pudgy cheeks. One day, she would have a family as happy as Ruby's was. She—

Her musings halted as she saw Charles Avery walking toward her. She smiled before touching a finger to her lips and pointing to the babies to indicate quiet. She motioned for him to sit beside her. In a low tone, she said, "It's good to see you. How are things going?"

"That's what I came to ask you," he whispered with a smile.

"Fine, so far, except that contradictory Steve Carr gives me a hard time once in a while. I have to confess it's partly my fault; sometimes I have trouble paying attention during class."

The tall, lean man just responded, "It's no wonder, my dear, after what you've been through lately and what you have staring you in the face soon. I'm sorry you're having a difficult time with him; he struck me as a nice fellow."

"He is, but I rub him wrong at times, too many times."

Charles studied the curious blush on her cheeks and grinned. "Ah, so that's how it is," he teased. "You like him a great deal. What about him?"

Ginny didn't feel uncomfortable talking about her romantic

feelings, as Charles Avery had a way of relaxing her. "I can't tell how he feels or what he thinks, *Father.*" They shared soft laughter. "Sometimes he's nice and seems to want to become friends; other times, he's cold and rude and distant. I don't understand him at all." She related the incidents that weren't too personal. "Do you see what I mean? I'm utterly baffled." She listened to the forthcoming advice from her trusted and respected friend.

"Be nice and cooperative, Anna; he has a heavy burden on his shoulders." The name of his deceased daughter rolled easily off his tongue. Lord, how he missed his child and wife. He liked this girl and would do almost anything to help and protect her. "He may only be intimidated around a real lady; I doubt he meets and deals with many genteel women. He could be afraid that a refined lady can't learn her lessons or might not hold up during the hardships on the trail or that she will delay everyone with spoiled ways."

Ginny knew where her assumed name had come from and guessed what Charles had been thinking and feeling when he paused for a moment. Her heart went out to him for his tragic loss. The eyes that filled with torment for a while were the bluest, clearest, and gentlest ones she had ever seen. She had no doubts he liked her and that she was safe with him. "You could be right. He's nice when I'm obedient and catch on quickly. He gets mad when I don't focus my full attention on him and class."

"If he wants total concentration on him, give it to him. It is to your best interests. Besides, you might have use of him later." At her quizzical look, he explained, "A skilled guide like him would make a good scout and protector for what you have to do soon. If you agree, I can loan you the money to hire him for that service."

"Let Steve Carr take me to Colorado?" she murmured as her head filled with thoughts of what could happen between them on a secluded trail.

"Are you afraid of him? Has he done or said anything to

make you think he's dangerous or untrustworthy? If he hasn't been a complete gentleman, I'll thrash him with a whip."

Ginny knew why the man got upset and why his face flushed with angry seriousness. She understood his concern. She appeased him with a touch on his rigid forearm and by assuring him Steve hadn't done anything improper or scary. *Not*, she added mutely, *like you mean.*

"He'd better not!" Charles declared angrily, balling his fists.

"I'm certain he won't, sir. I just don't want to distract him from his duties with disobedience, mistakes, or romantic overtures." Ginny turned to check on the Amerson children, who had stirred to the disturbance, but she settled them down with light pats on their backs and a soothing tone.

Her last few words told Charles Avery that she was powerfully interested in their guide. Since Carr struck him as a decent fellow, he wasn't worried about Ginny leaning in the man's direction. After all, Carr could be of great help to her soon, especially if her deception in Texas failed and if her father was truly dead. From overhearing talks between the two girls before Johanna Chapman died, he knew more about Virginia Marston and her dead friend than she realized or had confided to him.

If he didn't have his own busy schedule and problems to resolve, he concluded, he would escort her to Colorado himself. Perhaps he could after they were handled. He would make sure she knew where to locate him in case trouble arose in Texas. But if he couldn't help her if she got into peril, the skilled scout was a path she needed to open and to keep cleared for use. He would continue to encourage and advise her to do so. With the interest Ginny seemed to show in him, that shouldn't be difficult. All he had to do, Charles planned, was to make certain the scout was just as enchanted by her as she obviously was of him. If so, Steve would do anything to help and protect her. They had a long trail to cover and plenty of time for him to push the two young people together, but only if he didn't change his mind and opinion about the expert trail guide.

When Ginny faced him again, Charles said, "I'm sure you'll be fine, Anna; you're brave and smart. You know what you have to do to succeed. You have a lot at stake, so you'll make the right decisions to accomplish your goals. If the war taught me one thing, it's to do what one must for survival, victory, and happiness."

"Those are my dreams and goals, Mr.— *Father,*" she corrected herself for practice. She returned his affectionate smile before continuing. "But sometimes I'm afraid I'll fail."

"That's only natural, Anna, but you won't," he assured her.

"You have more confidence in me than I do," she confessed.

"Because I know you're a strong and courageous person. Before this journey and challenge end, you'll be convinced, too."

"I hope so."

"I know so." He changed the subject. "Martha sent you a fine meal and a whole dried apple pie. I put it in the wagon before I joined you here. Is there anything else you need? I'll be returning to town soon to reach there before dark. No need to tempt evil forces to attack me."

"You will be careful and alert, won't you?" she asked with concern.

"Of course, my child, and I'm well armed for trouble."

Ginny eyed the weapon he exposed and smiled in reassurance. "I can use driving gloves. Mine are too thin for protection."

"I should have thought of that. Give me a pair of yours for size and I'll bring them tomorrow."

"I have to watch Ruby's children, but they're laying on the wagon seat." She told him about Steve loaning her an extra pair of his.

Charles grinned in pleasure. "Yes, sir, a real gentleman, just like I thought. Anything else? Don't worry about money; I have plenty."

"Only if you let me repay you later."

He smiled. "It's a deal. I'll keep an account, if you insist."

"I do. I can use pants for climbing around on the wagon; a full skirt gets tangled up and immodest at times. You can use the green riding skirt on top of my trunk for size. And boots, if you can find sturdier ones to fit. Open the trunk on the left side facing front and pull out the slippers on top. Will that be too much trouble?" she fretted aloud. "If so, I'll understand. I never considered proper attire for the trail or the training before I left town."

"Martha will assist me if I need help filling your requests. Don't worry, Anna, it's no trouble at all; honestly."

"Thank you, sir. I don't know what I would do if not for you."

Charles was touched by the unshed tears that shone in her hazel eyes. "You've been a joy to meet, to get to know, and to help, Anna. I haven't felt warm sunshine in my life since my daughter . . . died, not until I met you and . . . You know what I mean. Thank you," he said with an emotional lump in his throat.

"We're both fortunate to have met each other in a time of mutual need."

"You're right, my girl. Well," he said as he stood, "I should get moving. Take care, Anna Avery, and I'll see you tomorrow."

"Good-bye and thank you." She watched him vanish into the trees between her and camp. With Charles Avery's help and generosity, her first deception would succeed, no matter how distasteful she found it to lie to friends. As he had warned her, it was possible one of these people knew or knew *of* her stepfamily or her father, so she couldn't risk confiding her identity and ultimate goal to anyone. As for her second deception, she wouldn't think about it until the time came to begin it.

The little girl stirred and awakened. Ginny lifted and cuddled the child to keep her from disturbing the baby boy. She didn't know how much a child of fourteen months could understand, but she said, "Momma's washing clothes; she'll be back soon. Do you want . . . Anna to play with you?" She lifted a hand-

94

made toy to use to entertain the toddler along with words in a soothing tone. The child relaxed and responded, and they played.

Steve approached, observing the tender scene that tugged unbidden at his stony heart. How, he asked himself, could he behave in a cold and disinterested fashion to a woman with such warmth and appeal? Yet, he must for the sake of his mission and to protect himself. He quelled his rebellious emotions to speak with her, to continue his cunning strategy of repel, attract, repel, attract. "Babysitting, Miss Avery?"

Ginny looked over her shoulder and answered, "Yes, sir, while Ruby does the wash. She has more chores than I do, and her husband was with you."

He propped against the tree. "Why do you call me 'sir,' " he queried, forcing a mirthful chuckle and grin to surface. "I'm twenty-seven and you're nineteen; that's only eight years separating us. 'Sir' makes me feel old."

Was he, she wondered, being subtly enticing again? "Sorry, Mr. Carr. Age has nothing to do with it; a show of respect to authority does."

"Ah, yes, your fancy schooling and fine breeding are responsible."

"True," she replied, but decided not to say more until she discovered what mood he was in this time. From his casual tone and expression, she couldn't guess how he meant his last words. She remembered one teacher saying: "A smart woman knows when and how long to be silent with a trying man." The problem was, Virginia Marston fretted, was she a smart woman when it came to a difficult man—to utterly bewildering Steve Carr?

"I heard your father came to visit. Sorry I missed him." He wished he had seen Charles, as he needed time with every one of his suspects. During the successful hunt, he hadn't gleaned a single helpful clue.

Ginny sensed that his full attention wasn't on her. He was like a train with engines at both ends, each trying to pull in an opposite direction. "I ordered gloves and pants as you suggested. Father will bring them to me tomorrow. When I get them, I'll return yours. And I told Father of your kindness. He speaks highly of you."

"Does that surprise you?"

She watched a squirrel play as she answered, "No, why should it?"

"We have had our . . . differences in the last few days."

"Only because I was distracted by other matters at the wrong time."

Steve watched her closely. She seemed to avoid meeting his gaze with hers on purpose. "You're taking full blame for them?"

"No, but most of the problems were my fault."

"Then you understand why I have to be tough on you?"

"For the most part." The toddler cried in boredom and from a lack of attention, or maybe the child sensed tension in the air and it unsettled her. As Ginny focused on quieting and comforting her, the unpredictable scout left after reminding her of target practice in thirty minutes.

Steve had tested and instructed all but one woman with rifle and pistol when it came Anna's turn. He said he had made her last again because the other women with children and husbands had more chores to do. He had set up a target area a half-mile from camp to prevent frightening and disturbing the youngsters. Since Ellie's oldest children were twelve and fourteen and could watch the two younger ones for a while, Stuart Davis took the other women on their two-mile trek to let them get finished with their training today. Steve said that he or one of the other men could walk with Anna Avery when she had completed her shooting lesson.

"You said you could load and fire a rifle, right . . . ?" Steve began.

"Yes," she replied, aware they were alone and out of sight.

"Show me."

Ginny accepted the Henry rifle and studied it.

"Anything wrong?"

"Nothing, just seeing how and where it loads; weapons do vary."

"It fires .44 caliber rimfire cartridges. It's a fifteen-shot repeater with lever action and magazine loading. Any questions?"

"None." Ginny loaded the rifle without trouble. "Ready?"

"Do it."

Ginny eyed the targets he pointed out, shouldered the Henry, and fired fifteen times. "It kicks like a . . . mule," she murmured, knowing she gained another bruise.

Steve walked to the targets and checked them, then returned to her. "You're right, a skilled shot, only two misses, and I doubt by much. How did you become such an expert marksman?"

Ginny had to deceive him. "The teachers at school thought ladies should know how to protect themselves; we were at war, remember?" Actually, she had been taught because hunting was a favorite sporting diversion of the English, one every well-trained lady was expected to master.

"What about a pistol? Do you know how to handle and use one?"

"I've only fired small ones a few times."

Steve withdrew one of his Colts, unloaded it, and handed it to her. "Forty-four caliber. Six shots. Hand-cock the hammer after each firing."

Ginny took the pistol. At over four pounds and with a nine-inch barrel, it was heavy and awkward to handle. She loaded the weapon, then looked at him in uncertainty. "How do I aim?"

"Extend your arm and lock your elbow. Line up the end of the barrel with your target and pull the trigger."

Ginny obeyed with difficulty because of the pistol's weight. She exerted pressure on the trigger and a loud bang filled the air. The force of the blast jerked her hand and arm upward, sending the shot wild and high. "Not even close," she muttered as she cocked the hammer again.

Steve grasped her right wrist and put downward pressure on it as she fired another shot. "Closer, but still off. Try again."

After ten minutes and two rounds of cartridges, Ginny hit the largest target twice. "Two out of twelve is a bad score," she murmured.

"You have to learn to control a pistol's power and offset its weight. A weapon isn't much good to you if you don't know how to use it. Make it your friend, as comfortable in your hand as your palm is. You can't protect yourself if you can't hit your target, and a live one moves."

She glanced at him. "I could never kill anyone."

"When and if the time comes, you will," Steve reasoned, "and you'll be glad you're alive instead of your enemy. Think of it as gaining revenge or justice. Some people believe you can do anything for those reasons."

Ginny assumed he was referring to the recent war and lingering troubles resulting from it. "They're wrong. The war is over; we've made peace, and we're heading for new starts. The past can't be changed. Revenge only breeds more problems for innocents to get entangled with and be hurt worse."

Steve saw an opening to draw out possible clues. "The KKK doesn't think the same way you do. Of course, it's turning sour fast, forgetting why it was formed. It soon might be as bad as those Yank bands who attack Southerners."

"I don't know much about the Ku Klux Klan, only what I've been told or read. But I think it's wrong to go after black men. Most are good, kind, and honest men who only want freedom and peace. You can't blame them for the actions of those who've been deceived and provoked by the Yankees into terrorizing and punishing their ex-masters. I realize some of those gangs have gone wild and they're killing or robbing any white person, but that doesn't justify what the Klan does to innocent ex-slaves."

"You're right, and smart, too, Miss Avery. Let's get back to

98

our task. Maybe your trouble is bad aiming. With powerful eyes like yours, you should be able to see how to do anything. Give it another try."

Ginny warmed at the almost-concealed compliment. She loaded and fired another round, and did better—three out of six. She grinned in pleasure as she looked at the scout and he commented that she was improving each time.

Steve leaned against a tree while she continued to practice. She seemed determined to become accurate and was thrilled with her success. After telling him she wasn't learning so she could kill anyone, he concluded she was trying hard only to please him. That was just what he needed . . .

When she emptied the box of shells and was hitting the target four times out of six, he said, "That's enough for today. Let's go on our stroll. I'm sure you're ready to get finished and on to relaxing or doing chores."

"Does that mean I pass the test, teacher?" she asked with a grin.

"Yep. Let's move out; we have two miles to cover."

They headed for the path he had marked earlier. Steve set the pace to match that of a moving wagon and stayed a few steps ahead of her. He didn't make small talk, as he'd been familiar enough with her for today. He was too cognizant of their solitude, the peaceful surroundings, and her appeal. If he wasn't careful, he might seize her and kiss her then and there. He would try that soon, but it was too early to get that friendly to win her favor. He had to keep telling himself that during the entire two miles.

Ginny stayed within a few steps of the tall man strolling before her. Since he didn't speak, she didn't, either. Obviously he wanted the silence and distance, so she let him have both. Besides, it wasn't wise to make an overture in this dangerously romantic setting, and she wasn't sure how he would take one from her. It was best to spend quiet and pleasant time with him rather than creating more friction between them. He was being nice and leaning her way, she realized, so she would leave it be for a while.

They returned to camp, dismissed each other, then parted.

Ginny gathered her things and went to the river for a bath. She discovered her monthly flow had ended, and she was glad. Soon, scrubbed and refreshed, she joined Ellie Davis to help finish cooking the fish the boys had caught and cleaned. She noticed that Steve had been invited to eat with the Jacksons tonight and wondered how he would tolerate the overbearing Louise and her quiet husband during the meal.

She had intended to give Steve the food Charles Avery had brought, but he didn't need it now. Two of Ellie's children didn't like fish, so Ginny gave the fried chicken to them. She saw the youngsters' eyes glow when she produced the dried apple pie from Miss Avery in town. "Eat all your dinner and you can have a slice," she advised the enthusiastic children.

Virginia Marston was relaxed and content following her successes today and Steve's easygoing manner with her. She didn't realize she was in for an enlightening and stunning lesson later that night.

CHAPTER 5

Almost every one of the men and a few women gathered around a colorful fire to talk about the evils plaguing the South. To keep from disturbing the children, the gathering was held away from the other wagons but was still close enough to hers for Ginny to overhear the chilling conversation. The barely waxing moon with its sliver of pale yellow did nothing to help lighten the setting. Only those near the blaze had their faces illuminated for recognition when they spoke.

When the talk became serious, Ginny put aside her book and doused her lantern to listen without being noticed at the side of the wagon where the canvas was slid up a few inches for fresh air.

"Some folks think strong actions should be taken to halt it, but I can't imagine what most people can do to change things. Not if they want to stay out of jail. Those Radicals are in power and they want everything done their way; they even have Secretary of War Stanton as their leader. You can't provoke a man in his position to come after you. I guess our hands are tied."

Ginny recognized Steve Carr's voice; she hadn't taken him for a man interested in or concerned with politics and reforms. Hadn't he implied he only needed and took care of himself? Odd. . . .

"Ain't much an honest man can do until the South is free of

Yankee control and we get our own governments back in power," Stuart Davis said.

Daniels disagreed. "What we need is stronger 'Black Codes' like ever'body voted in 'cept Tennessee. Like them Mississippi boys said, we live under the threat of Yankee bayonets and crazy words from misguided foreigners. We done did away with slavery, so why can't ever'body be happy and leave us be? Ex-slaves can't be citizens of this great country; they can't socialize with us or rule us from political offices handed to them by crazy Yanks. We'll do as we're ordered, let 'em be safe, but we don't have to like it or be friends with them or have 'em crammed down our throats."

"Us Georgia boys don't cower to Negroes. If they're caught lazing around, we arrest 'em and jail 'em or fine 'em. It's all legal, too."

Ginny couldn't see who had made those remarks. She wished she could, as a Georgian might know— Harry Brown's explosion halted her thoughts.

"Hellfire, our own President can't help us! The Army Act won't allow him to give it orders; they have to come through General Grant. I say, a President, no matter how I hate him, should be in control of the country, not them contrary and greedy Radicals. Hellfire, the South's been chopped up into five military districts with a general over each, all because we wouldn't accept that Fourteenth Amendment. They expect us to agree that Africans are citizens and can vote? They can hold office and we can't 'cause we fought against the Union? We can't file claims for slaves they took away or for property they burned and looted just for the meanness of it. We can't even get loans to see us through bad times; they let carpetbaggers steal our land and homes on unpaid taxes they levy on us to pay for a war we lost. We're all dead broke. Why should we vote in and then obey laws that go against us? Hellfire, we ain't even part of the Union again! Africans have more rights than we do! If we even pass air the wrong way, they punish us."

"They do the same to businesses," Ed King added, "They

keep us disfranchised and rule every manner of transportation and sales. With those carpetbaggers running over us with the help of scalawags, we don't have a chance of recovering. They stole my dairy business, but I'll build a new one in Texas. They won't get that one without a bloody fight."

"You think those Yanks will ever pull out of the South?" Ellie asked.

"No conqueror ever retreats or gives back what he's won. They think they did us a favor with that Amnesty Act, but it only helped the rurals."

"I know what you mean, Ed," James Wiggins said. "Any man who was a high officer or had money before the war has to personally beg the President for one. I refused to bend my knee to him or any Yank."

"We could have won the war if Ole Jeff Davis and most of us hadn't been so genteel," Jeff said. "If we'd done forays into the North before Abe hired such good generals to fight us, they would have been too weak and scared to strike."

"The Yanks ain't got no room or right to be high and mighty!" Daniels fumed. "They're forgetting they had slavery, too, nigh unto 1805. When they leaned toward industry, they didn't need slaves no more; but we did for our plantations. They asked us to abolish it, that whole institution of slavery, but we couldn't. They ruffled lots of feathers when they demanded it in '30. I never knowed any southern gentleman who abused his property; they was too valuable to beat and cripple, like they near crippled my leg from no treatment in that prison. The Yanks had no right to take our property away and attack us. They just used slavery as an excuse to destroy us, to come down here and take over. They ain't nothing like us, so they don't understand us. They think we're stupid and backward 'cause we talk slow and easy and different."

"Hellfire," Brown spat. "They don't care about Africans! They're already abandoning and ignoring their *rights*. We'll make it back in spite of them."

"It all started with that Missouri Compromise in '50," Ed

King said. "We should never have agreed. Then, the way they acted over that Dred Scott case was stupid; it didn't matter if his master moved to a free state; that didn't give him a right to sue for his freedom or become a citizen. But when they blockaded our ports and captured southern territory, they challenged us beyond restraint, even those of us who didn't have slaves and never would. We had to join our friends and families to battle them."

"Weren't much of a country anyway," Daniels said. "We had one constitution and a President and congress, but not much unity beyond them. States and towns handled their own affairs. What did the government do for us? Very little, so why should we be more loyal to the Union than the South?"

"It was the railroads' and telegraphs' fault. Progress be damned! Made everybody get too close and cozy, too easy to reach and control."

"You're right, Ed," James said. "Every section was being threatened or exploited by another. We were being pulled apart at the seams, which weren't strong to begin with. The Englanders hated the westerners because too many folks were moving that way and could raise and sell crops cheaper than them. The westerners knew the easterners were using them and considered them trash. The South was rich and genteel and powerful so those Yanks couldn't stand it. Yes, sir, they used slavery as an excuse to attack. They even praised that vicious John Brown when he made that bloody attack at Harper's Ferry on whites to free his own kind."

The quiet Samuel Jackson spoke up. "I've seen the papers, so I know the real figures: less than three hundred fifty thousand out of six million Southerners owned slaves; fewer than two thousand had one hundred or more; most only owned four or less."

Again, Ginny couldn't recognize the voice of the speaker in the shadows who said, "It didn't help Georgia none that she was the power of the Confederacy. Her rails, port, and three arsenals kept our side alive until Sherman destroyed them. He even captured Jeff Davis at Irwinville."

"The Yankee bastard should have been shot!" Daniels shot out. "He ordered and allowed his men to do things beyond cruelty, even for wartime."

"I bet the KKK would love to get their hands on him for a few hours," George said. "They're big in Alabama where we'll be passing soon. Right in the heart of the Confederacy's birth, our first capital at Montgomery."

"If you men got rid of Radicals, carpetbaggers, scalawags, and that Loyal League," Cathy scoffed, "we wouldn't have to pull up roots and move; we wouldn't have to tuck our tails between our legs like beaten dogs and flee. This is our land, so why hand it over to greedy Yanks? We can all join the Klan and fight back. The Invisible Empire is strong and fearless. The soldiers have to catch you before you can be jailed or punished. If we're clever, we won't get caught. It's worth a try. Surely somebody here knows how to reach members."

Ed King changed the subject after scowling at his beautiful wife and scolding, "Don't be foolish, Cathy. Those are dangerous words to speak aloud. You never know when spies are around. Besides, you don't know what you're talking about; the Klan is as dangerous as it is helpful. I heard that Sherman and other Union officers have been assigned out west to whip the Indians like they whipped the Rebs. Word is, everybody's demanding Indian control by placing them on reservations or by destroying them. With so many citizens moving west, the government will have to respond."

"Yeah," Daniels scoffed, "Sherman is commander of the Military Division of the Missouri. I hope them redskins lick him and his troops worse than they did us. Serve 'em all right to get killed and scalped after what they done to us. Maybe those redskins will do a job on them we couldn't."

"Mrs. King is right to a point; if we could fight back, we wouldn't have to leave. But we can't; it's too dangerous. That Klan is going crazy."

"How is that?" Steve questioned Mattie Epps's husband.

"Yeah, Joel. I hear they're doing a good job of protecting Southerners and running out bad Yanks and Africans. Hellfire, they done got the vote and got themselves schools. Next, they'll be taking over," Brown sneered in disgust.

"Schooling might help them," Ellie reasoned. "Learning helps anybody. Even if you don't believe that, it's wrong to burn their schools and churches and homes. It'll only provoke more of them to attack whites."

"I hear only educated and rich men are Klan members," Louise remarked. "That's why they wear hoods, so they can't be recognized and caught. They only raid troublemakers and Yankees, and those traitorous scalawags. Half the things they're accused of doing are actually done by those Loyal Leaguers in disguise. I think they deserve praise for their courage and cunning. I wouldn't mind being a Klanswoman. If I were, I'd lead my group to great victories. Our name would be known the country over."

"So would news of your captures and hangings."

"We wouldn't get caught, Ellie, we'd be too clever. We'd scare the pants off those Yankee thieves and killers."

Again, Ginny struggled to pierce the darkness to see who spoke next. "Those Yankee courts don't help us; they only help their kind and Negroes. If it wasn't for the Klan, we'd be in sorry shape. Most say General Dudley DuBose is the leader in Georgia, but the law can't prove it. I say they're patriots, good men being forced to fight evil any way they have to."

Steve marked Carl Murphy off his mental list of suspects, even though he hadn't been included on it earlier. No culprit, he surmised, was fool enough to say an important leader's name aloud. He listened as Louise Jackson began spouting her knowledge of matters.

"I saw their creed published in a newspaper. Some journalist got his hands on a copy and exposed it. It didn't help the Yankees' claims against them because it said it was to 'protect the weak, the innocent, and the defenseless, from indignities, wrongs and outrages of the lawless, the violent, and the brutal,' and so forth, 'especially the widows and orphans of Confederate soldiers.' It even said it was to 'protect and defend the Constitution of the United States, and all laws.' It sounds good to me."

"Me, too," Daniels said. "You don't see the 'so-called' *law* capturing and punishing those Loyal Leaguers or gangs of 'so-called' soldiers. But catch a Klansman and he's strung up high on the spot or tossed into the worst hellhole of a prison they can find. You're in deeper trouble if you're a high officer, say a Grand Dragon. Or a Den member of the Red Magnolias."

Steve wondered why John Daniels would mention the very unit the law was trying to expose. Most feared to even whisper the name of that secret society. *A trick,* he pondered, *to throw off suspicion?*

"Who are the Magnolias?" Cathy inquired.

"A small but powerful Den. Their symbol is a white magnolia blossom dipped in blood or one painted with red dripping from it. Their costumes are scarlet, a fearsome sight to behold. If you ever find one of their signs on your porch, you best run for your life."

"It's the war." Ellie ventured, "That's what did it to them. Made them cold and hard. Made them willing to do anything for revenge."

Jeff Eaves asked Steve if he was in the war.

"Yes, like most men."

"For which side?" Harry Brown asked.

Steve had to reply, "Wasn't but one right side, the Confederacy."

James Wiggins asked him where he had fought.

"Here and there, mostly in Mississippi, Tennessee, and Kentucky."

"Let's not talk about the war anymore tonight," Ellie suggested. "It's late and everybody's unnerved. George, why not play us a relaxing song?"

"Sure, ma'am, be happy to." Ruby's husband lifted his fiddle from his lap and began a merry tune to calm everyone before bedtime.

As he listened, Steve knew why he hadn't told them he had been captured at Shiloh in April of '63 while trying to save a man's life. Nor would he mention how he had been imprisoned and harrowed, and most of all how he had been released to become a Galvanized Yankee. He knew how most Southerners hated and viewed such soldiers as traitors and cowards.

He told himself he shouldn't have been in the war in the first place, so why stay in a "hell hole," as John Daniels had called Union prisons? Why be tormented emotionally and physically or watch others be treated that way? Why watch men die in fear, pain, and denial when you could be out West in fresh air, free, far from the horrors of war, and doing good and brave deeds instead of rotting away for years? Who wouldn't accept the Yanks' offer? Other Rebs had done the same thing for a variety of reasons. Some were fed up with war and killing, some realized how futile and wrong the fighting was, some were plagued by utter despair, some were suffering from lost courage, some wanted hope for new roots elsewhere, and some didn't want to be forced to change sides to battle family and friends as the other price for release.

Despite the good Galvanized Yankees had done during the war—helping with road and fort building, stringing or restringing or guarding telegraph lines and relay shacks, carrying mail, protecting and guiding survey crews, rescuing Indian captives, and other jobs—they were labeled yellowbellies and betrayers by the South and they were pushed aside by the Union they had helped. Dishonored and discouraged, many had become outlaws, rustlers, gunfighters, and worse after their releases in '65; some had become his missions to track down and halt.

Steve felt he was one of the lucky ones, and good fortune hadn't been too kind to him in the past. The compromise had given him a place to work, a way to earn respect, to get survival training, to hone his skills and instincts, and to make a few good friends. He could have escaped at any time, as he had often worked alone, but he hadn't. It wasn't because of loyalty to his releasers or fear of recapture, but out of what he was gaining from the situation. It had suited his needs, so he had done his assignments; he had continued to do most of those same tasks afterward.

Steve sensed eyes on him from the Avery wagon. He wondered what Anna thought about all she'd heard. If her father was the villain he was seeking, did she know about his evil involvement with the Red Magnolias? Did she approve? Had she been duped into believing the Invisible Empire was doing good and necessary work? He wished Charles Avery had been present tonight to air his opinions. He hoped Anna's father could be eliminated as a suspect. If he was the guilty one, what would happen to the refined beauty?

Steve told himself he couldn't worry about that possible future predicament, couldn't worry about the repercussions to families and friends of *any* criminals who were slain or imprisoned. He had been easy on her today. Tomorrow he must be repelling, but not rough, just ignore and avoid her enough to concern her and challenge her.

Practice began at nine. When all women showed they were proficient in harnessing, driving, and circling up, Steve said it was time for their next lesson: handling runaways, stampedes, and calming terrified teams.

The women emptied one wagon of its load so three at a time could practice: a driver with two assistants standing behind her. The others waited their turns in a group but were ordered to pay attention, not chat.

"Mrs. Jackson, you be our first driver. Mrs. Amerson and Martin, you two be the riders. I'll spook the team with gunfire. Usually it's gunshots from raiders or thunder that sets them off. When one team takes off, the others generally follow. The lead wagons must get their teams slowed and controlled as quickly as possible. Just do as I say." He spoke to everyone at once, but only Louise nodded with smugness.

"If you lose the reins, hang on to the seat until I halt the team. You observers make sure your drivers don't fall off. Grab an arm or handful of clothes to keep her aboard. Pull her back into the wagon with you if need be. Any questions?" None came, so the scout asked if they were ready to leave.

Louise sent him a confident nod. Ruby and Mrs. Martin braced themselves for the wild ride ahead.

Steve drew his pistol and fired shots within inches of the mules' hooves and whizzed bullets past their twitching ears. The startled animals bolted instantly, jerking the wagon into motion. The pounding of hooves, squeaking of wagon, and women's yells filled the air. Dust and severed grass were flung up by hoof and wheel alike.

As instructed, Louise Jackson "let them have their head" to see if the frantic beasts would overcome their fear and settle down or get winded soon and slow by themselves. Steve galloped alongside the runaway team to be nearby if help was needed and to protect the women from injury.

When the winded team began to slow, Louise pulled back on the reins and shouted commands for them to halt. At the right moment, she worked the brake lever and the wagon stopped.

Steve looked at the grinning female who grated on his nerves most of the time. "Good, Mrs. Jackson. Now, drive it back for the next team to do it."

Lucy Eaves drove for Mrs. Hammond and Mrs. Brown without trouble.

Ellie drove for "Anna Avery" and Mary Wiggins, again without trouble.

When it came time for Cathy King to be the leader for Mrs. Murphy and Mrs. Franks, she fretted, "I'm so scared, Steve. Must I?"

"Don't worry, Mrs. King; you're in no danger; I'm here."

"That's the only reason I have the guts to try this," she told him.

"You'll do fine, just like the others did," the scout encouraged.

But the dark-haired beauty didn't "do fine." She lost the reins almost immediately and screamed for Steve to rescue her.

Ginny watched the racing team speed up as the reins dragged the ground. She was glad she hadn't been assigned as a driver, but only because she hadn't wanted to make a mistake. Ellie had managed the team with skill and courage, and she had bragged about her friend. She had the wicked suspicion that Cathy King had let go of the reins on purpose. She watched the sultry beauty lean over and grab Steve by the neck, forcing him to take her onto the saddle with him to keep her from falling to the ground from the lofty seat. The other women must have suspected the same ruse because they glanced at one another and frowned.

Steve turned the control over to Mrs. Carl Murphy and put Cathy inside the wagon from the rear. He told her to go forward while the other woman did the demonstration. "Pay close attention, Mrs. King. You might need this knowledge later. This lesson could save your life."

"I won't have to do it again, will I?" she pleaded.

"Not today. Maybe later. Let's get moving." He took his position by the team. "They're winded already, Mrs. Murphy, so they shouldn't bolt long. I hate to scare and run them again, but you all didn't get a good enough lesson. Ready?" he asked, and the woman nodded.

When the wagon returned, Mattie Epps was told to drive for Mrs. Daniels and Hackett. The constant whiner glared at the boss and declared, "It's too dangerous. I won't get injured before we even begin this stupid journey. You didn't make Cathy do it, and I won't, either."

Steve gritted his teeth and clenched his jaw. "Mrs. Daniels, why don't you show your team how it's done?" he said. "Stampedes don't happen often, so everyone doesn't have to do it. You just need to know how to respond if it does. Watching is enough for now."

"I'll do it. I ain't scared. No worse than battling a Yankee attack."

"Hang on, ladies," he told the other two, and Mattie scowled at him.

Ginny was amazed and pleased Steve didn't make each one of them drive. She was impressed by his expert horsemanship and physical prowess. She wondered if there was anything the skilled man couldn't do. She had no doubts they were safe in his care, no matter the perils ahead.

"I was terrified," Cathy said. "I could have been thrown off and broken every limb in my body." When no one replied or gave her sympathy, she was miffed. "You pulled my hair, Sue Murphy," she chided her teammate.

"That was the only thing I could grab to keep you from falling."

"It still hurts," Cathy complained, rubbing her scalp.

"Stop groaning and pay attention," Louise scolded her.

"You have room to talk; you know about teams and wagons. We don't."

"If you kept your mind where it should be, you would, too, by now."

"What does that mean?" Cathy demanded, eyes blazing in anger.

"You know very well what I mean. Now, be silent."

Cathy glared at Louise Jackson, then at "Anna Avery" for a moment.

Ginny wondered if the dark-haired vixen was jealous of her, as that was the look she had been given.

While the others were eating lunch and after he'd finished his, Steve went to scout for appropriate river locations for the women's lesson in water crossings this afternoon. During his absence, Charles Avery came to deliver his "daughter's" order and to see how she was doing with her lessons.

Ginny took a stroll with him so they could speak in private.

112

She told him about the training and her successes. She thanked him for the items and supplies he had brought, but assumed the food he'd given Ellie was a thank-you for all the meals she—"his daughter"—had shared with the Davises. Afterward, she related the alarming talk she had overheard last night.

"That would be Carl Murphy," he enlightened her to the Georgian's identity. "He's a hothead, so avoid him. I hope the others hush up about this Klan business; we don't need a spy in camp pulling down the Yanks on us."

"Is what they said true, sir?" she asked in concern.

"In a way. Some men have gotten into the Klan to wreak revenge on Yankees and their cohorts for the horrible things done to them during the war and after it ended. Some are reckless and downright mean and trying to settle personal grudges. But most are honest and decent men who just want to protect Southerners from more cruelties."

"But killings and burnings aren't the right way to obtain justice."

"What would you suggest they do?"

Ginny gave that question deep and serious thought. "I don't know."

Charles smiled and advised, "Well, don't worry your pretty head about it. Soon, we'll be far away from such perils."

"I'm glad, sir, because I don't want trouble to interfere with our journey. We both have grave matters to handle."

"And we will, my girl, you wait and see. But I'd best get back to town. I have a last business meeting this evening. I'll return for good in a few days. Yessiree, this will all be behind us next week."

"We'll be on our way soon," she murmured, dread and excitement filling her from head to foot.

"Any more problems with our handsome guide?" he queried as they headed back to camp.

"Not really," Ginny replied. "Right now, he's ignoring and avoiding me as much as possible."

"That tempted by you, is he?" Charles jested.

113

"If you say so, sir."

"He is, mark my words. Give him the space he thinks he wants and needs while coaxing him toward you, girl. Don't forget what I told you; you might need him and his skills one day soon."

That idea both thrilled and alarmed her. "He'll probably be hundreds of miles away from me when and if that time arrives."

"Somehow I don't think so," Charles murmured, his grin broadening.

She told her racing heart to slow. "We'll see."

"Yes, sir, we surely shall. Good-bye, Anna."

"Good-bye, sir. *Father,*" she corrected with a warm smile.

When Steve returned to camp, Ginny handed him his borrowed gloves and thanked him for them. "Father brought me these," she said, holding out the new pair. "Are they all right?"

Steve grasped one hand as if he was examining them for quality and sturdiness. "Yep, I see I missed his visit again." He released her hand.

Ginny was moved by their brief contact. "Yes," she murmured, "he didn't stay long. He'll be joining us soon."

Steve eyed her closely. "I'm sure that makes you happy."

With a blend of truth and deception, she responded, "It does. We've been separated for six years. It's time to get reacquainted. We had so little time together after my return home from boarding school."

"What kind of man is your father, Anna?"

"Just how he seems: kind, generous, charming—a gentleman."

"You aren't biased in his favor, are you?" he teased.

She returned his smile. "Isn't it natural to be so?"

His tone and expression altered uncontrollably. "I reckon."

Ginny surmised that he didn't sound convinced and decided he might be an orphan, which would explain why he was such a loner. She was intrigued and touched by the bitterness that

114

glittered like black ice in his dark eyes. A clue to him? she wondered.

"Have you eaten?" He suddenly veered away from the topic of parents, and after she had nodded in the affirmative, he said, "We go to work soon. I'll see you later."

"Steve?"

He stopped and turned. "Yes, Miss Avery?"

"You're doing a fine job with our training. Thank you."

He tipped his hat, didn't smile or thank her, turned, and departed.

What an enigma you are, Steve Carr! Should I try to solve it?

At two o'clock, the women met at the river in their wagons. Steve halted them at the first location he had chosen. They gathered around him as he gave his final instructions. "We'll start shallow and work our way to deeper areas. This first site will give you a feel for moving through water and soft bottoms. Once you approach the bank, keep going; don't allow your team to stop to drink or rest. If you do, your wheels will mire down. Goad them extra hard on entering and leaving; that lets the mules get a quick grip when they're changing surfaces. Some rivers will be the most treacherous ground to cover. If your wagon starts leaning to one side, don't panic; you're probably just hitting a low place. Keep your pace steady and don't let your mules slack off or sense you're not in control of them. When we hit deep water later, if we have problems, I'll explain then how to deal with them. Along our route, we'll probably have to hitch up extra teams to get enough power and strength to cross some rivers. That causes delays, but it can't be helped. If there are no questions, let's get busy, ladies."

By the time that lesson was over and their two-mile walk was behind them, the women were exhausted from the arduous exertions. Most of them flopped down on grassy areas to rest before beginning evening chores.

Ginny prepared a plate from the food Charles Avery had brought to her and left it on the rock ring that enclosed Steve's campfire. She knew he would return soon from selecting a deeper site for their river crossing practice tomorrow. When he did, he would find a nice meal, including apple pie, awaiting him. She hoped that would please him.

She joined the Davises for dinner, and delighted the children with another tasty dessert. After the dishes were done, she helped Mary Wiggins repair torn clothing for her four children. She had noticed and questioned Ellie about the fact there were no children in the camp between the ages two and six. Ellie had explained that those ages would correspond with the war years, when so many men were absent! Those few born at the war's end or shortly afterward were the results of men returning home earlier than other soldiers because of injuries.

She hoped things would settle down for the devastated South. It would be wonderful for life to get back to normal. She prayed nothing would happen to create new hostilites and troubles. If wicked and well-intended groups on both sides ceased their vengeful and greedy attacks on each other, peace and healing could come. *Please, Lord, let it be so.*

When she and Mary had completed the task, Ginny smiled at the perky woman with bouncy curls and said, "I want to thank you and the others for helping me learn my chores. It'll make it easier for me on the trail. I'm afraid household tasks weren't part of our studies at school. They depended on mothers to teach them to their daughters."

"You said your own mother has been dead for a long time?" Mary queried.

"Yes, since I was eleven. I still miss her." Longing filled Ginny's heart, so she changed the subject. "Sometimes I feel so ignorant not knowing the things most females do."

"You can't be blamed for that, Anna, so don't feel bad. You were away a long time. I'm sure you're happy to be home."

From the corner of her eye, Ginny noticed Steve leaning against a tree nearby and wondered how long he had been standing there and listening, and why? She pretended not to see him and said what she must, what would mask any possibly unusual behavior between her and Charles. "Yes, I am. I missed my father very much. It's been too long. We've both grown and changed during our separation; it's almost . . . like meeting for the first time and having to learn about each other all over again."

"That could be fun, like a game," Mary ventured.

"You're right; I hadn't thought of it that way."

"The others are gathering soon for conversation and maybe some music," Mary reminded her friend. "Why don't you join them? I'll be along as soon as I get the children tucked in. And thank you for the help with sewing."

"That's one of the few feminine things I can do," Ginny quipped.

"And do very well," Mary complimented her skill.

They exchanged a few words before Ginny left. As she did so, she noticed Steve was no longer around the Wiggins area. *Quiet as a mouse, you stealthy creature. What reason do you have to be furtive with me?*

As she headed for the meeting spot, Ginny pondered if she could be mistaken about thinking he watched everyone in a curious manner, and her more than the others. After what she'd heard last night from her wagon, she fretted about him being a Loyal Leaguer who was trying to ferret out Klan members. Ed King had warned his talkative wife to silence for that very reason. Others had mentioned how spies were used to gather "evidence" against Rebel whites to justify an attack on them. It didn't matter, she reasoned, that the scout had a southern accent, as plenty of them had sided with the Union.

You're being silly, Ginny. Steve is too expert to be a fake wagontrain leader. Maybe he just likes to know his charges well, pick out the possible troublemakers, and deal with them to prevent problems along the way. Or maybe he has a personal interest in you. For certain, there's more to that cunning guide than meets the eye. Whatever the answer, you need to solve the mystery soon, before you become more ensnared by him.

"That's mighty heavy thought, Miss Avery. You really pull deep into yourself when you're distracted. I've been walking beside you for fifty feet and you didn't know I was here. Be glad I'm not an enemy or you'd be in danger. I'm worried about this saddle-napping you do."

Ginny halted and looked at him. With scant moonlight and illumination from the fire, she could barely make out his expression; after she squinted and strained to do so, it was unreadable. The combination of his darkly tanned flesh, ebony hair, and black garments made him almost as invisible as a new moon. He smelled fresh, as if he recently had a bath. She was impressed that a trail man took such care with his body and clothes. The only things ever a little slack in his grooming were a habit of not shaving until evening and of mussing his hair with his fingers, yet those things oddly enhanced his appeal. Her study only required seconds, but it seemed longer. "Don't be worried, Mr. Carr. I simply have a special matter on my mind tonight. I didn't realize I needed to stay alert in camp, not with an expert gunsman and plenty of guards around to protect me. Besides, with your enormous skills, I bet you could sneak up on a bird and capture it."

Steve was aware he had been scrutinized, and it aroused him. He murmured in a husky tone, "Is that a fancy way of complimenting me?"

Ginny felt warm, shaky, and tingly being so close to him in the dark. How she wished things could settle down between them, but perhaps it was best if they didn't. The stars fall down if he wasn't already too tempting! If he ever pursued her seriously, she'd never be able to resist him. "No, you're the one with that skill, too. I wouldn't be surprised if you sneaked up on me so you could scold me for another lapse of attention."

He chuckled and grinned, revealing snowy teeth. In a mirthful tone with left hand over his heart, he said, "Why, Anna, you wound me deeply with that accusation."

Ginny frowned at him for his jest. "Do I indeed? I would imagine few things get to you, Mr. Tough Scout."

Steve fingercombed his hair as he prepared his answer. "You're right, but those few things are real special or they wouldn't work on me."

She struggled to appear poised and unaffected by him and his words. "I would certainly hope so."

Steve gave her a swift and close eyeing. She was as enticing as a wagon of gold. Her hazel gaze sparkled with interest and conflict. Her light-brown hair, or maybe dark tawny, snaked its way from her crown to her waist in wriggling curls and waves. Her lips called to him to kiss them. Her flawless skin urged him to stroke it. Could he? Should he? Not yet. "You're a strange filly, Anna Avery, different from all the others."

"I hope so; I'd hate to be exactly like everyone else. I'd prefer to be a pink cloud in a sky filled with white ones."

"Ah, pink, a soft and warm and lovely color, not stand-out bold and fiery like red. Good choice. What color would I be if I were a cloud?"

Ginny was surprised by his question and response to her whimsical remark. To let him know how he often treated her, she said with bravery, "Black. You're stormy, unpredictable, threatening, and powerful."

Steve took her comparisons to have dual meanings, as her mood implied. "That sounds about right. You're a good judge of character."

She had half expected—more accurately, *hoped for*—him to refute, explain, or apologize. "I hope so," she murmured again to pique him. To escape the disturbing banter, she left him to join the others, and he tagged along without another word.

Following light conversation, one of the men asked Steve to tell them about Texas.

Steve knew it was the duty and custom for leaders to entertain and enlighten travelers with stories and information. He used an easygoing manner as he complied. "She's big, with mountains and valleys westward, forests in the eastern part, and desert in the western section. Lots of flat, open prairies and grasslands. Most areas have rivers or streams. You have to be careful of flash floods in low-lying sections; they can sweep away horse and rider or even a wagon in the blink of an eye. Her weather isn't ordinarily bad, but she can boil your brains in summer and freeze your bones in winter if she takes a mind to. She's like a divided horse, half tamed and half wild."

Steve had everyone's attention and interest, so he assumed he was doing a convincing job. "Cotton, cattle, and farming are her big interests. The Revolution with Mexico for independence ended in '45. *Bandidos* still raid across the Rio Grande sometimes, but they stay near the border for a quick escape, far from where any of you will settle. Right now, she's still excluded from the Union; she tried to get back but they wouldn't allow it. They elected a Unionist governor last year and voted on a new constitution that renounced slavery. Hasn't helped yet. Military law rules her under Radical control and that new Reconstruction Act but there's little trouble from either one. General Sheridan is in command of the Texas-Louisiana district; I'm sure all of you recall his name from the war."

"Damn right we do!" Brown sneered, and others nodded agreement.

Steve didn't give the men time to start rehashing their grievances. "Texans are proud, stubborn men who know how to fight," he said, and related their deeds during the war. "She had legendary lawmen who could face down an entire mob or gang alone; the Union put Rangers out of power fast to prevent any threat from them."

"You said there wasn't much trouble there?" a man asked Steve.

"Very little trouble with gangs of soldiers or raiders like you have here. Texans have occasional problems with rustlers on ranches and outlaws along stageline routes. She's too big and spread out to entice many villains to work there; they'd have to do too much riding."

"Do you do this kind of thing—escort wagontrains—all the time?"

"Not all the time," Steve answered Mrs. King's question, "but I've made my share of trips across country. Mostly I've taken trains from St. Louis to the Far West, to Arizona and California or to Colorado and the Oregon Territory. It's mostly gold and silver that draws folks there. Outlaws, too."

"What do you do when you aren't escorting wagontrains?" Cathy asked.

"A little bit of everything and anything, ma'am."

The dark-haired beauty persisted. "Such as?"

"Guard for gold and silver shipments or freight lines, shotgun for stagecoaches, scout and guide for the Army or private companies, Indian fighting: you name it and I've probably done it or will do it." He chuckled.

"Indian fighting?" Cathy's husband echoed. "In Texas?"

"West Texas has problems with Apaches and Comanches, but none of you are heading there. Most of the trouble is northward in the Dakota lands. The Sand Creek massacre in Colorado started the worst of it. The Indians made treaty in '51, but it's been broken too many times and ways to count. They're working on a second one now and hope to have it signed by fall. It'll be a wise move; those Indians are powerful and cunning and fearless; they won't surrender their lives and lands without heavy bloodshed on both sides. You'd think everybody had had enough of killing."

Ginny fretted over the knowledge of fierce Indian trouble in the area where her father supposedly lived. Without help and protection, how could she get there safely? She halted her frantic musings to listen to the rest of Steve's revelations.

He talked about Chivington's massacre, the Indians' retaliation, and the Bozeman Trail conflict. He finished with the tale of a cocky officer's fatal battle with the legendary Crazy Horse. "Fetterman was led into a cunning trap with his men and slaughtered with the ease of throwing a stone. Some of his troops were part of Sherman's bloody campaign through this state."

"Served 'em right after what they did here!" the Georgian declared.

"Yesiree, maybe them redskins will take revenge for us," Brown murmured with a happy smile and a glitter of hatred in his eyes.

"You said we won't have trouble with outlaws in Texas?" one man asked.

"Not much, maybe a little along stage and mail routes."

"You ever killed an outlaw, had a shootout with one?" another asked.

"I try to mind my own business and keep out of trouble. You should never challenge a man or provoke one to challenge you unless you're certain you can outdraw and outshoot him. Never covet a gunslinger's reputation. There's a saying: 'Live by your guns and you die by them,' and it's true."

"You surely know how to handle your weapons," someone else observed.

"It's my job. Besides guiding you folks, I have to protect you." Steve took the interest off him by saying, "The bad ones work the Missouri, Kansas, and Arkansas areas. Most of them are leftover Jayhawkers or men from Quantrill's raiders."

"We've heard of him, read unbelievable stories in newspapers," Jeff Eaves said. "He was killed in '65, wasn't he?"

"Yep, in Kentucky. He led federal troops on a wild chase for years. People's opinions of him differ from good to bad, from misguided patriot, to heartless thief, using the war for his own profit and glory. His band killed innocents and burned and looted both sides: that's been proven," he added when two men looked about to argue in favor of the notorious man.

When neither spoke, Steve continued. "War taught men to kill and some to enjoy it. Some outlaws seem born mean and greedy; others are driven to it out of revenge. Folks say the worst ones from Quantrill's band haven't stopped killing and robbing innocent folks since the war ended."

Steve noticed that no one asked about the Jayhawkers: plundering marauders who had been antislavery raiders in Kansas, Missouri, and their bordering states. He began tales about notorious outlaws and their criminal deeds.

"They must have people giving them shelter or they'd be caught by now."

"I'm sure they do, Mrs. Wiggins," Steve told Mary. "Some folks see them as famous, and others are afraid to turn down their . . . *requests*."

"They should be Jim Crowed like Negroes are. Segregated, like we do those Galvanized Yankees! You ever met those traitors during your travels, Steve?"

"Plenty of them in the West."

"You mean they admit what they done?" Brown scoffed.

"They don't think they have anything to be ashamed of, Harry. Nor do most folks out West; those men did too much good to be rejected and insulted. Much as you and others despise them, it might be wise to keep those feelings to yourselves or you'll offend new neighbors and friends who might have personal reasons to like them. You have them everywhere out there: many stayed after the war and made fresh starts alone or sent for their families. Most won't return to the South because they are viewed as traitors."

"We sure didn't *want* them back here, the stinking polecats! Nothing but a bunch of betrayers and gutless weaklings. I won't befriend one."

"What are Galvanized Yankees, Mr. Brown?" Lucy asked.

"Let Steve tell you; I can't stand the taste of the words on my tongue."

Steve explained what they had done out West.

Ginny, who had listened quietly and intently, spoke up. "I don't understand, Mr. Carr. If they did so much good and all they wanted was to get out of horrible Yankee prisons, why was that so bad?"

"Hellfire, girl, are you crazy?" Harry Brown shouted. "They betrayed our side, went against their own families and friends."

"How so, Mr. Brown?" she pressed to learn more about her Galvanized Yankee father and his possible motive for remaining out West.

"They went over to the side of the damned Yankees who was killing their people and robbing them or burning them out! A decent and brave man don't do nothing to help his enemies. Nothing!"

"You're saying you think it would have been better if they had stayed in those awful prisons instead of doing good work that didn't harm the South?"

"I spent plenty of time in a prison, but I wouldna ever gone over to the Yankees' side. About cost me my leg, too!"

"But what they did out West will help all of us who are going there. Isn't that worth something, worth forgiveness and compassion?"

"Hell, no, girl, it ain't!"

Steve was about to jump into the hot talk, as he didn't like how Brown was looking at or speaking to Anna Avery, who was only asking questions to grasp the tragic situation. She had a tender and compassionate heart that moved him. He was relieved when both people went silent so he didn't have to cause any conflict.

As people chatted about less serious topics, Ginny drifted into deep thought. She knew the embittered and vengeful man couldn't be reasoned with or appeased. It was evident a few others present didn't like what those ex-Rebel soldiers had done but those didn't feel or react as strongly, thank goodness. She realized that if she was faced with a similar choice, she would have done the same as her father had, following his capture at Stones River at Murfreesboro in early '63. That was how Mathew Marston had gotten to Colorado, and tonight's revelation could prove a partial answer as to why he had remained. He had done some of the jobs Steve Carr had mentioned, and she was proud of him for doing so. She was glad he hadn't stayed in prison and suffered needlessly. Why couldn't these men see that it was better to live and build rather than kill and destroy? She could hardly wait to reach her father's side and be reunited. No joy could be greater than to see his smiling face again.

Ginny sneaked a look at the virile scout, who was silent and alert. After what she'd learned, could she take Charles Avery's suggestion about hiring Steve as her guide and protector? Perhaps she shouldn't keep her deathbed promise to Johanna Chapman. Perhaps she should head straight to Colorado to begin her search. Maybe she should make her final decision after she got to know the mysterious scout better, and after she learned if he was indeed available to be hired.

For all she knew, Steve could be heading back immediately to escort another wagontrain to Texas or farther west. That would place enormous distance between them. What if she never saw him again after this journey ended? Despite their many conflicts, that wasn't what she wanted. She wanted— *Stop thinking such foolish things, Ginny Marston! It's impossible for more reasons than you can count on both hands. Forget about winning Steve Carr. Forget your silly romantic notions. Your goal is to reach Colorado and find your father, not find a husband along the way . . . Certainly not a quicksilver and enigmatic male,* her mind added.

Ginny told herself she was inexperienced and, maybe even ignorant when it came to men and romance. She had been instructed to think of serving and pleasing her mate first and her family second, never herself, to defer to her husband's whims and desires at all times. One was to look and behave her best at all times: be charming, demure, ladylike, and servile. One's only goal should be to find the "proper" man, wed him, bear his children, and cater to his needs. It was believed that a woman was nothing without a husband, no matter if she had talents and skills elsewhere. She must have a mate to be respectable and accepted. She must be taken care of, not fend for herself. Only females in the lowest class supported themselves and remained unwed, even if not by their choice, but the result of cruel fate.

Surely, Ginny thought, there was more in life for a woman.

There must be other challenges and rewards. Why was wanting and needing more than a husband so wrong, so unacceptable by society? What made a man stronger and smarter and braver? Didn't their lessons this week prove a woman could do the same tasks and take the same risks men did? Why must a woman only cower, bend a knee, and serve?

Until she met Steve Carr, she hadn't been tempted to pursue a man. She hadn't met one who caused such flames to burn in her body or such hungers to torment her soul. But dare she follow through with her temptation? Dare she risk a broken heart if she lost the chase, as Steve was probably unattainable? Dare she risk tossing obstacles into the difficult and dangerous path she must travel?

CHAPTER 6

Steve guided the women to an Ogeechee River location where the water was deeper and swifter and where the banks had more of an incline. After repeating their instructions of the previous day, he added a caution he had forgotten: "Watch out for large rocks in stream beds; they'll bust a rim or a spoke. If a river is too bad on the trail, we'll have to use an extra team to help pull wagons across. That causes delays but can't be helped. We'll have to ferry or float wagons across the worst sites; it slows us more when wheels have to be removed along with loads then replaced on the other side. Now, if nobody has a question, let's get moving."

Ginny was apprehensive but not terrified. Her biggest worry was making a mistake that would cause Steve to scold her. She kept her concentration at peak level and used everything he had taught her. Paying attention was simpler when the handsome man wasn't close.

At one point, Steve had to climb aboard Cathy King's wagon to get it unstuck after the dark-haired woman let it halt in midriver and mire down, on purpose Ginny surmised with annoyance. She watched how the two of them had to sit close and snug on the short seat with bodies touching. She witnessed how Cathy brazenly and wantonly gazed into the scout's eyes and thanked him for rescuing her. She fumed, knowing she would have been scolded whereas Cathy didn't receive the slightest reprimand. For all she knew, the guide didn't care about the woman's marital status; Cathy certainly didn't. If the sultry flirt had her way, she would entice Steve into the woods to roll on the ground, and he might go! In England, she had heard gossip about men having mistresses or fiery moments in the arms and beds of wedded women. Her anger mounted with her jealousy. She warned herself to cease her distraction.

After the women made two successful crossings in a row, the smiling teacher told them to take a break then meet for self-defense lessons.

The women gathered near camp, some reluctant about this class. But even with scowls or pouts, everyone listened to Steve's instructions about how to fight and defend oneself. When he asked for a volunteer to help him demonstrate several ways to respond to an attack and to gain escape, Cathy King almost leapt forward with eagerness for contact with him.

Ginny observed as Cathy giggled and practically fondled Steve as he showed them what to do if someone grabbed them. She fumed more and more as time passed.

When Steve had finished his demonstration, he turned to the women. "The secret is to be quick, to take your attacker off guard and by surprise. If you can't find something nearby to use as a weapon to club him with, react fast and flee . . . Who's next?"

As if by prearranged signal, Ellie, Lucy, Ruby, and Mary pushed Ginny into the human circle and shouted, "You, Anna."

Ginny balked and protested, "I paid attention; I don't need to do it."

"If she doesn't want to, Steve, I'll continue to be your target," Cathy said coyly.

"That's all right, Mrs. King, but thank you anyhow. Come and give me a try, Miss Avery. Prove you wouldn't be helpless and vulnerable if you were to be attacked."

Ginny was challenged to make an attempt to best the grinning man. She prayed she could do it, but the supplication wasn't heard above. As she tried to do as Steve had instructed and shown, she was tossed to the ground and pinned there with a knee to the small of her back while he roped her like a calf for branding. With her hands and feet bound behind her and lying on her stomach, she was relieved she was wearing pants today, thanks to Charles Avery's generosity. She wanted to scream curses at the chuckling man but refused to be goaded into bad behavior before others.

Steve withdrew the knife from his boot and sliced through the short rope he had snatched from around one gunbutt and used to capture the now-infuriated woman with blazing eyes. "See, without training and practice, you can be taken quick and easy by a determined man. Try me again."

Ginny tried to entangle his ankle and flip him over her shoulder. She found herself lying on the ground with Steve straddling her and his hands imprisoning her wrists to the hard earth. She felt his knees touching her sides and was staring up into a cocky—seductive?—expression. She wanted to shriek for him to get off her! She knew no one could see his face, the look he was giving her. For a crazy instant, she wished they were alone and wished he would lower his body to hers and . . . Turbulence raced through her as she feared he was playing with her, trying to humiliate her in front of the others. She narrowed and chilled her gaze.

Steve was inflamed by the contact, by the way she first looked at him. Her breathing was rapid and shallow, and her chest rose and fell from exertion, straining against the taut material of her shirt. Perspiration gleamed on her exquisite face, and she was dusty. Her hair was flared around her head like a light-brown pillow. *Shu,* what he would give to bend forward and kiss that parted mouth. He would give even more to rest his body atop and within hers. He had stalled her release too long, so he stood and pulled her up with him. "Try me again."

"This isn't a fair test, Mr. Carr. You're on alert, whereas you said our real opponents wouldn't be. How can I take you by surprise when you're awaiting my attack and prepared to parry it?" Before he could answer, Ginny lowered her chin as if to catch her breath and calm her anger. The moment Steve relaxed, she lunged forward and slammed him in the gut with her head, knocking him to the ground. She fled to the safety of the ring of women and turned to gloat at him for her clever escape.

Steve looked at her from his seat on the grass and said without smiling, "See, even a man on guard can be fooled and beaten. Who's next?"

When it was time to break for lunch, everyone had practiced with Steve. As Ginny headed for her wagon to wash up for the meal, the roguish scout caught up with her and murmured in a tone only she could hear, "You need a bath, Miss Avery; you're a mite dirty and sweaty after scuffling with me."

Don't let him provoke you to say or do something foolish, Ginny. "You're right, as always, but it will have to wait until this evening. If I'm late for afternoon class, I'll be curtly scolded," she retorted and kept walking.

Steve dropped by the Davis campsite before her arrival to thank Ellie for the food she had left for him last night, which had included apple pie.

"It wasn't me, Mr. Carr; it was Anna. Her father brought it to her. Since she eats with us, she gave it to you. She's a kind and thoughtful young woman. She's really trying hard to do good with her lessons. It must be terribly hard for a girl who hasn't had a mother to teach her much, and she's been away from home and her father for so long. She's lived such a sheltered existence, so this challenge must be difficult for her."

"You're probably right, ma'am. Thank her for me, will you?"

"It would mean more to her if it came from you," Ellie suggested, as she sensed the attraction between them and thought them a good match.

He nodded and left. He wondered why Anna would do such

a kindness and keep it a secret. Wouldn't she want the credit? Of course, he mused, she figured he'd seek out the thoughtful person and discover it was her! She was a sly and wily female after all.

That afternoon they walked for three hot and tiring miles. Ginny passed Steve as she entered camp and refused to glance his way or speak. She told herself that maybe he couldn't decide how he felt or how to behave. If she ignored him for a while, maybe that would coerce a decision from him.

Dark, threatening clouds moved overhead before meals were cooked and served and evening chores were done. The wind increased in force and intent; it yanked at limbs, clothes, hair, and canvases. A heaviness in the air warned of an imminent storm. Menacing rumbles said it would lash out at them any moment. Everyone hurried to prepare for its assault. Baths were skipped or taken swiftly. Possessions were either stored inside or placed underneath the wagon on waterproof cloths.

Ginny took all the precautions with the animals and wagon she had learned. While she was checking and securing the mules' ropes and stakes, the storm struck with a fury. A torrential rain poured down in a rush before she could finish and dash inside. The beasts were startled by the loud thunder and flashes of lightning. She patted and spoke soothingly to them until they calmed. When she turned to head for the wagon, she saw Steve running toward her, as drenched as she was.

"Anything wrong?" he questioned, gazing at the water dripping from her face and at the soaked curls plastered to her face. Her shirt did the same clingy task on her chest but he pretended not to notice.

She explained what she was doing over the loud and combined noises of rain, wind, and thunder. "I'm finished now and going inside."

"You don't have your tarp on the front. A rain this heavy will seep inside and ruin things. I'll help you." He grasped her hand

and pulled her to the wagon. He climbed onto the tongue, lifted the jockey box lid, and withdrew a large waterproof cloth. He showed her how to toss it over the box and seat, then secure it in place. The way he positioned one edge created a valley that allowed rain to run off left and right of the wooden bed. "Let's get inside and see if anything needs moving out of the water."

Steve leapt aboard the tailgate, hauled her up as easily as lifting a feather, then closed the opening behind them. He saw that the center of the wagon was clear of obstacles, as she hadn't put down her bedding yet. He moved forward and checked for puddles at the front. "Nothing to worry about, just a little damp." He handed her several items that needed moving out of possible harm's way if wind ripped the cover loose. "That should do it. You best get dried off and changed before a chill sets in."

"Thank you for the help. I'm sorry I didn't know about the tarp."

"Think nothing of it, Miss Avery; it hasn't been the subject of a lesson yet."

As they stepped over a crate, Ginny's foot was snagged by the fastener and she lost her balance. Steve grabbed for her, and both began falling toward the back. The motion of their actions caused the bedding to topple to the floor before they reached it, softening their landing. Steve was half atop Ginny, so she was captive between him and the soft bedding.

Steve chuckled and remarked as he patted the feather mattress, "That was good timing; or both of us might have been injured."

Ginny noticed that he didn't move off her; nor did she push him aside. "Thank you for the rescue," she murmured, unsettled and wary.

"You're welcome, Anna." He pushed wet curls from her face as he smiled. "You're soaked."

Ginny couldn't help but smile in return. "So are you, Steve."

Without lifting his elbow from near her shoulder, he leaned

his head forward and fingercombed his sable hair. "A mess, eh?"

"No," she heard herself murmur. His virile body felt like a copper bedwarmer on a wintry night. She couldn't break his powerful hold on her gaze. His dark-brown eyes were glowing and his mood was entreating. It was almost as if she could hear them beckoning: *Kiss me; love me, Ginny.* Her eyes drifted over his rain-slick face and settled on his mouth.

Steve observed her actions and felt her tremble. "Cold?" he asked, though he knew she wasn't. He wondered if she realized he was also aquiver with desire. His body felt aflame. A curious tension held him rigid and refused to allow him to leave her. He knew that was what he should do, and pronto.

Ginny's hands rested against his broad chest. She felt his heart pounding against her fingertips and palms; it surprised and pleased her to have such a powerful effect on him. Her gaze was drawn back to his as she finally shook her head to his query. His mood was mellow and enthralling, as was his dark gaze. Almost against her will, her fingers seized his shirt and pulled him toward her.

Steve responded to the unspoken invitation. His mouth covered hers and parted her lips. His fingers wiggled into her drenched hair, clasped her head, and held it still as his mouth worked hungrily at hers. A groan escaped his throat as he pressed closer and tighter against her. The lightning outside couldn't be charged with more energy than he was.

Ginny's arms banded the dazing scout's waist. She clung to him, stroked his back, and urgently returned his kiss. A surge of unfamiliar heat licked over her flesh. Love claimed and ruled her heart.

A thunderbolt crashed loudly outside and vibrated the wagon. The mules nearby brayed in panic. Steve came to his senses and leaned away from Ginny. Her cheeks were flushed with passion and her eyes were glazed by it. She wanted him as much as he wanted her. If they weren't in a camp filled with people—any one of whom could approach any second and discover this reckless scene—he would make her his. He would brand her with a love she would never forget, remove, or match.

Ginny blushed as reality and his withdrawal destroyed the dreamy illusion. She didn't know what to say or do; they had gotten carried away by desire. She recalled she had been the one to initiate it, to encourage it. What must he think about her, a so-called lady entreating . . . seduction?

"I've been wondering for days what that would taste and feel like. You've learned your wiles well, Miss Avery; you're one powerful temptation. I'd best get out of this hot box before we both say and do something foolish."

"You're right, Mr. Carr. I apologize for . . . behaving so badly and rashly. You're also a powerful temptation, and I'm unaccustomed to . . ." Surely he recognized an innocent without her admitting to being one. "I don't know what possessed me to act that way," she lied. "I'm ashamed and embarrassed. Please don't tell Father I lost my wits."

"Don't worry, Miss Avery, I won't. He might horsewhip me for letting the situation get out of control. I promise it won't happen again." He told himself he was only inching closer to her because of his mission, and he dared his troubled mind or racing heart to argue with him.

"Thank you, and I'll also make certain it doesn't." She watched Steve loosen the cord and hop over the tailgate. She heard the thud and squish of his boots against the softening ground. She commanded herself to get up and resecure the opening against the bad weather.

Ginny flopped down on the bedding and rested a forearm over her eyes. She had the urge to cry in frustration but fought it down. *How could you have been so stupid, so wanton? You rebuke Cathy King, then behave as badly or worse. Whatever got into you, Virginia Marston? You've never acted like this before. Damn you, Steve Carr, you have too strong of a pull on me. I have to be extra careful around you in the future.*

134

When the storm lessened near dusk but still didn't cease, tents of tarp were put up for cooking underneath. Grassy spots were chosen to cut down on mud. The men built fires, and smoke soon curled around the shelter's edges. When the flames were right, meals were began by the women.

Ginny put on a rain slicker and helped Ellie Davis as usual. She doubted anyone had seen Steve enter, remain too long, and depart her wagon; the storm had been in full force and all wagons had been closed tightly against its intrusion.

As she worked, she wondered whether Steve was attracted to her and just being defensive, or if he had, as men were said to do, merely taken advantage of something offered, or if he truly wanted her to leave him alone. She was to blame for the heady incident, so she shouldn't fault him for responding. Still, it would be unfair—was *cruel*—for him to play with her emotions, to abuse her weakness for him. She ordered herself to forget about Steve and the intoxicating moment for now.

The scout was joining the Kings for supper. From the corner of her eye, she saw Steve and Cathy laughing and chatting. She couldn't forget how the woman clearly craved him. Nor could she halt the flood of envy and jealousy that surged through her. It was almost as if Steve knew of her gaze upon him and was behaving that way on purpose. She should be angry but it tormented her.

It rained most of the night, and Ginny slept little. Part of her restlessness had to do with the two Davis girls sleeping with her. They were active even in slumber and she was unaccustomed to bedmates. She had offered to let them stay so Ellie and the others would have more room inside their cluttered wagon where the weather had driven them. It had been a kindness that was taking its toll on her. As dawn approached, the weary Ginny was exhausted and tense.

Ginny watched Steve chat with Cathy after breakfast. What difference did it make, she fumed, that the bold woman had approached him? That Steve didn't say a few polite words and walk away as he should have to prevent suspicions in others, particularly in Ed King, who had to be blind or stupid not to be aware of his wife's flirtation? Maybe the Kings wanted something special from the scout and Cathy was softening him up to get it.

How far, she worried, had the relationship between Cathy and Steve been taken? Had they stolen kisses and caresses during walks when they were last to return or those times he had gone back to fetch her? Had Cathy sneaked into the woods to meet with him? Would Steve Carr do such a wicked and dangerous thing? Surely not, as he took his job too seriously and was too proud to risk humiliation.

Besides, the virile male had spurned her in the wagon yesterday when she had practically begged him to seduce her. She had lost her wits and self-control, and he had been the one to use his to halt their behavior. *Just because he didn't want you that way doesn't mean he doesn't want Cathy. After all, she's experienced and hot-blooded, you're only— Stop it, Ginny; you're letting this get to you too much.*

The next morning, Steve said, "Thanks to a timely rain, this is the perfect day to practice driving through and getting out of mud." He gave them instructions before they hitched their teams and began the lesson.

Since keeping the correct pace and avoiding perilous spots were the main two safety measures, Ginny paid the most attention to them.

* * *

It was almost time for lunch. Once or twice they had halted to rehearse getting started again after a stop with wheels sunk into mire. Only a couple of women had gotten stuck or couldn't get moving again and had required Steve's help. Neither of them was Cathy King who, Ginny assumed, was smart enough to realize she couldn't be all over the scout all the time.

They headed for rest and food. Two wagons became stuck in the overworked ground, as Steve had chosen a saturated dirt area that had been trampled by them into mush. One was Ginny's, who tried her best to free the captive wagon so he wouldn't have to help her in her foul mood.

Steve sent the others onward to camp with Louise Jackson in charge. He helped the other woman first, as she wasn't mired down as deeply.

Before the scout reached Ginny, she took an ax and trudged through graspy earth to chop off pine limbs from nearby trees. She hauled them to the wagon, got down on her knees, and worked them around and under the captive rim; that would give it something to grip for pulling out of the mud hole. She had seen carriage drivers in England use this method. She was about to climb aboard to test her solution when Steve arrived.

He looked at the draggled female, eyed her work, and said, "That's clever, Miss Avery, but what if no tree limbs are around on a prairie?"

Ginny mused a moment, then walked to the side. She ignored the mud she was getting on her hands and clothes to kneel and remove the limbs. She went to the front, opened the jockey box, and took out a hammer. She walked to the back and climbed inside, then unloaded a sturdy crate and shoved it to the ground. She didn't say a word as she took the box apart and laid the hammer and nails on the tailgate. She used the wood slabs as she had the limbs. Within minutes, she was free, and no wooden piece had been broken, only one cracked a little. She hopped down—glad she was in pants and boots again today— and put the crate together again. She left it in the back to wash off the mud before replacing the items she had removed. When the hammer was returned to its location, she climbed aboard and said, "All done. See you in camp."

Steve had observed in silence. He was impressed by her quick wits. She was definitely learning how to take care of herself. As he watched her, he couldn't get the passionate scene in her wagon off his mind. He had to make sure it happened again soon. He rode up beside her and unwisely teased, "You and your clothes will need a good scrubbing, Miss Avery. I'm surprised a lady would roll in the mud like that."

Her overcrowded mind retorted, *Better than rolling in the grass with another man's wife! Don't let him provoke you, Ginny. You're just tired and edgy and miserable, and angry. Show him you can control your temper.* "I know it's unlike a lady not to look her best, but there are times when she can't; this is one of them. It's more important to do my lessons and appease my teacher than to look ready for a Sunday stroll."

"Then you've learned one of the most important lessons of all: never let anything or anyone stand in the way of doing what you must."

"That advice couldn't come from a more appropriate source."

"Appropriate . . . suitable," Steve murmured. "Yep, you're right."

For a moment, Ginny had thought he didn't know that word, and she was amazed he did. But actually, she admitted, he seemed quite educated.

After they reached camp, Ginny unhitched the team and led them to the river to drink. She carried a bucket along to rinse off most of the mud, as it would surely be uncomfortable after it dried. She staked them near her campsite as usual and stored the harnesses underneath the wagon. Just to pique Steve, she didn't take a bath, only washed her face and hands. Nor did she change clothes or brush and rebraid her mussed hair. She was relieved the other women didn't groom themselves, either.

* * *

The women took their three-mile walk following lunch, because Steve said it was going to storm again later and they needed to get their chores and meal preparations completed earlier than usual.

Ginny hung back with Lucy Eaves. Her bad ankle was swollen and slowing her friend's pace. Ginny knew it must be aching and suggested she fetch Steve to give Lucy a ride to camp.

Lucy thanked her, but refused. "I have to do this for myself. It'll be fine by morning; it always is. It's just the wet weather bothering it. Why don't you go on ahead? I'll be fine. I'm ruining your pace."

"I don't care about that. Our demanding teacher will understand," Ginny told her, but wasn't convinced he would. She never knew what to expect from the unpredictable creature.

Steve didn't say a word to either woman as they entered camp. He knew why they were slow. He saw how brave and determined Lucy was and how thoughtful Anna was. An idea came to mind and he went to work on it.

"You don't have to do this, Anna," Lucy protested, but she was inwardly delighted.

"Yes I do. We're friends. You keep that foot in saltwater soak while I do the chores. Just correct me when I go astray. You know I'm not well trained in the kitchen," she reminded with a laugh.

After the Eaves family and Ginny ate the meal she had cooked, Ginny made Lucy sit down while she did the dishes and put things away. She helped Jeff prepare everything for the approaching storm.

Afterward, she sat on the ground and rubbed liniment into Lucy's ankle, foot, and calf. "Am I hurting you?" Ginny asked as she gently but firmly massaged the aggravated area.

Lucy smiled and sighed almost dreamily. "No, and you're so kind to tend me this way. I feel like a pampered child; it's heaven."

"You deserve good treatment. I'll do this again tomorrow."

* * *

Ginny hurried to get her own chores and preparations finished, then gathered her things and headed for the designated bathing area to scrub off the mud and to wash her filthy garments. She wasn't about to share her bed with mud or to dirty the wagon with it. When she heard voices around the bend in the path, she ducked behind some bushes after she recognized one as Cathy's and the other as Steve's. She told herself the action was silly, but she didn't want to meet and speak with either one. They passed her concealed location and stopped ahead, out of hearing range. Ginny refused to risk exposing herself. She must wait in concealment until they left and hoped that would be soon.

Steve was annoyed with the dark-haired beauty for seeking him out in the woods. He knew, if discovered, it would appear improper and could be hazardous to his mission. He was tired of the woman grasping at him and offering herself. He suspected he was going to have to be harsh with her to make her behave. When she pleaded for a stop to the exhausting walks, he told her, "You need the stamina, ma'am. You'll soon be doing it daily on the trail, so you'd better get used to it now."

"You could tell the others I have a good reason I can't do it, perhaps a bad ankle or leg like Lucy Eaves has."

"I don't lean toward lies and tricks, Mrs. King; they cause trouble."

"I could reward you," she purred, pressing her body close to his and lacing her fingers behind his neck. She tried to kiss him.

Steve grasped her hands and worked them free, careful not to get any telltale scratches from her nails. He captured her chin to keep her from rising to attempt another kiss. "Don't do this, Mrs. King."

"Why not? I want you, and you want me."

"That isn't true. Don't force me to embarrass you with the truth."

Ginny couldn't watch any more. She hated the way Steve

cupped the woman's face. She couldn't bear to see them kiss, so she gingerly slipped from her hiding place and escaped the tormenting scene.

The rain began before Ginny finished washing her shirt and pants and cleaning her boots. Her clean skirt and blouse would get soaked before she reached cover but she didn't care; they would dry. The drops felt cool, refreshing, soothing, even stimulating to her weary body and troubled spirit. She stuffed her things into a cloth sack and flung the laundry over one arm to head back.

The downpour increased and played mischief with her vision. Peals of thunder boomed overhead and lightning flashed in zigzag patterns. She assumed everyone was inside their wagons by now so there was no one who knew she was gone and would worry—or so she thought. She almost collided with Steve Carr as she hurried along the path. Blinking away raindrops as she looked up into his sullen expression, she said, "I'm coming; I'm coming."

"Get to your wagon, woman! Don't you realize it's dangerous to be away from camp alone? With the storm's noise and everybody inside, a scream for help wouldn't be heard. If anything happened to you, Anna, I'd be held to blame. Why take this foolish risk?"

"I was helping Lucy. Her ankle looked awful. She can't walk like the rest of us. You're mean to force her to aggravate it with exercise."

Steve knew what she had been doing. "There are times she'll have to walk, Miss Avery. She knows and accepts that; she doesn't complain."

"She wouldn't, and you know it," Ginny told him. "She won't have to walk. When she can't drive her wagon, she can drive mine, and I'll walk."

"What about your father?" Steve reminded and tested her.

"He has a horse; he can ride him. There are times when a

person can't do his share of the work and others have to help them."

Steve sensed anger and tension. "You're in a foul mood today."

"Why shouldn't I be? You pick at me half the time. I don't appreciate being hog-tied for your amusement or constantly corrected like a bad child. You're mean to me and Lucy. Since you obviously don't like me, Mr. Carr, why not leave me alone? Stop playing spiteful games with me."

"What do you mean?" he asked, looking confused and intrigued.

"Do you want the truth?" she challenged, egged on by her strain. *Be honest, Ginny, so you can clear the air.*

"Of course," Steve murmured without thinking of the consequences.

"A few times you've reacted too strongly, even if you had just cause for your annoyance. You have a heavy responsibility for a lot of people; I realize that. But you and I rub each other wrong. I'm a friendly and open person; you're the opposite; our differences somehow offend and irritate you. You mistake those traits as false pretenses and womanly wiles. In clear terms, you think I'm a fake, spoiled, can't or won't learn the lessons, will delay the journey, make you look bad, and will be too friendly to you. You don't believe a lady can carry her weight on the trail. Whether or not it's intentional, you're tougher on me than on the others."

"How do you know what I think or feel?"

"Actually, I don't," she admitted, "because you keep me in a constant state of confusion and tension with your contradictory behavior, but that's the impression you've given me. Correct me if I'm wrong."

"I thought you had confidence in me."

"I do. I believe you're a very capable teacher and skilled guide."

"But you have a low opinion of me as a person?"

142

"No. I just don't think you like me or trust me or that you're fair to me."

"Do you think I should give you special treatment?"

"That isn't what I mean. Louise and Mattie and . . . others give you a hard time, unjustly I'll add, but you aren't mean to them. Why single me out to be scolded and embarrassed so many times?"

Steve came up with a logical explanation. "You need toughening up the most. Your distractions endanger me, yourself, and the others; I've explained that to you. What Mrs. Jackson, Epps, and . . . others do is annoying but not dangerous. I see no need to make them behave worse by reprimanding them. But with you, corrections improve your progress and you don't get spiteful and rebellious, or I didn't think you would."

"I'm to take that as a compliment?" she scoffed, ignoring the storm.

Steve did, too. "Why, Miss Avery, I do believe you've been hiding a naughty and defiant streak. You have more sides and surprises to your personality than a box," he teased to relax them both. As he did so, he cupped her face as he'd done with Cathy while setting the vixen straight.

The same scene came to Ginny's tormented mind and she was provoked to warn, "Don't make fun of me, you bastard."

Steve went rigid and glared at her. He was piqued into a rash reply. "Yep, so I guess it comes natural for me to act like what I am."

Ginny was stunned and she gaped at him. He was serious! Telling the truth! On purpose? Was that the root of his—

"Sorry if I shocked you, Miss Avery; it slipped out."

Even though he was the one to apologize for a change, he did it with a sarcastic tone and expression. Her pleading heart went out to him. "I'm sorry, Steve; I didn't mean to say that. You made me angry with your amusement at my expense. I like you and want to be friends, to have peace, a truce."

She looked genuinely contrite but he discarded her plea. "Don't be sorry or feel pity for me. I'm not the only bastard

143

alive. The way some men and women carry on, who can be sure of their parentage? Take that King woman; her children could be fathered by three different men. If she doesn't stop working on me to become number four, she'll be sorry."

Was that what influenced his feelings and behavior toward women? Toward her? At least, she had misunderstood the scene she had witnessed earlier. "I'm sorry you hate your mother so much."

Steve stared at her strangely. "I don't; I love her."

She realized he didn't mention his father, if he knew who he was. She didn't query him about the touchy subject. But why blame and hate the man involved and not the woman? Odd . . .

He was so drawn to her that he rebelled. "Just a friendly warning, Anna, if you have your sights set on me, don't. I'm not available."

"You're married or you have a sweetheart?"

"Neither; past, present, or future. No place in my life for either one. A man like me only needs himself to tend."

"That sounds awfully cold and hard and lonely, Steve."

"Maybe so, but it suits me fine. I never allow myself to become vulnerable to other people's demands or put myself in a position to suffer defeat. You shouldn't, either. Be strong and smart, and you won't."

"You don't trust anyone or let anyone get close?" she asked.

"Nope, I just trust myself."

"That's a hard way to exist, Steve."

"Hasn't been so far."

"You don't ever want to change your life?"

"Nope."

"I don't believe you."

"Why not?"

"Who would want to live that way on purpose?" she reasoned. "Besides, you're too special to be alone forever."

"Am I? A man like me will take whatever a woman offers him, even if he doesn't feel the same way she does. Beware of devils like me, Anna Avery. We're dangerous and untrustworthy and selfish." *And I'm worse things you don't even know about.*

Afraid of me, are you? "Is that a challenge to find out? To prove to you that you're wrong about yourself?"

"Maybe so, because you're one tempting woman, but don't accept it. When you've had time to think about me carefully, you'll realize I'm right, that I'm worse than any violent storm could be. Get back to camp now; the storm's getting worse and it isn't safe out here alone. Don't do this again."

Ginny grasped double meanings in his words. "Ste—"

"Don't push, woman, or you'll be sorry. Better listen to me and heed my words while I'm in a rare generous mood. Git!" he ordered.

Ginny obeyed him, but didn't want to leave him or stop talking.

Steve watched her hurry out of sight when what he really wanted was to yank her into his arms and cover her mouth with kisses. He leaned against a tree and took several deep breaths to calm himself. He was angry for making his reckless admission and for behaving like a fool. *Nuguyaa,* he must have a head full of stones! But his heart no longer felt like one, and that worried him. Whyever had he told her such a humiliating and bitter secret? Because she had unsettled him—taken him off guard—with her words, expressions, and allure. But she was *ntu'i izee,* bad medicine.

After she tossed her sack inside the wagon, Ginny hung her soaked garments over a rope she had suspended between two trees to allow them to dry. Drenched, she checked on the nervous mules and went to the Davis wagon.

After leaving Steve and while she was doing her tasks, she pondered this man she desired. She could imagine the anguish and hardships he must have endured without a loving father's name, guidance, affection, and influence. It must have been a terrible cross to bear. Perhaps his mother had been ravished, or

145

been a "soiled dove" who had gotten pregnant on the job, or had chosen to love and surrender to an unattainable man, one like her son had become.

Steve Carr was clearly a man in torment, with deep resentments, a scarred heart and troubled soul, and a tragic past. By his own admission, he didn't want to trust or get close to anyone, especially a woman. She was beginning to grasp why he was so moody, defensive, and wary. He had become self-contained, stubborn, and tough to protect himself against being hurt again; but he was unaware that he was his biggest enemy and torturer. Without realizing it, he had become more like his father than he knew, or wanted to be, or would admit. She was positive he didn't comprehend how much he needed love, comfort, and peace. Maybe his slip hadn't been an accident; maybe his lost soul was reaching out to her for those things.

When Ellie responded to her call, Ginny said, "Give me a minute to get into dry clothes, then let Stuart bring the girls over for the night."

"We don't want to be trouble, Anna; we'll have to sleep this way on the trail during bad weather."

"No need to be cramped before it's necessary," she teased. "Truly, it's no bother and everyone will be more comfortable."

Ginny sat in a nightgown on the mattress with the two girls. She was tired and needed a good night's sleep, but she needed a diversion more. The youngest provided it because she was afraid of the loud rain and thunder. "Let's play a game," she suggested. "Let's close our eyes and make guesses what the storm sounds like to us. Ready?" Ginny asked when they agreed. When both answered at the same time, she said, "I'll be first. Listen to the rain; it sounds like your mother . . . frying chicken or bacon. The thunder sounds like . . . your father hunting and firing his rifle."

"It sounds like furniture moving upstairs," the oldest ventured.

"You're right," Ginny said, and the game continued.

Afterward, she entertained and distracted them with stories her mother and father had told her as a child. At one thunderous boom, the youngest girl leaned closer to her. Ginny embraced her and soothed, "Snuggle close and I'll protect you. When I was a little girl and scared of storms, my mother left a candle burning and sang to me."

Ginny had the light low and the lantern secured to prevent an accident. She sang softly to the girls until both were asleep, one on each side of her. She smiled in satisfaction and closed her eyes, relaxed and weary enough to slumber herself tonight.

Steve moved away from the Avery wagon, wishing he could be cuddled in Ginny's arms. She was right; he was too tough and inconsistent with her, but he had good reason and he wasn't certain he could stop his ruse. She was the most invigorating breath of air he had ever taken. She had good and enticing traits. He liked being with her and talking with her. He warmed under the shine of her smile. He quivered under the sound of her voice. He flamed with desire for her.

A wife, home, and children were things he hadn't ever considered or wanted for himself. Then, Anna Avery had appeared on the scene and made them come to mind too often, made them look and feel compelling at times. That was crazy, he told himself. He had no room for them in his life, no place for them in his embittered heart. He resented the fact she even teased such dreams over his mind. Perhaps being around so many families was also to blame for him thinking so wildly and foolishly. What did he know about romancing and loving a woman, a lady like Miss Anna Avery?

Love . . . Jump off that stallion before you break your neck trying to tame it. Don't go near her with thoughts of capturing and mastering her.

Steve quelled his rebellious emotions and went for a ride on Chuune. He would finish the women's training tomorrow, give them Sunday for final preparations, then pull out on Monday, April first. He hadn't unmasked the culprit he was seeking, but he would during the journey. If it turned out to be Charles

Avery, he might kill the man for endangering and involving his daughter! What would he do about her, with her, if Charles was guilty? The spirits help both of them if she was part of the crime in progress!

As he galloped along on Chuune's back to release his tension, he knew that several people were in for big surprises in the morning.

CHAPTER 7

Saturday morning, Ginny went to help Lucy Eaves with chores before their final training began. The woman showed her the sturdy crutch Steve Carr had made for her to help her walk better during the daily exercise and on the trail. She heard of how the scout had offered to let her friend skip that difficult task, and that Lucy had refused. Ginny was pleased but dismayed with herself for her verbal attack on him about the matter. Why hadn't he told her about this? It wasn't something he'd done since her criticism of him, which revealed he possessed compassion. Again, it was made clear he wanted to conceal or deny good traits. Remorse and guilt flooded her. As soon as she completed Lucy's chores, she sought him out.

"Steve, I want to apologize for what I said on the path yesterday. Lucy told me what you've done for her. I was wrong to misjudge you and to be so hateful. I was in a wicked mood from lack of sleep. I shouldn't have taken out my tension on you. Please forgive me."

"There's nothing to forgive, Miss Avery. It's my job to see that everyone does their jobs. She needed help, so I provided it."

"You can pass it off lightly if you wish, but I won't. In spite of what you think your motive was, it was nice and thoughtful. You aren't as cold and heartless as you believe and try to pretend to be. I'm sure you must have suffered in your life, but you can let the past go if you want to badly enough."

"With your help and sacrifice, Miss Avery?"

Tears glittered in her hazel eyes as she looked at him. She tried to convince herself it was a defensive action, but it hurt; it hurt for him. Her voice was strained as she replied, "I know it's hard for you to accept words of gratitude, but these come from the depths of my heart."

"Don't do this to yourself; don't make me out to be something I'm not. Being responsible for people you're in charge of doesn't mean I have a tender heart like you do. That's fine for you, just not for me. I've told you and shown you what kind of man I am, a bastard in more than birth."

Ginny shook her head in disagreement. "If you think kindness and compassion are weaknesses, you're wrong, Steve. Sometimes people do get hurt when they take risks, but life isn't much without the times you succeed. If you aren't the man I believe you to be, you would have taken what I offered and cared nothing for its effect on me."

Gazing into her entreating eyes and lovely face, it required a moment for him to think clearly enough to find a deceitful reply. "I care about my survival and my job; playing with you could destroy them."

"You can tell yourself that was your motive, but I don't believe it."

He locked gazes with her. "What do you think my motive was, *is?*"

Ginny decided to gamble for the whole pot. "I think you feel the same way I do and that scares the dickens out of you."

Steve narrowed his eyes and he dared not ask her what those feelings were. "You think I'm a coward, a weakling?"

"Only with your feelings," she explained. "You're willing to risk everything or anything—even your life—on physical challenges, but refuse to risk anything on emotional ones. Taking physical chances can kill you; emotional ones might only wound and can heal with time and another try."

"Some wounds never heal, Anna. Never."

"Because you pick at them, keep them open and raw, untended. You refuse to allow anyone to help treat them."

He realized he had to extricate himself from this unsettling talk. "Unless you've lived my life, you'd never understand it or me. Advice is easy to give, but taking it isn't. Even if I did feel as you do, whatever that is, it wouldn't change things. I'm a loner and I'll remain a loner till I die."

Ginny feared she couldn't reach him, and perhaps that was for the best. It was selfish and reckless to try to convince him to take a risk that could hurt both of them if it failed. "You aren't the only one who's scared of risks and who's suffered and been cheated in life."

Something in her voice and expression reached deep into his gut and twisted it. "How would a lady like you know anything about suffering?"

Tears pooled along the rims of Ginny's eyes, but she kept them from overflowing and spilling down her cheeks. "It would shock you."

"Teasing from Yankee girls and being away from family for years in an expensive boarding school isn't the end of the world, Anna."

"It has nothing to do with that. Yes, I've had what most people would believe is a pampered existence, but you don't really know me or what . . ." Ginny lowered her lashes to compose herself before she revealed too much to a beguiling stranger. She had the overwhelming urge to sob. When she lifted her eyes again, she was poised, but curious anguish was still visible to the man before her. "Forget it," she said. "I just came to thank you, not unload my burdens. Your shoulders are too full as is. Besides, we don't know each other well enough to share such a serious talk. I'll see you later, Mr. Carr."

He grasped how he had hurt her and spurned her. He couldn't help but reach out to her, even though he told himself it was only to save his mission, to repair the bridge needed to get to her. "Anna, tell me—"

She didn't face him while replying. "No, Mr. Carr; you solve your problems and I'll solve mine." She walked away with head held high.

Steve ran certain words through his keen mind: "Problems . . . Unload my burdens . . . Other worries . . . Feel the same way I do . . . Suffered and been cheated . . ." What had she been about to tell him, to let slip? Why hadn't he allowed her to confess whatever troubled her? What would "shock" him? Her "burdens" had to do with more than him, and he should have let her expose them. She could hold valuable clues to his case and he had forced her to keep her hands balled. He wondered if it had been intentional on his part; once he solved this case, he would be gone.

The group met around a wagon in the next clearing: they used the Avery one because it had fewer things to unload, and Charles had the necessary tools for today's training task. Before they started the lesson, Steve told the others how "Miss Avery" had gotten free of the mud hole and praised her wits; that surprised and pleased Ginny.

"You should remember those tricks in case you need them later. Now, let's learn how to remove and replace a wheel. We won't break anything here to learn how to do repairs, but I'll tell you how they're done."

"Why learn this? Our husbands and the other men will do it."

Steve explained to Mattie Epps and others, "If your husband is alive and uninjured, you're right. And, if you don't get stranded or leave the wagontrain for some reason, you're right. But what if you're wrong?"

"Why would anyone do that?" the complainer asked.

"Husbands can get hurt and killed and too sick to work. If one of those hardships strikes, sometimes people don't go on, or they decide to head to the nearest town to settle or recover there, or they decide to give up and turn back. Once you leave the wagontrain, you're on your own. If you break a wheel or part, who's going to do the change or repair? Are you going to sit there waiting and hoping for help to come along? Supplies could run out or robbers could come by before that happens. I won't force any of you to learn this lesson, but don't say I didn't give you fair warning it could be needed."

After those words, no one left the area or refused to participate in the lesson. They used Charles Avery's jack to lift the wagon by the axle assembly. They took turns turning the crank, removing the wheel, replacing the wheel, and lowering the contrivance.

When every woman knew the procedure and could respond accurately to questions about other repairs, they broke for lunch, then took their four-mile walk. Afterward, Steve met with them for final instructions.

At four o'clock, the scout announced, "You're trained and ready, ladies. Be sure to practice and hone your new skills on the trail; don't let them get rusty. This evening and tomorrow, get your final chores and preparations done. We leave Monday morning at seven sharp. You're dismissed until that time, except for your exercise tomorrow; you don't want to get stiff and soft by skipping a day. I'll be heading to town soon to tell the grain wagon drivers we're finished and to join us tomorrow. If any of your husbands want to come along to get supplies, he's welcome to ride along with me. All of you did a good job, so I doubt anyone will have trouble along the way."

Loud cheers rose among the women.

Ginny climbed aboard the wagon, drove it back to her campsite, and unhitched the team. She went inside to make certain everything was in its correct place and was secured, as others had helped her reload.

"Miss Avery?"

She turned, walked to the back, and knelt to speak with the scout.

"Do you have a message for your father I can deliver? Anything you need him to bring when he comes tomorrow to join us?"

"Nothing I can think of, Steve, but thank you for the offer."

"See you later."

"Good-bye, Steve, and thanks."

He tipped his hat, nodded, and left.

So much for not having human kindness, Ginny thought with a smile. It slowly faded as she mused, *Or did you only want an excuse to see where and how you think I lived? Checking me out, my inquisitive guide? Why?*

Ginny shook her head in displeasure. *Don't be so suspicious of him. Just because he's being nice doesn't mean he has an ulterior motive.* Yet, she had a strong feeling he did; perhaps it had been something in his tone of voice or in his expression that gave her that feeling. After all, Steve Carr wasn't a man to do anything without a good reason, his own reason.

Ginny let the matter drop and went to see Ruby Amerson. "Why don't I watch the children while you get your wash done?" she offered. "I don't have as much, so I can do mine afterward."

"That's so kind of you, Anna. It'll be a big help. George went into town with Mr. Carr to replenish some of our supplies."

"It will be fun and educational; just tell me what to do."

Ginny scrubbed her clothes at the river. After she finished each item, she laid it on a blanket to keep from soiling it while she worked on the others. She realized ironing was impossible in camp and on the trail, so she could imagine how some of the cotton garments would look a rumpled mess soon.

She heard a distant gunshot and remembered some of the men had gone hunting. She was relieved they hadn't had any trouble while camped there, and prayed they wouldn't on the trail.

* * *

Steve leaned against a tree at his campsite. His supplies and gear were ready to move out; they always stayed ready for a quick departure. None of the men who had gone into town with him had done anything suspicious. Either the gems were hidden in a wagon, concealed near camp, or would arrive with Charles Avery tomorrow. He had stopped by the boardinghouse for a minute on the pretext of telling Charles their schedule. The man hadn't been home, so his older sister had taken the message. The friendly woman had sent Anna some treats and a shawl that he would pass along to her when she returned from chores.

Steve concluded the boardinghouse was clean, large, and had been successful, but not enough so to earn wealth or provide a high social status. From Anna's possessions, schooling, and genteel breeding, he had expected something very different. He told himself it was because Charles, preparing for this move west, had sold his home and business and moved in with his sister. Steve wished he could have gotten a look at something indicative of Charles's old lifestyle which could tell him more about the man. He also wished he had arrived in time and had the chance to do more study on Avery and the other men. At present, he didn't know who to watch most carefully.

Steve joined Ginny as she hung her wash to dry. She glanced at him and smiled. "It's hard to believe we'll be heading west on Monday."

"You're looking forward to it?"

Ginny gazed into space over the rope clothesline as she thought of seeing her father. "Yes, very much. I can hardly wait to arrive."

"Better enjoy the journey. After you get there, you'll have lots of work to do . . . Your aunt sent you some surprises; I put them in your wagon."

Ginny halted work to look at him, "You went to see her?"

"I dropped by to tell your father we'd be leaving Monday. He wasn't home, so I left word with your aunt."

What if someone had told him Mr. Avery's daughter was dead when he asked for directions? she fretted. What if someone mentioned a recent death and burial of another girl, a stranger who had just docked from England? Surely not, as the scout didn't appear or sound suspicious of her. "That was nice of you," she said and concentrated on her task.

Steve wondered why she looked unsettled by his mention of the visit to her home. Maybe she had lost more because of the war than she had hinted at and hoped no one in camp discovered they were near what she might think were dire straits. He'd keep alert to—

"What's this, Mr. Carr?" one of the Davis boys asked as he drew Steve's knife from his boot sheath while the scout was distracted.

Steve reacted instantly by grasping the blade and yanking it from the startled child's hand. "That's sharp and dangerous, Son; don't ever play with knives or guns."

"I'm sorry, sir; I won't do it again. I better go."

Ginny and Steve watched the embarrassed boy run off to play with the others. She looked at the scout's hand as he replaced the weapon and saw red staining his palm. "You're bleeding. Let me see your hand."

Steve looked at the injury. "Just a nick. Doesn't hurt much."

Ginny captured and eyed his hand. "It needs tending. I'll—"

"Don't trouble yourself."

"It won't be any trouble."

"I can take care of it; I always take care of myself."

"That blood should prove you're human just like everyone else. You don't have to be so strong all the time. It won't hurt to open up a little and let people in. You might be surprised to learn you like it. That wound could become infected. It will be easier for me to bind it. Besides, I need the practice; you can tell me what to do. I insist, Steve, no arguing." She captured his

156

wrist and pulled him toward her wagon. "Sit up here while I take care of it. Let me fetch the medicine box."

Steve did as she said, sat cross-legged on the tailgate. He watched her get the medicine box and a basin of fresh water.

Ginny washed the oozing scarlet area with gentleness, but blood continued to flow from the cut. "It doesn't look deep enough for stitches, so that's good." She dapped stinging medicine on the slice, but the man didn't wince or move. She wrapped a clean bandage around his hand, then used his thumb and wrist to secure it in place. "That's better. I'll check it and change the bandage tomorrow."

"Thanks, Dr. Avery, you did a good job."

Ginny returned his smile and quipped, "See, it wasn't so bad to let someone help you for a change. You do it plenty for others."

"I suppose not," he relented a little. He realized she hadn't released his injured hand yet; it was cupped tenderly in hers, and the contact felt wonderful. Too stimulating, he warned himself and moved it.

Steve eased off the tailgate and turned to her. "The things from your aunt are over there." He pointed to a small pile. "See you later."

Ginny observed his retreat before she tossed out the bloody water and put away the medicine kit. She returned to hanging up her laundry. She was amazed he had given in to her request, spoken as an order. It had been enjoyable, despite the circumstances, to tend and to touch him. The more time she spent with him, the more she wanted him to remain in her life.

The sliver of a moon attempted to give adequate light to the shadowy landscape; its task was aided by fires here and there whose colorful flames leapt upward and sent curls of smoke in the same direction. The ebony sky was filled with bright stars. A refreshing breeze stirred mosses, branches, and grass blades. The ground was still soft from two days of rain. Nocturnal birds, insects, and creatures sent forth their sounds into the night. Frogs and crickets were particularly abundant. Some wagons were aglow from lanternlight inside. Laughter and voices could be heard wafting on the wind. Most seemed content to rest and relax tonight at their own campsites before doing their final chores tomorrow.

Ginny strolled into the shadows opposite her wagon. Steve joined her immediately without startling her. She grinned and explained, "I wasn't going far, boss; I remember your caution about the danger of being away alone. I love nighttime: the stars, the moon, the shadows, the nocturnal sounds, the calm of it all. You have to be in the darkness to experience them better."

"If we were out West, you wouldn't be safe even this close to camp and guards. A trained warrior could sneak up to kill you, rob you, or capture you without making a sound to alert others."

"Then I'm glad we're here tonight. Have you . . . tangled with many Indians in your travels?"

"Yes and no," he replied as he envisioned her as his captive.

"Explain that," she encouraged to keep him talking.

"I've done Indian fighting, and I've also made friends with some."

"Friends?" she echoed in surprise.

"I do have some, Anna. I just don't make them easy and often."

"You constantly amaze and confuse me, Steve Carr. Who are you?"

"Nobody, so what do you mean?" He tensed as he wondered if he had done or said something to cast suspicion on himself, on his mission.

"Where are you from? How do you live?"

"Out West and by whatever catches my interest. I stay on the move so I'm not in one place very long."

"No home? You travel all the time?"

"Yep, I prefer it that way."

"Where did you attend school?"

"What?"

"You sound educated to me."

"That surprises you for a cowpoke, a trail duster?"

"Nothing I learn about you should surprise me. You're quite a puzzle."

"My mother."

It was her turn to be baffled. "What?"

"My mother taught me and had me tutored. Thought it would help get me accepted in the 'right' places and with the 'right' people."

"From your bitter tone, it didn't. So you instantly dislike people like me? I'm sure life was tough and painful for you on your own."

"Despite what you think, Anna, I haven't had a bad life. I'm good at what I do, and I like it."

"Do you ever hire out as a private guide?"

He was intrigued. *A clue?* "Why?"

"Just wondered. Do you?"

"I have, and I'd do it again if the money and challenge were there."

Ginny dropped that idea for the moment. "You said you don't let people get close so you won't be vulnerable and get hurt. How could I hurt you?"

"Don't you know, Anna?"

"I hope so, but I'm not sure. Do I make you as nervous as you make me? Do you push me away because you don't like me or because of Cathy?" The last question slipped out before she could prevent it.

"Mrs. King? Ah, yes, so it is noticeable to others. I was afraid of that. I set her straight when she waylaid me in the woods yesterday. I'm lucky I didn't get clawed up by that coy little cat when she was grabbing at me. I had to struggle to control my temper. I don't like women who paw me."

"I imagine many women chase you during your travels."

"Some."

159

"Do you . . . spurn all of them?"

"Mighty nosy, aren't you?" he jested and gently tugged on a curl. "Should I start questioning you about your lovelife?"

"I don't have one and have never had one."

"That's hard to believe, a beautiful and desirable woman like you."

"It's true, by choice. I've never met a man I wanted to get to know better, until now."

"Until now?" he repeated, asking himself if he should press onward to ensnare her or retreat to avoid this sensitive topic.

Ginny's gaze fused with Steve's. "Until you."

"You want to get to know me? Why?"

"Because you're interesting, different, appealing. Because I like you. Because I think we could become good friends. Is that being too bold?"

"It's mighty direct for a lady."

"Is that why you're afraid of me, because I'm a lady?"

"Ladies give men like me trouble and aggravation."

"How so, Steve?"

"For all reasons you mentioned last night when you scolded me, and because they want and need what I can't and won't give them."

"Why is friendship so terrible to give?"

Steve clasped her face between his hands, gazed deeply into her eyes, and asked, "Is that all you want from me, Anna Avery? I don't think so."

"I honestly don't know *what* I want from you, Steve. It's confusing."

"I know, Anna, and it's trouble for both of us; it's impossible."

"Why?"

"I'm not the settling-down kind. Look for a husband in Texas."

"What was it you said to me; 'Advice is easy to give, but hard to take?' I'm not searching for a husband, Steve, in Texas or here with you."

"You're not the kind to have . . . unmeaningful . . . amusement."

She was relieved when he chose his words with care. "I . . ."

When her words trailed off before refuting his statement, Steve bent forward and kissed her. His tongue danced with hers. He pulled her tightly against him. Scorching heat licked over his body. He yearned to possess her then and there. He felt her tremble in his embrace. She was so warm and willing and eager with her responses, with the way she kissed him, with the way she clung to him, with the way she stroked his back. He knew it would be wonderful to teach her lovemaking, to experience it with her. But what would happen after she surrendered to him? Would she endanger his mission? Would he become too distracted by her to solve it? Would it blind him to the Averys' possible involvement in his case? Would she become clingy and demanding, or would she get painfully hurt by him?

The intensity of Steve's kisses and hunger, and those of her own, alarmed Ginny. Strange and powerful longings filled her, and she knew their names were Desire and Passion. She wanted to be introduced to them; she wanted to get to know them. But they could be enemies, could be dangerous, could be captors. She relished his fiery kisses and tender caresses as long as she dared without losing her wits. When she realized the hunger was increasing, as was the pleasure, she pushed away from him. "I can't . . . do this, Steve."

"I know, Anna; that's what I was trying to prove to you."

Ginny looked into his eyes and doubted his claim. He couldn't convince her he wasn't as aroused as she was. "Just because I can't do something reckless here and now doesn't mean I don't want to, Steve."

"Wanting something badly and taking rash action to get it aren't the same, woman. Keep a strong will and a clear head, Anna Avery, and don't allow a man like me to take advantage of you."

Ginny knew he had the power to capture her heart and claim

her innocence if he really tried; the fact he wouldn't do either told her he cared about her more than he realized or would admit. "That's easier for you than for me, Steve, because you're experienced with these things."

"Not with a woman like you, Anna. You should steer clear of me; I'm untrustworthy and dangerous." He was trapped between two forces. One urged him to take what she offered and what he wanted for his own pleasure and to aid his mission; the other warned and pleaded for him to let her escape his clutches to be kind.

Ginny didn't know if his advice was an evocative challenge or an honest warning. "Couldn't we become friends and take this slow and easy?"

"I'm tempted, but it wouldn't work. I won't mislead you, Anna."

"Are you telling me to come after you at my own risk?"

"No, I'm telling you I'd probably let you catch me for a while, but only for a while, Anna. That I know for certain. You strike me as a woman who'd want more from a man, who'd suffer later."

"So you're spurning me to protect my feelings?"

"Maybe. I just know it's crazy to leap on a stallion that can't be tamed."

"I believe you have the skills to master anything you want to. Doesn't a man keep a valuable stallion after he's tamed it and branded it?"

"Some only love the challenge of breaking them in. Then they sell them or release them back into the wild."

"And it never bothers you that it carries your brand?"

"Hasn't yet."

"But it might with me so you don't want to take the chance?"

"Maybe."

"You never want to commit yourself, do you?"

Steve studied her for a moment. Maybe she was smarter and braver than he knew; she had learned her lessons well in the past week. Maybe she was using cunning wiles he couldn't

162

perceive to lure him into her clutches to get him, as she'd subtly hinted, to guide them to the Averys' contact out West. She could be working with Charles on an evil scheme, out of loyalty to her father or out of a misguided belief the Klan was doing good things. As with most Southerners, she did have cause to hate Yankees and to seek revenge. There was only one way to find out: challenge her to pursue him, let her think she'd caught him, and see what happened. If he was wrong about her and she got hurt from his ruse . . . He'd deal with that possibility later. If she didn't need him for something important, his immi-nent words should frighten her and send her running for cover! "How's this for being clear as a mountain stream? Damn right, I like you and you get under my tough hide. Damn right, I want you, and want you badly. Damn right, I'd take you if given the chance, and take you every time I could. Damn right, I'd leave when the time came for us to part ways; and it would come, Anna, never doubt that for a moment."

Ginny watched his retreat with an open mouth and stunned wits. He had admitted his affection and desire for her! He would love her and he would leave her.. Or would he? Could she change him? Or not so much change him as help him get over the past. What would it be like to love him, to win him, to marry him, to have his children, to share his life, to take him to Colorado with her?

Ginny milked the cow as Ellie Davis had taught her, then helped with breakfast and the clean-up chores.

A religious service was held under the trees with Bible read-ing, singing, and praying. In spite of many complaints, they had begun their training last Sunday on the "Lord's Day." By this one, the men and women were ready to begin their trek the next day.

The women took their four-mile walk while husbands watched children. Afterward, the men took theirs. It was every-one's last task before making all final preparations to depart.

They had the remainder of the day off, to work, to rest, and to have fun.

The two grain wagons and drivers arrived in camp: Hollister and Brent. The leader met with them and gave them their instructions.

After lunch, Ginny and other women went to the river for a last bath and shampoo before hitting the dusty and demanding trail. She lathered her long hair as she thought about Steve and last night. He had been distant again today and that troubled her. She couldn't decide whom he was trying to protect the most: him, her, or both of them? Would she ever understand and reach him? He wouldn't be afraid of her and avoid her unless . . .

Don't push it, Ginny. It might complicate matters and you don't need more problems. You don't know him well enough to reveal your secrets. Doing so can paint you black to him. He already doesn't trust people; then you confess you're a deceiver! He'll think you're like the others—or worse.

While Ginny was gone, Charles Avery arrived and joined the group.

Steve walked over to speak with the man who was attaching his chicken pens to his wagon and stowing supplies. "Good to see you."

Charles glanced up and smiled. "My sister gave me your message; thanks for coming by yesterday. I was already planning to head out today. I thought it was best to let Anna have privacy during her training. How did she do, Steve? Any problems?"

Steve was intrigued by what he thought was a slip: how could she "do badly" in front of him if she'd been away at boarding school for six years and had just returned? "No problems to amount to anything. Training was tough on all the women, but Miss Avery did fine. You should be proud of her."

Confusing the two girls as he sometimes did—his lost child and Virginia Marston, his alleged daughter—Charles answered with remarks about both. "I am; she's a smart girl; she can do anything she sets her mind to. She made the best grades of her class. They wanted her to become a teacher, but Anna wants more of a challenge in life."

"Such as?" Steve asked casually as he helped with the task.

Charles centered on their ruse, as he honestly liked Ginny. "She doesn't know yet, but I won't be surprised by anything she attempts."

"She'll do fine at whatever she tries if she keeps her mind on it. The only trouble she has is with bouts of distraction."

"She told me she had trouble concentrating and you scolded her."

Steve gave the same explanation he had given her, and no apology.

"I fully understand and agree, and I told Anna so. She promised to do better and obviously she kept her word." Charles glanced around to make sure no one was close enough to overhear what he was about to say. He had decided to get the scout and Ginny matched up for she would need the man's help and protection soon. He was sure Carr would keep his confidence, as he seemed that kind of man. "This is between us, Steve, but it might explain why she behaved like that in the beginning. When she came to camp, she'd just lost her best friend since childhood, she died in Anna's arms right before I started my training. That's really why I left her in town with my sister; I thought she needed privacy to grieve and begin to recover. Don't tell her I told you; it would upset her to know you'd be nice because of her suffering. She's a proud girl. She also has me to deal with; we've been separated for six years, so she's having to get used to me again. While she was up North, she lost her home, and the war ravaged everything she knew and loved. I collected her and I'm rushing her off to the Wild West. She just needed time to adjust to all those changes. Do you understand?"

Steve nodded and continued helping Charles to secure the fowl pens. He knew what it was to lose a best friend, a home, and more. He now knew the reason why she'd been weeping that night; and she'd had no one to comfort her. Twinges of guilt for his behavior and suspicions chewed at him. He had been too tough and cold; she was so very vulnerable. It was surprising she'd come to like him. She should have confided in him about her troubles. She probably assumed he wouldn't understand or, if he did, it wouldn't make a difference in his treatment of her. Yet she had tried, he remembered, and he'd prevented it. Lost a best friend to death . . .

At least her best friend had died, he mused with bitterness, not been murdered and . . . But the cold-blooded killer would be tracked down and punished as soon as he completed this mission. He had promised himself: no more defeats, distractions, and unfinished business to prey on his mind. He would—

"That has it done, Steve; thanks for the help. You promise you won't tell Anna what I told you?" the graying man reminded.

"You have my word of honor, sir."

"That's the most important thing a man can have and give to another."

"Yep, but the war almost took it away from us Rebs. We promised to do a lot of things—protect our homes, families, friends, and land, but we couldn't keep those vows. I guess we'll all accept that defeat one day."

"One of the hardest losses a man can suffer is that of his pride. Things wouldn't be so bad in the South if the Yankees would let us have a little bit of it back. They're determined to keep us cowered and conquered."

Steve listened and watched for clues. "I don't see that there's much we can do about that, sir, until they change their minds and actions."

"I'm afraid you're right, Steve, and it really sticks in my craw."

"Mine, too, sir. But as you said, there's nothing we can do about it. Of course, some of the men here think differently."

Charles came to alert. "What do you mean?"

Steve tried to sound and look nonchalant. "Oh, there's been a lot of wild talk at night about the Klan and what they're doing. Some of the men think they're in the right."

"And you don't?"

Steve pretended to think a moment, shrugged, and replied, "I'm not sure what I believe, sir. A man can't always trust everything he hears and reads, so I don't know if they really do all they get blamed for."

"Would you ever join up with a group like that to punish the ones who've made us suffer and continue to make us suffer so much?"

Steve faked deep thought again. "I can't honestly say one way or the other, sir. I've never run into any Klan members. I don't know the truth about them."

"I have. They struck me as decent, honest men who are protecting their friends and families and what little they have left from the war."

"But what about all the lynchings, burnings, and lootings they're blamed for?" Steve reasoned.

"I don't suppose they're doing anything worse than those Yankee marauders and foragers, like Sherman and his troops did here in Georgia."

"But isn't the Klan attacking innocent men?"

"From what I hear and read, it's carpetbaggers, scalawags, Loyal Leaguers, cruel ex-officers, and troublemaking Negroes they focus on."

"Does that give them the right to retaliate in such a deadly way? They could make mistakes and kill innocent people, and some don't obey rules."

"Who can say what's right or wrong when it comes to war, hatred, revenge, and justice? If things were set right in this country and courts didn't go against us, there wouldn't be a place or need for societies like—"

Ginny returned and halted their conversation. She glanced at Steve, then looked at Charles Avery. She behaved as she thought she should. She smiled and embraced the older man. "It's good to see you, Father."

"It's good to be here, Daughter. Steve was telling me how well you've done with your training. I'll get a look at it for myself on the trail."

She stood there with Charles's arm around her shoulder. "It was hard, Father, but we all survived his lessons."

"If you two will excuse me, I have chores of my own to tend. Good day, Miss Avery, sir." Steve nodded at the woman and left them alone.

"That young man likes you, girl," Charles told her.

"He what?" she asked. "Did he tell you that?"

"Not exactly, but he was softening up your father to get to you."

"What did he say about me?"

"Nothing much; just bragged on how well you'd done this week."

"It's about time; he's usually stingy with compliments or he walks them through the back door."

Charles laughed. "That's because men get skittish around girls they like and want; they're scared of making mistakes and scaring them off while they get up the courage to court them."

"Court me?" she repeated and laughed. "I can imagine a moody loner like Steve Carr coming to our wagon at night to ask your permission to take a stroll in the moonlight with me," she teased.

"He might surprise you and do just that."

"Surprise me? It would shock me to wits' end."

Ginny helped Lucy Eaves cook, serve the meal, and do the dishes. She and Charles ate with the couple and their three children. They enjoyed talking with Jeff and Lucy, and they seemed to enjoy the Averys.

Afterward, almost everyone met in the camp center around a glowing campfire to sing, chat, listen to music, dance, and laugh—except those few who believed it was wrong to dance on Sunday. It was a celebration of the end of their work and the beginning of an adventure, and all were in a cheerful and relaxed mood. Music came from a harmonica, a "squeeze-box," and George Amerson's fiddle. Toes were tapping on the ground. The older children observed or joined in on the merriment.

Charles talked with Ed King, and Ginny did so with her women friends.

"Go ask him to dance," Ruby suggested with a grin.

"I couldn't. He might not know how and might be embarrassed. Besides, it would be forward of me," Ginny replied, knowing George's wife meant Steve. She was greatly tempted to be bold.

Steve wished he could check out the chicken coops Charles had brought with him. He knew the birds would make too much noise. He had attempted to inspect them while helping Charles but failed. When he saw Cathy King eyeing him, he knew she was about to ask him to dance. He prevented that by approaching and asking Anna Avery, who looked astonished. Steve grasped her hand and pulled her forward to join other couples.

As they moved around the campfire, he chuckled and whispered, "See, woman, no broken or stomped toes. I can do a few refined things. If you're still interested, we can be friends, Anna, but take it slow and easy."

Ginny dared not look up into that handsome face. She was amazed by the revelation of this new skill: he was an excellent dancer. She was also amazed he had chosen her as his first partner, shown interest in her before the others. She decided not to play coy. Instead, she murmured, "Slow and easy it is, sir."

Steve loved the feel of her in his embrace, savored her hand in his, feasted on her beauty, enjoyed her hair grazing his arm, and inhaled her clean and perfumed fragrance. "We leave tomorrow at seven. Make sure you're ready so I won't have to ruin our truce with another scolding."

Ginny had difficulty thinking about anything but the irresistible man she was touching and smelling. He was reaching out to her, however cautiously. "I'll make certain I'm ready for any challenge by morning."

"*Any* challenge, Anna?"

She met his roguish gaze. "Yes, Steve, *any* challenge."

CHAPTER 8

"Wagons, ho!" Steve shouted, and signaled them with a wave of his tan hat to follow his lead as they left the campsite near the Ogeechee River on April 1, 1867. His deception was in progress but hadn't provided much information to date. Soon, he promised himself, the case would be solved.

Seventeen wagons—fifteen families and two hauling grain—moved out to head west. Of the eighty-four people present, those old enough to be aware of things were happy to be seeking fresh starts away from the war-ravaged area. Steve Carr on his sorrel led and scouted the trail. Men and women either drove their wagons, walked beside them, rode for a while on them, or sat astride nearby horses. Some older children walked, too, for as long as they could, while toddlers and babies rode inside. Few talked, in an effort to conserve energy. Cows and horses roped to tailgates ambled along at the pace set by leader and mules—a few times sending forth whinnies, moos, or brays. Occasionally a chicken clucked or a rooster crowed, startled by unfamiliar movement and noises.

Water sloshed back and forth in covered barrels secured to the outsides of wagon beds. The wide rims of wheels rumbled along easily on the mixture of grass and hard dirt beneath them. Sounds of trampling hooves, shaking canvases, creaking leather, jangling harnesses, and squeaking wood were heard.

The Old South of Georgia was being left behind, as were

previous lives. New starts were before the travelers, who assumed they would never return to their lost homes. All of that was gone, just as the Indians who had once lived in the area, who, too, had been pushed westward, but to reservations in the Oklahoma Territory. The days of gentility, chivalry, hospitality, culture, charm, wealth, and leisure were things of the past; or so everyone present believed. The "Planter's Society" that had made the South great had also destroyed it.

Miles south of middle Georgia, the flat terrain was covered in a sandy topsoil over hard clay and with verdant grass and scattered wildflowers. Virgin forests of pine, oak, and other hardwoods greeted travelers with a vision of green. Here and there, graceful magnolias and dainty hollys joined the scenery to beautify it. They journeyed through woods, meadows, and fields, where cotton, cattle, corn, and other crops once flourished; many were now overgrown with weeds.

As Ginny walked beside the Avery wagon, she reflected on her last talk this morning with the man driving it. He had asked if she was ready for the "challenges and adventures" that lay ahead. She had said, "Yes," but a mixture of emotions filled her: panic, doubt, excitement, and sadness. *I wish I could forget my problems and promises, get on a horse, and ride to Colorado.* Yet, more trouble and peril could await her there, especially if her father was dead. It was frightening to think of being stranded alone in that wilderness with its many hazards and threats. It was scary to think of becoming a target for her father's enemy. Yet, each mile trekked took her closer to her father and hopefully to success. She wanted to tell her friends the truth, but it would get her and Mr. Avery kicked off the wagontrain and stranded without its protection and guidance. She couldn't do that; the kind man had done too much for her and Johanna.

She wanted Steve, but if she confessed the truth to him, he'd never believe her or trust her again. She didn't want to increase his bitterness and mistrust or risk him thinking horrible things about her or risk breaking her heart. It was better to let him see and remember her as Anna Avery, a lady, a tempting romance, a friend.

Ginny wondered if Johanna's adopted brother was anything like Steve Carr. Perhaps all western men were similar in character and behavior. He was two years younger than Steve, but he could have fought in the war and been changed by it as so many men had. Were he and Mr. Chapman as close as they had been years ago? Had losing Johanna altered the rancher's feelings and actions? Mr. Chapman had given up his only child for another man's son; he had given up his wife for a mistress. Had he ever regretted those decisions? What kind of man would want two women at the same time? Ginny didn't think she was going to like or respect Johanna's father.

She looked at the man silhouetted against the blue sky. Last night had been such fun, but he was ignoring her today. Steve sat astride his sorrel and kept a steady pace. A rope hung from the butt of his sheathed rifle. His saddlebags bulged with clothes and other small possessions. A blanket, slicker, and bedroll were secured behind his cantle. A cloth sack with supplies and cookware swung from the horn. Two Colts with his initials were strapped to his waist and thighs, and the knife was resting in its boot sheath. His red shirt could be sighted easily by anyone needing him.

Ginny walked as much as she rode or drove, and she was glad now that Steve had insisted on daily exercise to increase her stamina and strength. But she worried each time he galloped past to check on everyone, always on the other side of the wagon and never glancing her way. At lunch, Steve didn't approach her; and he left early to scout the trail ahead for problems. They crossed the Canoochee River and other streams and creeks without trouble or delay. Along the waterline she saw cypress trees with lacy moss draped over their branches and with their gnarled roots exposed.

On the land outside of Savannah, they passed lingering reminders of Sherman's "March to the Sea." She viewed signs of the horrible and tragic destruction: burned and looted plantations and homes, collapsing barns, weather-beaten sheds and outhouses, lonely churches, and broken-spirited Southerners who were trying to eke out a living in the midst of ruins. Some farms and once-grand houses were deserted and rundown or occupied by squatters. Many fields hadn't been replanted, but some—belonging to carpetbaggers, she presumed—showed tiny green sprouts. A few had workers in them, white and black, but paid for their labors now, not slaves. She wondered how Green Oaks had fared the war and Cleniece's ownership.

I wish I could go to Texas, tell Johanna's father the truth, then head for Colorado, with Steve. Would you hold me to my promise, Johanna, if you knew I had fallen in love, and honoring it might destroy that love and me? I wish you were here so we could talk and you could tell me what to do. Everything has gotten so complicated. I made a promise to you and I have to keep it or I'll feel guilty for the rest of my life for letting you down; I owe you that much. I have to stay silent on the journey because I owe Mr. Avery that much. To confess the truth to my friends and Steve wouldn't change things; it would only make them worse.

Penniless, homeless, alone, Ginny had no current alternative except to continue on to the ranch. She couldn't keep taking advantage of Mr. Avery's generosity. She couldn't force Steve to love her. She had no choice except to carry out the secret she had promised Johanna that sad night.

At dusk, Steve halted them to camp in the edge of a cool and shady forest. Charles built the fire and she "cooked" their meal, opening and warming two jars of canned soup with ham from his sister. She mixed and fried cornbread in a skillet and prepared coffee as Ellie had taught her. They also drank milk Charles had purchased from Stuart Davis.

After the meal, Ginny used water from the barrel to wash the dishes. At that point, she didn't have to worry about conserving it, as they would pass enough rivers and streams for refills. She helped Charles grease the axles and tend the team after she fetched grain in a bucket from Hollister. The mules also grazed on grass, but had to be supplemented daily with feed to keep them in good condition. She thought Steve was smart for providing the feed service so wagons wouldn't have to bear the extra weight of heavy grain sacks. When both finished, they went their separate ways.

As Ginny chatted with her four women friends, she noticed that Charles Avery had spoken with Ed King and was with Harry Brown and John Daniels at present. Later, he visited with Carl Murphy, the Georgian.

When he returned to their site, she expressed her concern about Murphy. "Do you know him? Can he expose our ruse?"

Charles patted her arm and coaxed, "Don't worry, girl; nobody can expose us. Nobody here knows my Anna's fate. No one knows you recently docked. Even if any checking was done on us, no one could discover anything."

That relieved Ginny, who didn't want to be caught in lies.

Within twenty minutes, the camp was quiet and slumbering.

Tuesday, the pattern and pace established on the first day became routine. The Georgia plains stretched out before them, an area that would have been a sea of white from cotton if the war hadn't occurred and if it were late summer. The terrain stayed flat and easy to travel. Trees of pine and hardwood remained the same. Sometimes they passed ponds with lilypads floating atop, creating a serene sight.

The next day, a landscape of various shades of green continued. A low hill—more of a gentle incline and decline—appeared once in a while. Only twice did the line of wagons journey on dirt roads. Usually it went through forests, over untilled farmland, and across unused pastures with torn-down fences. They crossed the Ohoopee River with its slow-moving black water and fifty-feet width and a swift stream here and there.

*　*　*

On Thursday, they traversed areas abundant in oak, flowering plum, cedar, and chinaberry. The only difference in the terrain were spots of uneven flatland. Everything was verdant and growing, as many trees and bushes were evergreens and Georgia's winters were mild. Sometimes they saw old churches with cemeteries. They were fortunate to have a wooden bridge for crossing the wide, deep, and swift Oconee River; they did it one at a time, given their heavy loads and its advanced age. More streams and creeks greeted them before they halted for their fourth day on the trail.

Ginny noticed that during the last few days Steve and the two grain wagon drivers camped together and ate together unless some of the families invited the men to join them for the evening meals. She had seen the scout visit around the camps each night, but he always seemed to reach theirs while she was away on chores or for chats. She surmised it was intentional and was twice tempted to approach him to ask why. She decided to let him unravel his defensiveness alone. She had seen him riding and talking with other men on horseback during the day, including with her companion while she drove the wagon. She was grateful to the guide for his tough lessons, as they were paying off.

Charles kept telling her how taken with her the scout was, but Steve's contradictory behavior didn't reveal or even suggest that. Four days, she fretted, without a touch, a word, a smile, or a kiss! She yearned for all, or for only one, of them. She couldn't grasp why he was treating her this way after what he'd said that last night in camp.

Ginny was tired each night and was sleeping well in the wagon, with Charles slumbering beside or underneath it on a bedroll. Few people talked after turning in because the closeness of the circle prevented privacy. Baths had merely been fast wash-offs, as they hadn't camped at a river site since leaving. Thanks to the jars of canned soups and vegetables from

176

Charles's sister, and to the simplicity of trail food, preparing tasty meals hadn't been difficult so far. The routine was set and would continue for weeks.

Friday, between long spans of flatland, more very low-rolling hills appeared than in past days; they were so gentle with their rises and falls that they presented no hardships for the strong teams and only required a slightly slower pace. They reached an offshoot of the Ocmulgee River, some dense patches of scrubs to their right and left, and soft spots Charles called "attempts at creeks."

In some locations, countless pines had concealed the ground with their dead straw and were currently sending out pollen to attack everything in sight. Ginny kept the wagon openings closed to prevent the yellow dust from covering their possessions. It coated canvases, sweaty animals, and perspiring people with sunny-colored grime. It caused some travelers to respond with sneezes, watery eyes, runny noses, and headaches.

In camp that night, Charles borrowed a horse and gear from Ed King to teach Ginny how to ride western saddle. Finally she had told him she walked when not resting or driving because she only knew sidesaddle and feared making a fool of herself or causing an accident with an error. She was delighted to discover how easy it was to master. They were gone twenty minutes when Steve joined them. Ginny was surprised and pleased, although he rode next to Charles, not her.

"Enjoying yourselves?" the scout asked from his sorrel.

"Most assuredly," the grinning Charles replied.

"Yes" came her succinct response. *Let him stew as I have!*

Steve leaned forward, looking past Charles to speak to her. "I see your training is paying off, Miss Avery; you're doing fine."

Ginny kept her gaze ahead, on the scenery and off him. "Yes, it is, and thank you for the many lessons."

The men chatted for a while before the sly and determined

older man said, "I think I'll head back now. This body isn't used to so much exercise. Steve, would you escort Anna back when she finishes her ride?"

Before the scout could answer, an embarrassed Ginny said, "That won't be necessary, Father, I'm ready to return to camp, too."

"I don't mind at all, Anna," Steve told her. "It's still early."

She didn't want him to think this ride was a ruse to capture his attention or be forced to spend time with her. "No thank you, Mr. Carr. I'm tired and have things to do before bedtime. Let's go, Father." Ginny pulled on the reins, turned her horse, and started riding.

Steve and Charles exchanged apologetic looks and shrugged.

"You have been ignoring her, son," Charles hinted, "and women are sensitive creatures who need attention."

Steve was surprised by the remarks. "Miffed with me, is she?"

"Yes, I'd say she's that all right. Too bad, because she likes you and misses you. I'd hate to see anything spoil your friendship."

"What are you suggesting, sir?"

"Anna can use good friends right now; she has a lot of adjusting to do, and they can help ease her burdens. During her training, she came to respect, admire, and depend on you. I guess she feels cut off from that strength and that shoulder to lean on she'd gotten accustomed to. I don't know what would become of her if anything happened to me. Anna's strong and smart and brave, but she's lived in a sheltered environment for six years under the guidance and protection of the teachers. I'm not sure she knows how to deal with people and situations. She left the South when it was beautiful and safe; she returned when it was scarred and dangerous. We love each other, but we're like strangers because we were separated for so long. She left as a girl and returned as a woman; I've changed, too. The war was on, so any letters we might have written to keep us acquainted couldn't even get through. Her best friend was with Anna at school; they were like sisters; her death hit her hard. She has a lot to learn about people and life, so I'd be grateful if you help her. See you in camp, Son. And will you join us for supper tomorrow night?"

"What will Anna have to say about that?"

"She'd be delighted, I'm sure. So will I. See you in camp."

Steve watched Charles catch up with his daughter and join her. He had a strong feeling the man was trying to push him and Anna together. He wondered why a gentleman would want a "saddle tramp," as he'd been called more than once, to court his most precious possession. Suspicion and curiosity flooded his body. A gut instinct told him Charles Avery wanted something particular from him. It could be help on his new ranch, as he'd be a greenhorn in his new existence. Or it could be as a guide to an evil rendezvous, as Anna had hinted earlier, if her query was more than casual conversation. Or it could be as a gift to his cherished daughter, if she craved him enough to seek and receive her father's assistance. Or it could be as a protector if an accident or death befell the man on the trail or until she was settled on the new ranch or needed returning to her aunt. Whatever the older man's motive was, Steve needed to learn it quick.

As they rode along, Ginny asked Charles what the two of them had said to each other.

"We were talking about guard assignments and what's ahead. I hated to come after you too fast after you took off like that, so I chatted with him a while. Why didn't you stay with him, girl? The perfect opportunity was there."

Ginny explained her reason, and Charles concurred and apologized. But the man knew he had sparked interest in the scout toward her, and he was glad of it. Most of what he had said about Ginny and her father was true, so he had sounded convincing, and he knew Steve wouldn't repeat it to her. Getting the skilled westerner bewitched by Ginny, Charles believed, would fill everyone's needs.

179

* * *

The wagontrain halted the next day at five, as some men needed to hunt for fresh meat while it was still light enough to do so. Charles Avery left with them after saying he was off to get rabbits for roasting over a spit.

A clear sky and early-rising full moon promised a lovely evening. While Ginny was cooking over the fire Charles had built before leaving, Steve approached the Avery campsite. She was frying cured ham, cooking biscuits in a Dutch oven, and getting coffee ready to perk. She glanced up at the smiling scout, then returned her gaze to her tasks.

"Did you need something, Mr. Carr? Father isn't back yet."

She was polite but cool. The things Avery had disclosed to Steve in confidence raced through his mind at lightning speed. "He invited me for supper. Is that all right with you, Anna?"

Her head jerked up, her eyes wide in surprise. "He did?"

"I guess he forgot to mention it to you."

She quickly recovered her poise and was courteous. "He did, but it's all right, if you don't mind what we're having tonight. Father wanted ham, red-eye gravy, scrambled eggs, biscuits, and coffee." Now she understood why Charles had asked for the simple fare; she could manage it without mistakes or much work. He should have told her about inviting Steve, should have asked her permission.

The man comprehended she was genuinely unaware of the invitation and assumed the sly Charles had kept it from her on purpose. "Sounds and smells delicious, if you have enough and don't mind my joining you two."

"Oh!" she shrieked as she realized the ham would burn soon if she didn't tend it quickly. "Don't say it," she warned the scout.

He was baffled. "Say what, Anna?"

"That I'm distracted again and ruining dinner," she replied.

"I wouldn't, not when I'm the cause—or hope I am." She didn't glance up or respond, so he ventured, "You're annoyed

180

with me, so I should explain my . . . 'contradictory,' you once called it, behavior."

"You don't have to tell me anything. You don't owe me excuses."

He noticed she said 'excuses,' not 'reasons.' "Yes, I do, Anna."

"Why?" she asked, stealing a quick glance at him. "You said 'take it slow and easy.' We've both kept our word, so there is no problem."

"I didn't mean we should have no contact."

"That hasn't been my intention or doing, Steve. Surely I'm not expected to chase you down to be friends. That isn't proper."

"I know it's my fault, but you've kept your word too well."

Ginny set the cooked meat aside and covered it. She shifted the pot to the edge so the coffee wouldn't perk over the spout. She had been taught by Ellie not to peek at the biscuits and let out the heat, so let them be. Pleased things were under control, she looked at Steve, who was hunkered down across the fire. "That's all until Father returns and I can cook the gravy and eggs. I believe you were talking about our avoiding each other. I'm confused, Steve. You get unsettled if I'm too bold, but you also get unsettled if I'm too reserved. Frankly I'm not sure what the middle ground is with you so bear with me until I find that tricky location. It's been six days since we pulled out and we've barely spoken or been near each other. Since you didn't come around, I assumed you wanted to be left alone for a time. You said making friends was hard for you, so I don't want to push. How exactly do you prefer me to behave? What exactly is it you expect and want from me? I can't obey rules when I don't know what they are."

He sat down and crossed his legs. "I'm sorry, Anna, but a man like me makes few, if any, female friends; I reacted too strongly. After we danced and talked so much that night, I was worried others might think we'd gotten too close and they'd be

181

watching us for mischief. The best two reasons for firing a leader are incompetence and . . . You know what I mean."

She hadn't been prepared for an apology and explanation from him. "You're avoiding me to protect your job?"

"It isn't amusing or unimportant."

"I didn't laugh or dispute you."

"Your eyes did, woman, and I'm serious. I can't lose this job."

"Don't you think it looks more suspicious to others for you to avoid me like cholera rather than to visit me as you do them?" Ginny reasoned.

He shrugged and admitted, "I hadn't thought of it that way, but you're right. With your father's permission and help, I can probably visit you without any suspicion." He leaned forward to whisper, "Some people would enjoy making problems for anyone. I've given some of them a hard time, and you're a woman to be jealous of. I can't anger them by showing special treatment to you." *For crucial reasons you don't know,* his mind added. He was having a difficult time deciding the best way to handle each person.

Ginny deliberated his words and concluded they had merit. Cathy could be spiteful after a spurning, or Louise or Mattie could be vindictive after stern and embarrassing words of correction, or one of the men could think they were trained well enough to go on alone if Steve vexed him too much. She certainly didn't want to do anything to get him fired. "You asked his permission to see me?"

Steve shifted in uneasiness. "No. But he guessed I wanted to, and gave me the opportunity."

"He likes and respects you. He sees no harm in our being friends."

"Maybe he's wrong to trust me around you," he muttered.

Ginny hoped she understood the meaning of those words. "Why, because you have wicked intentions of leading me astray?" When he frowned at her jest, she said, "I was only teasing. You can't do that without my agreement and coopera-

182

tion. He trusts me and doesn't tell me what to do or think, so stop worrying. Now I have to fetch the eggs."

Steve leapt to his feet, took the basket from her grasp, and said, "I'll do it for you. I need a breather. Serious talk tenses me." He ducked under the wagon to the inner circle where the pens with cushioning nests of hay were attached to the bedside. He checked each one to see if a bag of gems could be hidden there: none. He removed the eggs and returned to her.

To calm the nervous man, she made light talk. "Thank you, Steve. You saved me from getting pecked again. One of those hens hates me."

He chuckled. "Not really. She's only a mother hen protecting her unborn babies."

Steve wanted to bite his tongue for replying, "That's what mothers are for, to defend their own." *Shu*, she was relaxing him too much!

With caution, Ginny inquired, "What's your mother's name, Steve? What is she like? You said she was still alive. Where does she live?"

He didn't look at her to answer, "Rose. She's beautiful, gentle, kind, and unselfish to a fault. She lives in Arizona. Your Mother is dead, right?"

"Yes, she died when I was eleven. She had the same traits as yours. I still miss her. I doubt anyone ever gets completely over the loss of a parent."

"It can be done if necessary." More rash words had shot from his lips unbidden, and he warned himself to clear his wits.

"Did you . . . Do you . . ." She halted on second thought.

"Know who my father was?" he finished for her, guessing her question accurately. Since he had made the slip, he'd test her feelings about his illegitimacy.

Ginny heard the bitterness and resentment plaguing the man she loved. She wished she hadn't begun the topic. "I'm sorry, Steve, that's being too nosy about a painful subject."

"Yes, Miss Avery, it is. For now," he added for some crazy reason.

"The last thing I'll say about it is that it doesn't bother me; it doesn't influence my opinion of you. I'm only sorry it torments you so deeply. I won't ever mention it again. How about a cup of coffee? I can't promise it's good, but I hope it won't be the worst you've ever had." She laughed.

"You're quite a woman, Anna Avery," he murmured.

Charles returned, grinning as if he was the happiest man alive. "Hello, you two. Did I hold up supper?"

"Not really, Father. It gave Steve and me time to talk for a change. Any luck?" she asked, noting his hands were empty.

"None, I'm afraid. But some of the others made kills; one even got a deer. That'll be sweet eating for days. I'll get washed up for supper."

As Ginny prepared the red-eye gravy and readied the eggs to scramble, Steve asked, "Does your father always stay dressed up?"

She laughed, then speculated, "A habit, I suppose, from years of being a businessman. I imagine a formal attire is like a second skin to him by now. Sort of like those pistols and knife are to you, my well-armed protector. I bet you're so accustomed to wearing them, you don't realize they're there, until you need them."

"Point made," he murmured with a grin.

"Does that make you a gunslinger? I've read books about them."

"Nope. A gunslinger earns his living by them; I don't, or try not to."

The food was eaten with enjoyment and little talk. Afterward, the men drank coffee and chatted while Ginny washed the dishes in a basin nearby. She listened closely to what they said.

"Where is your ranch, sir?" Steve inquired over sips of not-bad-tasting coffee.

Charles was impressed with the manners and intelligence of

184

the man before him. He realized Steve Carr wasn't an ordinary man or drifter. Somewhere in his past, the scout had been schooled and taught. Yes, he assured himself, Steve was a good match for Ginny. Charles finished his coffee and set the cup aside. "Outside of Waco. I got a good deal on it. One hundred acres with seventy-five steers, a few cows and horses, and two pigs. It has a nice house and barns, but I'll have a few repairs and changes to make. The hands and foreman have agreed to stay on; they'll teach me what I need to know about raising and selling cattle. It's called the Box F now, but I'm told it will be simple to alter that mark to the Box A with a special branding iron."

"Yep, that'll be easy to do. It sounds good to me, sir."

"It will be, Steve. You're welcome to come by anytime to visit."

"Maybe I will, sir. I'd like to make sure you get settled in all right. You'll like Texas and that area. War hardly touched it. You won't see the ugly scars there that you see in these parts."

"How glorious, praise the Lord. It certainly will be nice not to have these same horrible reminders in the place where we're trying to make a new start. Ever thought about ranching, Steve? Or ever been a foreman or cowhand?"

"I've been just about everything, sir. I like ranching, but haven't decided if that's where I want to be when I shake the last trail dust from these boots. I have a roaming spirit, too restless to stay put long. Guess that's why I enjoy leading or scouting for wagontrains; always on the move."

"What about your homestead and parents, Son?"

As Charles leaned forward to refill his coffee cup, he didn't see the look Steve sent Ginny, but she did and understood its meaning, its plea to conceal the humiliating secret he had told her.

"They're dead, sir. Been on my own since sixteen." That was why he still scolded himself for joining the Confederate Army; he had no home and land to defend. He had done it to protect those of friends and his mother.

Charles looked surprised and intrigued. "You're mighty well bred and cultured for a man who was an orphan on the road."

Steve smiled and feigned a look of modesty. "Thank you, sir; that's mighty kind of you. I put eight years of schooling under my belt and hat before . . . and I do read most of the time, try to learn all I can. I've been lucky to have smart friends along the way who've taught me plenty."

"Like dancing?" Charles asked with a sly wink.

"Yep. A major's wife at one of the forts where I was scouting forced me to learn. She said that was one skill every young man should have. When she first took hold of me, I thought I had four feet and they kept getting tangled. She used music boxes for practice, and I finally got the know of it. I knew I had to or she wouldn't let up on me. Strange as it sounds, the crabby driver of freight wagons was the one who taught me how to mend my clothes and take care of them."

Ginny had the feeling that most of what he was saying was the truth. That bewildered her. How could he have done so well for himself and been touched by so many others, yet still be so tormented and such a loner? He was a complex and mysterious man. She wished she knew more about him, *everything* about him. She dared not press for more information and cause him to close up to her. She must allow him to reveal things at his own pace. After all, she had plenty of secrets of her own! She dared not expose them, not when he was learning to trust her. Besides, there was a strong probability that he would leave her behind when the journey ended, no matter what happened between them.

After Steve left the wagon, Ginny and Charles took a stroll to speak in privacy.

"Why did we tell everyone such things?" she asked him. "You purchased a mercantile store in town. What will Steve and the others think when they learn we deceived them about a ranch as well as being kin?"

"It won't matter; by then, you'll be safe at the Chapman ranch. I want Steve to believe we're rich in case you decide to hire him. Besides, westerners think more highly of ranchers than of storeowners."

"Won't he think it's odd I'm going to Colorado without my father?"

"Not if you tell him you have a brother there who you're going to visit while I get the ranch fixed up. When you reach your destination, you can confess the truth, if you wish. Don't tell him anything before then, Anna. He'll think that if you can lie about one thing, you'll lie about another, about *all* things. Never forget that he's a wary and proud man. You don't want him to get his feelings and pride hurt and take off leaving you stranded."

"You're right, and I'll be careful. But—"

"Listen well to me, Anna: some people put on good fronts when inside they're bad, or just confused and misguided. They'll use you and trick you, then get rid of you by discarding you or killing you. Steve Carr seems like a good man, but we could be wrong about him. Don't risk getting hurt or betrayed," he urged. "Wait until you're convinced beyond even a tiny doubt that he's totally dependable and trustworthy."

"I agree, sir, and I'll follow your good advice. What I was about to question was the lie about a brother. I don't want to make up one now in case I don't need to use that ruse; it could complicate matters for us if we mention details about him that don't match. When and if the time comes to hire Steve, I'll think of something credible to tell him. I'll say we didn't mention such a close family member because you two had a serious disagreement years ago and don't have anything to do with each other anymore."

Charles was intrigued. "About what?"

Ginny mused a moment. "Your son, my brother, sided and fought with the Yankees, so you disowned him in a moment of anguish, anger, and disappointment, and he's angry with you for being a Rebel, a traitor to the Union and his country. That actually happened with some families, so it should work. I'll say that now that the war is over and things have calmed, I'm going to see him to try to make peace between you two."

Charles beamed with excitement and pleasure. He grasped her hand and squeezed it gently. "You're quick and smart, Anna. It's perfect. That way, our stories won't conflict and expose us."

"I'm getting good at deceptions. Too good," she murmured in dismay. "I don't like having to lie and trick people, especially friends."

Charles put empathetic pressure on her hand. "Sometimes it can't be helped, girl. With so much at stake, this is one of them. You can't allow anything or anybody to stop you from accomplishing what you must do. I'm proud of you, girl; Anna and you would have been good friends; you're so alike."

Ginny watched him drift off into melancholy thought. She knew that her similarity to his daughter was part of the reason Charles Avery liked and helped her, and it was why he could be trusted implicitly. He was a good and kind man. Charles didn't realize that Steve would refuse to be hired by her when he discovered she wasn't Anna and there was no ranch, nothing but lies. Nor would either know how or where to locate the other when her departure time arrived or if he decided to visit the nonexistent ranch. She didn't know why the mercantile store was a secret, but she assumed Charles had a private reason for keeping it one, and so would she.

They journeyed over matching terrain on Sunday, except for crossing the Ocmulgee River five miles from camp. Although very wide, it wasn't deep, so caused no delay. They had a short religious service during the noon break then continued traveling until dusk to camp forty miles south of Macon. Meals and chores were completed and visits began.

Ginny took a stroll, and Steve joined her when she was out of sight of the others.

"Sorry I had to lie to your father last night," he said. "If he

188

knew the truth about me, he would make sure I didn't get within fifty feet of you."

"I understand. We've been apart for so long and we've both changed so much that I can't honestly say if you're wrong or right. But it's best to take no chances. Besides, it's none of his or anyone's business."

"But it doesn't bother you I'm a . . ."

She watched him lower his head and take a deep breath. "No, Steve, I swear. It wasn't your fault, or even perhaps your mother's."

"She chose him of her free will. Knowing the awful truth about him, she . . . yielded to him and bore his bastard son anyway."

Ginny detected anguish but no bitterness toward his mother. Would he feel the same about her if she "yielded" to him and got into trouble? Would he do as his father had long ago and refuse to wed her? Would he let anyone or anything saddle him with responsibilities and restraints he didn't want? "She must have loved him deeply."

"She did, and I can't blame her for that."

"But you blame him for . . ." She stopped and said, "I'm sorry, Steve; I promised not to do this again, nose into your life."

Vexed with himself, he admitted, "I started it, like a fool trying to switch himself with a limb."

Ginny ventured in a tender tone, "Maybe because you need to talk about it to someone who cares and understands so you can get rid of your torment and deal with the truth. You've kept it pent up for years. It's ready to burst from confinement."

"You're right, but I'm not ready to talk about it, not yet."

"When the right time comes along, you will," she contended. "I know you will." He didn't look convinced. "Maybe it's had a good side, Steve; it could be what's driven you to become so strong and independent. Troubles have a way of doing that for us. If everything in life was easy, where would we get our strengths and courage? What would hone our skills and wits?

What would make those good things and times so wonderful and rewarding?"

Steve's gaze locked with her hazel one. "For such a young and sheltered woman, you know a lot, Anna Avery."

Ginny sent him a bright smile. "That's one of the best compliments you could pay me. Thank you."

"No flattery, woman, just the plain truth."

The moon was full. A breeze wafting over them was cool. The green and quiet setting was romantic and private. They were alone.

Steve's alert ears checked for sounds of anyone nearby. He heard nothing to stop him from pulling her into his arms, and she came willingly and freely. They shared several kisses, their eager lips meshing with gentleness and leisure, then swiftness and urgency. Their fingers caressed, giving and receiving pleasure. He trailed kisses over her face, then claimed her pleading mouth once more.

When he realized they were becoming too aroused, he ordered himself to recover self-control and to clear his wits. He rested his cheek against the top of her head while hers nestled against his broad chest. He felt her tremors of desire. He wanted and needed her so badly. He wished they were alone somewhere else so he could make love to her. Yet, that might be a painful experience, to know her and lose her. If he got that involved with Anna, it could mean trouble and pain for both of them. He didn't have anything to offer her, not yet, not any time soon, if ever. Without his changing, a bond between them was impossible; and he wasn't sure he could change or *wanted* to change. If he couldn't make a promise to this special woman, how could he take her?

Ginny felt and heard Steve's heart thudding rapidly and heavily in a fierce need that matched the one storming her body. It felt good, right, perfect in his arms. She knew she wanted more than hugs and kisses from him and, if they were elsewhere, she would challenge the unknown. He had lied to her "father" for a good reason, so perhaps he would be forgiv-

190

ing and understanding of her deceits. She had to learn if he was softening toward her.

"When this is over, Steve, why not come with me to . . . work?"

He noticed she hadn't said with *us*. "Where?"

"To . . . the ranch or wherever."

He caught her hesitation and prayed it didn't mean anything sinister. Surely the Klan wouldn't send a woman to do their task! But who would suspect an innocent-looking beauty? His heart pounded in dread and his guts twisted into painful knots. To evoke information and clarification, he said, "I have another task waiting for me when I finish this one."

"Is there anything I can say or do to change your mind?"

Don't make me wrong about you, woman. "I can't, Anna; I made a promise, and it's important. I will come to visit you afterward."

She understood important promises and having to honor them, but a "visit" wasn't all she wanted from him. Yet, it was a good start. "How long will the next job require?" she asked.

"Maybe weeks, maybe months. I don't know yet."

"What if, . . ." *I need you, pay you, persuade you?* her mind enticed.

"What if what?" he asked when she halted and tensed.

"The ranch doesn't work out and Father moves again or returns to Georgia? How could we locate each other?"

"Leave a message for me with the Waco sheriff."

She looked at him wide-eyed. He was acquainted with the lawman where Charles alleged to own a ranch? "The sheriff? You know him?"

Steve worried over the sound of her voice, the expression in her eyes, and the way she went almost stiff in his embrace. He knew there was something he must check out when he reached Columbus and could send a telegram. "No, but most towns have one," he lied, "and that's how messages get passed. Give him a dollar and he'll do the favor for you."

191

"We'll need a guide if we return to Georgia or move elsewhere."

"Then I'll make sure I stay in touch; I'd like to have this same job again."

"How did you get it in the first place?"

As he toyed with long curls, he murmured, "Newspaper."

"What do you mean?"

"The company that arranges and outfits wagontrains advertises in newspapers in the South and East. They knew of me, so they hired me as leader and scout. A lot of folks are moving west these days, but most to the Far West. I usually head out of Missouri on the Oregon, Sante Fe, or Mormon trails. This trip sounded good for a rest and change. No prairies, mountains, or Indians to worry about. The company tells the leader where the best stops are and has preparations made for him along the route."

"You know the Midwest well, don't you?"

When she focused on that particular area, Steve's anxiety increased. He had been told that Missouri was the rendezvous point for the villain to meet his contact. "Yep, traveled most of it many times. Tell me where you need to go and I can get you there safely. Maybe even for no charge."

Ginny hated to leave him, but it was perilous to remain longer in the tempting location. "If I ever need to make a trip there, I'll hire you. It's getting late. We should return to camp before we're missed." She kissed him again before they parted.

Steve lay on his bedroll staring at stars and clenching his teeth over and over until they ached. *Getting later than you think, Anna, because you're becoming too inquisitive about certain things.*

CHAPTER 9

On Monday, the soil became redder and harder on the western side of Georgia but the shape of the terrain altered little. They saw few snakes and animals; no doubt the approach of the noisy wagontrain frightened them away. They skirted two areas where fenced cattle grazed and finally reached the wide and deep Flint River and camped, as it was too late in the day to begin the lengthy crossing. That allowed people to have extra time for chores and relaxing and for thorough baths. Many had worn the same garments several days so this was a welcome stop.

Women gathered in different areas at the water to wash clothes. Lucy, Mary, Ellie, Ruby, and Ginny chatted while they worked together. Ginny helped Ruby tend her babies while her husband hunted with some of the men. In camp, other husbands or older children tended small ones so the women could work. Steve rode to the farm nearby to let the owner and his helpers know they had arrived and would be ready for ferry assistance in the morning as prearranged.

Ginny asked Lucy about her ankle and learned it was doing fine, giving credit to the support crutch Steve had made for her. She heard from her friends that the irritable women in the group had behaved themselves.

Ruby looked at Ginny. "Our handsome scout has been paying you much attention, Anna." The redhead grinned, as did the other three.

"Is that bad?" Ginny asked, testing his worry about dissension.

"Only if you don't want him to," Mary answered. "You do, don't you?"

"I like him," Ginny admitted with a light flush to her cheeks.

"That's good," Ellie told her. "He would make a fine husband."

"Husband? We haven't gotten that close and I doubt we ever will."

"Keep trying," Ellie encouraged, and the others nodded agreement.

"I'm not certain Steve Carr is the marrying kind."

"You can convince him otherwise," Ruby said with confidence.

"I'm sure you can, Anna," Lucy added in a coaxing tone.

"If a man is shy or reluctant, a woman has to lead him with cunning bridle to the trough to drink from her charms, just like a stubborn mule."

"But how does a woman capture a man's total interest?" Ginny asked.

Ruby smiled at Ginny and replied, "Just be yourself, Anna. How could he help but like you and want you? He isn't blind, old, or taken. And you have an advantage, girl; you're the only single lady available."

"That doesn't matter to Cathy," Ellie whispered, "but she must have gotten a stinging rebuff because she's left him alone for a while."

"She has to know our scout is enchanted by Anna," Mary said.

"If she's the jealous and spiteful type, she could cause trouble for us."

"Don't worry, Anna, we won't let her."

"Thank you, Ellie. I wouldn't want anyone to get the wrong idea and try to have Steve fired out of vindictiveness."

"You work on him with all your might, and we'll make sure no one interferes. Right, ladies?" Ruby, Mary, and Lucy nodded their agreement.

After their baths, the two Davis boys entreated Ginny to fish with them. "If we catch enough, Momma says we can cook 'em for supper. Please help."

Ginny looked at the elder boy and realized he had a case of boyish infatuation on her. She smiled at him and said, "Why not? Let's go, but you'll have to teach me how."

Hooks had been baited and lines tossed into the river many times with good results when Steve returned and joined them. The scout grinned at Ginny and noticed how the boy was disappointed by his arrival.

"We can use another fisherman, Mr. Carr. If we catch enough, we're frying them for dinner. If you help, you can join us," she tempted.

"How could any man resist an offer like that?" he replied. He located and cut a sturdy limb, then attached line and hook. As he secured a small hunk of old meat as bait, he said to the subdued boy, "You're skilled at this, son; I'm sure your parents are proud of you. I bet you wouldn't have any trouble fending for yourself and them if need be." The boy beamed with pride and pleasure, and was won over to Steve's side.

Ginny hauled in a catfish with laughter and squeals that amused and delighted Steve. The fish thrashed in the air, then on the bank. "I'm not taking him off," she murmured with more laughter. "The last one pricked my fingers with those sharp fins."

The fourteen-year-old removed the fish and rebaited her line. He added it to the growing string that dangled in the water to keep them fresh.

When the task was finished, the group had plenty of catfish and two other kinds to feed nine people. Steve and Stuart skinned or scaled, gutted, and cleaned the mess. Ellie and

Ginny rolled them in a mixture of cornmeal, salt, and pepper, with a smidgen of flour. As the fish began cooking, a delightful aroma wafted over the area. Ellie prepared hushpuppies, and Ginny provided several jars of canned vegetables.

While they all worked or observed, Ginny asked Steve, "Does the Klan really do all those awful things some of the men have mentioned?"

Getting worried about helping them? "I don't know. Why?"

"Mr. Brown and Daniels and a few others speak so strongly in their favor that I'm confused. The North did do horrible things to the South, so I'm not sure I can blame them feeling as they do. If the Loyal Leaguers and other gangs—white and black—continue to terrorize Southerners, who will stop them if not the Klan? The Yankee-controlled courts and laws don't protect them. I wonder which is worse: do nothing or risk overdoing? People have suffered so much already; I hate to see more."

Steve was in a quandary: If he spoke against the Klan, she would hush if guilty; if he didn't and she wasn't involved, she'd get a bad opinion of him. Luckily he didn't have to answer, as the meal was ready.

Mattie scowled and complained as she unpacked her wagon at the riverbank, "Why couldn't we cross on a bridge? This is lots of work."

"Bridges north and south of here were destroyed by the Yankees and haven't been rebuilt, ma'am," Steve explained once more. "We'd have to travel too far out of our way to take the next one."

"More time than it takes to unpack, ferry across, and repack?"

"That's right, Mrs. Epps," Steve responded. He was hard pressed to control his annoyance with the whiny woman who'd carried on childishly since they began this task after eating breakfast and cleaning up the campsite. Travelers worked together on both banks to unhitch and reharness teams and to unload and reload wagons. Hired men from nearby towns helped ferry the people, teams, wagons, and loads across the eight-foot depth on separate trips because of their heavy weights and large sizes. Steve was in an unsettled mood because no one had acted strangely, as if they were protecting valuable gems. He'd hoped this chore would provide him with a clue.

Later, they crossed railroad tracks that stretched between Macon and far below Andersonville. They camped not many miles above the site.

After the evening meal and chores, men chatted about its significance. It was a well-known Confederate prison camp for captured Yankees. Nearly fifty thousand of the Northerners had been incarcerated there, and thirteen thousand of them had died during captivity and were buried on the vast acreage.

"No more died there than Rebs died in their harsh prisons. Woulda been more if not for those traitors who joined 'em. If them Galvanized Yanks hadn't done all their work out West, we'd have had less of 'em to fight."

Harry Brown snarled like a wild dog. "Hellfire, the Klan ortta go after them traitors, too! If I was a member, we would."

Others gave their opinions until rain sent the men and women rushing to their wagons for cover. Later, some sat beneath them to play cards.

One man watched and listened. He absently touched his waist where a pouch was secured under a blousy shirt. Soon, he vowed, the Red Magnolias would have the arms and ammunition needed to seek and punish the Yanks for what they did to the South. His Den would make those vicious attackers only too happy to pull back of the Mason-Dixon Line! When he reached Dallas, the plan would go into motion. He would meet his contacts and journey with them to Missouri to exchange the gems.

* * *

197

Two days later at four o'clock, the wagontrain halted to camp near the Chattahoochee River, a few miles south of Columbus on the border. They had journeyed two hundred twenty miles in eleven days to cross Georgia, the largest state east of the Mississippi and the lengthiest one to traverse.

Some of the men headed for town to restock supplies. The grain wagon drivers did the same. Women tended chores and children.

Charles talked Ginny into going to Columbus to eat, bathe, shop, and stay at a hotel overnight. She did her chores and secured the wagon openings against rain. She took a small cloth satchel with her possessions, mounted a borrowed horse, and they left.

The scout met with a stranger—Luther Beams, called Big L because of his size. The real leader would pose as Steve's helper and be ready to take over if the special agent solved his case and had to leave. Luther had agreed without hesitation to assist the crucial mission that riled him.

"I'll tell the others you're to be obeyed as quickly as I am. You'll be in charge tonight. I have to ride into Columbus to send two telegrams. I won't return until morning. One of my suspects is staying there overnight, so I'll need to watch him." He was glad he hadn't said *them* or *her.* "You keep your eyes and ears open here for anything suspicious."

Steve approached Ginny's door to invite her to take a stroll. He was relieved her father was at the other end of the hall and had turned in for the night, early. One telegram was on its way to the Georgia agent to have him investigate if Charles Avery really had a daughter, one this woman's age. It was possible her name wasn't Anna Avery and she wasn't kin to the older man. If she wasn't Anna, he'd have a strong clue to work on. If she was, he could breathe easier. The second telegram was on its way to a Texas agent, asking him to investigate if Charles Avery had purchased the Box F Ranch near Waco. He had requested answers as quickly as possible, and said he would check for them in Montgomery and Jackson and Vicksburg. He anticipated those responses with a blend of dread and hope.

Steve tapped on the door marked with the number the desk clerk had given to him, and Ginny responded. She appeared surprised to see him. She peeked into the hall, saw no one, and pulled him inside in a rush. She closed the door, locked it, and looked at him.

Ginny was so glad to see Steve that she acted without thinking about what she was doing—bringing a man into her room, and in her state of dress! "We can't be seen talking this time of night in a hotel. What are you doing here? Why aren't you back in camp?"

Steve noted how she was attired, in a white cotton nightgown patterned with dainty and colorful flowers. It had long sleeves, buttoned to the throat, and reached her ankles, so she was well covered. Yet, the reality of what the garment was and the heady setting enflamed him, almost caused him to lose sight of his mission, his real reason for coming—to get closer to her. The uncertainty about her was driving him wild; he had to be convinced she was what he hoped she was: an innocent beauty attracted to him.

"No one saw me; I was careful. Your father went to his room and doused his light fifteen minutes ago. My partner joined me here, so he's in charge of camp tonight. I came to invite you to take a stroll. I didn't think you'd be turning in so early."

"I wasn't. I couldn't go out alone, so I planned to lie in bed and read. We had fun. We shopped and ate grandly downstairs and took long baths. I wish I had known sooner and I wouldn't have gotten un— Oh, my goodness!" she said with a blush as she remembered what she was wearing. "I don't have a robe with me. I only answered the door because I thought it was Father. Dear me, this is most improper and embarrassing."

Steve smiled and murmured, "You look beautiful, Anna. I'm sorry I intruded on your privacy. I'll leave so you can read and relax. I'll see you in camp tomorrow. We have a lot of busy days ahead."

Without privacy, her mind hinted. "You didn't intrude, Steve, and I'm happy to see you. I'd rather talk with you than read."

Steve looked her in the eye. "I'm not sure it's wise for me to visit with you here. You're much too tempting, woman. All I can think about is yanking you into my arms and kissing you."

"Why don't you?" she enticed with bravery as her wits dazed.

"If I did, I would be too ensnared by you to quit there. I want you, Anna, more than I've ever wanted a woman before, for any reason. Every time I see you or hear your voice, I catch on fire."

Ginny lifted her hands to caress his face. He turned his head to kiss the palm of one, then did the same with the other. She trembled and he did, too. His fingers closed over hers and he gazed deeply and intently into her hazel eyes. She didn't attempt to pull away.

"You have too much power, Anna. How could I not want you?"

"How could I not want *you*, Steve? You make me feel so strange, so weak and shaky. When you touch me, and sometimes when you only look at me or speak to me, I feel as if I'm standing naked beneath a blazing sun and it's scorching my flesh. My heart races like a runaway carriage. I can't think clearly. It feels good and it feels scary. Why do you do this to me?"

The more she said, the more Steve's eyes glowed and the more his smile broadened.

Somehow, both knew what was going to happen between them tonight, what they had craved for what seemed more like an eternity. They no longer had the strength—or desire—to resist. Each knew they could part forever soon. Each also knew loving would bring them closer, a bond each needed.

Steve cupped her face and kissed her with tenderness and

longing. Ginny responded joyously. It only took moments for their kisses to become urgent with rising need.

Ginny wanted this night with all her soul and she loved this man with all her heart. Johanna's death had taught her that life could be short, cruel, and demanding. She had to seize this precious moment while it was available. She murmured against his lips, "I don't know what to do. You'll have to show me."

Her shyness and admission touched his heart. Near a whisper at her ear, Steve said, "Don't be afraid of me, Anna, or of making love. We can't deny what we want and need. Resisting each other is too hard." He drifted his lips down her throat and back to her mouth.

Ginny's hands encircled his waist and she pressed closer against him. Her mood encouraged him to continue arousing her. Her fingers stroked his back and relished the feel of his hard frame. She felt aswirl in an unfamiliar and yet instinctively familiar pool, with powerful currents of desire and mystery lapping at her body.

Steve's hands slipped into her long and thick tresses. Each kiss fused into another and another; each caress led to an even bolder one. He guided her toward the lamp and doused it, all without interrupting their kisses and caresses. He thought it would be better for her this first time if there was darkness to protect her modesty and to ease her introduction to a man's naked body. As his mouth lavished adoration on her neck, his deft fingers unfastened the buttons of her gown. He worked the garment off one shoulder, his hand tugging on the sleeve. She assisted him by withdrawing one arm then the other. The gown slipped to the floor around her bare feet. He worked the bloomer laces free and allowed them to join the other garment. He felt her movements as she stepped out of them and nudged them aside with her toes. Contact with her bare flesh heightened his desire and increased his pleasure. His hands were like greedy and starving creatures who feasted on her breasts and soft curves.

Ginny was amazed by how brave and bold she was being.

She was glad he had put out the light so she could use her other senses to get to know him this first time. But next time, she planned ahead to her surprise, she wanted the light on so she could see him. Her breasts were taut and tingling and their buds stood out in rigid yearning. She learned why when Steve kneaded and kissed them. Her body reacted to the blissful new sensations from head to foot.

Steve lifted her and laid her on the bed. Rapidly, he was out of his clothes. He lay on his stomach with his hips beside her and with his chest over hers. Some instinct or past advice told him to kindle her smoldering coals into a roaring blaze before he took her. He trailed his lips and fingertips over every area of her face, neck, shoulders, and breasts. One hand stroked her abdomen, along her thighs, and inched its way up their inner surface. He used evocative stroking to arouse her to a writhing and breathless state, one which wouldn't allow her to halt him when he touched her most private places.

Ginny couldn't have halted him; her will was stolen, along with her breath. She wanted him so much that a curious bitter-sweet torment flooded her mind and body. She realized this tantalizing period was leading to something wonderful. She felt her body straining and pleading for something more, much more. Steve was being so gentle, so skillful, so tender, and so filled with the same desire for her.

Steve knew there was no turning back for either of them. He wished he could view the expression on her face, within her greenish-brown eyes. He wished he could send his gaze on a leisurely journey over her body. His hands were mapping and exploring her well, but seeing it all would enhance his delight. He savored every touch with hand, body, or mouth.

Ginny's lips teased over his shoulder and nibbled at his neck. Her fingers roamed the same welcoming territory and trekked onward into his silky hair of midnight black. She didn't need the lamp's glow to tell her how he looked; she had memorized every inch of his face. It was time to seek and yield to her destiny.

"Whatever comes next, Steve, I'm ready to challenge it," she murmured in an emotion-strained voice.

Steve thought she was moist and eager enough to be prepared for his entry. He believed he would be able to please her, even though tiny doubts chewed at his mind, as he'd never been with a virgin before. Anna was different, innocent. He gently moved atop her, kissing her deeply as he eased inside her. He halted when she moaned in discomfort.

Ginny realized why he stopped. "I've heard it only hurts a moment," she whispered, "so do what you must, quickly, then wait a minute."

Steve followed her advice. She gasped, winced, arched her body toward his, and clenched her teeth. He didn't move, fearing he had injured her. He didn't know what he should say or do at that point. He waited while she brought her erratic breathing under control and relaxed. He seared her mouth with kisses, branding them as his own.

"It's all right now," she murmured, hoping that was true.

With gentleness and caution, Steve moved within her, and was relieved when she didn't flinch or cry out or tell him to withdraw. He worked with slow deliberation to rekindle her doused flames. Soon, she was responding feverishly again, and he increased the pace of his thrusts.

Ginny's discomfort vanished and pleasure returned—no, *heightened*. Her fingers trailed over his face and torso. His broad chest was hairless and firm; it teased against her swollen and sensitive breasts. She had assumed this physical act would be wonderful with Steve, but it was beyond measure or description.

Steve labored lovingly until she writhed and moaned with need. Pride and joy surged through him when he fulfilled it. Toward the end, she had caught his pace and matched his rhythm until rapturous release came. Her mouth and body clung to his to extract every moment of the glorious experience. He did the same, reveling in the throes of ecstasy, in the wonder of her total surrender to him.

As they lay nestled together, neither knew what to say—if words were even necessary in the golden aftermath of something so beautiful and special!

After a while, Steve kissed her and finally spoke. "I have to leave, Anna. We don't want anyone to find me here like this. I'll see you in camp tomorrow."

Ginny surmised he was tense and uncertain about the intimate situation, probably feared what demands she would make on him. It should surprise and please him when she made none, not yet anyway, not aloud. She smiled into the darkness and murmured, "Good night, Steve."

The sated and anxious man calmed a little when she responded in that careful manner. He couldn't say what the future held for them, but he knew he wanted her again and again. He rose, dressed, strapped on his pistols, and told her good-bye. "Lock the door after me, and don't open it again without asking who's there. I don't want anything to happen to you."

Ginny saw him in the hall light when he opened the door and slipped out quietly. She went to obey his protective order. She leaned against the door for a minute, took a deep breath, then returned to bed. She cuddled against the pillow where his head had rested; his scent clung there. "I love you, Steve Carr," she whispered, "and I want you so much. Please let this bond you to me. Please love me and want me, too."

Steve listened outside Charles Avery's door to make sure the man hadn't sneaked out to meet anyone. He heard snores from inside and relaxed. He had allowed himself to get distracted again by Anna Avery, and he wasn't sure that tying her so tightly to him was a smart idea at this point. But he couldn't help himself, and that worried him even more. It was bad for him if she was guilty; it was wrong of him if she weren't.

After crossing the powerful and sometimes treacherous Chattahoochee River by ferry, the wagontrain was in Alabama, birthplace of the defeated Confederacy. They had skilled help from local hired men. Yet, the strong currents, depth, and width of the river made it an almost all-day task. Again, Steve observed the travelers with a keen eye, but no one behaved as if he or she feared the loss of valuable gems. He wondered if the reports had been wrong or if the Red Magnolias' plans had changed.

As soon as the ferrying was completed, everyone rested before chores and meals and visits. Steve spent that time with Luther Beams, something Ginny noticed and assumed was another defensive action.

For the next four days, they journeyed through an area that appeared evergreen with a thick plant cover, countless pines and some hardwoods, and widespread mistletoe on branches. At rivers and ponds, they saw black cypress and waterlilies and willows; in many locations, they encountered bamboo and cane thin enough not to block their way. They passed north/southwest railroad tracks and traveled through sleepy rural communities where homes were scattered, people were poor, and farmers and sharecroppers worked fertile fields. As with other southern states, Alabama had a long and mild growing season, a hundred days more than in the North.

At first, the eastside landscape was a mixture of low, gentle hills, stretches of flat lowlands, an occasional steep incline or decline, dense forests, rivers, and streams of various widths. The Indian Trail, oldest one to the Atlantic, was pointed out to them, along with churches and cemeteries.

Then, a section of consistent hills appeared and caused them to move slower for a while. The dirt became redder, a sturdy clay. They crossed spots that though marshy, gave no one trouble, nor did the endless creeks. More oaks and magnolias began to blend in with pines and cedars. Farms were being worked. Abundant morning glories on fences and bushes greeted them each day in pink, white, blue, and lavender.

Everyone noticed the lack of war devastation in the rural location. It gave them a time to relax and forget it for a while. The talk in camp at night was genial and hopeful. Music and stories were heard more than complaints or grim memories.

On Tuesday evening, they camped fifteen miles below Montgomery, birthplace of the Confederacy and its first capital. It was a land of white-supremacy beliefs, but under military rule now because Alabamians had refused to ratify the Fourteenth Amendment, as had most other southern states. It looked as if war hadn't touched this area or, if it had, damages had been repaired and concealed.

Ginny helped her companion with their daily chores; greasing axles, fetching grain and tending the mules, checking the water barrel supply, cooking, and washing dishes, and making any repairs needed to the gear. In the past four nights since entering Alabama, she also had assisted her friends with chores or by babysitting, as that helped to distract her from Steve's behavior.

Those who hadn't gone into town in Georgia to restock supplies did so. Steve also went to Montgomery, and in a strange mood, she noticed. Since Charles, her "father," didn't suggest going, she had no way to meet with the man she loved again. She missed him and longed for him. She feared that their intimacy and brief closeness had Steve panicked. She didn't know how to convince him otherwise. It had taken a lot of patience and self-control to let him have the space he needed, but she didn't know how long she could exist in . . . limbo. He was so capable of dealing with the problems and needs of others but not with his own. As for exposing feelings, she fretted, he made sure he didn't commit that mistake, that weakness. But why, she reasoned, was it so terrible for their unwed scout to court a single lady?

Steve was keeping his distance again. He always seemed on alert and inquisitive. Sometimes he appeared to look for a reason to visit with certain men. She felt as if there was a particular motive for him being so watchful and curious, one she couldn't surmise. She hoped and prayed his mystery didn't include ensnaring her to aid it.

After eating, she chatted with Luther "Big L" Beams. "How long have you and Mr. Carr been partners?" she asked.

The real wagontrain leader smiled and replied, "This is our first job together, but surely not our last. I'm enjoying working with Steve. He went on ahead to train all of you while I brought up the rear with preparations. From what I've seen, he did a fine job of teaching everyone."

"He did, Mr. Beams, and we're all grateful . . . How did you two meet?"

"The company hired both of us."

Ginny talked with him a while longer and realized she wasn't going to learn anything new about Steve, as she had hoped. She saw how skilled and experienced and easygoing Luther Beams was by observing him with others around camp, on the trail, and while relating stories at night. It seemed to her as if the company should have hired Beams as the leader and Steve as scout and assistant. She wondered why they hadn't.

In Montgomery, Steve observed the three men who were his suspects as they shopped and talked with locals, but nothing out of the ordinary took place, to his disappointment. He wanted to be in camp with Anna; no, in the nearest hotel room with her. He couldn't get their passionate night off his mind. She was closer to him than anyone ever had been except his mother, and, as a child, his deceitful father. He wanted to get even closer to her, but determined not to do so until he had the truth about her, and until his next task was finished. The telegram in his pocket from Georgia informed him that Charles Avery had a nineteen-year-old daughter named Anna, but that didn't mean "his" Anna was that woman. If only the telegram from Texas had been awaiting him, he would know if Charles had purchased the Box F Ranch in Waco, would know if they were honest, would know if she was worth risking his heart and soul to pursue. It would be a long and tormenting stretch to Jackson and a reply, if one was awaiting him there.

Steve knew he was avoiding her too much again, but he couldn't be near her without wanting her, without fear of betrayal chewing at him, without risking exposure of his feelings by the look on his face.

For the next three days, Ginny stayed busy during the daytime rotating drive shifts with Charles Avery and James Wiggins because Mary came down with an illness that plagued her with vomiting, diarrhea, dizziness, and weakness. The three Wiggins children spent time during the day in the Avery wagon to prevent an excess burden on James's team with Mary and the toddler riding inside. At night, she tended to her ailing friend's chores and children. Only the youngest one—eighteen months old—gave any problem, as she couldn't seem to understand why her mother couldn't take care of her.

The driving hadn't been too difficult for Ginny, even the numerous back-to-back streams at one point or the creek with its boulders to be avoided to prevent broken wheels. In the lush location, they had sighted armadillo, fox, rabbit, squirrel, a few deer, one bear, and several poisonous snakes.

That night, they camped at the Alabama riverbank where they could bathe and do washing. Ginny and her friends insisted a slowly recovering Mary rest while they did her laundry along with their own.

Steve watched the generous woman as she worked so hard and long to help her friend. He had done James's hunting several times, and the man was grateful for the fresh meat for his family. In spite of his apprehension about discovering that Anna was involved in criminal mischief, Steve joined her as she finished her washing. His heart pleaded: *Please don't confess anything terrible to me when I probe for clues.* "You've been mighty busy these past few days, Anna. I bet you're exhausted and sore.

208

James tells me his wife is better, so you shouldn't have double duty much longer. I'm sure you can use the rest."

"You've been a big help to them, too, Steve. And please don't say, 'It's part of my job.' Accept gratitude and compliments when they're deserved."

"Yes, ma'am," he drawled, and chuckled. "You all right, Anna?"

"Of course. Why shouldn't I be?" She glanced at him and smiled, as his tone and gaze waxed serious and concerned.

"Have you ever done anything you know was wrong or realized later it was; something you're sorry for and wish you could change?"

Ginny stared at him as she tried to read his expression. Was he referring to their lovemaking? Was he seeking a kind way to reject her? "Not that I can think of on the spur of the moment. Have you?"

Steve noticed how she tensed and her smile faded. "I suppose an answer depends on who's judging the situations. People have different opinions about what's right and what's wrong. Even Christians don't honor their Ten Commandments all the time. They say not to kill and steal, but the North and South do it to each other, the whites and Negroes do it to each other, and the whites and Indians do it to each other out West. Some folks think it isn't stealing if you take something from an enemy. The Brownses and Danielses say it's a sin to work or have fun on Sunday, but they talk about hatred, revenge, and killing half the time. Where is the line drawn between right and wrong? Life can be a bad place to live with people stirring up more trouble."

To understand, she asked, "Like the Klan and other secret groups?"

"Can't really say. What do you think?"

Ginny assumed he was searching for anything to talk about except their feelings for each other. *For now, let him.* At least they were together. "I suppose the Klan has good and bad points."

Why mention only that one? "Would you side with them?"

"Me? Not unless I had a strong motive for doing so."

"Lots of folks think they do. It's expanding and spreading."

Ginny locked her gaze with his. "That worries you, Steve? Do you think they'll give us trouble along the way?"

"I hope not."

"Why should they? We're Southerners escaping Yankee perils."

"Innocents get injured and killed during a war, Anna, and the Klan has declared war on their conquerors."

"Somehow I can't believe Southerners would attack loyal Southerners."

"Like you believe Galvanized Yankees aren't traitors and cowards to be hunted down and punished by Klan members?"

Did he know who she was? Who her real father was? Was he tracking down Virginia and Mathew Marston for . . . Surely not. Her father's enemy couldn't know she'd be on this wagon-train or even back in America! And surely he wasn't a secret Klansman seeking "traitors and cowards" to slay in revenge! "Of course they aren't. Why would you think of them?"

Steve noticed her change of tone and expression, as if fear and doubt of him had entered her mind. Odd . . . "It jumped into my head while I was making crazy talk to keep me distracted from you." He grinned wryly.

Ginny relaxed but wasn't sure he told the truth. "Ah, yes, I do recall you don't like distractions. That means I certainly don't want to be one."

"But you are, woman. A big one."

"I'm sorry. What can I do to correct my innocent mistake?"

Steve drifted his gaze over her silky hair and skin. He yearned to stroke them. "Be patient and understanding while I work out a few things."

Ginny read desire in that almost-black gaze, and she warmed with it herself. "Don't pull you closer but don't repel you, either?"

Steve's hands itched to touch her. "You're smart, Anna; thanks."

210

"I'm trying to be, Steve. It's hard at times because I miss you."

"Miss me? But I'm around every day. My mind couldn't be any closer to you."

She wanted to ask, *What about your heart?* "The same is true for me."

"Then we're both in good shape or in deep trouble."

Ginny laughed and replied, "That's an unusual way to put it, but I get your meaning, and you're right . . . Now I have to go see if Mary needs anything before bedtime. It's getting dark."

Steve hadn't noticed; he'd been too absorbed with her. "I'll walk you back to your wagon."

"Is that a wise idea?"

"Probably not, but I'll do it anyway."

She gathered her things and returned to camp at her lover's side. "Good-bye, Steve."

That word twisted his gut. "You mean, good night, don't you?"

"Every time we part, it's like a short and painful good-bye."

"One day . . . Good night, Anna."

Ginny watched his retreat. *One day we won't have to say good-bye?*

Crossing the wide, deep, and swift Alabama River the next morning was slow and treacherous work. So was crossing the Tombigbee River two days later. Without bridges or hired helpers at either site, the wheels and possessions had to be removed, the wagons floated across, the goods and mules and people rafted over, and everything replaced. Under the supervision of Steve and Luther, the travelers worked in groups to speed up the task. Nothing went wrong, and the scout gathered no clues for his mission.

For a time, the terrain was swampy as they journeyed over hills and "lumpy" land, as Charles called it. They traveled to the state line, having traversed two hundred miles across Ala-

211

bama in ten days. They camped there for an extra day for rest, chores, and repairs.

Ginny was delighted by the lengthy stop, which gave Steve the opportunity to eat dinner with them one night. Afterward, he remained to play cards and chat with Charles. She even fried fruit fritters from canned Georgia peaches for the men to enjoy as dessert with steaming, rich coffee.

Both men smiled and complimented her, and she beamed with joy and pride. She observed Steve as he visited with Charles. Every day she came to love, want, and need him more and more. She savored his friendship and glowed under his glances. *Two states down,* she told herself, *and two and a third to go before parting or committing.*

A new state came. Mississippi was much like Georgia and Alabama: pines and oaks, red clay, rich vegetation, mostly flatland with an occasional rolling hill, and many streams.

On the third day in the lush area, trouble struck.

Charles felt the jolt as a rear wheel dropped hard into a deep pothole and he heard weakened wood snap. He pulled out of line and halted his team, then he leapt down and looked at the damage: two busted spokes. He knew a change was needed or the unsupported area of rim would bend. He yelled to the last wagon driver, "Keep going, Carl; Anna and I will change the wheel and catch up by camptime. You won't be far ahead."

Carl Murphy nodded and continued on without stopping to help.

Ginny eyed the damage. "We can do it; Steve taught us how."

They worked swiftly to unload everything heavy. They moved light things aside to reach the extra wheel and jack. Charles positioned the jack beneath the axle and began turning the crank to lift the wagonbed.

Steve glanced back and saw the Avery wagon off to the side of the rutted trail. He told Luther Beams to continue onward while he went back to help them, as camp was less than an hour away. He galloped to the location and dismounted. "You should have signaled me."

"I was afraid gunfire might spook the teams. We have rifles nearby," he said, pointing to two on the ground. "Anna said you'd trained her to help out, so I figured we could change it and join you in camp."

"She's right, but it's dangerous to be too busy to stand guard."

They changed the wheel and reloaded the wagon. Ginny had to relieve herself before heading out and entered the woods to do so.

Within minutes, Charles and the scout heard a scream, then her voice shouting, "Steve, help me!"

"Get your rifle! Guard the wagon while I see what's wrong. Stay here!" Steve ordered, drawing his pistols and racing into the forest.

Charles wondered if it was a cunning trick by Ginny to get Steve alone. He'd do as told until someone shouted for assistance.

Steve was frantic as he headed toward her, yelling he was on the way to rescue her. He saw her backing away from a log positioned between them, her face pale and her wide gaze on the ground. He heard the reason why: a timber rattler. "Don't move, Anna," he commanded and was relieved to see her obey. He turned and shouted to Charles, "A snake, but don't worry. I'll get him."

Charles grinned and mentally thanked the crawly creature. He leaned against the wagon to savor what he hoped was a lengthy wait.

Steve reholstered one of his pistols. He killed the snake with the other, then bent to remove its rattlers with his knife. He stuffed them into a shirt pocket before joining the trembling woman. "Are you all right?" he asked gently.

She watched him wipe the snake's blood on his fingers onto his pants leg. "I am now. I was going to skirt him, but he moved right or left every time I did. I was afraid he was going to take off after me."

"They do that sometimes when you spook them." He pulled her into his arms to comfort her, overwhelmed by desire for her.

His mouth closed over hers, and she responded eagerly. One kiss fused into another until both were breathless and quivering with a need for more. They dared not lose their wits, as time was short. They kissed and embraced a final time, then parted with reluctance.

"*Shu*, woman, what you do to me," he said in a ragged voice.

"And what you do to me, Steve Carr," she responded with a smile.

In camp, Mary Wiggins met them. "You two are joining us for supper. It's the least I can do to repay all the wonderful care you gave me."

Ginny and Charles ate with the Wigginses while Steve ate with the Davises. The yearning couple didn't speak again that night, and very little during the next two days before they camped south of Jackson.

Charles suggested they visit a hotel in town for relaxation, and Ginny readily agreed, as Steve was going into town himself.

It was ten o'clock when Steve approached her room. He was dismayed that a telegram from the Texas agent said he'd been delayed in his task and to expect an answer when he reached Vicksburg in three days. The troubled man knew it was reckless, but he had to see and hold her tonight.

Ginny responded to the soft knock at her door, assuming and hoping it was Steve. She smiled when she saw him. "I'm glad you came," she whispered, and pulled him inside the room.

"I brought you a present, something for protection." He held out a small derringer in a miniature holster. At her confusion, he explained, "It straps to your thigh or calf for concealment.

214

It's always better if an enemy doesn't know you're armed. Wear it every day, Anna. Please."

His concern touched her deeply. "Why don't you show me how to strap it on?" she suggested, lifting her nightgown to above her knees.

Their gazes meshed and both knew what they wanted to show each other.

CHAPTER 10

"You can strap the derringer on here," he began, securing the short belt to her shapely calf, "so you can reach under your skirt or pants to grab it quickly when needed. Or," he continued as he unfastened the buckle, "you can put it here." With quivering fingers, the scout placed the small holster a few inches above her knee. "A dress will hide it, and you can get to the pistol easily." His hand remained on her silky thigh.

Ginny withdrew the derringer, studied the weapon, and reholstered it. She kept her foot propped on the bed so he wouldn't move his hand away. "That's very clever. Thank you, Steve."

He pulled a box of low-caliber cartridges from his vest and held them out to her. "Here are the bullets for it. If you have a pocket in whatever you're wearing at the time, keep a few extras handy. I have another box to use for target practice. I wanna make sure you can put a few holes in whatever you aim at." When he saw the same expression he had during her weapons lesson, he added, "At least wound and stop an enemy if you can't force yourself to kill one."

Ginny undid the buckle and laid the holstered weapon on the table, along with its ammunition. "This is very kind of you, Steve, but I should pay you for it. You work hard for your money. I'll ask Fa—"

"It's a gift; and I can afford it. Didn't cost much. Besides,

Miss Avery, I did it for a selfish reason: I wanna be sure you stay safe and alive."

"That kind of selfish is wonderful, my protective scout. The only present I have in return is this," she murmured, and kissed him.

When it ended, she gazed into his eyes, as dark as night and as fiery as black coals. His nearness and touch were breathstealing. Her fingers traced his rugged features. "You're the most handsome and irresistible man I've met, Steve Carr. You make me think and do crazy things. You have a powerful hold over me, and I don't know whether to be happy about it or afraid."

Steve stroked her flushed cheek and drifted his forefinger over her parted lips. "You do the same to me, woman." His arms tightened around her body and his mouth covered hers. Exhilaration filled him.

Ginny knew she loved him and wanted to marry him, but was sure he wouldn't consider such a dream until he worked through his troubles and resolved the reasons for his bitterness. This was perhaps the last time they could share intimacy before the journey ended; she needed to bond him to her as strongly as possible, to soften his heart and to open his mind's eye to the reality of his feelings for her. A loner like Steve wouldn't do and say such things as he had if they didn't have deep meaning behind them. She had to get him past his fears so he'd recognize and accept the truth. She pressed tightly against him, kissing him with feverish desire and hugging him with soul-deep feelings.

Steve's mouth feasted at hers with ravenous hunger. He also realized how short their remaining time together was, perhaps shorter than either of them knew. It was difficult not to yank off their garments, fall to the bed, and ride away to splendor within her. She was eager and responsive. He had dreamed day and night of having her again; now that precious moment had come.

Thoughts of Ginny's troubles vanished in the golden glow of their loving. It was as if thousands of butterflies were trapped inside her body and fluttering against her skin as they sought to break through to freedom. Simultaneously she felt relaxed and tense as her anticipation mounted. No man had ever made her feel this way, and probably no other man could. She craved his kisses, his embraces, his touch. No flames could sear her body and heart as his possession did. She yearned to become one with him again tonight, and for countless times in the future. Even if her behavior, her uncontrollable surrender, was dangerous and reckless, she could not stop herself from claiming what she needed.

Steve relished her sweet mouth, and clean skin. His lips varied between long and firm kisses where their tongues touched, to light and brief ones where his lips scouted hers from end to end. He wanted to take her fast; he wanted to take her slow; he wanted her completely. His hands roamed her clothed body with stirring caresses as he increased their suspense, until he could endure the barriers between them no longer. He removed her gown, with her eager assistance. He stripped off his weapons, boots, and garments—again with her bold help. He lifted her and carried her to the inviting bed and placed her there. For a moment he felt vulnerable without his ever-present Colts and knife, and knowing his wits were dulled by passion.

Ginny had already tossed aside the covers. She kept her gaze locked to his as he smiled down at her. She had to read what was exposed in his eyes, to see it was tenderness and desire. She didn't ask him to put out the lamp, and he didn't do so. With courage and elation, her gaze slipped over his masculine body. His bronze physique appeared flawless; the few scars here and there did not detract from his near perfection. His muscles were well honed, creating a potent landscape of ridges, valleys, and plains. His weight was ideal for his height. She noticed that he had little body hair growing on his arms and legs, and none on his tawny chest. Yet, his ebony hair was thick and lush, his stubble when he needed a shave was heavy and black, and the crispy fuzz around his . . .

Ginny blushed as she realized she was examining him like she had seen gamblers do with prize horses before placing their bets at the races. Her feminine curiosity had gotten the better of her. When her gaze rejoined his, he seemed to be savoring every inch of her the way she had visually adored him.

Steve had expected her body to be as compelling as her face, but it was even more exquisite than he had imagined. Her complexion reminded him of a ripe peach from her home state. Some would call her hair lightest brown and others, darkest blond. Her eyes were like pools of green with brown magic submerged in them. No artist could have created a more lovely beauty; one probably could mix colors forever and not find the correct shades to capture her. The seven-inch difference in their heights made her the perfect size to fit in his embrace. From the glow on her cheeks and in her eyes, she was as pleased and enticed by what she saw as he was. Obviously she recalled how much pleasure he had given her and was too highly inflamed to be either modest or afraid at the sight of his arousal.

Steve lay down half atop her. His mouth roved her face, neck, and shoulders. His lips returned to hers and sealed them in a kiss that could enlighten her to his deepest and most protected feelings. The contact with her bare skin caused him to tremble with swiftly mounting desire. He trailed his fingers over her as they mapped and explored her terrain. His mouth trekked with leisure down her throat and to her breasts.

Ginny moaned in bliss at the wild and wonderful sensations. Her fingers wandered into his ebony hair and thrilled themselves with its softness. They left the midnight location to roam his sleek torso. He was strong and firm, but supple. She was consumed by an overpowering need to be locked against him, but couldn't seem to get close enough after his mouth returned to hers. He was like a sorcerer working his spells and enchantments on her, and she didn't want to break them, ever.

Steve cupped and stroked her firm breasts. He quivered with joy every time his hands or mouth touched them, as did she. His body was awash in a flood of tormentingly sweet sensations. He hadn't experienced such feelings with saloon girls, as only his body had sought and found physical release with them. With Anna, his heart and mind were involved in taking her. She seemed more relaxed and eager tonight, as she knew what lay ahead—that thrilled him, as it said how much he had pleasured her last time. He kissed her closed eyes, the tip of her nose, the crest of her chin, the ridges and hollows of her cheeks, her ears, and her mouth. He let his tongue dance with hers, as he had danced with her in camp.

Ginny thrashed her spinning head and aching body. He was assailing her wits and heightening her desire. Her strained voice urged, "Please, Steve, take me before I die of longing."

His lips captured hers as he slid his manhood within her. Obviously there was no discomfort this time because she arched to meet every thrust and clung to him. She was yielding herself freely, totally, and ardently. He took her in those same ways.

Passion's flames leapt and scorched their bodies as they caressed, kissed, and moved as one. Love's fire burned out of control. The tension within them built to an almost staggering point as they reached the pinnacle together. Their pulses quickened, as did their pace. Bursts of ecstasy shot through them. Their kiss went on and on, making them breathless and lightheaded until, at last, they rested in each other's embrace.

Steve's voice was husky and tender as he murmured in her ear, "That was the best experience I've had in my entire life, Anna. Thanks."

Ginny was overwhelmed by her love for him. "You're a good teacher in many areas, Steve Carr," she replied, aware it was still too soon to press him for a permanent relationship or an admission of love. "Of course I have a lot more to learn, if you don't get weary and bored with my lack of experience and vexed with my distractions. Blame yourself. You are quite witstealing, my talented scout."

Steve propped his elbows on either side of her head, careful not to entrap and pull her touseled hair as it spread out on the pillow. "You're the big distraction, woman. Half the time, all I think about is you."

"Only half the time?" she drawled, putting on a look of disappointment. "You control my thoughts and feelings most of the time."

"If I thought about you any more than I do, we wouldn't travel ten feet safely. As for getting 'weary and bored' with you, it will never happen, woman. If you gave me any more pleasure than you do, I'd go wild. You best have mercy on me and take it easy or I'll be stalking you day and night."

"I wouldn't mind. That might be fun."

"But bad timing, Anna," he responded in a serious tone. He needed to prevent either of them from saying revealing words too soon.

"I know, for both of us. After we get things settled in our lives, we can see if we want more from each other than this. Is that fair?"

Apparently, he decided, his necessary caution had worked, and he was relieved. "Sounds like a good offer to me. What do you have to settle?" he asked as his mind shifted with reluctance from romance to his mission.

"Starting a new life. How about you, my secretive scout?"

"Secretive? Me? What do you mean?"

Ginny wanted to do probing of her own but quickly learned it would be futile. "I've seen how you watch people. You're mighty inquisitive for a scout. You look as if you're trying to discover everyone's secrets."

Steve chuckled. "Only those that could cause me trouble on my job."

"Like *I* cause you trouble?" she teased, his answer unconvincing.

"This kind of trouble, I like," he replied and nibbled at her neck.

Ginny used her hand to smother her laughter. "Me, too."

Steve leaned back and gazed into her merry eyes. He pondered how he had gotten to this refined lady so quickly—unless she wanted him to do so. Was he *all* she really wanted from him? How could he know for sure? They were so different: she,

221

a genteel, pampered southern belle; he, a half-breed bastard and all saddle tramp. *Are you real, Anna Avery? Can I trust you? Can I accept the consequences if you're—*

"Why are you staring at me like that?" she inquired, feeling unsettled by the intensity of his gaze.

"Like what?" he murmured, kissing the tip of her nose.

"Like you're a voracious predator who's searching for my weaknesses before attacking me."

"I am. Haven't you realized that by now?" he jested.

As Steve's mouth and hands returned to her pliant body, Ginny had an alarming feeling he had lied or masked his real meaning. What, she mused in panic, did she really know about this man she loved? He could be anybody, anything. Should she trust him? Would he use, betray, and discard her when they reached Dallas? But how could he make love to her so tenderly if he didn't care about her? She reasoned it was probably only her guilt about deceiving him that played tricks on her mind, or maybe he had been probing his intimidating feelings for her before he had spoken. Soon, she was lost in the wonder of what he was doing to her.

The group stayed camped below Jackson the following day for several men to make repairs on their wagons. The grain supply was replenished, chores were done, and visits exchanged.

Ginny wished she could have remained in the hotel room with Steve all day and another night, but that was impossible. Several men from town had arrived to chat with the travelers, to gather news from Georgia and other locations, and to relate all the horrific details of the Yankee conquest of that area and the fearsome destruction it had caused.

Ginny wished the depressing talk would stop. She didn't want to imagine what had been done at beautiful Green Oaks in Georgia, her lost home. She wasn't surprised when a query was voiced concerning the existence of the Ku Klux Klan in Mississippi.

The local man answered that "no group had been organized yet, but that if things got worse or didn't improve, they would indeed form one."

As Ginny listened, she was glad she'd hadn't witnessed and endured those tragedies and terrors. Since entering Mississippi, she had viewed lingering and chilling reminders of vast destruction, still visible two years after it had ended. She heard and saw bitterness and hatred in the Mississippians, as she had in Georgians. It had been war, she admitted, but some things couldn't be justified even under that word. She was sitting in the dark in the Avery wagon and knew she couldn't be seen, but she saw Steve standing near the conversing group of people. She observed him closely as he took in every word spoken, every expression used, and every person present. What, she mused, had the scout so intrigued?

They broke camp on time Tuesday morning and crossed the wide Pearl River without problems, as it wasn't deep or swift.

Steve was edgy and alert. He surmised that he might not unmask the culprit until Dallas, their termination point, unless the telegram he was expecting in Vicksburg gave him a clue. The closer he came to a response, the more he dreaded what he might learn.

Ginny continued to study the moody and mysterious scout who had won her heart. This morning, he had ridden close enough to touch her calf and find his present to her missing. He had scolded her, telling her in an almost curt tone, "Put that pistol on during the next stop and never be without it, not even in camp. Wear it dawn to dusk, woman; I mean it."

She told herself she should be happy he was so protective of her, but his concern seemed to have an underlying motive she couldn't grasp.

* * *

On Wednesday, May first, they crossed the Natchez Trace and Big Black River. Widely spaced rolling hills of mostly pine and cedar with a few magnolias allowed for a comfortable ride and steady pace. As the sun was setting, they halted near Vicksburg: "Gibraltar of the Confederacy" whose conquest had begun the gradual fall of the South. Because they were close to civilization, they didn't have to circle-up as on the trail, which allowed for welcome privacy between wagons.

The Mississippi River wasn't far from camp. Its width and depth and its swift and unpredictable currents would make it the most treacherous and time-consuming crossing. This was where accidents and losses might occur. The famous river was down a steep slope with countless evergreen trees between it and camp, so the water wasn't visible. The hilly terrain was dotted with numerous mounds, some manmade earthworks from the war; the men called them redoubts, redans, and lunnettes. Damage by gunboat blasts to land, trees, and property was still noticeable and heartrending, although Mother Nature and local inhabitants were doing their best to heal the numerous scars. Twice they heard horn blasts from steamboats that plied their trade on the river. They had journeyed for seven days to traverse one hundred forty miles of Mississippi, and the sight of the famed river and nearby town filled everyone with excitement.

"We'll rest tomorrow and get ready to challenge our most dangerous river on Friday," Steve announced. "I suggest a night of fun and rest."

Everyone happily concurred. Meals were eaten and chores were done with haste. Music, merriment, and dancing began as soon as children were put to bed.

Steve stayed in camp, hating to imagine what he would discover in the morning. He realized that if the villain he must defeat was Charles Avery, that could call a halt to his relationship with Anna. This might be the last enjoyable evening with

224

her. Besides, he excused his reluctance, the telegraph office was surely closed by now.

Residents who had seen or heard the wagontrain approach came to visit and bring treats for fellow Southerners. They joined in the fun.

One related that Vicksburg had been a gambler's paradise at one time because of the riverboats. When crime became a problem, the locals had put an end to it in '35 by ordering them out of town within a day or face brutal consequences of "thirty-nine lashes at the public whipping post." He reported with a comical grin how the threat had worked on almost all of the professional gamblers and their "fancy women." He went on to entertain the travelers with colorful tales of famous thieves who had worked the Mississippi and the Natchez Trail.

Conversation naturally veered to the past war with the North. Another local told them about the steamboat *Sultana* that picked up released Yankee captives in April of '65. "She took on too many fur her size and power: twenty-five hunnerd prisoners and others piled aboard. More 'an eager to git outta the dangerous South. Squeezed into her tighter 'an blood in a tick after a good feeding. She blew up near Memphis, burned, and sank. Word was fifteen hunnerd went down with her. Some couldn't swim and some was too weak to do it, and that river has powerful currents in some places no man could survive."

Ginny listened until she couldn't endure any more grim talk. She was relieved when several men took up their instruments and played cheerful tunes. She saw couples dance and others snack on the sweet treats of southern hospitality. Many chatted, laughed, sang along, clapped hands, or tapped toes.

"Why don't we join them?" Steve suggested to Ginny, nodding to the dancers.

"Dare we risk being so close?" she jested. "I might lose my wits."

Steve grinned. "Who can blame me for yielding to temptation?"

"Or me," she replied, and slipped into his beckoning arms.

Their first dance was fast and lively; the second one was slow enough and with sufficient distance from others to permit whispered talk.

"We're lucky we haven't had any problems with storms and mud," she remarked. "Bad weather always seems behind us. I hope it stays that way."

Steve didn't know if he agreed or not, as storms would slow their progress. If he received good news tomorrow, it would give him more time with Anna, but would lengthen his mission and delay his other task. He wanted both jobs finished so he could . . . He frowned as he realized his future action was controlled by the information in that telegram. "Less than three weeks and four hundred miles to go, Anna," he murmured.

She wondered what Steve had been thinking to bring such a scowl to his handsome face. He was so tense tonight, and that worried her, yet he had asked her to dance twice and appeared reluctant to leave her side. Something heavy was weighing on those powerful shoulders, and she feared the burden somehow had to do with her. She tried to relax him with light talk. "I know; Father told me today. It sounds like a long time, but it will pass so swiftly. These last four and a half weeks have raced by."

Steve pushed aside his worries to concentrate on her. "That's because you stay so busy and are having so much fun," he jested.

"In spite of the work and hardships, Steve, it *has* been enjoyable. I'll never forget this journey. Of course, since we've encountered no perils, I'll have to embellish it to make it colorful for my children and grandchildren. I'm sure you'll have countless adventures to relate to yours one day."

Words the haunted man had thought and believed for years leapt from his lips before he could halt them. "I don't plan to have either one. I wouldn't make a good father, or a good husband."

Ginny assumed he had taken her innocent statements as pressure for a commitment. She faked merry laughter and

226

teased, "You could be right; a trail man wouldn't be around enough to fill their many needs."

Steve forced chuckles, too. She was generous to release him from his trap. "That's a fancy and kind word for saddle tramp."

Ginny broadened her smile and slipped a seductive tone into her voice. "A saddle tramp doesn't work to earn his living or have routes and schedules to follow. You do lead a free life without attachments, but you aren't an idle wanderer. You aren't ill-kempt, worthless, or irresponsible."

Steve leaned back and stared at her. He grinned and asked, "What brought on those compliments?"

Ginny sent him a beguiling look that said she wasn't going to answer. "Father says we're going into Vicksburg tomorrow to spend the day and night. If you're going, too, perhaps we could share the day."

Steve squeezed her hand and lowered his voice even more to whisper in a husky tone, "What if I want more than the day with you?"

Ginny trembled with desire and her cheeks glowed. "I hope you do. We only have Shreveport left between here and Dallas."

Steve caught her meaning: one more town and one last chance to have privacy. "Let's have lunch, a long stroll, sup—dinner, and . . ."

Ginny's body felt as if he was setting it afire with his provocative words. She couldn't wait to be alone with him again. She had only a few chances left to win his heart before they arrived in Dallas. She wished they could sneak from camp to kiss and embrace. They didn't have to make love every time they were alone, only be together.

"Well?" Steve prompted. "You want to spend time with me?"

She gazed into his dark eyes. "Sounds perfect to me, Mr. Carr."

Steve reacted to the intoxicating plans in the same manner. He was aching with need for her, and more than physical need.

227

She made him feel good in many ways. "Sounds perfect to me, Miss Avery. Now, let's change the subject before our expressions expose us as naughty children."

"Sounds very wise to me, Mr. Carr," she replied, and grinned.

Steve left the following morning before the Averys did. He picked up the telegram and read it. His emotions were a mixture of anger and sadness, of disbelief and confirmation of doubts. As he had suspected, Charles Avery had not purchased the Box F Ranch, hadn't purchased any ranch or property; there wasn't a Box F near Waco! He had been deceived! Ginny's father was the sly culprit.

Dread washed over the scout's body and anguish flooded his mind. What remained to be learned was if Anna knew the dirty truth about her father and—Spirits help him—if she was involved in the vicious scheme.

All he could do was wait for them to reach town. In bitter resentment, Steve resolved to take advantage of Charles's encouragement to pursue his daughter. He must confront her in private. *Shu*, he hated to search for the truth! Either she was innocent and would despise him for duping her and arresting her father, or she was guilty of complicity and of tricking and betraying him and would go to prison with Charles. Even if guilty, could he condemn her to such a terrible fate? Didn't love and loyalty to her father and misguided beliefs count for anything with the law? How should he know, as he didn't have love or loyalty to his father?

Be innocent, Anna, or I can't help you, not without destroying all I've worked for and without sacrificing vengeance for my best friend. If you've lied to me and used me, how can I ever trust you again?

"We're here to see Mr. Avery," a stranger said to the oldest Davis boy.

"That's his wagon over there, sir." The youngster pointed to it.

"Much obliged," the gang leader said, and guided his friends that way.

As five roughly clad males approached the wagon, Ginny eyed the well-armed and crude-looking men who made her nervous even at a distance.

"We're looking for Charles Avery. Is he here?"

Ginny's wary gaze drifted from man to man. "My father went to view the river with some of the men. He'll return soon."

"Your father? We didn't know he was bringing his daughter along."

"You know him? You're friends of his?"

"Yep, we've come to get him and take him to a meeting."

She was confused and apprehensive. "What do you mean? We're heading for Dallas on the wagontrain. Was he expecting you to meet him?"

"Yep, but we're a mite early. We have a business deal."

Ginny was uneasy. She didn't like the unkempt . . . *ruffians*, she decided with aversion. "What kind of business do you have with my father?"

"Private, Miss Avery, 'less he's already told you about it."

"He hasn't mentioned anything like this to me." She glanced around to see if anyone was close enough to rescue her if these men presented a threat. She saw the group returning from the river. With relief, she said, "Here he comes now . . . Father, you have visitors."

Charles looked the five men over as he asked how he could help them.

Ginny grasped that the leader had lied, that they were strangers. Her anxiety increased.

"We're here to take you safely to where you need to go."

Charles was as angry as his look and tone sounded. "This wasn't part of the plan. You're supposed to meet me in Dallas."

"Plans changed, Avery, and we had no way of getting in touch with you. This one's better. It'll save everybody a lot of time and saddlesores. Graham will meet you in Little Rock 'stead of St. Louis."

Ginny was more worried about Charles leaving with such crude-looking men than she was concerned about this unexpected event playing havoc with her own plans. "What's going on, Father?"

Charles patted her arm and smiled. "Nothing for you to worry about, Anna. You boys will have to meet me in Dallas as prearranged; I can't change my schedule. I have to get my daughter there and see her settled in before we take our little business trip."

"Afraid that ain't possible, Avery."

"And why not?" Charles demanded.

"I have orders to bring you with me. And we've already been seen here. Too many dangerous questions will be asked. Too many suspicions aroused. You catch my drift?"

"Then you shouldn't have come here. Everything was going fine, just like we planned. No one suspected me. This will bring trouble to me and to my daughter after we leave."

"Can't worry about that. The good of the cause is the only important thing. Ain't that right?"

Good of the cause echoed across Ginny's mind and alarmed her. She surmised Charles Avery had a deception of his own in progress, one he hadn't told her about. He was vexed by this kink in his scheme, whatever it was.

"Get the goods and your gear and let's move out fast. Bring her along."

"She stays here. She isn't part of this." Charles grasped her hands in his. "Anna, you take the wagon on to Dallas," he ordered. "You'll do fine alone; you're well trained. I have to go with these men. Don't fret, girl, Steve will take good care of you if you need help. You do what you have to do."

Ginny gleaned the clues in his words for her to carry on with her deceptions. "What's going on?" she pressed in fear. "What's wrong? You didn't tell me about this trip."

"Nothing to worry about, Anna, just do what you came to do."

"Ain't smart or safe to leave her behind," the leader said. "Not after people get curious about you."

"They wouldn't have if you'd done as planned," Charles scoffed.

"Time's important, Avery; you'll find out why very soon."

"Nothing is as important as keeping my identity and mission a secret."

"Too late to worry about that. Let's get moving. Get your stuff ready to pull out, too, Miss Avery."

"I told you she isn't coming with us. Anna stays here and goes on to Dallas on the wagontrain."

"She's coming with us, Avery. The law could be on to us anytime. We might need her for cover. You got the goods with you?"

"In a safe place. I'll turn them over to Graham when I see him."

Luther Beams had been observing the incident and catching a strange word here and there. He walked over and asked, "Got a problem, folks?"

"I'll be leaving the wagontrain with my friends," Charles said. "Anna is continuing on to Dallas with you and will wait for me there to join her. I trust you and Steve will look out for her?"

The gang leader fingered his gun butts. "No, sir, that ain't a smart idea. Your daughter is coming along with us." When Big L started to bring his rifle upward to ready it for trouble, the leader warned, "You don't want to do that, mister, too many nice folks around here might get hurt. Why don't you lay aside that rifle until after we're gone?"

"What's this about, Avery?" Luther Beams asked as he obeyed.

"Private business," Charles replied.

From what he'd been told by the authorities who asked for his help, Big L realized what was taking place, but he dared not

231

risk challenging five armed men who looked as if killing could be second nature to them.

"You two get your stuff and let's get out of here. We need her along for protection. Nobody will follow and shoot if a woman prisoner is with us."

"Prisoner?" A wide-eyed Ginny repeated the chilling word.

Charles comprehended he couldn't change the men's minds. He looked at Ginny. "I'm sorry, Anna, but you'll have to come with us for a while. Don't worry; you'll be safe. I promise."

"What about my things, Father? Are we taking the wagon with us?"

"Nope," the leader answered for Charles. "We're riding horses."

"I don't have a horse," Ginny told the man who had been doing all the talking.

With a wicked grin, the boss said, "I'm sure one of these nice folks will lend you one. They don't want any trouble with us."

Ginny grasped his meaning, as did Big L and Charles. *"Steal* one?"

"Borrow is a nicer word, Miss Avery."

That would entice the authorities to pursue them, Ginny knew. Once questions started being asked, the entire truth about her identity might be exposed. "Stealing is against the law," she protested. "We'll get into trouble."

"You don't have to steal; I will. Rollie, you and Slim find her a good mount. Avery, you and your daughter stuff some things in a bag. Now."

"What about all my possessions?" Ginny persisted.

"The wagon will have to be left here," Charles answered.

"What if they're stolen before we return?"

Big L surmised that Anna didn't know what was going on and was being taken as a hostage by the ruffians. "Don't worry, Miss Avery; your friends will take turns driving your wagon to Dallas. Your belongings will be waiting for you at the company office in a few weeks."

"Thank you, Mr. Beams, but I can't put you all to such trouble."

"Won't be no trouble at all, miss. You've done plenty for others, so they won't mind helping you out. You best go with your father and his friends; we don't want trouble and injuries in a camp of women and children. Steve will take care of everything when he returns from town."

Ginny caught his hints. Fear gripped her heart as she thought about Steve getting weary of awaiting her, returning soon, and having a gun battle with these . . . outlaws. Nor did she want to endanger any of the people in camp. She had placed herself in Charles Avery's care; now she was in the midst of his troubles. "You're right. Thank you, sir."

Ginny climbed into the wagon, lifted a cloth satchel, and packed clothes for the trail in it. From the corner of her eye, she checked to see if she was being watched. Not close enough, she concluded, for the men to see her drop extra cartridges into her skirt pocket for the holstered derringer strapped to her thigh. She was told to rush by the man at the tailgate.

Ginny realized she was helpless to disobey, but, thanks to Steve's tough training and precautions, she wasn't vulnerable in other ways. She would do as she was told and await the opportunity to escape. She must watch the route taken carefully so she could retrace it afterward. She admitted with sadness that she had misjudged Charles Avery in some areas; he obviously was up to no good and had used her as a protective cover for his "mission." Yet he had tried to help her, to have her left there. His failure meant he had no control over these rough villains, a realization that frightened her.

Within five minutes, she and Charles were mounted and being led from the campsite. She was on a horse taken from a wickedly smiling Cathy King, as Ed was in town. Ginny waved to her four watchful friends and sent them a look that said she wasn't leaving willingly.

The seven galloped south for miles to a stream and rode in it for a time. They veered northeast, with one man hanging

233

behind to cover their tracks, skirted Vicksburg, and headed northwest toward Arkansas.

Ginny feared no trail or clues were being left for anyone to follow and come to her rescue. She glanced back at the large city perched on steep hills, and its cobblestone streets. Her last sight of town was of the Greek Revival courthouse on its highest point. Before concentrating on memorizing their route, she thought of Steve Carr futilely awaiting her arrival in town to share the day and a glorious night together. What would he do when he discovered she had been taken against her will? He couldn't quit his job and cast aside his responsibilities to chase after Charles Avery's daughter. No matter what Steve felt about her, his duty and job would come first. She was sure he would allow the local law to take a course of action.

Steve paced at the corner of Clay and Washington streets as he watched for the Averys' arrival. Time passed, too much. It was after the lunch hour, so Charles must have changed his mind about the diversion. He mounted up and rode for camp, to be told a shocking story there.

"What do you mean, Anna was abducted by her father's friends?"

"Miss Anna was taken captive, Steve. I could tell she wasn't involved in these evil doings. Mr. Avery tried to leave her behind, but that leader—a bad sort—wouldn't let him. They stole Mr. King's horse and forced her to go with them. She looked real scared and worried, but she didn't have a choice. They hinted they would shoot up the camp if she refused or I challenged them, so both of us obeyed. They rode south hours ago. When you took so long, I sent one of the men to search for you in town. You must have missed him on the way back." Luther related all he'd heard and seen.

"I have to go after them, Big L; you have to take over here."

"Don't worry about us; we'll do fine. Just catch those devils and help Miss Anna. One more thing, Steve. As they were mounting up, the leader whispered a warning to me. He said if anybody followed them, Miss Anna would be killed. I think he meant it. Out loud he told me they'd release her soon. He lied and she's in big danger. I don't believe Mr. Avery has any control over them, but he don't know it yet."

They talked a few minutes before the troubled man gathered his possessions and supplies and took off after them.

Steve rode south, hours behind them. He speculated they were heading for New Orleans to exchange the stolen gems for arms and ammunition. That would give Avery access to a ship to transport his cargo to Savannah and into the clutches of the Red Magnolias. He couldn't allow that to happen. He must not fail in this mission.

Steve rebuked himself for not keeping his mind on the assignment. If he'd returned to camp after getting the revealing telegram, he could have captured the gang and recovered the gems this morning. This case could be settled by now. Instead, both the villains and gems were gone. So was Anna. He wondered if she had promised to meet him in town to get him out of the way so they could join their contacts. Maybe what Luther Beams witnessed was nothing more than a pretense to conceal her involvement. Maybe she cared for him, suspected trouble, and had kept him out of danger with a pretty lie. Or was that too much to hope for, her love and innocence? He'd know the truth when he caught up with them soon.

CHAPTER 11

Virginia Marston and Charles Avery were ferried across the wide Yazoo River on a large raft that **didn't** seem sturdy enough to the trembling female to bear their weights or to be safe in the tricky currents. Rolling hills of lush grass, wooded knolls, and sand-colored soil gave way to fertile black flatland of the delta region where cotton grew in abundance and the moist ebony dirt clung to hooves and was kicked up behind them. They journeyed westward of a dense forest of mostly pine, oak, and willow, with occasional magnolia and dogwood. They crossed numerous creeks where cypress with huge bases grew at their sides. They passed plantations at a distance, some repaired and some fallen into ruin during and since the bitter and bloody conflict with the Union. They saw fields of rice and corn. To Ginny, it looked as if the residents of this area were recovering slowly from the horrors of the war.

The group of seven traveled as fast as the terrain would permit and took few rest stops. The gang continued to watch for pursuers over their shoulders, and finally stopped concealing their getaway trail. They rode in close proximity that warned Ginny, along with Bart's words, not to "make a break for it." She was glad her body was in better condition now than it had been before her intense training period with Steve and from weeks of exertion on the wagontrain.

So far, the ruffians hadn't given her trouble. The leader

promised her safety on the trail and release in Little Rock, but she distrusted him and his men. Although the muckers talked and joked with Charles and he with them, an intimidating tension filled the air. Charles tried to mask his apprehension, but Ginny's worried senses penetrated it.

She was afraid, but assumed it was best to put up a brave front. She discouraged any conversation and disdained all attempts at friendliness. She knew that haughtiness often kept even roughened types at a distance. She hoped that pretense would work for her. But every mile of the way she was conscious of the holstered derringer strapped to her right thigh and the extra bullets in her skirt pocket, cushioned by a handkerchief. She wisely did not expose it and wouldn't until the right moment presented itself. She knew she could not take on five armed and dangerous men. She must wait to get one alone, disable him as Steve had taught her, and flee. She hoped she would remember the route they were taking and paid close attention to it.

By flatboat, they crossed the mighty Mississippi, a river to evoke wonder and terror. The ferrymen kept on alert for treacherous "boilings" and eddies in the swift blue currents and for ever-shifting sandbars. It was noisy at both banks where sucking and gurgling sounds chewed ravenously at land and debris and where vegetation was thick and verdant.

In Arkansas, they encountered a heavy tracery of rivers and streams in the lowland that would, Ginny prayed, slow their progress for a while. Yet the flat and open landscape allowed for a lengthy visibility, and she saw no one in pursuit. At dusk, the leader halted them not far inside the watery stateline: fifty miles from Vicksburg, the man she loved, and her possessions.

Ginny was exhausted and sore from a nerve-wracking and long ride. The food being cooked—fried salt pork and grits, served with strong coffee and warmed biscuits—did not appeal to her even though she was hungry. She knew she must keep up her strength, though, so she forced herself to eat. She heard frogs and crickets and saw fireflies flickering here and there. She studied her surroundings carefully in case she was compelled to flee trouble. This area did have sluggish creeks and stagnant ponds and names with "bayou" attached, but it was nothing like those in southern Louisiana, Georgia, and Mississippi. The terrain was called swampland, but it wasn't what she'd imagined a real swamp to be. In spots the ground was wet, spongy, and densely vegetated, but she'd seen no uncrossable marshes, quagmires, alligators, poisonous water snakes, or other bog creatures she associated with one. Yet this area was spooky at night and fraught with hidden perils, so she must escape during the day when she had light to guide her steps.

An inquisitive fox darted back into the trees and vanished before one of the men could shoot it with his drawn rifle and a mean grin on his face. She hated to imagine how these men would act in a few days after they wearied of her arrogance. If they tried to ravish her, she would fight them to the death.

Death . . . Ginny trembled, thinking the word. They might silence her with death to protect their evil scheme. She might never see her father again, or Mathew Marston could be dead already. Steve could be murdered if he came after her. To stay alive and safe to return to her loved ones, she must remain alert and cautious and brave. She must depend on the skills her lover had taught her for protection and freedom. At the time, she hadn't realized how important his tough training would become to her.

Ginny massaged her grumbling shoulders and neck and the muscles at the back of her waist. Riding horseback all day, she decided, was more demanding than walking and driving a wagon, or perhaps it was only a reaction to the activity. During the day, they had encountered boatmen, several riders, hunters, and fishermen, and had seen workers in fields, but she hadn't shouted for help from sources she considered futile. She was in a perilous predicament, but she must survive and find her father and Steve Carr again.

Charles joined her away from the men. They lay on bedrolls beside each other. "I'm sorry I got you into this, Ginny," he whispered. "Don't be scared. Those men are hired to do a job and wouldn't dare betray their boss. Don't worry, they won't harm either of us."

He didn't sound convinced to her. Ample space between them and the bandits and the excessively loud croakings of many frogs allowed them to speak softly without being overheard. The separation was permitted because the horses were close to the gang and Bart had pointed out that, "nobody's fool 'nough to escape into a swamp at night."

"What is this all about, Mr. Avery?" she asked. "I have a right to know why I was abducted."

He reasoned she would discover the truth soon, so it wouldn't matter if he revealed it now. "I'm a carrier for the Red Magnolias. I have a crucial mission to accomplish for them."

Ginny stared at him, his features visible beneath a three-quarter waxing moon. She recognized the name of a powerful unit of Klansmen. During the journey, she had learned that most Invisible Empire members honestly believed they had formed the secret organization to combat Yankee and ex-slave terrorism in the vulnerable South. But as in all large groups of rebels, the Ku Klux Klan had members who went beyond protection and justice to obtain personal revenge and greedy desires. "Carrier? For what?"

Charles patted his waist, "Gems, mostly diamonds, worth a fortune. We're exchanging them for arms and ammunition from Timothy Graham in St. Louis, and we're hiring scouts to track down our enemies."

"What enemies, sir?"

"Men like Sherman, who ravaged the South, and Loyal Leaguers, who are still ravishing our land. We're going to punish them, kill them, so they can't do this to anybody again."

"Track down and . . . assassinate them?"

"Punish them for what they did, for what they're still doing to us. To stop Negro gangs they're inciting, arming, and training to loot and kill us. They're sicking embittered ex-slaves on us like starving dogs on juicy meat. Most of us didn't even own slaves; those who did, never abused them. They didn't believe in cruelty, and such property was too valuable to maim. We can't take attacks lying down like cowards. But we can't risk fighting back in the open or exposing ourselves as Klansmen. If we succeed, the South will rise to her past glory. We'll be free, safe, and powerful once more."

"But what you're planning to do with this . . . 'mission' is murder, Mr. Avery. You can't be a part of it. You're too good and kind; too gentle. The war is over; let it die."

"Like my Anna died? Raped, beaten, and murdered by Yankee soldiers. She's not the only woman that happened to because of the war. Other members have wives, daughters, mothers, and sisters those beasts have ravished or terrorized or slain. With these," he said, patting his waist again, "they can be located and punished. My sweet and innocent Anna and others can be avenged."

"With *what*, Mr. Avery? You have the gems hidden on your body?"

"In a pouch around my waist. I don't want those men to know what I'm carrying or to where. They probably think it's money or a voucher or a promissory note. Once our scouts find the bastards we want, they're dead."

Scouts? her mind echoed. Steve was a skilled one for hire, and Charles had constantly and eagerly pushed them together. She fretted over the possibility of their being secret cohorts. Steve had been inquisitive and observant; he could have been interrogating her and spying on everyone else for this very reason. He could have gotten wind of this "mission" and been seeking the carrier, a boss to approach for his next job. Steve had insisted she be armed at all times. Had he suspected this trouble and prepared her to defend herself? No, she argued with herself, he wouldn't take a wicked job like this.

"Were you wooing Steve Carr to become one of those scouts?" she probed. "Is that why you wanted him ensnared by me, your daughter?"

"No, Ginny girl. I meant, hire detectives. I only wanted Steve

240

to be willing to guide you to your father. You see now why I couldn't, and can't, go with you. Steve Carr is a good and honest man, a skilled guide and expert shooter. I thought you might need his help and protection after we parted and if things didn't work out in Texas." Charles sighed heavily and frowned. "After this, he probably wouldn't let you hire him for any amount. He's also proud and stubborn. If you meet again, you'll defeat any hope with him if you continue being Anna Avery or if you confess you lied. Either way, he'll never trust you again. Men can deceive, then expect and get forgiveness, but if a woman deceives them, they take it as an attack or unforgettable treachery. Besides, it's dangerous and foolish to travel with a man who feels that way about you. You'll have to find another way to get you to Colorado. I'm sorry I messed that up for you."

Ginny feared those grim words were true, but only time and Steve's reaction could convince her. She worried over what her friends at the camp were thinking about her. Possibly they had added up the clues and realized her "father" was committing a more terrible deed than horse-stealing. They might even think she was a clever and disguised party to it. Her four friends . . . She missed them already and hoped they wouldn't believe such awful lies about her.

No doubt Cathy King was delighted to have her gone. And no doubt the theft of their horse would give her an excuse to cry on Steve's shoulder!

Steve . . . Would he try to trail and rescue her? But how, when fourteen families were in his care? Would the law come to help her soon? Would they be fooled by the false trail the men had marked southward?

The following day they were riding again by eight o'clock. The Arkansas lowland was green and beautiful. Past or present crops of cotton, rice, and maise stretched before their gazes for what looked like miles in several directions. They skirted inhabitcd areas to avoid contact with farmers and sharecroppers, just as they did where cattle grazed on lush grass. The few hills they crossed were so low and gentle that they could more accurately be called uneven terrain. Sprinklings of hardwoods broke what sometimes seemed like prairie land. They spooked deer, quail, squirrel, and rabbit, a few times, turkey and opossum.

During one rest stop, Bart told her that people in the northern and western sections of the state were fiercely independent and suspicious of strangers. He said many, especially in isolated mountain regions, were backward, poor, and rough. He disclosed that Union loyalty had been "strong and thick" in the northern region, and fights still broke out between ex-Confederates and ex-Union sympathizers. "You don't wanna git caught by none of them mountain boys, Miss Anna," the leader ended his chat. "You'd never see a town or friendly face again. You'd be kept like a slave to 'em till you die, or git too old or belly-fat to serve 'em."

Ginny didn't have to be told what "belly-fat" meant. She shuddered as she realized she could escape one peril and fall into another one.

Friday night they camped west of Barthalomeu Bayou at dusk, having used all hours of daylight available.

The following night they camped fifteen miles southwest of Pine Bluff. Charles tried to persuade Bart to allow his "daughter" to ride into town where she could take a comfortable steamboat or keelboat down the Arkansas River to the Mississippi to Vicksburg or upriver to Little Rock and meet them there. Bart used the possibility of danger to her as an excuse to continue holding her captive. He claimed that too many Union troops had stayed in Pine Bluff or returned there since its capture in '63 for her to go unnoticed. Bart alleged the big town, where some of the first shots of the war had been fired, was perilous because of rough landing workers and tricky gamblers who plied their trades on the riverboats that docked there.

* * *

Sunday night they halted on the Ouachita River. Hills were steeper in this area, some with rocky sides exposed. Woods surrounded the site. Many trees had branches low to the ground, and underbrush was thick, telling her there were excellent hiding places nearby if she could escape.

By that time, Ginny understood what Charles was doing and why, but she did not agree and told him so. She was worried about his sinister plans with the Red Magnolias, worried about him, and worried about the bold, lustful looks the men had been giving her since Friday.

It had poured yesterday, and her soaked shirt had clung to her breasts. The offensive men had sent her lewd smiles, nudged each other and winked, and licked their lips as if in anticipation of tasting a treat. She had chided herself for not packing a slicker but hadn't thought about it at the wagon during her panic. She had used a dripping blanket to cover her shoulders and halt their leering. She knew time for action was slipping away and that she must escape the next day. She couldn't wait for aid to come. Even if someone was pursuing them, she reasoned, they had traveled too fast to be overtaken.

Ginny knew she looked a mess. She intentionally didn't groom herself and risk creating more appeal to the ruffians. She was miserable in the dirty, sweaty, and mussed state. She yearned for the day it would no longer be a necessary precaution.

"Ginny, I don't trust these men," Charles whispered. "We're heading west now, but Little Rock is northeast of us, so they aren't taking us there for a meeting. Tomorrow, I'll demand they release you. If they refuse, I'll hold a gun on them until you make your escape. When I give you the word, you ride out of here and keep riding as fast as you can, northwest to Hot Springs." At her baffled look, he explained, "I've been to Little Rock and Hot Springs before and, best I remember, the mineral springs should sit at eleven on a clock from our present position. If you're afraid you'll get lost, just follow the river. It's a longer route but will get you there. Once we begin our ruse, no matter what you hear, don't look back or return."

"I have a derringer strapped to my leg, Mr. Avery," Ginny revealed in a whisper. "Steve gave it to me and taught me how to use it. If I help, we can escape together. They'll kill you after I get away from them."

Charles exposed what was necessary to persuade her to cooperate, as he felt it was the horrible truth. "I think that's what they already have in mind for me very soon. I don't believe they're guiding us to Timothy Graham; I think they've turned greedy and traitorous and plan to take the payment for themselves. I'm not afraid to die, girl. I faced death many times during and since the war. I love you, girl, and I don't want to see you hurt. I'm more concerned about your safety and survival than I am about failing this mission. Another member can replace me, but nobody else can save you. You know what these men will do to you the moment I'm dead. I can't let happen to you what happened to my sweet Anna."

Tears clouded her hazel eyes. "I can't let you risk your life for me."

"I got you into this and I'll get you out. Please don't argue. Even if we both drew on them, these men won't care if we shoot two of them while the other three gun me down to rob me and . . . hurt you."

She admitted he was right. It pained her to know he would probably die helping her, as the cutthroats would have no reason to hold him prisoner. She was angered by their helplessness, terrified of the grim fates looming before them in the morning. "All right, sir."

"Good girl. Get some sleep. You'll need it."

Ginny lifted her satchel. "I'm going upriver to take a bath and change clothes. I'll return in about twenty minutes."

"Halt, Miss Anna!" the leader shouted at the departing

woman. "You don't wanna go trying nothing crazy and riling me."

Ginny looked at him and scoffed, "Attempt escape without a horse, weapon, or supplies and in an unfamiliar wilderness? I'm not a fool, Bart, and my father is in your care. I can't stand being so filthy and disheveled a minute longer. I'm going, so don't try to stop me or I'll pitch a fit."

Bart scowled but said, "Slim, you go guard Miss Anna. And behave yourself or you'll answer to my fists and irons."

Ginny found a site close to the woods for hiding after she made her break. She trembled in suspense and prayed for Charles's endangered life. She waited a few minutes, then called out, "Slim, a snake!"

The outlaw joined her in a hurry, "Where?"

"There, at the edge of the bank near those weeds and my things."

Slim stepped closer to the water and looked in that direction. "I—"

Ginny clobbered his head with a large rock. She tossed one pistol into the river so he couldn't use it on Charles and kept the other. She was tempted to return to camp and help him escape with her, but that would be futile against four men. She assumed he didn't stand a chance of saving himself and that troubled her, so much that she changed her mind.

Ginny bound the unconscious man's ankles and wrists with his shirt and belt then gagged him with his bandana. She drew her derringer, as she felt she could control her accuracy better with its lighter weight. She checked the bullet chambers and sneaked to camp, a weapon in each hand. To avoid startling and distracting her companion and giving the bandits time to react, she must wait until the right moment to expose herself. Charles had said he would delay the men when they became suspicious of her lengthy absence and decided to investigate. While she was reasoning what to do next, Bart took matters out of her hands.

"That gal of yourn is taking too long. Rollie, go check on 'em."

Charles drew his pistol. "Don't any of you move," he ordered.

"What the— Don't be a fool, Avery; it's four to one. You can't shoot all of us before the rest clear leather and fire."

"Ah, yes, but which one will it be who dies?" Charles bluffed. "You probably can't hit the side of a stage anyway."

"But I can, and I will," Ginny vowed coldly as she stepped into the clearing with two weapons pointed in the men's direction. "Let's tie them up and get out of here, Father," she said, accustomed to calling him that.

"Mount up and ride, Anna. I'll keep them covered then follow you."

"We leave together. Unbuckle your gunbelts, you scoundrels."

"You're making a big mistake, girlie. You—"

"The mistake was yours when you kidnapped me. See that canteen beside you?" Ginny fired at it and water gushed from . bullethole. "Does that convince you I know how to use these? And I will if you don't obey me fast and easy with one finger only." Ginny cautioned herself not to get carried away with her daring ruse. She wasn't "Little Pearl" from the ten-cent pocket novels she had read, about a fictional western heroine who could do anything a man could and most of the time better. She was lucky her reckless demonstration had worked; it wouldn't have if Steve hadn't insisted on weapons lessons and target practice.

"Do as the lady says, boys."

"What?" the other three shouted at the same time.

"Do it," Bart snarled like a provoked animal. "We don't want to be sleeping on our bedrolls like Slim probably is. She's serious."

All four unfastened and dropped their holsters to the ground.

"Step away," Ginny ordered, and Bart made his men obey again.

Charles collected the holsters and backed to the horses. He kept glancing at the outlaws as he saddled two of them in a rush. He mounted while Ginny kept her weapons aimed on the scowling men, then did the same for her. He glanced at the alert woman, smiled, and thanked her for coming back for him. They kneed their mounts to gallop to safety.

Having grasped Bart's hint, the men dashed for their bedrolls and fetched rifles from beneath covers as the leader gave his orders. All aimed and fired. Charles was wounded in the shoulder and fell off his horse, which kept galloping. Ginny's mount was shot in the neck and leg and both tumbled to the ground.

"Run!" Charles told her as he tried to get to his dropped weapon.

Ginny glanced back and saw the four men racing toward them. She couldn't help Charles further. Nor could she take time to aim and fire, as four armed villains were approaching them with haste. She ignored Bart's shouts for her to halt as she raced toward the woods. She heard the leader order a man to go after her.

While Rollie searched for her and Ted fetched the runaway horse, Bart scoffed at the wounded Charles, "You're a fool, Avery, if you think we'll let you git away with the money."

"I don't have any money. I only wanted to get us away safely."

"You musta figured we was going to take it from you today."

Charles winced in pain. "I had the feeling you'd try. You're the fool, Bart. The Klan will hunt you down and kill you for this outrage."

"We ain't afraid of no men in silly costumes."

"You should be; they're powerful and dangerous. They'll find you. They'll make you wish you'd never had a greedy bone in your body."

"We'll tell 'em we was attacked and you was killed. If you had any money with you, we don't know nothing about it."

"Money" would be the exposing word, and Charles smiled

at knowing he'd be avenged. "They'll know you're lying. You're dead men."

"Nope, *you* are," Bart said, and shot him twice in the heart. "Search his stuff, Kip. Let's git that money and the gal and ride outta here. We'll enjoy her in camp tonight, make her sorry she ever gave us trouble."

Kip grinned and stroked his crotch.

Bart chuckled. "Calm yourself; you'll get your turn after me."

Kip tossed Charles's things in all directions but found no money.

"He must have it on him," Bart suggested.

Kip yanked off the dead man's coat and checked it. "Nothing, boss." He searched Charles's pants pockets. "Not here."

As Bart flipped Charles over, he felt something besides flesh beneath his dark shirt. He ripped it open and grinned when he saw the leather pouch. He removed it and looked inside. "What the devil!"

"Cut a lizard in half, boss, them's diamonds and more."

Bart chuckled. "Yep, and I bet they're worth plenty. Lookie how they sparkle. Ain't they real pretty. We're rich, in high cotton."

Rollie joined the two men, looking mad and breathing hard. Slim trailed him with a bloody injury and embarrassed expression. Ted rode up with Charles's horse and dismounted. All five eyed the glittering treasure.

"Where's the gal?" the leader asked. "You got her tied to a tree?"

Rollie exhaled in annoyance. "I cain't find her, boss, but Slim's all right. She wacked him bad with a rock. Needs binding."

"Did you search real good? I got me a score to settle with her. After I finish, you boys can have yore fills, too. After we git tired of 'er, we can give 'er to some of them mountain boys if they give us any trouble."

"She's hiding better 'an a coon with hunting dogs sniffing

after her. She's real smart, but she'll have to show herself soon. We'll wait."

"Yeah," Kip agreed, "we'll outwit her. I'm second with her, boys."

"Why you?" Ted asked, licking his lips in eagerness.

Kip reminded, "I was last with the other girl. She was 'bout used up when it came my turn to shoot in her. So was the two before her."

Bart looked at the gems and thought about a posse coming to recover them and the chestnut, as horse-stealing was a serious crime in the West. "With these, we can git us all the women we want, women we won't have to force to do what we want and like, women for each of us. Anna cain't git far without a horse or supplies. We'll leave her to the buzzards. Probably wouldn't be no good hump no way. Let's git moving."

Rollie didn't know how right he was, as Ginny had climbed a tree and concealed herself among branches with thick foliage. She'd shinnied up many a tree as a child and was relieved she remembered how and could still accomplish the feat with speed. She'd heard two shots and guessed what they meant: Charles Avery was dead. She had eluded Rollie but hadn't relaxed her guard. She assumed the gang would come looking for her again, and she feared their retribution. She heard horses gallop away but dared not show herself in case it was a trick to lure her out of hiding. Even if the evil men were gone, she was still in a dangerous predicament. Life had never looked blacker for her than it did at that moment.

Ginny remained in the concealing tree until late afternoon. She finally climbed down, drew her pistol, and sneaked to camp, praying the ruffians were gone. She watched and listened for another hour before assuming they had left her to her fate. All horses and gear had been taken, except for the mount shot from beneath her. She knew the bullets hadn't gone astray; the men had wanted her alive to . . . She shuddered at the thought.

The distraught female walked to Charles Avery's body, knelt, and wept for his loss. He had been a good and kind man, only a misguided and tormented one. After what he'd suffered during the war and the tragic murder of his daughter, she understood what had driven him to this desperate act. She had no way to bury him, was not even able to cover him with rocks or a blanket to protect his body from scavengers.

The Kings' horse had died during the day and she raged at the men for not putting him out of his misery. She knew that was true because Charles had three wounds to his body, the one that had felled him and two in his chest, those she had heard from her hiding place. It was obvious the men had found his concealed cache and stolen it, which was no doubt their intention all along. They had taken his money and watch, too. They had left nothing behind for her to use: no canteen, blanket, or food.

Don't panic, Ginny. You'll get out of this mess. Think.

She remembered the satchel she'd left at the river. She hurried there and recovered it. At least she had a change of clothes, soap, a washcloth, and a brush. In her pocket, she had extra cartridges. And safety matches, she realized with a smile of relief. She had the river for water to drink. She had two weapons with which to hunt for food. She had strong legs, thanks to plenty of exercise on the trail and Steve's lessons, to walk to civilization and help. It was early May, so the nights wouldn't get too chilly. The thing to remember was to stay alert and to keep moving.

You can't head northwest to Hot Springs, Ginny reasoned, *that's the way their tracks lead. You don't know where or how far away Little Rock or another town is. There's nothing back trail for miles, and if you don't stick close to the river, you won't have a water supply and you don't know how far the next one is. You could use— No, the Kings' horse didn't have any saddlebags to use as makeshift canteens.*

She couldn't think of any use for the left-behind saddle to aid her survival. She'd heard and read that Indians used animal stomachs and bladders for water containers, but she couldn't

250

cut open the horse to do the same. Besides, she didn't have a knife.

Think, Ginny. She should get as far from there as daylight permitted. She prayed for Charles Avery's soul and began walking in a knee-high section of the Ouachita River to hide her tracks. She didn't remove her shoes and was glad she was wearing ones that laced snugly above the ankle and prevented excessive water from filling them. Her skirt tail was pulled from the back, between her legs, and looped over the waistband in the front to keep a soaked hem from slowing or tripping her.

It wasn't long before that precaution didn't matter; the water level reached her waist and then her breasts. Fortunately it was a clear blue hue that didn't cause her to worry about invisible creatures and perils. Balance was difficult and arm strain was the result during those minutes when she tried to hold her satchel over her head to keep it dry. Soon that was also futile. A few times she swam side-armed through deep areas to keep from leaving the water and giving a persistent villain a trail to find, which proved to be tricky with the satchel she refused to discard. Once she even hitched a short ride on a floating log that allowed her to rest except for kicking her legs to keep her moving. She realized her action would also deny the law a trail to follow; that couldn't be helped. She wasn't going to take any risk of being captured again.

It was dusk when she halted and climbed onto the bank where the Caddo River joined with the Ouachita. She ached all over from trudging and swimming in the river. She lay on her back for a while and rested. Her stomach growled in hungry protest.

"You'll have to wait until morning when I can hunt something to cook," she murmured as she stroked it.

Ginny used eye and ear to check the location and detected nothing to alarm her. Miserable, she stripped off her garments and bathed in the river, aware her modesty had lessened since meeting Steve Carr. She used wrung-out clothes for wiping off and donned clean but slightly damp ones. Pants would have been better for riding, but her concealed weapon was easier to get at with a skirt. She was relieved to find the satchel was waterproof, as promised by the seller, though some moisture had sneaked inside around the opening. Having brought along two skirts and shirts, she draped the water-dabbled extra set over tree limbs to dry.

Ginny felt better after taking a bath and brushing the tangles from her long hair. She braided it to prevent more during the night, then scrubbed the soiled clothes and hung them over branches to dry. She put aside her belongings, gripped the derringer in her hand, and lay down on the grass to sleep. She used the satchel as a pillow and one of her garments to cover her shoulders and arms. The heavy bag had been a nuisance to carry all day, but she might need the changes of clothes or Slim's confiscated pistol with its six bullets. Many times she had quelled the urge to toss the weapon aside and was lucky it hadn't gotten waterlogged.

At last her empty stomach and fatigued body allowed her to fall asleep. Her hand relaxed and the derringer slipped from her grasp.

Ginny heard birds singing. Her stomach growled. She yawned and stretched. Reality flooded her and she opened her eyes with reluctance to test it. She was lying on the ground beneath a tree, so it hadn't been a bad dream. She caught sight of a dark figure from the corner of her eye, shrieked in surprise, and jerked to an upright position against the tree. She gaped at the man sitting cross-legged nearby. "How did you find me? I traveled in water all afternoon."

"A Comanche warrior taught me how to move across the land without being seen and how to know somebody had passed before me even if he covered his tracks with skill," Steve explained. "Be it on dirt or in water or by foot or on horse, it matters not to me. But you did a good job, Anna. The average

252

man or tracker couldn't have located you, or surely not this fast."

Ginny realized it was only confidence in himself that caused him to speak the truth without conceit or thought that it might sound like bragging. One thing she was certain of was that Steve possessed enormous prowess. But one thing he didn't possess was a proper greeting. There wasn't a glad-to-see-you or comforting smile in return, and she wondered why he seemed . . . almost cool and wary. His ebony gaze, as usual, was as impenetrable as a moonless night. He appeared on rigid alert that was understandable under the circumstances. Except for a tan low-crowned hat lying beside him, he was attired all in black, even down to his gunbelt and holsters. His sable hair was finger-tousled, and dark stubble grew along his jawline and above his mouth. If not for his aura of mystery and reserve, she would fling herself into his arms and cover him with kisses. "I had a good teacher, a very demanding scout. I'm happy to see you. I was afraid no one would come after us or would be misled by that false trail Rollie made."

He caught her use of the man's first name and wondered why she seemed so calm after what she'd endured. He had expected her to leap into his arms with joy and shower him with praise and thanks, and was miffed when she didn't. He was mystified by why she looked and behaved as if nothing out of the ordinary had happened. "That false trail didn't trick me for a minute. I realized in a hurry you weren't heading for New Orleans or someplace southward. Took me a while to get the news and to catch up because I waited in town for you until one. They pushed you hard and fast, but you didn't hold 'em back any. It would have helped me if you had found cunning ways to slow 'em down a mite."

Ginny asked herself if his tone and expression had bewildering edges of accusation to them. "I dared not provoke them, Steve; they were evil men. I tried not to call attention to myself. I even skipped all my customary grooming until last night. The way they were eyeing me was scary."

Steve noticed how beautiful and fresh and desirable she looked, too much so for his troubled and doubting state of mind to handle. "You've had a rough time of it. I could tell what happened back there in the last camp."

Ginny's thoughts had been diverted by her rescue and handsome lover. His remark brought back the horror of yesterday. "They killed . . . him. We tried to escape, but . . . It was awful. I didn't even have a way to bury him."

As she cried in grief, Steve pulled her into his arms. He was glad he had finally gotten a normal reaction from her. Perhaps she was in shock; he'd seen Indian and war captives act strangely upon their rescue. To get at the truth, he must be patient and sly. The telegram from Texas sparked suspicions about her, as did possible slips by her during the wagontrain journey. It was hard to believe she didn't know in advance there was no ranch in Waco, no fresh start ahead. Yet he didn't find it impossible that her own father would misuse her this way; his had deceived and betrayed him long ago. He also knew from experience that women could be cunning and dangerous criminals. He had chased, exposed, and captured a female rustler, a murderess, and a bank robber. Those vixens had done their deeds willingly and eagerly, but Anna might have been ignorant of the real situation or acting out of loyalty to her father.

Ginny snuggled into Steve's strong and protective embrace. She allowed the cleansing tears to flow for a while. She had endured a terrible ordeal, but she was safe now. Her love was holding her and was stroking her back with tenderness. After she composed herself, she asked, "What about the wagontrain? How could you leave it?"

Steve was affected by her contact, her smell, her voice, and the pain of possibly having lost her. "I put Big L in charge; he's better trained than I am."

Ginny's heart fluttered. "You left to come after me?"

He used a misleading answer. "Did you think I wouldn't?"

She looked up into his dark eyes and murmured, "Thank you, Steve. I was so scared. I tried to remember everything you

254

taught me. Your training was the only reason I survived and was able to escape. I'll never again complain or refuse any lesson you want to teach me."

Pride flooded him from her sincere words, at least he presumed they were honest. If she was only a good deceiver, he worried, he could be wrong. "I'm glad you finally understand and accept why I was so tough on you. This untamed land can be a dangerous place, Anna."

She stared into his softened gaze and her heart warmed. "You're the best thing that's ever happened to me. Thank you for being here when I need you." She craved him so much that she couldn't stop herself from pulling down his head to seal their lips.

Steve's body flamed with a need that dulled his warring senses. In spite of his anger and doubts about this woman, he had been desperate to locate and rescue her. He had been filled with anxiety during every mile he traveled, praying he wouldn't come upon her discarded body along with Avery's, praying the gang wouldn't be so intoxicated by her beauty that they brutally ravished her. If the villains had harmed her, he would have tracked them to the end of the world and slain them, slowly and painfully as the Indians had taught him long ago. Guilt over deluding her had been his riding companion, and would be until he was certain she was totally innocent. If she was cleared, she might never forgive him for tricking her. He might never possess her again. That thought drove him to surrender to her.

Ginny's heart pounded with excitement and her flesh burned with desire. She was glad she had bathed and changed clothes last night. Steve's unspoken summons for her to yield her all to him was clear, loud, powerful, and irresistible.

He was as consumed by her as she was by him. They experienced an urgent, almost desperate, yearning to fuse their bodies into one. Their mouths meshed many times with hungry, deep, and feverish kisses. They sank to the grass, locked in each other's arms.

Steve's eager hands stroked her breasts through the material

255

of her shirt. His lips worked over her face, her ear, and down the silky column of her throat. His tongue teased into the hollows there as his quivering fingers unbuttoned the fabric obstacle and found no chemise to create another one. His cheek nuzzled her bare chest until his mouth reached a rosy-brown peak and fastened onto it. He lingered and stroked it for a minute, then drifted his tongue toward the matching bud nearby. He lavished delight between the two mounds and caused her to moan and thrash with white-hot passion. His hand traveled downward and worked its way underneath her skirt, which had been hiked up by her movements. His fingers inched to her warm moistness, entered it, and stimulated another peak to pleasure.

Ginny was adrift on a spellbinding cloud of enchantment. She ached to merge her body with his, as the core of her womanhood demanded almost immediate appeasement. Everything he did to her heightened her hunger for him. She stroked his hair, neck, and shoulders. Her fingers wanted to clutch him tightly to her. She had feared never seeing him again. What had seemed the darkest moment of her life was becoming the brightest one. Ever so often his stubble scratched her skin, but she didn't care, if she noticed. She was too lost in the wonder of Steve Carr and the power of what he was doing to her.

Steve's mouth returned to hers. His teeth nibbled at her lips. He kissed her several times, short and light, then long and deep. Tension mounted within him. Self-control was difficult to maintain any time he touched her. Her responses and satisfaction made it even harder to master himself. His heart thudded forcefully. No challenge had ever been as potent as she was. No nourishment as filling. No experience as rewarding. No fear as great as losing her to death. She was his! For now.

Ginny clung to him, wanting and needing him fast. She savored his taste and feel. Her actions coaxed him to take her swiftly. She didn't know how long she could accept this bittersweet torment.

Troubled hearts, dazed minds, yearning souls, and ravenous bodies craved and sought comfort. Ginny relaxed her thighs as Steve's hand nudged them apart. Both trembled in suspense and eagerness. They kissed as he unfastened his pants and, with her help, slid them past his hips. Without removing her garments, she assisted him with getting through the privacy opening in her bloomers. They tingled with rapture as they were united. In minutes, they were moving almost fiercely, with Steve embraced securely by her encircled legs. Their pace was swift and rhythmic, building to a climactic and stunning release. They relaxed in each other's arms, not moving or speaking until their erratic breathing and racing hearts returned to normal.

Then Steve withdrew and rolled to his back. He didn't know what to say or do following the heated episode that had taken place so unexpectedly. "We'd best wash up," he said, trying to sound composed. "You must be starving."

Ginny also felt slightly awkward after the uncontrollable coupling. She was glad he didn't apologize for his feverish behavior, as she'd evoked it. "Your perception and skills are enormous. You see and know everything."

"I wish I did, woman," he murmured, then stood, stripped, and entered the water. After he had washed and had left it, he dried off with the skirt she tossed him. He sent her a half-smile and nod of thanks, then put on his clothes.

Steve built a fire and warmed beans while she freshened up in the river and redressed. When she finished, he said, "Let's eat and get moving. We have a long way to travel before dark."

Ginny assumed he didn't want to chat because this total privacy and recent intimacy had made him skittish again. Yet, she allowed it to tell her he must care deeply for her or he would pass it off casually. The fact he couldn't discuss it and it made him nervous misled her, warmed her heart.

After they finished the scant meal and loaded his gear, Steve coaxed them to get moving. "Mount up with me until we find you a horse," he said.

She smiled. "I'll be so glad to get back to the wagontrain."

257

Steve noticed she had forgotten about her father, a proper burial for him, and the brutes who had abducted her and stolen the gems. "We aren't heading to rejoin the others. I'm going after that gang."

Ginny hadn't forgotten about Charles Avery but had pushed the man and his murder to the back of her mind to avoid suffering over them. She couldn't ignore the fact there might have been something she'd done wrong that had gotten him killed. Nor did she want to think about where she would be at this moment if she hadn't escaped and Steve hadn't rescued her. "Please don't, Steve. Let the authorities catch them and punish them. You don't have to take revenge because of me. I wasn't harmed."

Steve pulled her up behind him, ignoring her words. "Hold on around my waist. We have lots of territory to cover; they have a good lead on me."

"Please don't," Ginny persisted as they headed off at a gallop to return to the last campsite to begin his frightening task. "There are five of them. They're well armed and dangerous. I have faith in your skills, Steve, but you're only one man. Don't go after them, at least not alone."

Steve's body stiffened. His voice was monotone as he revealed, "It's my real job, Anna. I have orders to go after them and bring them to justice."

Somehow Ginny knew his two words had nothing to do with being a wagontrain leader and scout. "What do you mean, it's your 'real job.' "

CHAPTER 12

Ginny's nerves were taut, her heart pounded, and she held her breath in dreaded anticipation of his response. Somehow she sensed there was a secret and powerful reason for him coming after them that had nothing to do with his love for her or wanting to rescue her. Somehow she felt his answer was going to be detrimental to their relationship. She wanted to cry and scream before he admitted some awful and damaging truth. She waited and agonized over the destruction of her beautiful dream.

Steve could sense the fear and doubt and the tension exuding from her. With his own large measure of those same emotions chewing at him, he responded, "I have to catch them and recover those stolen gems."

Ginny told herself she shouldn't have been shocked by his reply but she was. "You know about the gems he was carrying?"

Steve surmised she would see and hear enough along the way to grasp what he was doing, so he might as well get his task into the open, here and now. He couldn't risk her distracting reaction at a perilous moment. "Yep, but I couldn't figure out where they were hidden or who the culprit was. Charles Avery had me duped good and that doesn't happen often. I figured the carrier would expose himself at river crossings while trying to protect his delivery. Your father never did. From the marks on

259

his belly, I know where and how he hid them, but that didn't occur to me earlier."

"I don't understand, Steve. You sound as if . . ."

"I was assigned to expose the man carrying the gems, get them back, and capture him and his contacts? I was, Anna, and I'll finish my assignment now that I have a clear trail to follow."

He sounded so nonchalant about such a serious matter! "Assignment?"

"Yep. I accepted a job to solve a tricky case for the law and a friend of mine. It sounded different and challenging. It's turned out to be more trouble and aggravation than I ever imagined. For a while there, I was afraid I would fail this time. The closer we got to Dallas without clues, the more concerned I became. Your father was very cunning."

"But you're a scout and guide, a wagontrain leader."

"Not this time; that was Big L's wagontrain I was using for cover. He's taken over and he'll lead them the rest of the way. He kindly allowed me time alone with everyone to get acquainted before he joined us in Columbus. It was important for everyone to accept me and like me as their leader."

"Using?" Ginny murmured, and realized how many times she was echoing his staggering words, words she didn't want clarified this way.

"Yep, to catch a Red Magnolia member and stop their evil plans. Big L agreed to let me pretend to be boss of his wagontrain until I exposed the culprit. It took longer than I figured. Big L was ready to take over the moment I had to leave. I shouldn't have wasted time in town waiting for you, but I wanted to speak with you in private after getting that telegram that pointed to Charles. If I'd headed back pronto, I could have captured all of them in camp and been on my way to my next job. I'm already late leaving, and there's another cunning man to . . ." He finished *unmask*, rather than *kill*.

He sounded eager to be done and gone, even from her. This "job" explained why he had seemed so inquisitive. She had agonized over deceiving him and others and how to confess the truth when he had been doing that same thing all along. She didn't know the real Steve Carr any more than he knew the real her. "You're a spy?"

Steve had half expected her to guess accurately: Special Agent for the Justice Department. For as long as possible, he needed to keep that identity a secret. "Sort of, with this particular job. I accept all kinds."

Including gunman for hire? "Can we stop to discuss this?"

"Nothing to discuss and no time if there was. Lost too much already hanging around town to talk to you and leaving their trail to rescue you. Every minute I waste they put more distance between them and me." Steve skirted the outlaws' last camp where her father lay dead and unburied to keep her from having to endure that bloody sight again. When he reached the authorities with his prisoners, he'd report the location of the body for proper interment for Anna's sake. He already knew which direction the cutthroats had taken, so he followed it.

Alarming suspicions and realities filled Ginny. Though Steve believed she was "the culprit's" daughter and surely suspected she might be involved, he had made passionate love to her this morning. He hadn't come to rescue her. He even sounded annoyed at losing time doing so. He had come after the Red Magnolia member, the gems, that gang, and the contact in . . . "His name is Timothy Graham."

"Whose name?" Steve asked, distracted while pondering if he should apologize for the fact his last statements sounded cold and cruel.

"The contact for the arms and ammunition. The meeting place was changed from St. Louis to Little Rock, or so those men told us. I doubt they spoke the truth; they only wanted to steal the gems for themselves."

Damn you, woman! "So you knew all along. I feared as much but hated to believe such a fine lady could be involved in something so wicked."

After all they had shared, Ginny was pained by his doubts of her. How could she have misjudged him so badly, and he, her?

He had beguiled her to aid his task, not pursued her from his own desire. That meant he was cold-blooded, ruthless, and would take any step necessary to help him achieve his goal. Her heart chilled for a time. "No, Mr. Carr, I knew nothing about it. I learned those things on the trail here."

The truth or a trick, Anna? "Why tell me?"

"To help you catch them and stop them from carrying out their plans."

"Why?" he asked, his neck bent to study the gang's trail.

"Because they're wrong and what they're doing is wrong."

"Including your father's part in it?"

Ginny refused to tell her traitorous lover the truth about her identity. He had lied to her, used her, and betrayed her love and trust. She had been shocked and hurt, and now she was angry. Yet she couldn't refuse to help prevent a horrible crime. "He was misguided, Mr. Carr, with what he believed was good cause. I'm sure he isn't the only one who ever made a terrible mistake." She could not stop herself from trying to evoke guilt and remorse in him for how he'd hurt her. "One of those causes was the rape, beating, and murder of my sister by a Yankee gang of so-called soldiers," she alleged. "The Loyal League-controlled courts and officials said there wasn't any evidence against them, so they went free. That was on top of losing our home, land, and business to Yankee deceits. Hate, he had reasons for it. Revenge, he craved it. Justice, he deserved it. Such things have happened to other members. But what he told me the Red Magnolias have in mind I know is wrong and can provoke worse cruelties against Southerners. One cannot fight evil with evil or hatred with hatred and win anything worthwhile. Most of the Klansmen believe what they're doing is right and necessary, but I admit there are wicked members who do things just as horrible as what Northerners and ex-slaves are doing to Southerners. I didn't know he was a Klansman or about his 'mission,' as he called it. If you don't mind, I'd rather not talk anymore. Besides, that's all I know."

Steve hoped she was telling the truth. The anguish in her

voice and tragic tale she'd told moved him to say, "I'm sorry, Anna, for everything. This matter is like a powder barrel and the Klan is holding a torch ready to explode it. I have to do my job any way I can."

Ginny fought back tears. Just as she thought there was a silver lining to the dark cloud she was under, Steve had vanquished it and blackened it even more. Some of her torment was replaced by ire. "That's supposed to excuse your traitorous actions, you bastard? 'Sorry' is only a word, and I doubt you have enough good inside of you to mean it. But what can one expect from a creature born and reared as you were?"

Steve tensed. He hated the sound of those cruel words from her lips, lips that had kissed him and had hinted at loving him. He had endured too many bitter disappointments and harsh experiences in his life to suffer another one with her. He had lost her, so he must protect himself against hurt. "I warned you long ago I was a sorry bastard in more than birth."

Ginny's warring heart accused, *No denial? No explanation?* "I should have believed you; it was probably the only time you spoke the truth to me. Are you arresting me?" Was that why he had wasted time to rescue her?

"Are you involved? I thought you were trying to tell me you aren't."

His asking the question told her he wasn't convinced she was innocent. If that was how he felt after being so close to her, there was nothing she could say or do to persuade him otherwise. "No, but I doubt you'll believe me. Don't worry, I'll have no trouble clearing myself."

"That's good, Anna, because you wouldn't like prison."

"You sound as if you're acquainted with such a place."

"I am. During the war those Yanks had fun with us Rebs at their mercy."

Ginny was shocked again. He had been a prisoner-of-war. There was no guessing what horrors and abuses he had endured. That atop his troubled past had hardened him. No wonder he was so self-contained and distant. No wonder he did as he pleased with little concern for others. How could she ever understand him, trust him, and forgive him? Or forget him? "But you're working for the Union now, your past enemies and tormentors."

"Yep."

"Trapping Southerners who are mostly trying to defend themselves?"

"There's only one side now, Anna, the right one. The United States."

"And you're a patriot doing a glorious mission to save it?"

"I'm a workingman who loves challenges, not much more."

"The infernal job! No one and nothing else matters but doing it with perfection. You didn't answer: Am I your prisoner?"

"Nope, it's just not safe to send you off alone and I can't spare the time to take you to a town. You're better off with me for a while. But do exactly as I say. Both our lives could depend on your behavior and obedience. After I capture those men, I'll take them and you to the nearest town. You can decide there what you want to do next. It would probably be best to return to your aunt in Georgia. There's no ranch in Texas."

"How do you know there isn't? When did you check on it?"

"I telegraphed the man who hired me when I was in town."

"When? Which stop?"

"Does it matter?"

To her, it did, considering their intimate relationship. "Yes."

"I don't think so. Why do you want to know when and where I learned you and your father were lying to me?" He felt her stiffen and her grip around his waist tighten. He didn't want to quarrel. He wanted her to have time to comprehend what he was doing and why it was so important; he wanted her to have time to settle down; he wanted her to have time to realize she must confess anything she knew that might be helpful to him, the mission, and to herself. "Would you stop the distracting chatter so I can concentrate on tracking that gang of outlaws?"

Ginny was provoked. "Why? You're so skilled you can probably do it blindfolded! You had no trouble finding and capturing me."

He noticed she didn't say, *rescuing* me. "None at all. If they hadn't been so stupid, they could have found you first. Hush up, woman, before they hear us coming and set an ambush. I doubt you want to be taken captive by traitors to the cause again. Despite what you think, Anna, I am trying to protect both our lives. Control your anger or you'll get us both killed. Don't blame me because your father got you into this crime and I'm the one solving it. Be glad I am or you could be in worse trouble."

Ginny stayed silent after that warning, but not totally because of it. She was confused by his words and mood. She didn't know what he was thinking and feeling. In fact, she didn't know him at all. Her heart kept telling her to confess everything and see how the truth affected him. But her mind warned that would complicate matters, and would cause him to doubt and disrespect her even more. Besides, he had proven himself untrustworthy and traitorous. She must wait and see.

Steve guided Chuune onward at a walking trot that allowed him to track the men. Anna's weight wasn't enough to be an added burden for the big and strong sorrel. He tried to keep his attention on his task, but the woman clinging to him made it difficult. He felt her, smelled her, touched her, heard her breathing, and desired her like crazy. He prayed she was innocent and honest.

Ginny was lost in confusion and anguish. *You're a hard and cold man, Steve Carr. I'm not sure I want to win you even if you beg my forgiveness. The bad instincts and feelings you've born, bred, and nourished for so long will always be stored somewhere inside you, ready to sprout and grow if the right provocation came along. I doubt anyone or anything can change you enough to . . . Let it go, Ginny. It's too late; he's seen to that. You can't trust him. I loved you so much, Steve. I wish you hadn't done this to me, to us.*

Ginny craved solitude so she could cry out her heart to alleviate the torment inside of it. She knew it would take a long time to get over this cruel experience and this elusive man. She had to be strong, brave, and work hard to succeed. Soon, they would part forever. Then she could start healing and forgetting, things she couldn't do in his presence. She had important challenges of her own ahead to distract her from him and to occupy her thoughts. She was bitter over his deluding her and she was tempted to seek vengeance. But spite and hatred were two-edged swords that could slice her more deeply than she was already cut. Besides, those wicked emotions were responsible for this bitter situation, for Charles's criminal actions, for her being here, and for Steve's troubled character. She hated the things that had made him this way, that had ruined their lives.

Don't let them destroy you, too, Ginny Marston.

The full moon that night illuminated their campsite. They hadn't halted until dark so Steve could use every ray of light for tracking. Ginny hadn't spoken to him after he silenced her, only nodded or shook her head to respond to his questions or comments. She hadn't trusted herself to speak without either crying or ranting at him.

They had stopped for a while to chew on dried beef and corn dodgers, downed with water from his canteen. They had ridden most of the time but walked on occasion for the sorrel to rest, with her on one side of the animal and him on the other. He had spoken a few times to tell her the men seemed to be riding slowly deeper into the Ouachita Mountains, and looked as if they were headed for Indian Territory. They were a day ahead of them, he had elaborated, and they might catch up in two days or less if the gang kept up its present pace and they could maintain theirs.

Steve roasted a rabbit over a spit that he'd shot, cooked johnnycakes, and perked coffee—all without asking her to assist him or looking as if he expected her to do so. Nor did she offer to help, as he was accustomed to doing his own chores and seemed to prefer it that way. It was apparent he knew what he was doing and had plenty of experience on the trail.

You're too self-contained, Steve; you don't need anybody.

After he handed her a plate of food and cup of steaming coffee, she took them and thanked him without meeting his piercing gaze.

Steve was unsettled by her silence and anguish. "So, you can still talk," he provoked. "I figured you'd lost your tongue back there."

Ginny glared at him and reminded in a toneless voice, "You ordered me to silence, remember? Since then, you haven't given me permission to talk and said our survival depended upon my strict obedience. Even if you had, I have nothing to say to you, Mr. Carr. You're a liar and deceiver."

He had expected her to feel this way, but it still got to him that she had reacted so strongly. Obviously she hated him now. "Don't worry, Anna, you'll have to endure me for only a few more days. That should please you."

"I'm sure both of us will be delighted to end this offensive matter."

His gaze narrowed as he retorted, "Is that a fact?"

Ginny determined not to let him provoke her into a silly or cutting quarrel. If he was trying to hurt her to push her away from him, she wouldn't cooperate at her expense. If he was being himself for a change, she didn't want to view that side of him. She ate her food and drank her coffee, and found everything delicious. She noticed Steve ate from the skillet and with his fingers because he had only one set of utensils and dishes. That told her the loner was not prepared for company. "You cooked, so I'll clean up the mess. It was good. Thank you."

"No need. Besides, I don't let anybody scratch my skillet. Doesn't cook good that way." He went to the stream, used sand to scrub it, then returned to grease and dry the surface. "A good skillet has to be kept conditioned. I've had this one a long time, seen a lot of things with me."

Ginny wanted to scoff, *How nice,* but she didn't. In fact, she was impressed by his many skills and the way he could take care of himself and others. Maybe she shouldn't blame him totally for the kind of man he had become. Perhaps she should blame his background and the cruel war and the many other unknown and embittering incidents. But people had endured times just as hard and hadn't become liars and deceivers and haters. *That isn't completely true, Ginny. Think about some of the people you met on the wagontrain, yourself, Charles Avery, and your own father. Everybody has a thirst for survival and battles obstacles in the only way open to them.* She certainly shouldn't have called him a bastard, as that fact was so painful; he had . . . trusted her with that secret in a moment of weakness and she had fired it at him like a lethal bullet. Why? Bad language and cruelty weren't normal responses for her.

Perhaps, she reasoned, it was because she was hurting so much and had struck out in pain. Perhaps all the untimely deaths in her life had changed her: her mother, Johanna's mother, her best friend, Mr. Avery, possibly her father, and almost herself. She had confronted so much evil and devastation since her return to America. Perhaps all of that put together was making her resentful and rebellious toward the cruelties in life and the harsh demands from fate. Soon, she would have to seek revenge on Bennett Chapman for her best friend; she had lost the man she loved; and she might that find her father alive. It wasn't fair to witness and endure so much pain. Why must it be—

Steve shook her arm to get her attention as she hadn't heard his voice. "You use the bedroll, Anna. I'll use the blanket. Take any spot you want, but not too far from me and my guns. Get settled now so I can douse the fire. We don't want it being seen by unwelcome visitors."

Ginny noticed how gentle his tone was and pretended to ignore it. "Don't trouble yourself over my comfort, Mr. Carr. I'll use the blanket or sleep on the ground. I don't want to take your bedroll." *Your smell on it will keep me awake all night and create fires I don't need!*

"I'm used to hugging the ground, Anna, you aren't. If you

don't get proper rest, you'll fall out of the saddle and delay me. It's a precaution not a kindness, so you don't need to refuse out of hurt pride or spite."

Ginny wasn't convinced his tender gaze agreed with his words. Was he being nice for selfish reasons or hiding his unwanted concern for her behind feigned ones? No matter the truth, she didn't argue and refuse. It didn't take her long to confirm the reason for her reluctance: the bedroll exuded his fragrance. Its manly smell made her flushed and restless. She damned him for affecting her this way.

"Here, it'll help you sleep," Steve offered fifteen minutes later.

"What is it?" Ginny didn't reach for the cup he held out to her.

"Whiskey, enough to put you out for the night. Neither of us can rest with you tossing around like that bedroll's full of biting ants."

"Is this supposed to loosen my tongue for a confession?" she quipped.

Unnerved, Steve snapped, "You said you didn't have one to make, so I'll take your word until you or something proves otherwise. You've been through a lot recently, so I thought it would help you relax. You don't have to worry about me taking advantage of you in a weakened condition."

"You've changed since this morning? How nice for the both of us," she scoffed, grabbed the cup from his grasp, and downed the strong liquid. She choked and coughed. Her eyes widened and watered, sending tears down her glowing cheeks. Steve tried to pat her on the back, but she yanked away and glared at him. Between coughs, swallows, and ragged gasps of air, she scolded, "Damn you! I . . . can't . . . breathe. My . . . throat and . . . stomach's on fire." She drank water from the canteen he held out and recovered. "You should have warned me to sip it slowly."

"You didn't give me a chance to warn you, woman. You'll be all right in a minute. Actually it's best to get it inside fast so it can get to work. Lie down, close your eyes, and you'll be asleep in no time."

Ginny did as he suggested. A mellow feeling spread through her body. A swirling sensation filled her head that made her feel as if she were drifting on clouds. Her lids were too heavy to open and she yielded to the effects of the potent magic. She was warm and cozy and serene. The gentle hand stroking her cheek and hair felt wonderful. But the heady kiss with sweet and soft lips was even better, though she could barely respond. She let the overwhelming sensations sweep her away.

Tenderness tugged at Steve's heart, knowing all she had suffered. He was well acquainted with torment and hatred that she must endure it. He owed it to her and to himself to help her avoid more. Perhaps she had made mistakes, but who hadn't? He must free her from this grim situation so she wouldn't wind up as he had. Inside, Anna Avery was a good person; she didn't deserve what could happen to her because of what her father had done. Maybe he wasn't guilty either, but it was too late to change that fact. If they had met under different circumstances and were different people . . . But they hadn't and they weren't. What he was, if or when she learned the whole truth, would kill any good feelings she had for him. He was dreaming, fooling himself, if he believed for one minute she could love and accept him. How could she, a stranger, when his own father couldn't?

"Good night, Anna, you'll be safe with me."

Unable to open her eyes or think clearly, Ginny murmured, "Good night, love." She sighed dreamily and went limp.

Steve sat beside her for a while, caressing her face and touching her hair. His fingers toyed with the wisps that had escaped her braid. He hadn't been able to stop himself from kissing her. He had seen her inhaling his scent on the bedroll and suspected—hoped—that was what had unsettled her. They had made such urgent and passionate love this morning; the heady episode was fresh in his mind, yet also seemed so far in the past. He could have been kinder and easier on her today; after all, she had just lost her father.

Fathers! he scoffed. *They can be more treacherous than your worst enemy. I want to trust, you, Anna, but I couldn't stand for you to betray me and reject me like he did. I don't know what I would do to you if you did. It's best if we don't find out who's the more skilled deceiver between us.*

Ginny chided herself for being too cognizant of Steve's closeness. The constant rubbing against him, hearing his voice, inhaling his scent, gazing at his handsome face, and speculating on excuses for his actions gnawed at her nerves and defenses against him. Doubts kept working on her. Maybe he was angry, disappointed, and hurt because he believed she had duped him. Maybe his behavior and words were his own kind of defense against being used and injured. Maybe he was afraid he would lose her if she had to go to prison, which was possible if a Loyal Leaguer court tried to punish her "father" and his group through her. Would the law believe her when she said she wasn't Anna Avery? Would it matter if she weren't? She had been with Charles and they had carried off a dangerous and cunning deception. The Yankee officials might not believe she wasn't informed and involved in it. After all, she had lost much to the war. If she had to summon her stepfamily as witnesses to her identity to save her life and avoid prison, that would expose her father's lies to them. With Mathew Marston missing in Colorado and possibly dead, she couldn't call on him for help. Her life had too many entanglements that could be exposed. Charles had warned her that to tell the truth or to continue her ruse was hazardous, so there was only one thing left to do. As soon as Steve released her, she needed to get far away from this threat, to go to the Chapman ranch.

Ginny covertly watched Steve. He seemed bothered, too. While riding and obviously in deep thought, his hand had covered hers around his waist and he had stroked them unaware of his action. Another time, he had thrown his arm behind her waist to steady her balance on a downhill section, then left it there longer than necessary. She sensed his thoughts were on her. He desired her, of that she was certain. But was it only a physical craving? Was it against his will? Had he been entrapped in his ruse to ensnare her for clues? Did he care for her more than he wanted to? More than he would admit to her or to himself? How could what they shared— *Don't do this to yourself, Ginny. It didn't mean the same thing to him it did to you.* She wished her heart hadn't added, *Not yet, not that he realizes. He can't believe someone could love him and want him as much as you do.*

Steve moved quietly to keep from awakening the weary woman until breakfast was cooked. He'd been compelled to give her some whiskey again last night as a sleeping potion. Something was wrong. She was too subdued for the woman he had gotten to know along the wagontrain journey. Where were her spunk and spirit? Why wasn't she yelling at him and cursing him? Why no demand for an explanation or more information? Was she silent and tense because she was grieved over her father's loss and hurt over his and Charles's deceits, or was she only afraid he'd discover her guilt as he continued to investigate this case?

Ginny stirred and inhaled deeply. She smiled and sighed in pleasure. Odors of coffee, biscuits, and bacon teased at her nose and stomach.

Steve nudged her shoulder. "Wake up, sleepyhead, or I'll eat all of this myself. I'm starting the eggs now, so get moving, woman."

Ginny sat up and rubbed her eyes. She looked in the skillet, then at him and asked, "How? Where?"

Steve grinned and said, "I have my ways."

"There's a town nearby?" she asked.

Steve misunderstood her surprise for eagerness to be gone from him. "Nope, only a farm. You don't want to go there. There's just a man and two sons."

"Did you steal those?" she asked, nodding at the eggs.

Steve glanced at her and scowled. "Nope. Why do you always think the worst of me, Anna?" He stirred the eggs swiftly in agitation.

She knew she'd piqued him. "Isn't that what you do with me?"

He looked at her again. "I have good cause, don't you think?"

"And I don't? I would never use innocent people the way you have, pretending to like them while spying on them." Guilt flooded her as she realized that was exactly what she planned to do to Bennett Chapman in Texas.

Steve noticed her curious reaction and strange expression. She wasn't being honest with him, but at least a guilty conscience made her cheeks color and her lovely hazel eyes blink too fast. "Like you did with me for your father? Distracting me so he could carry out his wicked task? Did you two suspect an agent might be after you?"

At that unsettling moment, she didn't notice the word he used to describe himself. "That isn't true! I didn't know about this crime!"

"So you do agree and believe it is a crime?"

"Of course it is!" Ginny ordered herself to calm down. "What did you mean when you said the gems were stolen? How did the authorities know a carrier was on the wagontrain?"

Steve saw no harm in answering her. "Stolen by bandits here and in England. Special Agents added up clues, investigated, and learned of the Red Magnolias' plot. Several of them were murdered for getting too nosy. The man who hired me knew your wagontrain was the cover, what the deal was, and where it was supposed to take place. What he didn't know were the names of the men involved; the agent died before revealing them. I was told to recover the gems and unmask the villains. It sounded simple and quick, but it hasn't been either one."

Stolen gems . . . That was why Charles Avery was in England and aboard the same ship to America! Agents murdered . . .

That meant the assignment was dangerous for Steve. He could be eliminated, too.

"Why did your father fetch you from that fancy boarding school up North? Was it to use you as his cover? You two weren't moving to Texas!"

"I didn't know he hadn't bought property there." Charles had told her he had purchased a mercantile store in the town of Waco, but he had lied. On the trail, he had confessed the whole truth to her, too late.

"I know you're his daughter, not just a cunning hired accomplice."

"You do? How?"

"I checked that out, too."

Ginny knew Anna's death was a secret to Georgians, as it had taken place in another state. "Before or during the journey?"

Steve wished he hadn't exposed that precaution. "During."

"Did you check out anyone else?"

"Nope."

"Why not?" Surely others had made him suspicious, too.

Steve dished up the food and poured the coffee. "After what happened between us, the reason for my action should be obvious."

Attracted to a suspect, she mused, or something else? "Perhaps to a man like you. When did you get your answer?"

He had to learn how much she knew and how deeply she'd been involved. That was the only way to find a means to extricate her from guilt. "In Montgomery I learned you were his daughter. In Vicksburg while waiting for you, I learned there was no ranch."

Ginny took the plate and cup as she reflected on those dates. He'd checked on her after their first night together in Columbus and on both of them after their second night together in Jackson. He had suspected her and Charles but had still made love to her at the first available opportunity. His suspicions had increased, yet he did so again. After being convinced Charles was his target, he had planned— "Were you going to confront me before or after we . . . were together in Vicksburg?"

His look said *After,* but his mouth didn't reply. He had taken her again after her rescue and before exposing his task. Why? A last time before his damaging revelations terminated their relationship? Again, why?

He realized she didn't say, *made love,* and that troubled him, along with her expression. No matter what he said to justify, excuse, or explain his behavior, it wouldn't change things and perhaps would make them worse. "Things and people aren't always what they seem, Anna."

She fused her gaze to his. "I agree, Mr. Carr. I think we've both proven that to each other, more than either of us realizes."

"Enough cutting talk, woman. Let's eat and then ride out."

Ginny decided she would be polite and friendly today to relax Steve with hopes he would open up to her so she could learn the whole truth. She asked at one break, "How can you tell how far ahead of us they are?"

He was surprised at her question and new, pleasant mood. "Condition of their tracks shows how long ago they were made." He explained his meaning.

"But how do you know if what's a day old here will be a day old a mile ahead? What's to prevent them from backtracking and ambushing us?"

He tensed. "Backtracking? How do you know about that trick?"

Ginny told him about the novels she had read to acquaint her with the West before moving there.

Steve smiled and relaxed but didn't laugh at her. "It isn't like that out here. Now would you mind telling me what happened in that last campsite? I haven't wanted to ask while your pain was too fresh."

Ginny related not only the episode there but all that occurred along the way since her kidnapping. She saw him paying close attention to her.

"I'm impressed, Anna. How did you learn to climb trees?"

"When I was a child. And I have you to thank for the other skills that saved my life. Despite the trouble between us, I am grateful to you for that."

He mellowed and warmed. "You used them well."

"Including the derringer you gave me."

"Are you wearing it now?" She trembled when he touched her leg.

"All the time, as you ordered, Steve. Afraid I'll pull it on you?"

He caught the switch to his first name. "That wouldn't be smart and you're no fool. I'm your only hope of getting out of here alive."

"I know, so I'll behave myself."

Steve grinned and chuckled. "I'm glad to hear that, woman."

"Were you around camp long after I left?"

"Worried about what your new friends might think about you?"

"Yes."

"Don't be; they like you and believe you were abducted."

"But you don't?"

Steve decided he should lighten up on her. "Actually, Anna, I do. I believe your father was, too." At her look of astonishment, he added, "Villains often betray each other. If they were good men, they wouldn't be doing what they do. That gang came after you two early just to rob you. They would have shot up the camp and taken you by force if you had both refused to leave with them. You saved innocent lives by complying and placing your own in danger. But that still doesn't excuse what your father was planning to do, what he would have done if he hadn't been killed. Even if you were involved or involved only as his cover, I'll release you soon as a reward for your unselfish actions in camp."

Ginny was dismayed that he continued to harbor doubts

about her. She couldn't persuade him he was wrong without revealing secrets about herself, secrets she didn't trust him with yet. Surely it would be worse if he suspected she was a habitual deceiver. Later, she would send him a letter explaining the truth and telling him her whereabouts in case he wanted to find her; she would send it in care of the wagontrain company. If he had gotten in contact with Luther Beams and they were close enough to do this task together, surely Luther would know where and how to find Steve. By that time, they would know how they felt about each other. Her intrusive challenges would be finished one way or another. If for no other reason, she would contact him to tell him how mistaken he had been.

They halted at dusk, close enough to overtake the gang the next day. In the last fading light of day, Steve scouted the area to make certain his assumptions were correct. He learned that no one was within striking distance of their campsite, north of Mena, a town of sparse population. They had encountered many streams, a few springs, and steeper hills today. The gang was headed into the rugged terrain of the Ouachitas, unique for stretching east to west rather than from north to south as most mountain ranges did. Not far ahead was Rich Mountain, the highest peak in the oldest and largest national forest in the South. He had no doubts they would overtake the outlaws before noon tomorrow, and he was grateful she hadn't slowed him down. He had been able to conserve Chuune's strength by skirting the bases or crossing the lower sections of the highest hills. He had trained her well, and she didn't complain when the going was hard. She was a remarkable, strong, and brave woman, the kind he would want. If only . . . *Don't dream!*

Steve returned to find the evening meal ready for him.

Ginny served the fried salt pork, biscuits, beans, and coffee. "It won't be as delicious as your food, but it'll save you time and work tonight."

"Much obliged, Miss Avery," he remarked, and sat down.

"Have you ever thought of carrying two sets of dishes with you?"

"Too much trouble and not enough space. Everybody I meet has their own provisions with them. Drifters like me have to travel light and fast."

"Don't you ever get tired of staying on the move and being alone?"

"Pour me some more coffee, will you?"

Ginny knew he normally would get it himself. It was a ruse to make her forget her question while he ignored it. She "obliged" him again.

They finished eating in silence, then did the chores together. As she took her place on the sleeping roll, she asked, "What will happen tomorrow when we catch up with those ruffians?"

Steve was lying within a few feet of her as he insisted on doing each night for protection, a pistol on either side of him. He looked at her as he answered. "You hang back and hide while I capture them."

Her gaze fused with his. "As simple as that, Steve?"

"Nothing is ever simple, Anna. Haven't you learned that by now?"

"Yes, but I wish . . ."

"You wish what?" he coaxed, quivering with desire for her. *Shu,* if things went wrong tomorrow, they could be dead before nightfall.

"I wish life weren't so hard and dangerous and cruel. There are five of them, Steve. You could be . . ."

"Killed?" Her worried gaze and use of "you" instead of "we" moved him.

"Don't say that!" she cried, then lowered her gaze from his.

Steve propped his right elbow on the ground and rested his chin on his fist. "If you stay hidden, Anna, they won't get you again."

"I wasn't worried about me. I meant, not only about me."

"Who else is there to worry about? Surely you don't care about those bastards who captured you and tried to rape you."

"Of course not."

"Then who?" he persisted, needing to hear her name him.

Ginny wondered why he was pressing her for an answer he didn't want to deal with tonight or any time soon—or perhaps never. Should she give him one more chance to recognize and accept his feelings for her, one last chance? She needed to know for certain there was no hope for a future with him. Perhaps more importantly, she needed to know if what they'd shared meant anything to him. She could always blame the potent whiskey for causing her to lose control. They could be dead tomorrow, so what happened between them tonight wouldn't matter. "I'm too tense to sleep. Can I have another drink from your bottle?"

"You're developing a bad habit, woman, depending on this."

"You're right, and I really don't want it. What I do want, is to know if what happened between us was all lies and deceptions?"

Steve's gaze locked with hers. "No, Anna, it wasn't. I care about you and want you. To ensnare you that way wasn't part of my assignment. You took me by surprise and I'm still not sure how to deal with you. As soon as this job is over, I have another important one I can't refuse. I don't know how long it'll take to solve. And I don't know where our trail could take us afterward, if anywhere. I've never ridden this road before and I'm not certain I know how. To tell the truth, I can't swear I want to ride it or *can* ride it. I'm a loner and that works best for me. And there are other things about me that can block the path between us."

Ginny watched and listened with a conflicting mixture of joy and sadness, with despair and hope, with courage and cowardice. He had sketched her a clear and honest picture. "Do they have to block the path between us tonight or until you must leave?"

Did he understand her right? "You can do better than me, Anna; you're a fine lady. I'm nothing" . . . *But a half-breed bastard who's broken plenty of laws to uphold others. I have nothing to offer you but*

279

trouble and hardship. No home, little money, and little respect from others.

"You're wrong, Steve; you're the best man I've ever met. You have so much to give if you'll only let yourself. Until you can open up, I'm not asking for any promises. I only want you for as long as I can have you. If you must ride away, I won't try to stop you. I'll wait for you to return."

Her words touched him deeply, but he was afraid to believe and accept them; his bitter past had taught him that much. "Don't, Anna. If I leave, I won't come back. Don't ruin your life waiting for something to happen that never will; I know from experience. I'm not worthy of a woman like you, so I can't keep pulling you to me. I realize now that's wrong and cruel."

He had said, *"If* I leave." "Will that stop how we feel about each other? How much we want each other? How much I . . . care about you?"

"Don't care about me, Anna, I can hurt you more than you realize."

"Your warning is too late, Steve: I care and I hurt now." She closed her eyes, causing the pool of tears in them to overflow and run into her hair.

Steve moved to her side. He stroked her hair and kissed at the tears as he entreated, "Don't cry, Anna; I'm sorry it has to be this way." His fingers cupped her chin between them and his thumbs dried the wetness on the flesh beneath her eyes. He kissed her forehead and the tip of her nose. The backs of his fingers lightly rubbed her flushed cheeks then drifted back and forth under her chin. They wandered down her neck and caressed its silky lines. "You're so beautiful and tempting." He trembled at contact with her. He felt weak and nervous, unsure if he should proceed.

Steve's fingers halted to rest along one cheek while his thumb moved over her parted lips. When she kissed, nibbled, and teased it with her tongue, his breathing grew fast and shallow. His body burned for hers as fiercely as the hot desert sun on the sand. His pulse raced like a wild mustang that was fleeing capture across hilly terrain. His heart pounded in his ears. He rolled to his back. *"Shu,* Anna, what you do to me."

Ginny couldn't let him withdraw and stop when she was trembling with anticipation and desire. Her skin tingled and blazed where he had touched it. She wanted all of him pressed to her. With boldness, she moved atop him, looked into his smoldering eyes, and kissed him with feverish need. Her eager hands roamed over his hair, face, throat, his whole body, then her lips followed the same trail.

Steve didn't know if he should lie still and enjoy her stimulating and unexpected siege or take control of it. Mercy, he couldn't lie still, not with her warm breath filling his ear and her hot tongue tantalizing it. Her brown mane surrounded his head and tickled him. Her body fondled his with seductively squirming motions. Her mouth and hands pleasured his flesh *in all directions*. He took a deep breath of what should have been steadying air, but it wasn't, not when she unbuttoned his shirt and let her tongue circle the nipples on his hairless chest. He hadn't realized that could be arousing to a man, but it was. He writhed as her fingers explored every inch of his torso. He couldn't suppress a moan when her flattened palm drifted back and forth across the evidence of his desire. He was astonished when she unfastened his pants and dipped her hand inside them to grasp his throbbing manhood. He shuddered. His head was dazed by hunger and his body ached with it.

Ginny was too aroused to travel this new adventure slowly. She felt brave and daring. She was just as aroused as he was. All her senses were aware of how much he wanted her.

Steve could hold himself pinned to the ground no longer. He grasped her by the forearms and guided her to her back. When his quivering fingers couldn't unfasten one of her shirt buttons, to his surprise, she seized both sides and yanked, popping off the last obstacle against his approach. She hastily undid the ribbons of her chemise and shoved it from his path. His mouth wasted no time in trekking down her neck, across her chest, and to the exposed mounds that beckoned his conquest. One of his hands hurried down her thigh, grasped a handful of skirt, and lifted it so his fingers could pass beneath. He called on all of his experiences, knowledge, and skills to pleasure her and himself.

Swept to a high level of urgent desire, they united their bodies. They kissed and caressed as they searched for the ultimate pleasure, and soon found it.

In the afterglow of their shared rapture, they cuddled together and slept on the bedroll in each other's arms.

Ginny recovered the button she had jerked off in her eagerness. She had bathed, dressed, and eaten. Steve had done so, too. They had exchanged smiles and casual talk this morning, but nothing was mentioned about their passionate lovemaking. As the sun came into view, they were loaded and ready to mount, to seek the perilous challenge ahead.

Steve climbed upon Chuune's saddle then assisted her up behind him. "No talking today, Anna. I can't be distracted for an instant. We'll catch up with them around noon, whether they slow or stop."

Five-to-one odds thundered inside her head. Ginny trembled.

"Don't be afraid; I'll protect you. Just do everything I say."

"Protect both of us, Steve." She snuggled her cheek against his back and embraced him tightly. As she loosened her grip, she laughed and quipped, "I'm finished now, and I'll behave for the rest of the day."

He was appreciative of the hug. "After I let you off to hide, don't show yourself no matter what you see or hear. Understand?"

"Yes, sir," she replied, knowing she'd obey him just as she had obeyed Charles Av—She winced as she recalled that her help hadn't saved his life and might even have cost it. She knew it was futile to beg Steve to turn aside from his job. *Help us to survive today,* she prayed. *I love him and need him so much. He feels the same way about me and will admit it one day soon. Please, God, protect us.*

Steve nudged the sorrel's sides and they headed toward an unavoidable confrontation with the cold-blooded gang.

CHAPTER 13

They passed Rich Mountain, where the view of the forested landscape beyond looked like a rolling sea of green waves with a hazy blue veil hovering close to their verdant crests. Wildflowers in many colors and sizes grew in abundance on hillsides where tall grass was moved by breezes. Broken white clouds with dark-blue bases and paintbrush splashes dotted the sky. Though emerald and azure bodies of water in streams and ponds were visible from that height, the Ouachitas weren't that high and rugged when compared to the north Georgia mountains Ginny had seen.

Steve halted his sorrel on a densely treed hill that allowed him to see without being seen. He dismounted, then helped Ginny down. "Wait for me here. I'll return for you as soon as I can. Keep alert for trouble." When she started to protest, his fingers tapped her lips. "No arguing. I can move faster and quieter alone. If I'm not back by three o'clock, start walking northeast to Waldron; it's about twenty miles from here." He pointed to the spot where the sun would be at that intimidating hour. He placed a compass in her hand and told her how to use it to find the town.

Ginny watched him unload his gear and remove his saddle.

"Why are you leaving those here? And why are you telling me how to reach civilization?"

"In case something goes wrong. I don't think it will, but it's best to be prepared for problems so you won't panic and fall into the clutches of that gang. I'll cover my trail so they can't find you. If it takes longer than I figure, I'll catch up with you on the way to Waldron. Make sure you take supplies, a blanket, and canteen with you." He nodded toward his pile of belongings and explained, "An Indian once told me to remove anything that makes noise when you're trying to sneak up on enemies. That's why I'm leaving them here, not because you'll need them if anything happens to me."

Ginny half believed him. She squeezed the compass and thought of his orders. He was showing care and concern again without being obvious. "I suppose he taught you how to ride bareback, too?"

He checked his pistols and knife. "Yep, that and plenty of other stuff I use in my work. Those tricks and skills are what's kept me alive so long."

"Let me help, Steve. I can shoot."

"You'd be too distracting. I trust your skills, Anna, but not mine with you in danger. Stay here. I mean it, woman, or you'll get both of us killed. Don't worry about me, I've done this plenty of times; have even gone after more men. They're not far ahead, so I'll return before you have time to miss me."

She stalled his departure by asking how he could tell.

He pointed to an area in the valley below their lofty perch. "Smoke about a mile away. Either they've decided to stay camped there for a while or they're getting a mighty late start today. Or maybe they're just nervous about heading into Indian Territory; they're almost sitting on its border."

"You sure that's the gang you're after?"

"Yep." Steve swung himself onto the sorrel's back. He hated to leave her behind, but he couldn't risk her life. Nor could he bring himself to admit anything rash.

Don't distract him with reckless confessions, Ginny! "Be careful."

Steve read more than a polite caution in her voice and expression. "Always, Anna," he replied huskily. "You do the same. I'll be back soon." He smiled at her and headed down the hill.

Ginny leaned against an oak and kept her frantic gaze glued to the smoke rising above the pines below. She didn't want to think about Steve getting killed. It was too far, even if she ran, to catch up with him and to assist him. He had left her this far away on purpose, as she'd told him how she'd disobeyed "her father's" orders to keep out of peril. All she could do was wait and worry, and pray she saw Steve Carr before three o'clock.

Steve sneaked toward the outlaws' camp. One man, supposedly out of sight to any visitor, was standing guard. He knew the others couldn't see either of them as he used stealth to approach and strike the cutthroat on the head with his gun butt. He bound and gagged his first prisoner: Rollie.

He slipped closer, relieved that dense underbrush concealed him. He observed the crude men, registering their names and speech patterns. It was apparent they intended to linger there at least for today, for horses were unsaddled, bedrolls were still on the ground, and a stew pot was simmering on the fire. The gang was lazing against trees while they drank coffee and whiskey. He couldn't rush four armed bandits, so he waited for an opening.

One came when Kip said, "Fry a lizard in oil, I gotta go take a grunt."

Steve made his way without noise to the spot the man had chosen. As soon as the outlaw finished, he clobbered, bound, and gagged his second prisoner. He was happy the task was being made easy for him, yet he knew it was reckless to get cocky or to lower his guard for an instant.

Mimicking Kip's voice and style of speaking, Steve called out, "Stomp a lizard's tale, my boot's hung in a foxhole! Help me, Ted!"

"Git yourself loose, you clumsy fool," came the unwanted reply.

Steve gave it another try before attacking the camp. "Lizard's toes afire, if I move, I'll fall into my grunt! Come on, Ted."

The outlaw grumbled but came to help. Steve captured his third man. He knew the others would get suspicious soon, so he prepared to take the last two with daring and hopefully by surprise. With a Colt in each hand, Steve leapt into the open and shouted, "Drop your weapons; you're under arrest." Bart and Slim grabbed for their guns, Slim's borrowed from Kip because their female prisoner had taken his. Steve wounded one in the hand, causing his pistol to drop to the ground. He winged the leader in an arm, but not before Bart got off a shot that went wild. Having disabled all five, Steve finally relaxed.

The Special Agent tended their injuries and tied them to trees. He fetched the others and did the same with them. He doused the fire and saddled a horse. "I'll be back for you boys soon." He mounted Chuune and rode to get his companion, taking along the roan stolen from Charles Avery for Anna to use.

Three shots echoed across the valley and caused Ginny to tense in fear. She strained to hear others but none came. There were five men, she fretted, so how could Steve defeat them with three bullets? Surely those vicious beasts wouldn't surrender to a verbal threat. Did that mean . . .

Ginny heard horses approaching. She concealed herself, the derringer in one hand and Slim's pistol in the other. Steve had told her long ago she could kill a man if her life was threatened . . . but could she? If it was those villains, recapture meant they'd—

"It's me, Anna. You can come out; everything's fine."

Ginny jumped from her hiding place and raced toward him. "Steve! You're all right. I was so worried. I heard three shots. What happened?"

The victorious man warmed to the hug she gave him; it kindled the desire to make love to her. This wasn't the time or place for being intimate, though, so he used nonchalance to quell the urge. He looked down into her anxious gaze as he related his tale.

"See, I told you not to worry," he said in conclusion.

Ginny wanted embraces, kisses, caresses, and tender words. She, too, realized she couldn't give or receive them at that time. She saw how reserved he was acting, how eager he was to get back on the trail as he saddled his sorrel and loaded his gear in a rush. Yet she hated to lose this opportunity, which could be their last time together. From here on in, they would have five ruffians with them. Once they arrived at their destination, Steve would take off to the other job he had mentioned. "You captured five dangerous men that easily and quickly?"

"Yep, but they weren't on guard and never got a chance to fight back."

"You amaze me," she murmured as she returned his compass and handed him a canteen to hang over the horn. "I certainly wouldn't want to be your enemy."

Steve glanced at her and grinned. "Thank you for the compliment. Now let's get moving. I don't want to lose my prisoners and have to track them down again."

As she mounted, Ginny inquired where they were heading.

"To Fort Smith, around fifty miles north of us. We should make about fifteen of those before nightfall and cover the rest tomorrow. With the terrain ahead and five men in ropes, it'll take longer than it ordinarily would. I'll turn them over to the commander there, then telegraph my boss they're in custody. He can figure out how to get them to the right prison."

Ginny had seen the long leather pouch dangling over his left arm upon arrival; he had rolled it later and packed it inside his saddlebag. "Your boss will be pleased with the good job you've done; you've recovered the stolen gems, captured the gang, and . . . unmasked the Red Magnolia member."

Steve glanced at her when she hesitated. "I'll notify the Army

288

to recover your father's body and bury it." He said, assuming that was the reason for her unease. "You won't have to worry about being arrested, Anna, I won't mention you in my report."

Ginny leaned back in the saddle and pressed her feet against the stirrups to balance herself on the downhill slope. "That wouldn't be wise, Steve; others knew about my presence on the wagontrain. You don't want your boss to think you're covering for me for a personal reason."

"You're right. I'll tell him I investigated you and found you innocent, so I released you. He'll accept my word."

She wished he had admitted what she hoped was the truth and was slightly depressed when he didn't. "Thank you, Steve. Be assured you aren't mistaken; I wasn't involved."

"Even if you were, Anna, I'd still let you go."

That admission touched her. *Tell me more, my love.* "Why?"

"Because I like you and it would have been a mistake on your part. Either way, you've suffered enough and lost plenty because of your father's evil deed, and I'm sure you wouldn't do anything like this again."

That wasn't the answer she wanted, but she didn't press for the desired one. "You're very kind and generous."

On level ground, he suggested, "Let's pick up our pace before you swell my head with more compliments."

They reached the campsite, where five sullen men were bound. Ginny saw Bart's gaze widen in shock, then narrow and chill. She noticed the wound on his arm and the one on Slim's hand. In a way, she was surprised Steve hadn't killed any of them, and she remarked on that.

The Special Agent used the Federal Marshal rule to explain. "Men like me get paid for the number of miles we cover to capture criminals and for live ones we turn in. If we kill a target or prisoner, we don't get paid for him and *we* have to pay to bury him." The truth was, he always tried to bring in suspects alive for questioning and punishment.

"I see you got help, eh?" Bart scoffed at her.

Ginny glared at the offensive man. "The best, can't you tell?

He captured all of you as easily as picking cotton from a ripe boll."

"Did he give you them gems he took from us?"

"No, they weren't mine; they were stolen. He's turning them over to the authorities to be sent back to their proper owners."

The leader sneered. "What you gonna do when we reach town and you join us in a cell, Miss Anna? Think you'll be safe from the Klan's reach? Or from the law's? One or the other will git you for what you done."

"I won't be in any danger from either side because I wasn't involved in Father's scheme or in yours. You'll hang for murdering him."

Bart feigned shock. "That's a damn lie, girl. Your pa wouldna been kilt if you two hadna gotten greedy and tried to git away with the Klan's payment. Your pa weren't the contact, *you* was. You can fool that hired man with you but you won't fool the law, and the Klan knows what you are. They'll make you pay good for trying to cheat them."

Ginny gaped at the man. "You're crazy, Bart."

"Crazy for not catching on to you afore it was too late. I don't see why you turned on us; we done just like your telegram said. We pretended to kidnap you to hide your part in this. We woulda split the gems with you two if you'da told us what you had planned. You're crazy if you think we'll keep our mouths shut and take your punishment atop ours."

Ginny realized Steve was keeping quiet and listening carefully to the brute's wild rantings. "Whatever you're trying to pull, Bart, it won't work."

" 'Cause you think the law will take a *lady's* word over ours? Once they capture Graham and he talks, your trick is up. You shouldna tried to run and we wouldna shot your horse and pa. And if he hadna tried to shoot me whilst he was down, I wouldna kilt him in self-defense."

"Self-defense? You murdered him in cold blood. You would have killed me, too, if I hadn't escaped."

"We was with you for days. We had plenty of time to kill you and rob you if that was our plan. Why would we haul you all this way to do it? When did we ever pull a gun on you or tie you up? Never! We didn't shoot till you two was galloping off with them gems the Klan needs. That's probably why Graham sent us after you two early, 'cause he knew you couldn't be trusted. You two was planning to disappear with them gems, wasn't you?"

Ginny looked at her love. "He's lying, Steve. He's only trying to save his neck by incriminating me. Besides, Bart, you made a slip; you said we telegraphed you to meet us early, then you said Graham changed the plans and sent you after us early."

"Graham sent us after we got that crazy telegram. You two musta needed us as guides and guards 'cause you had the law closing in on you. I bet you was planning to escape us soon as we got you clear of trouble."

Steve finally intruded. "You might as well hush up, Bart. I've been investigating Miss Avery for a long time; I know she's not involved. You're wasting your breath trying to trick me."

"She's the one tricking you, lawman," the leader argued. "What did she give you to git you on her side, a good roll or two in the grass?"

Steve's gaze darkened and narrowed and his body stiffened in warning. "Don't push it, Bart, or you won't make it to the Fort Smith stockade."

"Akst the boys; they'll tell you like I did."

"It would be lies like yours are," Steve retorted. "Let's go."

Ginny was relieved by those confident words and Steve's anger. Surely that meant he believed *her*, not *them*. She was glad Bart fell silent and the others didn't speak up to concur with his ruse.

They journeyed through woodland to open spaces. Steve kept control of the gang by roping their horses together by their bridles. The captives sulked and sent the quiet and alert couple lethal looks.

Ginny was tense the entire ride, fearing the law wouldn't be as trusting and generous with her as their hired man was. She prayed that Bart wouldn't continue to claim she was a Klan member and carrier and, if he did, they wouldn't believe him.

At dusk, they halted to camp on the Poteau River. Steve and Ginny prepared a meal large enough to serve all of them. They ate first, then he stood guard over the gang without cutting their hands free while they devoured their food. Steve bound them to trees to spend the night in a secure state. The couple took their places near a cozy fire to pass the dark hours in light slumber until morning came.

Ginny had noticed Steve's ability to fall asleep and awaken instantly. She also noticed that his features seemed to become hardset the closer they came to town, and she wondered why. Something she couldn't read was reflected in his gaze and revealed in the stiff way he sat in his saddle or moved about when dismounted. This shadow closing over him worried her. She wished he would explain his curious mood.

They ate a quick and light breakfast, saddled up, and got underway by seven to cover the last leg of their journey to Fort Smith, Arkansas.

They traversed more forest land and rode into open, wooded terrain, with trees scattered about. They took the Waldron Road and passed near Massard Prairie, where Rebels had routed Union troops in July of '64 in a glorious victory. They skirted the western edge of town and headed for the fort. They arrived at six o'clock on Saturday, May eleventh.

Ginny couldn't understand why Steve was taking the prisoners to the army post at Fort Smith instead of to the town marshal or sheriff. She didn't want to query him before the captives, though, so she stayed mounted as ordered while Steve spoke briefly with an officer at such a distance they couldn't be overheard.

Ginny gazed at her surroundings. The post consisted of both

292

two- and one-story buildings: officers' quarters, soldiers' barracks, storehouses, commissary, guard house, hospital, kitchens, bakery, telegraph office, stables, and other structures she didn't recognize. A pole about a hundred feet high with a large flag that displayed only thirty-six stars until Nebraska's would be added soon stood prominently dominant. In the open terrain, she realized it could be seen for miles, as was intended. A rock wall about four feet high encircled the fort that was nestled in a bend of the wide, blue Arkansas River. Situated on a high sandstone bluff, it was safe from flooding and could repel attacks by water. Ruins of an earlier one were visible on a nearby knoll. From the sizes and amount of structures and the number of men she saw moving about, she guessed about two thousand soldiers were assigned there. This time of day, it was quiet.

She recalled what Steve had told her about Fort Smith during their midday break, and his alleged motive for doing so. The original fort had been constructed as an outpost in enemy territory to handle problems between the neighboring Osage and "intruding" Cherokee Indians, following the "Trail of Tears" from the South. A military presence became more important in '39 when immigrants feared Indian uprisings and demanded more show of force in the area. The increase in Indians in nearby Oklahoma Territory was due to the influx of tribes from the southern states. Steve told her about a Grand Indian Council in '65 where new treaties were written to take effect last year, an action that cost the Indians half of their promised lands and was based on their siding with Confederates during the war. He related tales of glorious battles fought by the Cherokees, mostly under General Stand Waite, an Indian who was now a tobacco grower and curer.

When she had questioned him about why he was revealing so much about Fort Smith, he had shrugged and claimed she might want to settle there and, even if not, she would be there for some time while earning money to get back to her aunt in Georgia. That wasn't the answer she had expected or wanted and didn't query him further about the town or her future.

She was convinced he was well acquainted with Fort Smith; for all she knew, he could have been born and raised here. Perhaps he wanted her to stay around while he decided what to do about her. If only he'd tell her how he felt and what he wanted from her, she could make a decision about him.

Her rambling thoughts halted as the captain took charge of the gang. She was relieved Bart and the others didn't try to implicate her again before they were led toward the guard house by a detail of three soldiers.

Steve mounted and said, "Follow me, Anna. Jake told me where to find a good hotel that's reasonable and safe."

Ginny's heart fluttered with excitement, but she didn't ask him why he didn't know of one since he was familiar with this town. *Alone at last*, she thought happily. But Steve registered her at the desk and paid the clerk, then said he had to return to the post to finish his report to the captain, Jake Cooper, and to turn the stolen gems over to the commander.

"Will you be back in time to join me for dinner?" she asked, a curious sensation of dread washing over her at his reserved mood.

He didn't glance at her as he replied, "Nope, so don't wait for me. I have a lot to do tonight. Good-bye, Anna."

Ginny's heart hammered in her chest. Her pulse raced. Her throat was constricted by warring emotions. He said nothing about seeing her tomorrow or later. In fact, his last two words sounded like a final farewell. With others nearby, she couldn't question him at the desk, and he left too fast for her to follow him outside to do so.

From the hotel porch, she watched him ride down the dirt street toward the fort, and felt as if he were riding out of her life. She wanted to chase after him, declare her love, and entice an admission from him. But she couldn't and she mustn't. When he was out of sight, she went inside and to her lonely room. She didn't fail to realize this hotel was on the far end of town from the post, too far to walk if she were tempted to follow him. One of the owner's sons had taken charge of her horse and, by now, it was unsaddled and stabled. It was foolish to saddle him again and go find Steve Carr.

Don't worry, Ginny, he wouldn't desert you like this. Would he?

Ginny ate a quick meal, then took a bath and washed her hair in the water closet on the second floor. She paced her room while worrying about Steve. She pondered where he was and what he was doing and why he refused to visit her tonight. She wondered if it was because his "assignment" was over and he no longer needed her for clues, or if he truly had business keeping him away, or if he was running scared again.

Ginny prayed he wasn't seeing a woman in one of the brothels she had noticed on their way to the hotel. There was no way she could search for him, for the town was too large and unfamiliar, her hair was wet, and it was too late and dark for a stroll.

Steve Carr, she decided irritably, was exasperating! It was past midnight, so it was clear he wasn't coming to see her. She was tired and edgy and should go to bed. If there was something to learn—good or bad—she would discover it tomorrow.

Sunday at dawn, Steve mounted his sorrel and rode out of town. Once more he was heading to roam the countryside to test his prowess against criminals. He had done it for years, but the glow of excitement didn't warm him today. Long ago he had chosen to pit himself against lawbreakers and perils to prove he was a man to himself and to his father and to the others who had scorned him because he was a half-breed bastard. He hadn't chosen to be a gunslinger because he didn't want the hassle of a reputation to maintain or to be always looking over his shoulder for someone who wanted to take his place. His badge and license proved he was a man of authority, one not to insult or challenge. He had solved many cases and been praised by many government officials, so wasn't it time he accepted and believed he was worthwhile, not a nobody or a nothing? If that were true, he wouldn't have this important job, wouldn't have friends, wouldn't have tempted Anna to surrender to him.

Steve told himself he couldn't risk seeing Anna Avery before he left, as the meeting could evoke too many questions he wasn't yet willing to answer. Being apart for a while would give them time to clear their heads and to probe their feelings. He had work to do before he let her fill his thoughts and rule his actions. He had telegraphed his superior from the fort last night and had sneaked to the hotel and left money with the owner for Anna to use for her room and board and other needs. He had left a note with Captain Jake Cooper to give to her and hoped she accepted his explanation. The words he had penned to her from his warring heart drifted through his troubled mind:

Anna,

I have to leave to turn in the gems I recovered and finish my assignment in Missouri. As soon as I capture those to blame and file my report, I'll return for you. Wait for me here and don't worry about me; I've done this kind of thing plenty of times. I left you enough money with the desk clerk to pay for food and board during my absence. If it takes longer to solve this case than I guessed, Captain Cooper's wife will hire you at her dress shop in town. Stay close to the hotel and be careful. I don't want anything to happen to you. Stay armed, woman. If all goes fast and well, I'll rejoin you within a couple of weeks. When I return, we need to have a serious talk about us.

Steve

They had been together almost all the time ever since they first met. He needed to put distance between them to test her pull on him. She had become his one weakness. He had to make certain his attraction to her wasn't just physical. He could accomplish that only away from the temptation of her. He couldn't stand it if she rejected him as his father had, and she might just do that after she learned the rest of the truth about him: his half-Indian blood. Too many whites hated and avoided Indians, and half-breeds were looked down on more than full-blooded Indians. Most wanted Indians killed or confined to reservations. If she had known he was worse than a bastard, she might never have made love to him. Before he revealed his intimidating secret, he had to make certain he would fight to win her, would do anything to persuade her it didn't matter. And if he was willing to go after her, he had to be convinced he wouldn't be facing a losing battle, because not once had she said she loved him and wanted to marry him.

Marry . . . That was a scary thought. If they did wed, what kind of life could they have? Where? He had so little to offer a woman who had had everything from birth. Why would she want him as a husband and the father of her children? Could he endure her scorning him? Could he find the courage before his return to Fort Smith and her to ask her to commit herself to him? Maybe the future depended upon what he learned from Timothy Graham. He was certain Bart's claims had been wild and vengeful rantings, and he prayed he wouldn't find out otherwise. *Be trustworthy, Anna Avery, or . . .*

As Ginny dressed, she reflected on the decision she had made during a restless night that included awakening many times and pacing the floor a few of them. She was going to tell Steve everything about her today, everything. Perhaps he sensed she was withholding something from him and that made him even more wary of her. If she opened up to him, maybe he would open up to her. Before things went any further between them or they went their separate ways, she had to know where—if any place—she stood with Steve Carr, the man she loved. She would confess everything. She would discover today how that information affected him and how he felt about her. She couldn't put this off any longer.

Ginny went downstairs to eat and to see if there was a message from Steve. Perhaps he was waiting for her. Anticipation and dread flooded her. *Don't let him be angry,* she prayed. *Don't let him reject me. Help him to understand and accept what I've done. Please let him feel the way I do.*

"Miss Avery, your brother left a message for you," the clerk told her.

Brother? That told her Steve Carr couldn't be from Fort Smith or his lie about their relationship wouldn't work on the man. "What is it?"

The clerk handed her an envelope. "He gave me this for you before he left town."

Ginny stared at him. "Left town? When?"

"Last night, Miss Avery," he replied, looking surprised.

"I thought he was leaving this morning. I suppose he was too rushed to wait or I misunderstood him," she said to conceal her pain.

"He said you'd be staying with us for a while. Is everything satisfactory?"

Those words calmed her a little, as she prayed the letter said to wait for him. "Yes, wonderful. Thank you." Ginny returned to her room to read the message in private. She ripped open the envelope and gaped at its contents: only money, enough to support her for a few weeks. She looked between each bill and inside the envelope once more as she felt there must be an enclosed scrap of paper with a few words. But there was nothing.

Ginny was stunned, her heart was tormented, and her mind was dazed. How could he ride away like this? No good-bye. No warning. No mention of a return. She stared at the money with parted lips and wide-eyed disbelief. She fretted that he was paying her off as some . . . *fille de joie.* Why hadn't he at least included a short note of explanation? Just a few words would have been sufficient. Gone . . . He didn't want her. He was deserting her, betraying her. He had told her he had another job waiting that could take weeks or months. He could be going anywhere, be miles away by now. He hadn't asked her to wait for him. She remembered his words on the trail; "If I leave, I won't come back. Don't ruin your life waiting for something to happen that never will." Had that been all the message he felt was necessary? He had said, "I'm sorry it has to be this way." So was she, undeniably more than he was!

After all that had happened between them, how could he do this cruel thing? He had turned in his prisoners, but what about the gems? They were worth a fortune, perhaps one large enough to tempt even an honest man, and surely a penniless drifter. Yet he had tracked and captured the gang easily and quickly like a trained expert. Was there still more to Steve Carr than what he alleged? Was there a crucial reason he couldn't expose the truth to her? How could she check out her suspicions?

No matter his motive, he had done her wrong. Anger seeped into her body and dulled some of the shock and agony. How dare he use her and discard her this way! What reason could justify his behavior? None, she concluded.

As the hours passed, she began to doubt herself and him. Maybe she wasn't what he needed and wanted. Maybe he never had real feelings for her, only lust. How could she have misjudged him so badly? Or had she? There was one place she could check for him or news of him. Until she gathered the truth, it was unfair to suspect him of wrongdoing.

Ginny went downstairs and had her horse saddled and brought to the front. She rode to the fort and asked to see Captain Jake Cooper.

The private in charge of the officer's affairs told her, "Sorry, ma'am, but he left about dawn to handle a sudden problem in Indian Territory."

"Did Steve Carr go with him?"

"Don't know any Steve Carr, ma'am."

"The man who brought in the five prisoners yesterday."

"Him? No, ma'am. He talked with the captain last night and left town. Is there a problem I can help you with?"

"Thank you, but no. When do you expect Captain Cooper to return?"

"About a week, ma'am. I can tell him you want to see him."

"That won't be necessary; I'll be gone by then. Thank you."

Ginny returned to her room. She paced and worried. *Mother, Father, Johanna, if only one of you were here to advise and comfort me.* She didn't know what to do or think. She realized she could stay there forever and he might never come back. If he needed time away from her, should she give it to him? Would that do more harm than good to their uncertain relationship? She wondered if she should go on to Texas. *Let him worry for a change. If he wants me, he has the skills to search for me and find me.* She asked herself if she should give him today, perhaps a few days, to change his mind and return. *Yes, that's only fair.* Perhaps he hadn't thought a message was necessary or had forgotten to include one in his rush to depart. Perhaps he thought she trusted him enough to realize he would come back soon. Maybe it was an innocent mistake. Surely he would grasp his oversight then send her a message by letter, telegram, or friend.

But the next day passed without word from Steve. Ginny's hope dwindled and her apprehensions increased. Her troubled thoughts and misty gaze kept shifting to the packet of money, causing her to dread its meaning. Though he had deserted her, he hadn't left her without funds for her support, at least for a while. Yet the money could have been left only to ease his conscience for what he'd done to her. But a man, a drifter, couldn't have much money to spare. Where had he gotten it? A bounty payment on the outlaws? An advance on his salary for his assignment? No matter, she could either use it to wait here for a miracle or use it to get to Texas. There wasn't enough to do both, so a difficult decision was at hand.

By Monday morning, Ginny had convinced herself she must accept reality: Steve had betrayed her and abandoned her, just as Bennett Chapman had done to Johanna. Now, she fully understood how her friend had felt. As Johanna had, what she truly wanted was a logical explanation and happy reunion, not revenge. Yet, it was different with Mr. Chapman. He was a father; it was his duty, responsibility, and moral obligation to love, protect, and support his own child. He owed his daughter something and she must collect that long-overdue debt as she'd sworn to do on Johanna's deathbed.

She couldn't force Steve to love her or to return to her. She couldn't do anything about his cruel desertion, as she could about Bennett's. If Steve was that kind of man, he was wrong for her. He would bring her more anguish than joy. She must put him out of her mind and heart. She must focus on her original goals of locating Bennett Chapman and Mathew Marston. It would not be simple or painless to get over Steve, but she must get him off her mind and set her important tasks in motion.

Besides, she had realized that Steve's boss, the government, might not be as trusting and lenient with her as the scout had been. Either someone might believe Bart's accusations or Timothy Graham could lie about her. She couldn't ignore the possibility that something might incriminate her. The law could come after her at any moment. There were no witnesses she could call upon who wouldn't create problems for her and her father. She needed to get to the Chapman ranch and stay there until the investigation was completed. She needed Johanna's identity to hide behind for protection of her life and freedom.

She considered telegraphing Bennett for travel money and refusing to accept Steve's, but she decided that required too long of a wait. She could repay Steve later, if she ever located him in the future. If they were fated to be together, destiny would cross their paths again. Until then, she had work to do. She mustn't spend valuable time, emotions, and energy on self-pity. She got busy on her new goal.

Ginny sent her two extra sets of clothes to a laundress. She put the money in her skirt pocket and pretended to take a stroll to view the town, as she dared not ask for directions. In spite of dirt streets and few sidewalks, she realized how large and lovely the town was. It was busy and noisy this morning, so she mostly went unnoticed. She passed many businesses and the people who worked in them, passed schools, churches, and houses she was certain were fancy bordellos.

She saw the Missouri & Western Telegraph office, but had decided against sending Bennett Chapman advance warning of her impending arrival, as a telegram could be recalled and traced. Steve had told her most of these businesses and merchants had been here before 1860 when the last census of the area was taken and listed the population at over seven thousand. She saw Federal Marshal Luther White's office, and cringed in anxiety. Steve had related information about that lawman: he had strong Union feelings and ties, had been appointed by Lincoln, and was also a doctor. Surely a fiercely loyal Union man wouldn't lean kindly toward a suspected Klanswoman. She hurried past that office.

The town seemed to be expanding to the south and east with rapid growth. She noticed construction in many locations where laborers worked with skill and efficiency. Steve had told her that outside of town were farms of all sizes. Soldiers, from the post and ex-military men from both sides in the war, were everywhere. She suspected a few of the rough-looking men were gunslingers and outlaws. She saw some Indians and remembered Steve had said the neighboring land was Indian Territory. She hoped there wasn't terrible trouble there that might delay her plans.

She halted and pretended to window shop so she could listen in on two soldiers standing nearby whose words had caught her interest.

One said, "I don't wanta be sent to Texas where them Injuns are kicking up a fuss again. Myers and his unit should be at Belknap by now."

"I thought Fort Belknap was abandoned before '60."

"It was, but Texas troops used her during the war, and the Army's using her again until Richardson is built near Jacksboro. Hell, that's only seventy miles from Injun Territory. The boys at old Fort Richardson were split up last month and sent to

Belknap and Buffalo Springs. They'll all go back to Richardson when she's underway in a few months. Some of the rest of us might be sent down afterward. I sure hope it ain't me."

"Did Myers take that pretty wife of his with him?"

"Cora's to join him in the next month or so was what he said. Too bad she won't have time to get lonely and lean toward you, right, Harry?"

"Maybe she will. Being so far out of town, she hardly sees anybody. Most folks around here don't even know she's alive and out there. She'll probably need help with the farm and chores, don't you think?"

As the two men drifted into lewd whispers, Ginny left the scene. She relaxed when she saw the sight she wanted. She went into the stagecoach office and purchased a ticket to Fort Belknap for Tuesday morning under the name of Mrs. Cora Myers. She told the agent she was going to meet her husband who had been transferred from Fort Smith to Fort Belknap. She assumed the man couldn't know every soldier at the nearby post, and he appeared to believe her. While he prepared her ticket, she chatted cunningly about what she had overheard the two soldiers say. She had studied the map and schedule on the office wall while he was busy with someone else, so she knew the Oxbow Route would put her about one hundred and twenty miles from Dallas. She could either go to the Texas fort and catch a stage to Dallas from there or she could catch one to her real destination, the Chapman ranch, on a spur route after they entered the Lone Star State. The trip would require four and a half days. By Saturday night, she figured, she would be near or at the Chapman ranch, out of danger from any repercussions from her ruse as Anna Avery.

During her return stroll, she entered a nearby store and bought one simple dress for the journey ahead, all she could afford. After she reached the hotel and put away her purchase, she took Charles Avery's horse and saddle to a farm near the edge of town and sold them for less than their value. She told the happy buyer she wanted to make certain her beloved animal had a good home and she couldn't be sure of that if she sold him to one of the stables in town. Her action would make tracking her harder for Steve or for anyone else, as he could be assigned to come after her if things went wrong. There was one last precaution to take: She told the desk clerk, who was also owner of the hotel, that she was departing on a steamboat for home the next day and paid him to give a letter to her "brother" when he returned.

Ginny readied herself to leave in the morning. She took a bath and ate a good meal downstairs, her last for many days. Her laundry had been returned, so she packed her scant belongings. She hoped the wagontrain would arrive in Dallas soon so she could recover the rest of her possessions. Of course, everything could be replaced except for the doll her mother had made for her as a child. She hadn't wanted to risk losing it on the trail with that awful gang, and she would be glad to be out of the same town with them. If possible, she could see her four friends again in Texas.

Ginny looked around the room. Every precaution had been taken. The skilled Steve might be able to track her movements and locate her. If he did come after her, she hoped it was for the right reason. She thought about the message waiting for him with the hotel owner:

Dear Steve,

If I've misunderstood your motive for leaving me here without a word or note, I'm sorry, but what am I to think? I don't want to believe you would use me, betray me, and desert me in this cruel way. But it appears as if I've been paid off like a strumpet you hired to share your bed on a few occasions or have been paid off to soothe your conscience for deceiving me. Perhaps I was wrong to think there was something special between us. Your disappearing without a word tells me I was mistaken about you and about us. Perhaps you'll have a reasonable explanation when we see each other again, if we do.

I was going to confess everything to you Sunday morning, but you deserted me and took away that opportunity. I'm not convinced you'll return and get this letter, but I felt I owed you this much, although you didn't do the same for me. You'll be told soon where to locate me, if you have a desire to do so.

I can't wait around to see if you'll come back because I have an important and secret task to do. After your desertion and tricks, surely you grasp why I'm not disclosing it. In about a month or two, I'll send you a letter in care of Captain Cooper to tell you where I am. Perhaps by then, we'll both be ready to be honest about our lives and feelings. We've duped each other more than once, but perhaps there's still a chance for us to forgive each other and have a happy future together. If you care about me like I care about you, check for my message later. I'll pray I didn't misjudge you. I'll miss you.

Love, Anna

On Tuesday morning, Ginny was assisted into the brown stagecoach with its sunny yellow trim by a polite and friendly gentleman. If any passenger knew or suspected she wasn't Mrs. Cora Myers, none called her bluff. Yet her heart raced, her body quivered, and her tension increased. She heard the driver give commands to the team by words and whip. The coach jerked and creaked. She was on the way to become Johanna Chapman and would soon decide if she must be cruel or kind to her best friend's traitorous father. She was leaving Fort Smith and her misadventures behind. If only she knew if she were also leaving her love behind forever.

CHAPTER 14

Arkansas was quickly left behind. The stage crossed into Oklahoma Territory, more frequently called Indian Territory because the Osage, the Five Civilized Tribes of southeastern America, and other Indian tribes lived there. At first they journeyed near the Poteau River which caused bittersweet memories to fill Ginny's head. Their last night on the trail had been spent on the banks of that river. She didn't want thoughts of Steve to trouble her, so she distracted herself with recalling as many as possible of the often amusing rules posted at the station for Stagecoach Etiquette.

As other passengers talked with each other and a few times with her, Ginny stuck to her fabricated story. It was obvious, to her relief, that no one knew Cora Myers or her husband because nobody cast her a doubtful or suspicious glance. Nor had the three men who were riding outside: a driver and two well-armed guards.

She gazed out the window as she realized a stage journey was more bouncing, bruising, and jarring than one on a wagon. The pace was faster and more dust was kicked up because of the rapid speed and any motion was more noticeable as passengers were jostled against each other. The confines were close and tight in the small coach with its three benches. Nine people were crowded together three to each hard wooden seat. Fortunately she had one of the best seats, located behind the driver.

The middle one had no back rest and those on it constantly bumped knees with those on the rear seat. With little breeze coming through the tall and narrow windows, she could imagine how the cramped interior would smell in a few days as people went without baths. She hoped it didn't rain, which would compel them to lower the leather shades and block off all fresh air.

A mixture of sounds filled Ginny's ears: luggage thudding against the wood of the coach, the jangling of harnesses and snap of a whip in the jehu's hand, the flick of reins on horse flesh. She listened to driver's shouts as he urged the animals to a faster pace, the rumbling of wheels and pounding of twenty-four hooves against hard ground, and the voices of passengers as they chatted to while away the boring hours.

A routine was established immediately upon their departure. The half-wild horses were run at a swift pace for sixteen miles. At the end of that leg in two hours, they halted at a relay station where the exhausted team was unhitched and a new one was harnessed in less than ten minutes while the passengers stayed aboard. The process was repeated twice more until a twenty-minute lunch break and driver change during their third stop. Two more rapid runs lasted about two hours, when they halted at almost primitive home stations for the night. The schedule allowed for eighty miles travel each day with five stops. In a little over four days, they would reach Fort Belknap.

It didn't take the Kiamichi region long to become a familiar sight of mostly flat terrain with verdant bushes, trees, and grass. A little variety came by lunchtime; with scattered rocks and a scrubland look where even cottonwoods, oaks, and redbuds grew along waterlines. Hills and ridges greeted them before their third short stop where biscuits with fried meat were downed with coffee and milk. The customary meal was a rushed and almost tasteless one; taken at the station near the end of the Poteau River and south of the San Bois Mountains.

Their next stop was at Wilburton, which according to one man was notorious for sheltering outlaw hideouts in the nearby sandstone cliffs and caves. Four passengers got off and two more got on the stage.

During the last leg of the first day's travel, buffalo, deer, antelope, and coyote were seen foraging. Ginny realized what lush and beautiful grazeland they were crossing, the property of the Indians by treaty. One of the men mentioned how cattle drives passed through this area on their way to market, which reminded her of Bennett Chapman and the reluctant deception looming before her.

Ginny was relieved that no Indians, outlaws, or rustlers attacked them while traversing this perilous region. She didn't know what kind of trouble had drawn Captain Jake Cooper into this neighboring territory in such a hurry, but they hadn't seen any trouble, nor had the station keepers' known of any. She prayed it continued to be safe for all of them.

Each time they halted, dust surrounded the stage and team and wafted inside the coach, causing most passengers to cough. At morning boarding, at lunch and at dusk tonight, polite men assisted her from the stage. The home station was comprised of corrals, stables and smithy for the horses, privy, and two crude shacks where the keeper, sometimes with a family and his workers, lived in meager conditions.

Following a scant meal, men slept on the floor, driver and guards on bunks, and women with the keeper's wife or in a separate room. Ginny longed for a bath and privacy. At least she had been allowed those treats on one wagontrain. That last word stirred up memories she didn't want to think about tonight, so she pushed them aside to get much needed rest and sleep.

They passed west of the Jack Fork Mountains, crossed several large creeks, and saw woods without the pines she had become accustomed to before entering Indian Territory. By the end of the second day, she learned there was little money available for feeding passengers a good supper. Mostly it was beans, corn-dodgers or biscuits, and meat the keeper had shot or trapped: antelope, deer, and rabbit which was usually cooked too long.

The third day, rolling hills didn't slow their progress as the stage skirted the highest ones. She saw where farmers were raising corn, maise, cattle, and horses. As they crossed the Red River, the Texas border, her anxiety mounted. She was exhausted and dust-covered by the time they halted for the night beyond the Gainsville stop where three passengers had gotten off and four had joined them. She longed to take a spur route to Dallas, but thought it best to continue on to her alleged stop to conceal her ruse in case the law investigated the missing "Mrs. Cora Myers."

On the fourth day, majestic mesas appeared between the east and west forks of the Trinity River. Abundant mesquite, cactus, rocks, flash flood areas, and lush grass greeted her. The lunch break was better, as it was on Main Street in Jacksboro where supplies were easier and cheaper to obtain, and three passengers deboarded. Including her, there were five left, giving them unaccustomed and welcome room in the coach.

But Ginny learned while eating that there was no town at Fort Belknap, so she'd be stranded there and noticeable to curious eyes of soldiers. Too, another stage was due at four o'clock, heading for Dallas, which was about eighty miles away. She made the decision to alter her plans. She went outside and told the Fort Smith driver, "I received a message from my husband. He wants me to await him here where accommodations are better. I'll need my satchel."

Ginny watched the noisy stage depart in a cloud of dust. She waited a few minutes, then walked to the adjoining office and purchased a ticket for her real destination as Miss Johanna Chapman. One more night on the trail, she mused, before she began her next deception.

As she sat on the porch to await her ride in an hour, doubts plagued her about her impending ruse. Perhaps it was wrong to take justice into her hands, and especially *revenge* if she discovered it was well deserved. There were terrible accusations against Bennett Chapman from the lips of Johanna's mother. Ginny reflected on them to motivate her. Stella had said it took her years to get pregnant with Johanna, then she'd dared to birth a girl as the firstborn. When Ben learned she could have no more children, especially a son, he ignored and mistreated her. She claimed he had married her only to be his "brood mare" and arm decoration. Ben had wanted a son so badly that he had adopted a ten-year-old boy who lived and did chores on the ranch. He and Ben had become inseparable. Ben had lavished all of his love and attention on the boy and he had taken a mistress. The time came when Stella could no longer accept such cruelties, so she took Johanna and left for England to be far from Ben.

Stella had told Johanna that Ben had even asked her if Johanna was his daughter and seemed to doubt she was. Ben had not forced them back home because, according to Stella, she threatened to expose all of his dirty secrets to his friends, neighbors, and even the law. Stella alleged that Ben loved his image and position and wanted to avoid a scandal so much that he left them in peace, and never contacted them again.

Ginny remembered her crying friend's painful words as they sat on the floor next to the trunk: "I was always told that Father didn't love me or want me, that he never wrote me or tried to get me back. But here are his letters to me and Mother that prove it wasn't true. If she lied about that part, perhaps she lied about other parts. I must learn why Mother left him. And why Father allowed her to take me away and keep me from him. I must seek the truth, Ginny, in America, in Texas, as soon as possible. If Father acted out of cruelty, I must find a way to punish him. If he is innocent of Mother's claims, I must tell him the truth about me and her."

Johanna's death had placed that task on her shoulders.

Ginny worried over how Ben would react to "Johanna's" sudden arrival. She fretted over what Ben's adopted son would think. She had made her rash promise to Johanna in a moment of weakness and anguish. She had left Fort Smith in a moment of panic and torment. What she should have done, she now realized, was head for Colorado to search for her own father, not come here to investigate and possibly punish or hurt the father of her best friend. But she had no choice but to go on with her daring scheme, as almost all of the money from Steve was spent. Nor could she remain in Jacksboro and work to earn enough to head further west.

She eyed her surroundings. She saw the building called Old Fort Richardson, which the soldiers had evacuated. The town was rowdy and noisy but had lovely sandstone structures from local sources. Many of the businesses must have been aimed at the soldiers who had pulled out recently, but now catered to rough-looking men of questionable character. She overheard tales of Indian raids that chilled her blood and made her glad she would be gone soon. She realized the close proximity to Indian Territory and the recent uprisings were the motives for reopening Fort Belknap and for impending construction of a larger Fort Richardson, a mile outside of town. She would be happy to leave this town.

Late the following day, the coach halted at the Dallas depot. Ginny collected her satchel and walked to a small hotel she hoped was inexpensive and clean. She found it to be both and sighed in relief. Despite her dusty and wrinkled appearance, she decided to have dinner downstairs before she bathed and washed her hair, as she couldn't go into the eating area later with her long tresses wet and they required hours to air dry.

After a delicious meal, she approached the desk clerk and asked if he knew of a man named Bennett Chapman. "He owns a ranch nearby," she explained.

"Yes, Miss Chapman, a fine gentleman. Are you kinfolk?"

"Yes, I am. I'll need directions to the Circle C Ranch tomorrow." Even if the clerk recalled the name she was using, it wouldn't seem odd for her to need directions, since Johanna had left Dallas at the age of two.

The man smiled. "Mr. Chapman will be in town in the morning for Sunday services at the church down the street. You could meet him there or have a message sent to the pastor to have him visit you here."

"Thank you, sir, that's very helpful. Good night."

Ginny took a long bath and scrubbed her light-brown hair. She wanted to look her best for the meeting, and she would find that difficult enough with the simple cotton dress she had saved for the occasion.

As she paced her room, Steve Carr took lodging in her mind. There was so much distance separating them, more than in miles. It was possible that nothing and no one could change him. Perhaps they would never meet again to find out if she was wrong. Perhaps he could never be the marrying and settling down type. Maybe all he could do was take whatever was offered to him then ride away, back to his self-imposed lonely existence. He was so complex, so contradictory: good and bad, strong and weak, giving and unrelenting, and tender and tough. If only he would soften up long enough for her to—

Stop fooling yourself, Ginny; he's probably unattainable.

Sunday morning she dressed with care. She was scared, nervous, and reluctant to initiate her ruse as Johanna. She scolded herself once more for not using Steve's money to get her to Colorado, then dismissed her error, which was too late to correct. At least she looked enough like Johanna and knew enough about her best friend's life to stand a good chance of duping Bennett Chapman and the people in Dallas. She had to find a way to get money to search for Mathew Marston. From the warnings in his past letters, she dared not telegraph him in

Colorado City. She was trapped; it was carry out her scheme or
. . . *What?*

Ginny walked to the church down the street and took a seat
near the back. Several people looked at her and smiled or
nodded. She almost felt as if she were holding her breath as she
quivered inside. A man across the aisle greeted a friend who
had just entered. "Howdy, Ben," she heard him say.

Ginny tensed and observed, in case it was her . . . target. The
man was well-dressed, nice-looking, and alone. His hair—a
blend of black and gray—was combed neatly. He stood just
under six feet and had a sturdy build. If he was Bennett Chapman, that wouldn't surprise her since he had carved a huge
cattle ranch from a wilderness while battling Indians, inclement
weather, and other perils. As the newcomer's gaze drifted over
the people nearby, she noticed he had brown eyes and a gentle
smile. Many furrows etched his forehead and numerous creases
fanned from his expressive eyes. If this was the man she sought,
Ginny couldn't guess if they'd come from an age of forty-nine,
his work beneath the sun, or from painful emotions. Surely even
a cold and cruel man, she reasoned, would suffer from the losses
and hardships Bennett Chapman had endured.

Two older women sitting beside her shared their hymnal
during the singing. After the preacher began, Ginny wanted to
flee the building. The last thing she needed today was a sermon
on the Ten Commandments about stealing, lying, "shewing
mercy unto . . . them that love me," and honoring "thy Father":
all the things of which she might soon be guilty. Yet the service
finally ended the torment.

Ginny hurried outside and watched the people leave. A few
stopped and greeted her, and she thanked them but didn't
encourage conversation. She listened for names and heard the
man she'd watched in church called "Ben" by some and "Mr.
Chapman" by others. Her heart drummed in suspense and
panic. She wondered if her mouth would speak and her feet
would move when ordered to do so. Would a guilty conscience
entice her gaze and expression to expose her bold lies? She must

keep reminding herself how important this ruse and her success were to Johanna and to herself. When he finally approached a buggy to depart, Ginny walked to him and asked, "Sir, are you Bennett Chapman?"

The man lowered his leg from an attempted mount and turned to face her. His inquisitive gaze locked to her guarded one. "Yes. May I help you?"

Be direct, simple, and quick, Ginny. "I'm Johanna. I've just arrived from England. Mother is dead. I wanted to meet my father." The man was stunned speechless. He stared at her as if fearing to believe his eyes and ears. Then, his brown gaze glowed and teared.

"You're Johanna? My precious, lost Johanna?"

She commanded herself to reply, "Yes, sir, I am." She watched him look her over from head to foot. "Please excuse my appearance, as I lost my things during the trip here. This simple dress was all I could afford." He continued to stare in silence that made her nervous. "Do you doubt I'm your daughter?"

"Of course you're my Johanna. You favor your mother greatly."

She didn't read the anticipated hatred in his softened gaze or hear resentment in his emotion-choked voice. Yet she probed, "Is that bad?" She calmed a little when Ben smiled at her and shook his head. She didn't know how to respond when he hugged her and laughed merrily. She felt uneasy when he held her at arm's length and studied her with a loving gaze.

"My child, you're home at last. I feared I'd never lay eyes on you again. I don't know what to say. This is such a shock. A wonderful surprise."

He looked genuinely delighted and moved. "I hope so, Father. I didn't know where else to go. I have no money left. You're my only family. Am I welcome here?"

Ben laughed and hugged her again. "Yes, yes, my girl. I've wanted you back since your mother stole you from me so long ago."

314

"Stole me?"

Ben glanced around, then suggested, "Let's go home to talk. There's so much we have to tell each other."

"I'm staying at the Klems Hotel. It's all I could afford."

"But you'll come home with me, won't you? Please."

This was her last chance to back out of the scheme. "I . . ."

"Of course you will, my only daughter. Let's fetch your things and be on our way." He looked her up and down. "You've grown into a beautiful young woman, Johanna. I'm so proud of you and so happy you've returned. Wait until Nan and Stone see you. They won't believe this wonderful news."

She feigned ignorance of those names. "You've married again?"

"No, no," he replied quickly. "Nan is my housekeeper and Stone is my adopted son, adopted before you were taken from me. Of course you wouldn't remember Nan and your brother; you were only two when Stella cheated me out of my daughter . . . What did she tell you about me?" he asked abruptly.

Ginny concluded he looked worried and scared. "Very little, Father. She didn't like to speak of you or the past, even to me."

"She's dead, you say?"

"Yes, in February, from a winter chill in the chest. I used what little money she left to sail to America. I came here by wagontrain and stage. It was horrible, but I'll tell you about my misadventures later."

"You won't ever have to worry about money or be afraid again, Johanna. I promise everything will be safe and wonderful for you from now on."

"Thank you, Father."

"Let's go home; you've been gone too long."

Ginny smiled and said, "Yes, Father, we've been apart too long."

* * *

Ginny stared at the stone arch as they drove beneath its large, encircled C. They had been riding on Chapman land for over an hour. The spread was beautiful and enormous, with fences, cattle, horses, and cowboys scattered here and there. Numerous structures came into view over a grassy hill: barns, outbuildings, corrals, and a large house.

Ben halted the horse on a verdant knoll and motioned over the terrain. "Home, Johanna. All of this will belong to you and Stone one day."

"Is my . . . brother here so I can meet him?"

"Not at present, but he'll be home soon. He's away taking care of some business. Stone's lived here since he was a child. He did a lot to make the ranch as grand as you see it. The boy needed a father, needed a family. He was so special that I adopted him when he was ten. He's like my real son, Johanna, but that takes nothing of me away from you. I hope you agree it's only fair to split the ranch with him."

Ginny wondered if Ben had indeed showered all his affection and attention on his "son" as Stella had told Johanna? Love for Stone was obvious in Ben's eyes and voice. "Of course I agree, Father. I'm eager to meet him."

"He'll be thrilled to see you. He adored you. I wish you two could have been raised together. He was sad after Stella . . . But let's forget that for a while." He clicked his tongue and the reins to continue their ride.

When she reached the house, Ben leapt down and shouted, "Nan! Nan! Come see who I've brought home! She's back! My beloved Johanna has returned to me!"

Ginny looked at the lovely fortyish woman who hurried onto the porch. Her silky black hair was in a neat bun at the nape of her neck. With her dark eyes, complexion, and hair, she looked Spanish to Ginny.

"Johanna . . ."

Ginny heard the name leave Nan's lips in a whisper of amazement. She watched the neatly dressed woman come to greet her with enthusiasm. They exchanged smiles and studied

316

each other quickly. Suddenly Nan embraced her with what seemed to be honest joy and affection.

"It's so good to have you home again, little one. Your father has ached and prayed for your return. This is a blessed day."

"Stella died a few months past, so Johanna decided to return home."

Ginny noticed a strained look on Nan's face at that unexpected news. The woman glanced at Ben as if to see how he was taking it. The two exchanged smiles that told Ginny they were close friends.

"I'm sorry about your mother. Come inside. Tell us everything."

The woman entered the house with her satchel. When Ginny glanced at Ben in bewilderment, the man smiled and explained to her that Nan had been with the family since before she was born. She's one of us. I couldn't do without her. You'll love her."

Once inside, Ben said, "Nan, show Johanna to her room. She can freshen up there before we sit down to eat."

Ginny followed the slim woman to a room that astonished her.

Nan smiled and said, "He has kept it ready in anticipation of your return since the day you left. It's cleaned every week and redecorated every five years as things get old and faded. He wanted it to be perfect when you came home, which he always prayed and believed you would. He selected everything in here himself. Sometimes I'd find him sitting on the bed thinking about you, sometimes crying over the loss of you. He loves you so much, little one. Every Christmas and birthday he bought you a present; they're all in your drawers. He never shipped them because Stella refused to . . . I'm sorry; that isn't something I should talk about. You must still be grieving."

"I'm recovered now, but thank you for your kindness. This room is beautiful." Ginny looked at the sensitive woman and murmured, "I don't know you, Father, or this house. It feels strange to be here."

Nan placed her arm around the girl's back and patted it. "You were only two years old, so of course you don't remember us or the house. Don't worry; everything will be familiar soon. I'm so happy you've come home, Johanna. Your father has missed you so much."

"What's he like, Nan? And is that what I should call you?"

"You called me Nanna, but Nan is fine now that you're grown. You've become such a lovely young woman, Johanna. He'll be so proud of you."

Ginny wondered if Nan didn't answer her question on purpose. "Why did Mother leave him and take me away?" she asked and saw Nan grimace.

"I shouldn't be the one to discuss such matters with you. Ask him. But wait a while, Johanna, please. The past is a terrible burden he's carried for years. Let him be happy for a while. He deserves some peace, and your return can give it to him. Allow time for you two to get acquainted. Let's go join him. We have a great deal of catching up to do."

Over a lengthy and delicious meal with Ben and Nan, Ginny related all that had happened to her: her voyage to America, her ruse with Charles Avery, her abduction by outlaws, her rescue by the scout Steve Carr, and her trip to Dallas.

"The man deserves a reward if he can be located," Ben said. "With all that trouble and danger, it's a miracle you survived. You've shown real courage and cunning, Johanna, a true daughter of mine."

"Thank you, sir. It was scary at times and hard at others. That scout was tough on us during training, but his lessons saved my life and got me here. If I had known what kind of evil plans Mr. Avery had, I wouldn't have gotten involved in them by pretending to be his daughter." She related more information about Charles, his motives and his scheme to help her get through this difficult meeting.

Ben sighed. "I can understand how the war could drive a man—may Avery's soul rest in peace now—to take reckless action. We all have moments of weakness. We were lucky the war didn't touch here much and that Reconstruction government, as they call it, doesn't give me or my neighbors any trouble."

"I'm glad, sir, because it's terrible other places. You can't imagine the awful sights and bitterness I've witnessed on the way here." She disclosed some of those things to him and saw him frown in dismay.

"I'm thankful I didn't join the fighting or see such horrors. The Lord's been good and merciful to me. He brought you back to me, with Mr. Carr's help. If we can reach him, I'll repay the money he gave you—probably a lot for a workingman like him. Tell me what happened to your mother?" he asked abruptly.

Ginny was surprised by the sudden change of subject. She glanced at the quiet woman nearby, her expression asking Ben if she should speak freely in front of Nan.

"It's fine, girl. Nan's been with me since before I met and married your mother. She's . . . like a sister to me, an aunt to you. We don't have any secrets between us; we live and work too closely for them to intrude."

From what she'd perceived so far, Ginny decided that Ben loved his daughter. He couldn't seem to take his glowing and often misty eyes off her. He smiled and laughed every few minutes as if he were releasing an overabundance of joy in his heart to keep it from bursting. That pleased, confused, and dismayed Ginny. Perhaps, she mused, his past mistakes had been the results of flaws that might have been corrected over the years. Either Ben or Stella—or both—had lied about the past. But which one, why, and about what?

"If you prefer, Johanna, I can leave the room."

Ginny realized her thoughtful silence had been misunderstood. She smiled and said, "No, Nan, that isn't necessary. Father says you're part of the family, so you should stay and listen. It's such a painful story that I didn't know if he wanted to hear it alone. I'm sure her death came as a shock to him, as did my unexpected arrival." Ginny summoned more courage to gather clues. "Please don't think badly of me, but I'm going to speak the truth, mean and ugly as it may sound. At times Mother was a confused, selfish, and impulsive woman. But you know that from experience, Father, and you must remember it, too, Nan. I loved her dearly, but she made many mistakes. It was wrong of her to leave home, to keep me so far away and out of touch, and to live as she did."

"Don't worry about speaking the truth, Johanna," Ben entreated. "We both know you're right about her. She married me because I was wealthy and successful. I married her because she was beautiful, genteel, charming, and should have made a perfect wife and mother. But what I saw on the outside wasn't like her inner self. I won't blame everything on her; we were both wrong in many ways. We were ill-suited, and it caused us both a lot of suffering. She had to be free and I couldn't hold her, short of ripping all of us apart. I kept thinking she'd come to her senses and return. I should have come and fetched you home. At first, I didn't want you trapped between warring parents, and I honestly believed a baby girl needed her mother more than her father. Despite her many faults, she was a good mother and loved you dearly. Time just got away from me. I was working hard to keep this ranch and to make it prosper. The country was getting in bitter turmoil over the slavery question; trouble was springing up everywhere all during the fifties. Then secession and war came along. I couldn't find it in me to take sides, as both were wrong."

He took a deep breath and released it before continuing. "I wasn't a coward, but I had to stay here and protect my ranch from Yankees and rustlers and land grabbers—your land one day, Johanna, yours and Stone's. I thought that if I didn't support Stella in the fancy lifestyle she loved, she'd tire of living hand-to-mouth and return home. I certainly couldn't see her working to support the two of you; she'd been too pampered. I told her I would send ship tickets anytime she wanted them. I let too many years pass without taking a stand for you. I'm sorry, Johanna, and I hope you'll forgive me. I never meant for you to go wanting, but I couldn't trust Stella to use any money I sent to travel home. How did you live over there?"

Ginny was disappointed to learn some of those facts. Ben hadn't known how they were surviving and he had the money for their support, but he had tried to use it for leverage against Stella. Yet he freely and apologetically admitted he was wrong to do so. Perhaps his intention to drive a penniless Stella home justified it in his mind. But why couldn't he have taken a month off from his precious ranch to check on his child to make sure she had food and shelter? As she had told Steve, sorry was only a word if the feelings inside didn't match it. "Mother spent all the money she took from you when she ran away. When it ran out, she became . . . the mistress of an English lord."

Ben straightened in his chair. "She *what!* Stella let my daughter see her living in sin? My God, Johanna, I'm so sorry you had to exist that way. I can't believe she would become a kept woman. She was too proud and vain. I assumed she'd married again under English law, without divorcing me."

"Mother believed he loved her and would eventually marry her, but it wasn't true. Perhaps that's why she never divorced you, in case she ever needed to return home. The older I became, the more the earl considered me an intrusion. He paid to have me placed in a boarding school in London when I was thirteen. I rarely saw either of them afterward. It wasn't bad there. I learned to become a lady and received a good education. I had a best friend who came from Georgia, she was like a sister to me; we returned home to America together on the same ship. After Mother died in February, the earl cut off my support. While I was going through her things, I found enough money to pay for my trip to Dallas. There was a letter inside one trunk from you, begging her to send me or bring me home."

Ginny saw the man tense and pale, as if in dread of what had been written in that letter. She doubted he could recall every one he had penned to her, so she told him what it said, and saw him relax. She wished it had revealed the secret he seemed to fear her learning, as his reaction told her there was a terrible mystery to be solved. "I wanted to meet you, so I came here. I suppose I can be as impulsive and reckless at times as Mother."

"You did the right thing, Johanna. The smart thing. I'm glad."

"It was scary after docking in Savannah and seeing what the war had done in America during my long absence. Mr. Avery seemed so nice and trustworthy. It was the only way I could get to Texas. The stage ride from Fort Smith was just as scary. I was afraid to telegraph you from either town, afraid you'd tell me not to come."

"How could you ever think I didn't love you and want you?"

Ginny used her feelings and worries about her own father to facilitate her answers. "It's been so long since we were separated. I don't even know you, and I didn't know you'd written me."

"We'll have the rest of our lives to get acquainted. We're together, Johanna, and I'll never let anything tear us apart again; I promise. I hope you don't blame me for your mother's wickedness and weaknesses. I know she had come to hate me and she wanted to leave me. I couldn't divorce her or deny you like she wanted me to. I kept hoping and praying she'd come to her senses, realize what she had here, and return."

For Johanna and herself, Ginny responded, "I wish she had. It's terrible for a daughter to grow up not knowing her father."

Ben finished his chilled coffee and smiled. "This has been a long and straining talk for both of us. You should rest after your long journey. We'll talk again tonight and tomorrow and for many days to come."

"You're right, Father; I *am* exhausted and this *has* been difficult." Ginny rose and left the table after smiling at Ben and Nan, who hadn't spoken during the strenuous conversation.

She entered what should have been Johanna's room and looked at her surroundings. The cherrywood furniture was of skilled craftsmanship. The floors were highly polished, with a

322

floral rug concealing the center of the room. The coverlet, chair, and curtains were also in a matching floral design in muted shades of green, blue, and pink on ivory. A silver comb and brush lay on the dresser, along with a vase of flowers and bottles of cologne. The oil lamp was hand-blown glass, and brass candleholders were on the wall on either side of a mirror over a low chest. It was an expensively appointed and lovely room, and Ginny wished Johanna were there to see and enjoy it.

She stretched out on the comfortable bed and prayed the worst of her deception was over. Not once had either Ben or Nan looked at her as if they suspected she was an imposter. She was surprised that neither one seemed to wonder if Stella had sent her here for revenge or monetary gain. They appeared to accept her with open arms, which sent twinges of guilt through Ginny. From here on, she needed to glean clues to make her final decision; but she must work slowly and carefully to prevent arousing any suspicions. And there was one more hurdle to overcome: Stone. She hoped he would be as easy to dupe as Ben and Nan had been. Considering what "his sister's" return could cost him, he might resent her presence. *If you can see me and hear me, dear Johanna, I hope I am doing the right thing. This is so much harder than either of us realized it would be.*

Ginny turned onto her side and looked across the room. Didn't what she see and all she'd learned convince her that Ben loved his daughter and was contrite over the past? She got off the bed and went to the dresser. She rummaged through each drawer, eyeing the presents Johanna had never received, had never known about. That tragedy pained Ginny's heart. There were dolls and other toys for a child. There were necklaces, scarves, fancy ribbons, books, a writing set, expensive stationery, shawls, beaded purses, broochs, and more items appropriate for the daughter of a wealthy parent. It would have made Johanna ecstatic to have received only one of these gifts. It was cruel and spiteful of Stella to have denied them to her daughter. It was selfish and cowardly of Ben not to have made certain she did get them. How terrible to be caught between two warring parents. Yet Johanna had done well on her own, partly because of Virginia Marston. They couldn't have loved each other more or been any closer if they had been sisters. Once more, Ginny grieved over Johanna's loss.

She had to quell the brief desire to hurt Ben as he'd hurt her best friend. What was the truth about Ben, Stella, and the shrouded past? Did he truly love and want Johanna? Was she more than property to him? If not for that coin stuck in the corner of Stella's trunk, she and Johanna wouldn't have even known her father had tried to reach her and recover her many times. Had Stella lied when she accused Ben of being abusive? How could a woman who had lived in open sin for years and who had threatened to blackmail her husband with a scandal be trusted? On the same hand, how could a man who had allowed himself to lose his daughter to avoid that scandal be trusted and respected? Who would have believed the Ben she saw could be cruel to his wife and baby? Yet Ben had feared that threat enough to give up his only child. If, Ginny mused, that was the only threat Stella had held over his head. Besides, Ben had Stone, who was loved and accepted as his blood son.

"Why shouldn't my traitorous father support and protect his daughter?" Johanna had asked her. "He refused to do so years ago. He forced Mother and me into a terrible situation. He sinned, and he must pay. My Mother is dead because of him. I've lived in loneliness and fear because of him. Promise me you'll learn the truth about my father and the past. Promise me you'll make him suffer as he made us suffer. But if he isn't guilty of the things Mother said, give him a little happiness before you tell him I'm gone. Let him see and enjoy me through you; we're so much alike."

Oh, Johanna, do you realize what you asked of me? What if I make the wrong choice? What if he kills me after he learns the truth? What if Ben's adopted son doesn't want me back to share the ranch with him? This midnight secret can prove to be more dangerous than either of us imagined.

*　*　*

The next four days passed swiftly and more easily than Ginny had imagined they would. Ranch life was fun and interesting. She came to like Ben, Nan, the foreman, Buck Peters, and all the hands. It was clear everyone admired and respected Bennett Chapman. She enjoyed riding the range, learning new skills, and getting to know Johanna's father. But the longer she continued her ruse, the more she came to trust and admire him, to be convinced he had changed over the years, to believe Johanna would have loved and accepted him, would have forgiven him. The longer her deceit continued, the harder it became to expose the truth and the deeper she became ensnared.

Ginny was certain it would break Ben's heart to discover the cruel deception and to learn his daughter was dead. She didn't know how much longer she could go on tricking him. This ruse of daughter and father caused her to yearn for her own father. She was so worried about him. The length of time between his last letter and her departure created doubts about his survival and fears about confronting his enemies. What if she couldn't prove he had been murdered and unmask the culprit? What if the silver mine had been claimed by someone else? What if she made it to Colorado and found nothing and was stranded there? Would it be so horrible of her to live out her days as Johanna Chapman? Yes, because she *wasn't* Johanna.

If only Stone would get back so she could study the two men together; she could discover then if the adopted man meant more to Ben than Johanna did, as Stella had alleged. She had sneaked into his room once to see what she could learn about him. There were plenty of clothes in the drawers and closet of the neat masculine room—casual and dress garments. Yet she found it strange and intriguing that most of them appeared new or hardly worn. She surmised Stone had those he favored and wore most frequently with him on his trip. She held up several items and decided he was over six feet tall and had a lean build. There were no photographs in his room or in the house to tell

325

her how he looked. But there was a portrait of Stella and Johanna hanging over the fireplace in the parlor, painted before they left home. There were many books in Stone's room, so obviously he liked to read. But she found no letters or keepsakes to reveal more about him.

She had noticed that Ben and Nan didn't talk about Stone. When she'd asked questions about him, they had told her they wanted her to meet him and form her own opinion. She thought that odd since he was "her brother" and Ben's acclaimed "joy and delight," according to Stella.

Ginny had ceased asking any questions and just observed. She knew Ben's room was on one end of the bottom floor of the two-story house and Nan's was on the other. No woman had ever been mentioned by anyone. Ginny wondered if he had a lady friend nearby as he didn't leave home except to ride with his hands. If Stella had told the truth about his lusty diversions, perhaps he no longer enjoyed them at his age.

Too, Ben could have become romantically interested in Nan over the years, living in such close proximity with her for so long. Ginny suspected Nan had a deeper and stronger affection for Ben than a cook and housekeeper who was like a "sister" to him would normally possess. Sometimes she caught Nan gazing at Ben with what appeared to be love and desire in her eyes. Now that Ben was free, perhaps they could explore their feelings. That would be romantic, Ginny decided with a smile.

Love and romance . . . Where had they gotten her? Into pain and loneliness, she replied to herself. *Where are you, Steve? Do you miss me as much as I miss you, or at all? Have you even returned to Fort Smith to check on me? Should I write or telegraph you, tell you where I am? No, not yet . . . as soon as I finish my task here. I love you and want you so much. Please feel the same way about me.*

Friday, news came that the wagontrain from Georgia had arrived in town. Ben persuaded her to let the boys recover her possessions to prevent friends of the outlaws from discovering her whereabouts and coming to seek revenge on her for helping to capture them. She sent letters to Lucy, Mary, Ruby, and Ellie. She explained the "truth" to them and asked for their addresses to write them in the future. She hated not seeing them a last time, but Ben's advice seemed wise.

When Justin "Buck" Peters returned with her possessions, Ginny thanked the foreman. She hurried to her room to read notes from her four friends with whom she had shared so much. Steve hadn't returned to the wagontrain, and the journey from Vicksburg had passed without trouble.

Ginny unpacked her clothes, and Nan helped her put them away. She lay her prized doll on the bed, her heart overjoyed by its safe return. She told Nan it was a gift from a friend at school, and the woman believed her.

As Ginny dressed for dinner, she thought of the money in the drawer nearby. Ben had given it to her so his "Johanna" wouldn't feel vulnerable again as she had since "her mother's death." Ginny knew it was a sufficient sum to buy a stage ticket to Colorado City, as she'd asked the agent the amount in Dallas before leaving the station. She had given Ben six days of happiness and release from his tormenting guilt. She couldn't punish him for his past deeds because she didn't believe he deserved it, as he had whipped himself enough over the years for his mistakes. Ben would have Nan and his "son" to comfort him after he learned the awful truth of his daughter's death. What reason did she have to stay on the ranch a day longer? She had fulfilled her midnight secret to Johanna as best she could. She had her friend's letter to back up her claims. Why stay?

The following morning told her: her monthly flow began. It would require three days to complete, three days better spent here than cooped up like chickens in a coach where baths weren't possible. Tuesday, she decided, she would make a decision about when to tell Ben the truth and when to depart, if the deception didn't cause him to throw her out instantly.

At least she wasn't pregnant, something she hadn't considered in the heat of passion with Steve Carr. How tragic and ironic it would be for his first child to be born in his father's footsteps, an embittered bastard. Love could compel people to do foolish and reckless things. But was love worth any price one had to pay, any sacrifice one had to make? She couldn't answer, considering what she had done and would do for the love of Johanna, her father, and Steve Carr.

She hadn't asked Ben why had Stella left; she would allow him to carry that damaging secret to his grave. She decided she would confess and leave the ranch next week.

At Fort Smith, the man in Ginny's thoughts and dreams was receiving grim news on his twenty-eighth birthday. Steve couldn't believe she was gone from his life. Her letter to him was bittersweet. He was angry she hadn't gotten his explanation; Captain Cooper hadn't returned until after her departure. No one had seen her leave. She wasn't listed as a boat passenger or a stage passenger. Her horse was gone. He had asked Jake if there was a soldier named Myers who had been sent to Texas, the only female traveling alone that day. He had despised hearing there was, and her name was Cora, a brown-haired woman of around twenty years.

Why, Steve worried, had she vanished? How had she done it with such cunning and thoroughness? Even with his skills, it was hopeless to track her now after so much time had lapsed. This loss, atop that of his best friend, gave him feelings of loneliness and anguish, more intense than any he'd endured before meeting Anna. She had told him he picked at his wounds, kept them raw and open, and refused to let anyone, including her, help tend and heal them. He had realized that was true. She had told him that when the right time and circumstances came along, he would be ready and willing and eager to let go of the painful past. He knew now that Anna was that circumstance and this was the time for a fresh beginning.

He admitted that his troubles had molded him into a strong man, as she'd said, even stronger than he had comprehended until she entered his life. The bitterness eating at him was destroying him, might have destroyed his only hope for a bright future if Anna decided not to contact him. Steve couldn't blame her for disappearing, as his behavior did appear uncaring and traitorous. That wasn't true. He had come to realize he loved and wanted Anna Avery. Now, she possibly was lost to him, lost because she didn't know of those feelings he'd been afraid to expose to her. He was worried about the mystery hinted at in her letter. She could be in danger this very minute and he was helpless to rescue her. Spirits, he hated that feeling.

He wondered what task she had to do, where, what lies she had told him, and what she had wanted to confess. If only he'd seen her that night before he left. If only he hadn't left her escape money or given it to Jake. If only he'd put his note in with the money. He had trusted the clerk with the cash but not with a private message he had feared a nosy person might read.

It was too late for hindsight. On the wagontrain she had reached out to him, but he had pushed her away. "You solve your problems and I'll solve mine," he had told her. He could have learned her secrets long ago if he hadn't been stubborn and defensive. She admitted lying to him in the letter so, when he found her again, she should be as understanding and forgiving as he would be with her. She loved him and wanted him; wasn't that what her message implied? The next month or two would be terrible for him, waiting and hoping she didn't change her mind. He had told Jake Cooper he would keep in touch by telegram. He could hardly wait to hear from her so he could go to her and tell her the overdue truth.

He prayed she hadn't deceived him about being involved with the Klan. Timothy Graham hadn't known anything about her when he was arrested in St. Louis, or claimed he hadn't. Surely she had been only escaping the traitorous gang when he rescued her on the trail. Surely she wasn't heading back South to aid the KKK again, to help them replace their losses, and to succeed where her father had failed. From what she'd told him, she had just motives for being vengeful. Wherever she had gone, he hoped she was safe and that he would hear from her sooner than she'd said. While he was waiting, he would take care of another tormenting matter, then complete one final job: finding and killing his best friend's murderer.

Ginny fretted over allowing twelve days to pass since her arrival without finding the courage to expose her identity and ruse to Ben and Nan. She accused herself of being a coward, afraid of causing Ben pain, afraid of leaving these happy surroundings to place herself in peril in Colorado on the slim hope her father was still alive. What if she wrote to Steve in care of Captain Cooper, told him where to locate her, and asked him to come guide her to Colorado? What if he hadn't returned to Fort Smith? What if he *never* returned to Fort Smith? What if he was dead, too, which was a possibility as he lived such a dangerous existence? Could she throw away all she had here on the ranch to chase uncertain dreams? She must, as she had no right to Johanna's life. She had given Charles joy by playing his Anna. She had given Ben joy by playing his Johanna. It was her father's turn to receive joy. Both deceptions had been trouble and anguish. It was time to be herself.

Tomorrow, she would go into town and send Steve a telegram. She would pray she meant enough to him for him to come help her out of this predicament. As soon as she heard from him or he arrived, she would tell Ben everything and hope he forgave her.

She continued to dress for dinner, one of the most enjoyable times of the day. Yet she was apprehensive and didn't know why.

Ben smiled and said, "Stone, you're finally back, Son. I have a surprise for you; your sister's returned from England. And Stella is dead."

The younger man looked stunned. "Johanna's here?"

"Yep, and she's beautiful. You don't have to worry; I told you half of this ranch is yours when I die. Nothing can change that; it's in my will."

Stone saw the glow in his father's eyes. He had to struggle not to let bitterness storm through him. "Did you tell her about me?" He watched Ben lower his head in shame. Well-deserved, he decided.

"No, Son, and you know why I can't. Please understand."

"Protection of the Chapman name is the most important thing to you," Stone accused. "Not me or Mother or your precious Johanna."

"It's your name, too, Son. You don't want it stained, either."

"Mine by adoption only. I'd rather have it the right way. Being your half heir isn't as important as people knowing what blood runs in my veins. All my life I've had to lie about who and what I am. How can you say you love me and want me when you've denied me since birth, when you made me a bastard in everyone's eyes? My mother has loved you and served you for almost thirty years. Even after Stella found out about us and left, you still refused to marry her. Now that she's dead, you'll probably still find excuses not to do it. Yet you claim you love her and want her, too."

Stone closed the distance between them to tower over his slump-shouldered father. He knew he was hurting the man, but he couldn't stop himself, as he wanted to open Ben's eyes. Now that he knew what love was, he had ammunition to fire at the man who had denied and hurt him and his mother, had hurt Johanna and *her* mother. First he had to wound his father, then help heal that injury for all their sakes. "How could a decent man take two women to his bed at the same time? You selfishly and cruelly used both of them, Father. You've cheated all of us. You still don't think Mother is good enough to be Mrs. Bennett Chapman because she's Apache, enemy and scourge of the whites. Because I carry your blood, I'm good enough to be adopted and to inherit half of your ranch, but because my mother is Indian and I'm a half-breed I don't deserve for people to know I'm your son, that I have the Chapman name by right of birth and blood. I loved you. I worked for you and with you for years. I would have done anything for you. I wouldn't have known the truth about myself if I hadn't overheard you and Stella quarrel that day because you'd have never told me. For the rest of my miserable life, you'd have let me think I was the bastard of an Indian . . ." He could never call his beloved mother a whore as most had whispered but never dared to say aloud because she was under the protection of Bennett Chapman. "I even had to pretend she wasn't my mother so no one would guess the truth about you two. That isn't fair, Father. Can't you understand that?"

"I've hurt you worse than I realized, Stone, and I'm deeply sorry. But this isn't the time to beat the past like a disobedient dog. Johanna will be down shortly, Son. She doesn't know about us and this isn't the time or way for her to learn that awful secret. Let's talk about this later, please."

"It is always 'later' with you, Father. Have you ever feared it might be too late for us when you decide to acknowledge me? When I have children, I want them to know who their grandparents are, what their bloodline is."

"Times and people change, Son."

"Not that I've seen, and I've been everywhere. People will always hate and reject Indians because people like you refuse to show your acceptance of them. I need peace, Father. That's why I came home, to seek it. If we can't settle this soon, it will be too late for us. Is that what you want?"

Ben looked at his troubled son. "Be patient with me, Stone. I know you're right. I've been a coward for too long about a lot of things. I love you. Let me find the best time and way to explain this to your sister before we reveal the truth to everyone. I will, Son, I promise. Soon there will be no more lies and denials. But let's drop it for now; I hear Johanna coming."

"All right, Father, one last chance." He needed a strong

drink to calm his tension after the difficult talk and before a reunion with his "sister."

As Ginny entered the room she noticed the man with his back to her and his head lowered as he poured a glass of whiskey from a liquor cabinet. She tensed when she surmised it must be Stone and deceitful work loomed before her.

"Your brother's home, Johanna. Stone, you remember your sister . . ."

The man turned and his jaw went slack. His dark eyes widened in disbelief, then narrowed in suspicion. What pretense was she pulling now? How had she discovered his carefully guarded identity? What did she want from his family with this daring ruse? Force them to force him to marry her for dishonoring her? Women did that. Before he could think whether or not to expose her, he murmured, "Anna Avery, what are you doing here?"

Ginny went pale and trembled. Her heart pounded. Her lips parted. Her eyes gaped at him in shock. Her gaze slipped to the two Colts with S.C. on their butts: not for Steve Carr but for . . . Stella had lied or been wrong about Stone's age; he wasn't twenty-five! He had deceived her all along! He had made her feel sorry for him by claiming to be an embittered loner, a penniless drifter, a worthless bastard! She had loved him, believed him, surrendered to him! He was just like his father, a selfish user of women! He had told those lies to justify deserting her after they . . . Heavens above, if she truly had been Johanna . . . "You're Stone Chapman, Ben's adopted son? You lied to me, you sorry . . ." Anger and resentment choked off her remaining word. How could he have been so cruel and cold?

"You two look and sound as if you've met before," Ben remarked.

Stone and Ginny looked at a curious Ben, having forgotten his presence during their shock. Both wondered what to say and do now.

Chapter 15

"We have, Father. He's the man I told you about, the one on the wagontrain," Ginny finally replied, "the one who rescued me from those outlaws during the time I was pretending to be Charles Avery's daughter. He told me his name was Steve Carr, and I believed him, believed everything he told me."

Stone realized she looked genuinely stunned to see him and to learn this news, but he hesitated to trust her and resisted believing her. He recalled how she'd invited him to come home with her, but never suspected she meant to *his* home. But she wasn't Johanna Chapman; she couldn't be Johanna; it must, his troubled mind reasoned, be another trick. "Pretended to be Avery's daughter?" he scoffed. "You're saying you aren't?"

Ben chuckled and said, "Of course she isn't, Son; she's Johanna. She told me all about her adventures with you while she was trying to get home to us."

Stone's narrowed and chilled gaze glared into the woman's eyes, which were filled with . . . panic and anguish. If she wanted him as a man, why claim to be kin? Of course, he was allegedly adopted! Was her scheme to insinuate herself into his family, win and wed him, then confess her deceit? What if the real Johanna came home and exposed her? Yet she looked so alarmed and so vulnerable, so betrayed by him. Maybe the little trickster hadn't known Steve Carr was really Stone Chapman. Could he allow her to carry out her pretense so he could have her? No, because there was a vital secret she didn't know that would prevent that. Only by exposing her could he have her, if he could trust and forgive her. "All about them, Father?"

"Yes," Ben answered, ignorant of the situation between them. He hurriedly glossed over what he had been told about the reasons she'd left England and how she'd made it home. "Saints be praised, I have you to thank for saving her life. She said you were tough on her, but we're both glad you were. Her daring ruse as Anna Avery held surprises she hadn't expected. I'm happy you were there to help her. One of those undercover jobs of yours, I suppose. It's dangerous to be a Special Agent for the Justice Department, Stone. I wish you'd give it up and come back to the ranch for keeps. We need you here, Son . . . Well, aren't you going to hug your sister?"

The last word sliced through Stone like a white-hot knife carving out his resentful heart. After hearing Ben's revelations—things only the real Johanna could know—he couldn't delude himself. When he'd told the Fort Smith hotel clerk he was her brother, he couldn't have imagined that would prove to be the case. Spirits help them, he had made love to his own half sister! Thank the Spirits she didn't know the wicked truth. Johanna believed he was adopted, no blood kin to her, so she didn't realize what they had done . . . Unless Stella had told her daughter the truth about him. If so, she knew and must be tormented to discover who Steve Carr really was.

As Ben went into deeper detail about their adventures, Stone didn't listen to the tale he already knew. He was angry and bitter that he'd finally found a woman to love, only to learn she was his sister and a future together was impossible. He had to find a way to forget his forbidden feelings for her. Worse, if she didn't know the truth, and he prayed she didn't, he couldn't tell her why he would reject her. If she had returned home for revenge or for profit, her greed and hatred had ruined both of their lives. If only they had trusted each other enough on the trail to confess their secret identities before things had gone too far between them. He had himself to blame; she had tried to confess to him several times, and he had halted her. He cursed Fate for allowing this cruel trick to be played on them. How could he accept what he had done? How could he stop desiring her? How could he forget she desired him, might love him, and might be devastated by the awful truth? He hadn't deserted her at Fort Smith as she believed, yet she planned to contact him soon. What was she thinking at this difficult moment?

Ginny wasn't listening to Ben, either; she was ensnared by doubts and questions. How could she expose her lies to her traitorous love and his deluded father? Yet anger at her ruse might soften the news of Johanna's death. She feared both men might aim their vengeance at her, perhaps have her arrested for her dishonest action, as it could be labeled fraud. If only she'd told "Steve" she was Virginia Marston. Of course that would have evoked a much different confrontation at this time. She would already be exposed by Stone. She didn't know or trust the man she loved, so she mustn't confess the truth yet, even to soothe Stone. She would leave an explanatory and apologetic letter behind when she left for Colorado. From what she'd observed on the trail, he wasn't one to dupe. After pretending to be Anna and Johanna, he'd think her a liar and greedy schemer; he'd never believe she loved him and had made reckless mistakes.

If Stone had feelings for her, he would behave differently at this moment. Being adopted, he had no reason not to reach out to her. Unless he couldn't get past the word "sister" and was worried about seducing his adopted father's daughter. They weren't blood kin, nor were Johanna and Stone, so they hadn't committed incest. Perhaps he resented her for being Johanna and for returning to share Ben's love and possessions. Maybe he didn't love her and feared she'd make demands on him. Perhaps it was only hurt pride over being fooled by her, and the belief the love she proclaimed was also a lie. She longed to reveal the truth about everything, but something about Stone compelled her to stay silent for now. Despite all he had done to her, she loved him and wanted him. There was so much she wanted to say and to ask, but not in front of Ben. She must speak with Ste—no, Stone—in private first. How could he scorn her when he was a liar and deceiver, too?

With recovered wits and poise, Ginny said, "Mr. Avery did have a daughter named Anna, Stone. What I said about her was true." She gave a partial explanation for her pretense as Anna Avery. "You know why I left Fort Smith if you returned there and was given my letter."

"I did, but you never got mine." He pulled it from his pocket and handed it to her. He quickly realized he shouldn't have, but he couldn't yank it from her grasp and evoke curiosity in Ben. "Jake Cooper had it but never got a chance to pass it along because he was called away on a mission. Doesn't matter. You're home now and safe."

Ginny was thrilled and astonished to discover he had left her a message; she could hardly wait to read it. She stuffed the paper into her dress pocket. "We'll talk later. We have a lot of catching up to do."

Stone caught a hint in her tone about what she wanted to discuss with him. He couldn't allow it, not yet. She had been duped by Avery and had been drawn to Steve while vulnerable and grieving over her mother's loss, not over that of a best friend as Charles had told him. "We'll have plenty of time to talk later."

"Maybe we should talk tonight, Son," Ben said.

Stone also caught the hint in his father's tone and gaze, and froze in despair. He couldn't let Johanna learn they'd sinned against the Bible and the law by surrendering to their feelings for each other. He'd have to convince his father to conceal their secret forever. It was ironic and agonizing that the reason he'd wanted it exposed had turned out to be the reason it couldn't: his love for this woman. He should never have lowered his guard and taken her. Spirits help him, he still loved and desired her! "No, Father, this isn't the right time to finish discussing that private matter. We'll do it at a much later date. Dead business is better left buried."

"If you say so, Son," Ben replied, confused but relieved. "You two chat a minute while I tell Nan to set another plate on the table. I'm glad you're home, Son; we can be a real family now."

After Ben left the room, Ginny and Stone stared at each other.

"Why did you lie to me?" she asked. "Was it only so you could seduce me then ride away with me thinking you were too embittered to commit yourself to me or to any woman? You have love, a family, and a good life here. All those things you told me were only to make me susceptible to your siege. You aren't a scout or hired manhunter; you're a lawman, a secret agent. You used me and betrayed me, Stone. Why?"

When tears filled her hazel eyes, he couldn't resist pulling her into his arms and telling her how sorry he was. She nestled her face against his chest, and he felt her tremble. He had to be gentle, compassionate, and comforting without confessing his love and while letting her down as easily as possible. He realized for the first time that he had honor, deep feelings, and a conscience. He was surprised to discover those traits and emotions within him. "I've never done this with a woman before and I didn't mean to do it with you. I was attracted to Anna Avery, but I didn't want to be caught by her; I tried to tell you that many times." *Shu*, it was hard to lie to her, to bring her more anguish, to touch her without kissing her, to master his craving for her. "I am a bastard by birth; I didn't lie about that part. My father has never claimed me, and Ben's adopting me doesn't make up for that denial. I don't live here and I only came for a short visit. Ben and I didn't get along. I came to settle our differences, then ride on to . . . do another job."

Ginny wasn't sure what he was telling her. She had to make him be clearer before she decided how to make her confession. "You don't understand, Stone; this is all my fault. I should have told you who I am. Things can still work out for us; we aren't kin. I want you."

Stone forced them apart. His turmoil was enormous and

knifing. He was consumed by love and desire for her. He had to end it here and now. "Forgive me, Johanna, but there can't be *anything* between us. I like you and I enjoyed being with you, but that's all. I can't love you. Our little deceits with each other were painful and costly. We have to forget what happened between us; and it won't happen again, I promise. If it were anybody except you who had duped me, I would kill her. Nothing riles my temper more than lies and ruses. You're a beautiful woman and a mighty tempting one, so I couldn't resist making love to you. I shouldn't have."

Was he saying his feelings had been nothing more than physical desire? How could he speak so coldly about "lies and ruses" when he himself practiced them? She fused her somber gaze to his impenetrable one. "Then you don't feel the same way about me that I feel about you?"

Stone forced himself to reply, "No, and I'm sorry. I couldn't tell you who and what I was on the trail, but I would have returned to Fort Smith and confessed the truth. Despite how I tricked you, I didn't want you pining over me. I had to complete my assignment and make certain you weren't involved. If you had been, you could have betrayed me to other Klansmen. I sensed you were withholding things, but I never suspected what they were. If I could change what happened between us, I would. Anybody who does what I did to you for selfish reasons isn't worth dried mud on your boot. You were suffering from your mother's loss and caught up in a scary pretense, so you turned to me because you thought I was a strong shoulder to lean on. I'm not the man for you."

She had to make a last, desperate attempt to reach him. "Yes, you are. We must believe we were thrown together for a special reason. We can resolve this matter. I love you, Stone. I've loved you and wanted you since that first day in Georgia. No matter what happens between us, I'll always feel that way. You aren't and you'll never be a brother to me. I want us to have a life together, here or anywhere."

Stone feigned a scowl. "Spirit help us if that's the truth."

"It is. I know I've deceived you in the past and you have cause not to trust me, but I swear I'm telling the truth about my feelings for you."

"Forget me," he ordered. "Forget what happened between us."

Ginny caressed his cheek. "Never, and I don't want to. I love you."

Stone stepped away from her disturbing reach and touch. "Then we're in trouble. I never meant to hurt you, Johanna, and I hate hurting you tonight. You'll come to realize I'm not right for you. I don't feel the same way about you. It was physical, nothing more. Don't ever tell Father you love me and we . . . If you do, I'll leave and never return." He knew he had to leave tonight anyway to put distance between them.

Ginny winced at the cruel disclosure and his threat. Yet something urged her not to believe him. She thought, *You're home now, so I'll prove to you you're wrong about us. I'll tempt you and chase you every minute I can. You won't be able to resist me.* But if what he said was true, she best not expose herself to this dangerous man.

Ben returned and smiled at both moody people. "Nan said supper will be ready in about twenty minutes." She'd also told him she'd heard her son arrive and had been listening to their talks.

"I need to see . . . Aunt Nan a minute," Stone said, "I'll speak with you later, Father. You, too, Johanna. It's good to see both of you again." Stone left the room to visit a moment with his mother before he left for a while.

Ben smiled at the nervous woman. "Did you and Stone have a nice chat? You both look a little edgy. Is there a problem between you?"

"No, Father. We just had a tiny quarrel before he left Fort Smith. I can't blame him; he did believe I was Anna Avery and that I might be involved in that assignment he was working on with the Klan. He is miffed with me for not telling him who I am, but he'll get over that soon. We thought we'd become

340

friends, even though we continued to deceive each other. I think that was because we both had some secrets we were afraid to expose."

Ben looked as worried as he felt. "You two aren't . . . I mean, you didn't come to like each other too much, did you?"

Ginny forced out merry laughter. "Of course not. Stone acted as hard and cold to me as his name. He was tough on me, but he's nice. I like him. I hope he'll be around a long time so we can get better acquainted."

"I hope so, too. We've had problems in the past, but we're ready and willing to make peace now."

"That's good, Father, because you both deserve it."

After a short while, Ben suggested that they go to the table.

Nan entered the dining room. "Stone had to leave, Ben," she informed him. "He's gone. He said not to worry, that he'll return in a week or two."

"Gone without a word," Ben murmured. "Is he all right?"

Nan smiled at the worried man to calm him. "He's fine, Ben. He just didn't want to say good-bye to you two. He only had a short time to visit. He's working on a very important job. He was in a rush, but promised to return very soon," she stressed. "Now, dinner is ready."

Somehow Ginny managed to eat the delicious meal and to make light conversation. She couldn't surmise why Stone had departed in such a hurry. Perhaps he needed to get away from her. Temptation or remorse? To give both of them time to adjust to and accept their real identities? At least he had said he would return soon, she could work on him then or confess and leave.

When the meal finally ended, Ginny needed to be alone. She might have found her love again, only to lose him to his unrequited emotions. She sensed a curious strain in the air, though Ben and Nan tried to conceal it. Something was afoot, she decided. The two looked worried and sad, and hadn't mentioned Stone again. Was it true he didn't live here? Was it true there were problems between the two men? Had finding her here—the blood child and other heir to the ranch—created more trouble? Perhaps Stone had given Nan a message to pass to Ben. "I'll help you clear the table, Nan. I'm exhausted tonight. So much has happened today."

"You go on to bed, Johanna. I'll help Nan."

Ginny pretended to do as he suggested, but his eagerness to get her out of the room intrigued her. She saw Ben rise to assist the unusually quiet woman. She pressed herself against the wall to listen to their talk.

"Why did he leave in such a rush, Nan? Was he upset?"

"I heard what you two said to each other before Johanna joined you. That was hard for him, *Tsine*," she pointed out, calling him "my love" in Apache as she always did in private. "You two must make peace. You must learn to forgive, to understand, to accept each other. He's your son, Ben. It's only natural for him to want everybody to know that truth. He's had to live a lie all of his life. People wouldn't dare insult Stone Chapman to his face, but they do so behind his back. If you hadn't adopted him, they wouldn't let him sit in the same room with them. People hate Apaches; that's why you couldn't marry me, why you couldn't lay claim to our son. He needs you, Ben, your love and acceptance. This bitter life he's lived has almost destroyed him. He's reaching out to you; reach back before it's too late."

Ginny couldn't believe what she was hearing: Stone was Ben and Nan's child. Ben had adopted his own bastard son. Nan was Apache, not Spanish. Stone was half Indian, what some people called a half-breed. He knew the truth and wanted his father to acknowledge him. Ginny's eyes widened and her heart thudded. That meant Stone was Johanna's half brother and knew it. That meant he thought he had made love to his . . .

"Do you think Johanna knows about Stone?" Ben fretted aloud.

"How could she, *Tsine*, unless Stella was that cruel?"

"Stella was cruel, cold, and vengeful. She stole my daughter from me when she learned about you and Stone. She threat-

342

ened a terrible scandal if I went after Johanna. Lordy, how I wanted that girl back. I loved her and needed her, just like I do Stone. I should have called Stella's bluff. I shouldn't have let Johanna suffer all those years. I shouldn't have let Stone suffer all those years. I've been a selfish coward, Nan. I should have married you and dared anybody to scorn me for doing so. How could I have been such a blind fool? How could I have believed I needed a white wife, a genteel lady? I'm partly to blame for Stella's wicked flaws."

"No, *Tsine*, she had them before she married you."

"When Johanna learns Stone is our son, she'll hate me and I might lose her again. She'll think Stella had good reason to leave a man who loved another woman and had a son with her."

"But you weren't married to Stella when we had Stone."

"But we loved each other when I married her and we've never stopped loving each other. Johanna doesn't know how evil her mother was. After she learned she couldn't give me any more children, she didn't want me to touch her again. But she let other men do it. She laughed in my face plenty of times when I accused her of what I knew was true. Every trip she made she carried on like a harlot. But she was smart enough not to be seen by the wrong people. I tried every way I could to get my daughter back: I threatened to expose her wickedness and I even tried to bribe her. I'm not even convinced she wanted Johanna, she just didn't want me to have her. Lordy, that woman was so cruel, I'm almost happy she's dead. How can I break my child's heart by telling her such things? But if I don't, she'll never understand about you and Stone, about why I didn't come after her."

"You fear Stone will tell her when he returns soon? He won't, *Tsine*, he understands why we can't reveal the truth."

"Does he, Nan? It isn't fair to him."

"You're leaving him half of this ranch. You gave him your name."

"That isn't enough for a father to share with his only son."

"Stone Thrower is a man, *Tsine*, a strong and brave man, a smart man. He accepts what cannot be changed. He told me this before leaving."

"You heard what he said to me earlier, so what changed his mind?"

"If you claim him, *Tsine*, he'll be branded a bastard publicly. Our sin and love for each other will be exposed. He only wanted to see if you loved him enough to take such risks. You were willing, so that filled his hunger. He said it would be wrong and painful to all of us for the truth to come out now. He urged me to beg you not to tell Johanna. He said he will be content to live his life as your adopted son."

"But will *I*, Nan? Stella hated him because she knew how much I loved him. She despised him because he was half Indian. Many times she tried to get me to send that 'little Injun orphan' away. That's what she called him! She didn't mind your being here because you served her hand and foot. She was jealous of every minute Stone and I spent together."

"Which were many, *Tsine;* Stone Thrower was like your shadow."

"He loved me so much before he learned of my deceit."

"He still loves you. If not, he wouldn't keep returning."

"Every time he leaves home, I miss him. I hope he returns for good, and he and Johanna get along."

"They did as children. No matter what Stella thought or said, you didn't give one child more love and attention than the other."

"I kept thinking if I let Stella have her way, she'd relent. But she never did. She died with her sins on her head."

"Stella could not accept you loved me, not her. She could not accept I gave you a son when she couldn't. She was proud and vain."

"I should have beaten some sense into her. I should have locked her in her room and never let her take Johanna away."

"You could never harm anyone, *Tsine*, not even her."

"Much as I came to hate and resent her, I'm sorry she ended

up in such a bad way. I'm sure she's scarred our daughter with her wickedness."

"Johanna seems fine to me. Don't worry about her. She's proven she has her father's blood, his courage and strength. So does our son. When he returns, we will be a real family at last. I couldn't love Johanna more if she were my daughter. I'm so happy she's come home."

"What would I do without you, Nan?"

"Or I without you, *Tsine*, my love?"

"We'll have to be careful with Johanna in the house. But one day it—"

"Do not speak such beautiful words until they can come true. When the hatred of my people lessens, then we can speak of a future as one. But things are growing worse these days instead of better. You must not risk your name and place in this land. People would not sell and buy cattle from a man with an Indian wife and half-breed son. The truth could destroy you."

"I'm not sure I believe that anymore. Stella is gone; I'm free. Why would it be so despicable to marry the woman I love, the woman I've loved for thirty years?"

"We both know why, *Tsine*, we both know why."

Ginny crept to Johanna's room, having risked eavesdropping long enough to glean a few clues to help her make her final decision. She asked herself how Ben could not grasp how hurt and humiliated Stella had been when she discovered his long-time romance with another woman, a trusted woman who shared their home, a woman who had borne her husband a son. Surely Stella's vengeance, even if wrong, was understandable, perhaps even normal under those circumstances. She pondered how Nan could be the lover of a man who had married another woman, could share a relationship with him beneath the same roof that his wife did. How could their son, because Stone knew who his father was, accept such conditions as laid down by his deceitful parents? Was he just as selfish and greedy? Did he only want his share of this wealth? He had his father's name and was

345

accepted as Stone Chapman, but everyone believed he was a bastard.

Bastard . . . Her lover hadn't lied about experiencing the sting of that word. Yet he was fortunate he was loved and wanted enough by his father to be at least half claimed by Ben.

Had he rejected her downstairs because he believed they were half brother and sister? Or did he truly not want her? It seemed as if Stone was always fleeing difficult situations rather than confronting them. He had been hurt so many times in the past that she couldn't blame him.

What will you do to me when you discover my deception? You'll be happy I'm not Johanna and you haven't sinned with your sister. You won't have to risk Ben thinking you seduced his daughter for spite. Will you be understanding and forgiving? Will you be angry and vengeful for how I've hurt and duped you and your father? Will you be glad you're sole heir to this ranch? Will you want me as Virginia Marston?

Ginny waited two days for Stone to get over his shock and return so she could speak with him before talking to his father. She couldn't stop thinking about the letter Captain Cooper hadn't given to her. Did it mean Stone loved her and wanted her, or was that interpretation wishful dreaming on her part? Was he only going to "return for you" to guide her back to Georgia to Miss Avery? Was his "serious talk" only going to tell her what he had said the other night: not to pine over him, that his seduction of her was only the result of a physical need and weakness?

By Saturday night, June first, he hadn't returned, and she realized he might not come back any time soon. He had told her his next job could take weeks or months; she couldn't wait that long to get on with her personal task in Colorado. With the truth in his possession and her gone, Ben could tell Stone, if he contacted his father, that he had no reason to stay away from the ranch.

Stalling the inevitable only made it worse for everyone, especially for her. She needed her father, and Stone might be lost to her. If that was not the case, he'd know this time where to locate her at least, as she'd written him an enlightening letter. Perhaps it would be best if Ben told him the truth and if she wasn't present for his reaction.

Ginny walked downstairs and into the parlor where Ben was reading. "Mr. Chapman, I have to speak with you about a grave matter."

Ben lowered his newspaper and stared at her in confusion. "Why did you call me Mr. Chapman, Johanna? Is something wrong?"

"Yes, sir. Plenty. I don't know how or where to begin." She saw the man tense and grimace in dread of what might come from her lips. From the corner of her eye, she noticed Nan halt in the doorway.

"Is it about you and Stone? Did something happen between you two on the trail? You both acted so strangely. Is that why he left so suddenly?"

Ginny's heart pounded in matching dread. She didn't ask Nan to leave, as Stone's mother had a right to hear the truth. "Yes . . . and no, sir. I honestly don't know why Stone left as he did. I don't know what he thinks and feels about me, but I love him and I'd hoped he loved me," she revealed.

Ben paled. The paper shook then fell to the floor. *"What?"*

"As Anna Avery, I fell in love with Steve Carr."

"But you can't love him; he's your brother."

"No, sir, he isn't. I love him and want to marry him. I'm not—"

"That's impossible!" Ben shouted in dismay. He glanced at Nan, who stood motionless at the doorway, her face pale and body shaky.

"Only if Stone doesn't love me and want me," Ginny replied. "The other night he coldly spurned me. But I don't believe he doesn't love me, even if he honestly thinks he doesn't. I think, I *hope,* he left for a while to prevent me from causing a scene by

347

pressing the matter. Only if I reveal the truth to everyone can we resolve this."

"He could never marry you. He's your brother, Johanna, by blood. He's my real son, not adopted, mine and Nandile's. Oh, my God, that's why he tore out of here like a blue norther! He loves you, too."

Ginny kept herself from blurting out the shocking truth too soon. "I hoped he was falling in love with me. He denied it and rejected me before leaving. I'm praying he deceived me about his feelings."

"Did you hear me, Johanna? You're his half sister. This can't be. The Lord is punishing me for my past sins. He's let my children fall in love. God forgive me for keeping such painful secrets. What shall we do?" he murmured, looking at his secret love who stared at them both in disbelief and anguish.

"I'm leaving, sir, tomorrow or Monday, whichever you say."

"You can't. We'll work this out. I love you and need you."

Ginny made her tone and gaze as gentle as she could. "No, sir, you love and need Johanna. I'm not Johanna. I'm not your daughter, Mr. Chapman. I'm Virginia Anne Marston. Johanna and I were best friends at school. She asked me to come here and pretend to be her."

"Is this an act of revenge?" He questioned in angry despair.

"Not at all, she didn't hate you. She wanted to come home. She couldn't, so she sent me. Everything I've told you about her and Stella is true."

"This was a test, eh? I'll write her to come home immediately."

"You can't, sir. Johanna is . . . She's . . . She died on March thirteenth in Savannah, shortly after we arrived from England."

Ben leapt from his chair, the newspaper crackling beneath his boots as he crossed to her. He grasped her forearms and fused his gaze to hers, "Why are you doing this, Johanna?" he fumed. "So you can have Stone? You can't pretend you are another girl so you can live in sin."

Ginny wanted to escape his firm grasp and pleading gaze but she couldn't even try to do so. "I *am* Ginny Marston, sir, I swear it. Let me tell you all I know, then we can discuss it." She guided him to the couch, helped them both to sit down before her wobbly legs gave way, and faced the astonished man. She related her story as slowly, carefully, and compassionately as she could. "That's the truth, Mr. Chapman," she said in conclusion. "I loved her as a sister and did as she asked. I couldn't let you go on believing I was Johanna." She stood and looked down at him. "I'll leave immediately. I didn't want to hurt you, but I can't remain here any longer as your daughter. I must go search for my father, and I pray he's still alive."

"You lying, scheming witch," Ben cried out in pain. "How could you be so cruel? My Johanna would never do this to her father. You thought you'd come here and trick money out of me after her death. You're only confessing now because you know Stone will unmask you and kill you."

"No, Ben," Nan said from the doorway. She walked hurriedly to them. "Ginny has given you a part of your Johanna you could never have had if she hadn't come here. Can't you see how alike they are? I believe her. You owe her kindness and understanding for honoring Johanna's last wish; it must have been hard for her. You owe them to her for being honest. If she wanted anything from you, she would continue her ruse."

In torment, Ben accused, "She thinks she can get her hands on my ranch through my son, have him and everything else she wants."

"That isn't true, sir. I don't want your ranch or your money; I didn't want to do this for Johanna. I do want Stone, because I love him and I've been good for him. Hate me if you must; maybe that will help you accept Johanna's loss easier. Stella lied to her all those years, but she still loved you and wanted to come home. You would have been so proud of her. She was the most wonderful person I've ever known." Tears welled in Ginny's hazel eyes and rolled down her flushed cheeks. "I miss her so much. We couldn't have survived those years alone at school if

349

we hadn't had each other. She . . ." Ginny couldn't control the tears and anguish that flooded her heart.

Nan embraced her and cried with her because she believed her. Now she grasped Stone's suddenly black mood and his rush from the house: her son loved and wanted this woman. Ginny had changed and softened his heart. Their Life Circles had crossed many times because they were destined to overlap and become one. To deny and resist the truth would bring great suffering and defeat to all involved. The Great Spirit was at work in Stone Thrower's life; His hand was guiding her son toward his rightful path and fate: to Ginny and to peace with Ben. She must convince all of them this was meant to be.

When a small measure of control returned, Ginny said, "She would have loved it here and been so happy. When I saw her room and all those gifts you'd bought for her that she never received, it almost broke my heart. You don't know how happy it would have made Johanna to have gotten only one of them, only one letter, one word, one visit. It was wrong and cruel of Stella to hurt her just to spite you. I met Stella many times, so I believe all you said about her. I never told Johanna I didn't like or trust her mother because I didn't want to hurt her. I wish she could have lived to be here with you. It would have meant so much to her.

"I don't agree with what you did in the past, sir, but I understand it. Marry Nan and be happy," Ginny felt she had to give her opinion. "Don't care about what others might say; life is too short to deny yourselves one minute of joy together. Acknowledge Stone; he needs that so much, sir." Her eyes teared again as she said, "Somehow I think Johanna can see us and knows you didn't abandon her . . . I'll leave now. I'm sorry, sir, truly I am. It seems I've made too many mistakes lately trying to help myself and others. I'll leave a letter for Stone on the bed; please give it to him. He deserves to learn the truth from me."

Nan told the man she loved what she had been thinking

earlier. "It is fate, Ben. Do not make it harder on our son to accept the truth."

Ben surmised that this young woman was what had changed his son and was the reason Stone had returned to make peace and why he had mentioned children and grandchildren. His beloved daughter was lost forever, but he still had his son. He had come to like Ginny, and her motive for fooling him had come from the heart. Nan was right; Ginny had given him his daughter for a while. And, if Stone loved her and married her, he could lose him by rejecting her. He mustn't allow anguish and resentment to color his judgment. He halted her exit. "Stop! Don't go, Ginny. Please tell me more about her," he added in a strained voice.

Ginny turned and looked at the anguished man. "I'll tell you all I learned." She took a seat again and related the story of how they'd met, become best friends, how they'd lived in England, and returned to America. She revealed how Johanna was buried under Ginny's name and where. She asked Ben to bring his daughter's body home for reinterment. "Ask me anything you wish, sir, and I'll try to answer."

"Why didn't you confess this when Stone arrived?"

That wasn't the question she had expected. She blushed. "It's very complicated, sir. I've told you about our adventures together as Anna and Steve. I fell in love with him, but he had such bitterness and pain locked up inside and refused to allow anyone to get close to him." Ginny related some personal details about her feelings, but left out their physical relationship, which they probably suspected by now anyhow. Surely they of all people realized love and passion were irresistible and powerful.

"When he came home, I assumed he had lied to me about his troubled past. I believed he had deserted me in Fort Smith. You see, he left a letter for me with a friend, but I never received it. After he impulsively gave it to me the other night, I read his words to mean he did have deep feelings for me. But he treated me so distantly, spurning me completely. And then he left. I'm ashamed to say I eavesdropped on you and Nan after dinner that night. I realized Stone thought he . . . was falling in love with his sister, at least I hope that's why he rejected me and was troubled enough to leave. You see, Stella never told Johanna that secret, and it wasn't in any of the letters from you that we found. I was trying to give you as much time with 'Johanna' as possible, but I realized I had to end this ruse to keep from hurting everyone more. I came to like and respect you so much that I even wished at one time I never had to tell you. I had trapped myself and didn't know how to get free. In hindsight, the entire deception was foolish and cruel. So much happened so fast that I didn't think clearly or act wisely, but that's no excuse for what I did to you. I should have come here, told you the truth, then left. I'll admit, knowing my father might be dead and being so happy here, it was tempting to stay where I was loved and safe, but I want my father. I love him and miss him. I'm so afraid for him."

As tears brightened her hazel eyes, Ginny admitted, "Maybe I stalled so long and carried out this ruse because I'm afraid to go to Colorado and discover he's dead."

"Is there anything I can do to help, Ginny?"

"You've been too kind and generous already, Mr. Chapman. I don't deserve that after how I've duped you."

"You brought me the truth and a period of sunshine. If you hadn't been with Johanna all those years, she would have been miserable, and she would have died alone and frightened in Savannah. And I would have died never knowing she loved me and tried to get back to me. I owe you something for that."

"There is one thing you can do, sir: you can loan me stage fare to Colorado City. I'll return it by mail after I find my father. If he's . . . gone, I'll take a job there and repay you."

"Of course I'll do that. But why don't you wait until Stone returns? He can guide you there and protect you along the way."

"I think Stone will need time to adjust to the truth after you tell him. I feel it would be a mistake to wait for him. Stone's a

352

proud and troubled man. I've fooled him many times before, so another time might be more than he can accept and forgive. In the heat of his anger, he could say and do irreparable damage to any future relationship we might have. Besides, I'm only hoping and praying he feels the same way I do. He's never told me he loves me and wants me. In fact, he's always tried to convince me of the opposite."

Ginny decided to be bold and brave to help Ben understand and reach out to his son. "He tried to tell me he was a nothing. For such a strong and confident man in most areas, Stone has a low opinion of himself. He can't stand the thought of defeat or weakness, yet he's vulnerable in ways he doesn't admit. He doesn't believe he has anything to offer another person and he doesn't want to risk being hurt by getting close to anyone. He keeps a tight rein on his emotions, but I've seen the good and gentle side of him. He tries to protect himself by being cool and reserved. But I've seen him smile, laugh, show kindness and compassion, and risk his life for others; I think he shocked himself when he recognized feelings in himself he didn't know he possessed. I think he's softened and changed since we met; I hope because of me. He's a very special man with a lot of love inside him."

Ginny knew she might be going too far but she had to help her love. "For Stone to accept himself and to discard the burdens of the past, you have to accept him, Mr. Chapman. He has to know you love him and will do anything for him. Now that I know the truth about him, it helps me understand him better. He loves you and needs you. I believe that only you can save your son. Even though you adopted him, he still feels rejected by you. As for me and Stone, if I've seen him for the last time, I want to remember him the way I knew him as Steve Carr. I don't want him to feel he has to hurt me to prove he doesn't want me. Until he loves and accepts himself, he can't love and accept me. Does that make sense?"

Nan smiled. "Yes, Ginny, it does. You know my son well, and I think you're right about leaving. It would be best for

Stone to have time to think this out before he sees you. People in pain often strike out at those they love, it is only they who have the power to truly hurt you. We'll speak to him when he returns, and I'm sure he'll come after you."

Ginny's heart fluttered. "You do?"

Nan smiled again. "I will be surprised and disappointed if he doesn't."

"So will I," Ben added, his heart too heavy to allow him to smile at that moment. "When do you plan to leave? And how much money do you need for your ticket and expenses?"

"Monday morning, sir, but the money you gave me is plenty."

"I'll give you another fifty dollars for any unexpected problems. Send for more if you need it. And if you don't locate your father, you're welcome to return here."

Ginny was surprised and touched at his kindness. "Thank you, Mr. Chapman, Nan. You've both been wonderful to me. I'll pack tomorrow and go into town by dusk. The stage leaves early in the morning."

"Buck will drive you, if you're certain you won't stay longer."

"I can't, sir. One last thing: I didn't want you to think I was using this to soften and sway your opinion of me, so I waited to give it to you." Ginny withdrew a letter from her pocket. "This is from Johanna to you, explaining what she asked me to do and why. She wrote it in case I needed help to get out of trouble with you and perhaps the authorities. Please remember she didn't know the truth when she wrote it. All she had to base her feelings on were Stella's lies and those hazy letters from you that contradicted Stella's false claims."

Ben took the letter, almost dreading to read it. "Thank you, Ginny."

"Good night, sir. Good night, Nan. Thank you both again."

Monday morning, June third, Ginny climbed aboard a coach in Dallas to head for Gainesville to connect with the Oxbow

Route to retrace her recent journey from Fort Smith. From there she would travel on to Tipton, Missouri, and across Kansas to Colorado City. It would require fourteen days to complete her journey.

She was dressed in a dark-green traveling skirt and jacket with a cream-colored blouse. Her long hair was pinned atop her head and partly covered by a fashionable ivy hat. Her money was pinned inside her chemise as Nan advised to protect it from stage robbers. She was taking only part of her possessions; the rest she left at the ranch, along with her doll. When Ben sent for his daughter's body, he would recover the rest of her things, along with Johanna's, from Martha Avery.

She had spent a restless night in the hotel after bidding Ben and Nan farewell yesterday afternoon. Ginny was glad the letter from Johanna had been a kind and loving one that would help Ben accept her ruse. The couple, despite their grief, seemed happy about the future before them.

Ginny had hoped Stone would appear before her departure, but he hadn't. When he returned home, he would be given the explanatory letter she had left with his mother. She prayed he would be understanding and forgiving, and that he loved her.

She caught herself from lurching forward against another passenger as the driver popped his whip and set them into rapid and jostling motion. She was on the way to her next and final deception, again using the name Anna Avery while she searched for her father—or his killer.

CHAPTER 16

Virginia Marston journeyed across the beautiful Ozarks, over rolling green hills, through fertile valleys, past famed battlesites, and onto grassland that would almost extend to her destination. While the fatigued and bruised Ginny prepared to spend a restless night near Fort Leavenworth, a tormented Stone Chapman dismounted at his home, and spoke a silent prayer. *Spirits have mercy on both of us because I have to get this settled for my sister's sake. I can't let her suffer like I'm doing.*

He entered the house to find his father sitting at his desk. The rancher looked at him, then blinked back tears. Tears of joy and relief? Stone mused. He watched Bennett rise as if an old and beaten man.

"I'm glad you're home, Son," Ben said as he approached him. "I was afraid you wouldn't return. I've missed you and worried about you." Since Ginny exposed the awful truth and left for Dallas a week ago, the house had been too quiet. It had affected him like losing his daughter a second time. Grief and loneliness had plagued him, as had a fear of also losing his son, both resulting from his foolish and selfish mistakes.

Stone didn't know what to do when his father embraced him. Taken by surprise and sensing something was terribly wrong, he asked in an emotion-hoarsened voice, "Where's Johanna?"

Ben's arms dropped to his sides and his graying head lowered as he barely got out the painful words, "She's dead." Ben's head lifted with teary eyes as he continued. "But I have my son back. I love you, Stone, and I need you. I know I haven't been a real father to you, but I want that to change. Please help me do it."

The younger man's heart felt as cold as ice and as rigid as his name. His father's words and mood had registered in his mind, but his pounding heart could respond to only one thing. "She's . . . dead? How? When?"

"She became gravely ill during her return voyage from England," Ben murmured in anguish. "She died shortly after she reached America. Lord have mercy on my soul, I didn't even get to see my child again."

Stone feared the man had gone mad with grief and guilt. "What are you talking about, Father? She was here when I left over a week ago."

Ben's wits cleared and he hurried to explain, "No, Son, she's buried in Savannah. The woman we met was her best friend, like a sister to my lost Johanna. Ginny is the one who tended and buried Johanna, with Mr. Avery's help. My child had been deceived by her wicked mother. Stella told her awful lies about me. Ginny made her a deathbed promise to come here to wreak revenge and justice on me for betraying her. But the girl was too tender-hearted to carry it out. After she learned the truth from me, she confessed her ruse. She told me and Nan everything after you left. When she discovered you and Johanna were related she realized why you took off so fast. She didn't want to hurt any of us, so she confessed to her ruse and left."

Stone's heart drummed. His mouth felt dry. His head was dazed for a few moments. "She isn't my half sister?"

"No, her best friend. Ginny was heart-stricken over Johanna's loss; she loved my daughter. She told me all about their years at boarding school and how she got here from Savannah with your help."

Stone was astonished to learn it was only a ruse, like the one she pulled on the wagontrain with Avery. The woman he'd made love to wasn't his sister. The cunning vixen was a skilled pretender to dupe him twice.

Ben was bewildered by his son's reaction. If Stone loved Ginny, he should be shouting with joy over this news; for some unknown reason, he wasn't. "She told me the truth after you left like a bandit in the night. She would have told you, too, if you hadn't sneaked off. She was very contrite, Son, and I understand her motive."

"She certainly took her time getting a guilty conscience and spilling the truth. I'll bet she wouldn't have done it if I hadn't shown up and scared her witless. She knew she dared not cross me again. She came here to torment and punish you, but you understand and forgive her?"

"Yes, Son. You of all people should comprehend vengeance and bitterness as powerful motives to hurt someone. We've done terrible things to each other, Stone; I want to end the past; I want peace. I love you and need you. I will never call you my adopted son again; I swear. You're a Chapman, my only flesh and blood and heir; this ranch will be all yours one day."

Those admissions touched Stone deeply, but he couldn't deal with them yet. "Where is this Ginny? She and I have a few things to settle."

"She left the ranch and Dallas after her confession and plea for forgiveness. We know why you ran from her and why she's giving you time to cool your temper." Ben related Ginny's disclosures and assumptions about him. "She loves you, but she's afraid you won't understand and forgive her. *Do* you love her?"

The younger man paced as those stunning revelations flooded his mind. She seemed to know him well, but he didn't know *her*, not the real woman. He'd met "Anna Avery" and "Johanna Chapman," but not this Ginny woman. What if she wasn't anything like the women she had pretended to be? She lied and duped with ease and skill. Or did she? Hadn't he always perceived she was being dishonest and had a dreadful secret? Did she love and want "Steve Carr" or the heir to the Chapman ranch and fortune? "Gone where?" he asked.

"To Colorado to join her father. That's where she was heading after a visit here with Johanna, but Johanna never made it home. She's afraid for his life; someone is apparently trying to murder him and steal his silver strike."

Stone's heart skipped several beats and his body chilled as additional suspicions gnawed at him. "What's her real name, Father?"

"Virginia Anne Marston. Her father is—"

"Mathew Marston," he interrupted, gritting out the name. Now he grasped why she had escaped him again, terrified of his wrath.

Ben noticed his angry reaction. "You know her father?"

"Yep, I know the bastard. He killed my best friend, Clayton Cassidy. They were partners in that silver strike she mentioned. I was chasing him before I had to leave to join Jo— Ginny's wagontrain to catch Charles Avery and his gang. I'm heading there now to . . ." Stone narrowed his gaze.

"My Lord in heaven, Son, you aren't going there to kill her father? You can't. If he's guilty of a crime, arrest him, but don't do this to Ginny."

"Her claims of love for me are only another trick to protect her father from me and justice. Matt probably told her about me and Clay, may have even sent her here to ensnare me. If Matt is dead, Ginny may believe I killed him, so she came to wreak revenge on me after Johanna died and gave her a path. How can I trust her again? She's lied too many times."

"You're wrong, Son. They were friends for years, since they were girls of thirteen. I read your sister's letter to me telling all about them."

"How do you know this Ginny woman didn't write it just to fool you?"

"She didn't, Son. Please don't be hard on her. She loves you. I'm sure she doesn't know about you and Clay and her father. She would have told me. You're afraid to believe her because you don't want to be hurt again. Ginny's known heartache, too. Let me tell you about her . . ." Ben related what she had revealed about her difficult life.

Stone wondered if what Ginny had told his father was true. If it was, did it change anything—change what she'd done, change what and who she was? "You want to protect the conniving woman who deceived us?"

"She had good call, Son, and a good heart. I told you her life's story, Stone; she's suffered plenty, as we have. Don't hurt her more. Please."

Hurt her, his mind shouted, *after what she's done to me? She let me think she was Anna Avery! She let me think she was my sister and I had made love to her! She's Matt's daughter, greedy and sly just like him! Well, I have a big surprise for you, Ginny Marston, one you'd never imagine . . .*

"She left a letter for you, Son. And something strange. A doll." Ben walked to his desk, withdrew both, and returned to hand them to Stone.

"Do you understand this?" Ben asked, nodding to the doll.

Stone fingered the keepsake in confusion and anguish. "No, I don't," he finally replied. He wondered if what he feared to believe was true: that she did love and want him. Yet every time a black cloud vanished, another one took its place over their heads: Mathew Marston and his crime would come between them and prevent any hope of a future between them. "I need to be alone for a while. I'm going to my room."

"You won't take off again without seeing me first?" Ben entreated.

Stone looked at his father; the man had been changed by this event; he read that in Ben's eyes, tone, and posture. "No, Father, I won't. It's past time for us to make peace. We'll do it before I ride out on my last mission. When I finish it and return home, it will be to stay."

Ben hugged his son once more, and this time Stone responded.

"I'll tell your mother the good news. You don't know how happy this makes me, Son. We'll be a real family at last. My beautiful Apache Sunflower has agreed to marry me. We'll wait for your return for the ceremony."

Stone was astonished again. "You're marrying Mother?"

Ben smiled. "As soon as you return. It's about time, past time. She's the only woman I've ever loved. It's time the world knew and accepted our feelings for each other."

"I'm glad, Father. Tell her I'll speak with her later."

Stone went to his old room and sat on the bed. His thoughts and emotions were in turmoil. Dare he open and read the message she had left for him? Would it be the truth, as she'd promised in her Fort Smith letter? Or would it be another cunning deception? Did she know who he really was—Clay's heir and avenger on her father—and wanted to trick him into not taking either of those roles? Would beautiful lies in her missive affect his feelings and actions in a foolish way? No, he vowed coldly as he cautioned himself to remember she wasn't Anna Avery or Johanna Chapman.

His half sister . . . She was dead, buried not far from where he had trained this beguiling vixen for her trip to torment him and his father. Stella had taken Johanna away when she was two and he was ten, but he remembered the child who had owned their father's heart and loyalty. He would never get to meet and know the woman she had become. Yet, he was grateful the woman he had made love to wasn't his sister. He would grieve for Johanna's loss in his own time and way. For now, he had to. . . .

Stone's hands shook as he ripped open the envelope:

Dear Stone,

You know the wicked truth by now and must hate me. To say I'm sorry will mean little or nothing to you at this point. I know giving you my two most prized possessions—myself and my doll—will not make up for the pain and bitterness you're feeling.

I admit I tricked you many times, but my reasons seemed right at those moments. You also tricked *me* many times. If you had told me you were Stone Chapman, I would never have done what I did to you, with you. So often I wanted to confess the truth but things you said or did halted me. I sensed you were hiding something powerful and I feared to trust you. After you dumped me in Fort Smith as if I were used-up supplies, I had no choice, I believed—except to come here for help. I was hurt and confused and afraid because I didn't know you hadn't deserted me. I also feared I'd become entangled again in the Klan crime and had no one to prove my true identity and innocence. I wanted to hide here until I was out of danger.

I'm sure your father told you he loaned me the money to reach *my* father in Colorado. He said he would explain my past to you so you'd understand why I left and where I'm going. I suppose I knew all along I couldn't carry out my promise to your sister, but I loved her so much that I agreed in a moment of anguish.

I was going to tell you everything in private before confessing to your father but you left too quickly. I'll be out of your life when you get this letter and I'll understand if you make that forever. Please don't allow the mistakes I've made to increase your torment. Make peace with your father; he's a good man, even though he made cruel mistakes. He loves you and needs you and he's sorry. Give him the chance to make everything up to you. This is the moment both of you have waited for, so don't throw it aside.

I hope you can understand and forgive me one day. I'll never forget what you've done for me and what you mean to me. I'll always regret what might have been between us . . .

Love, Ginny

Stone read it again then squeezed his eyes closed. *Do I believe you this time, Ginny Marston? It won't matter after I do what must be done to your father. I understand love and promises between best friends; that's why I'll have to kill Matt, if the snake's still alive.* Stone rose from the

362

bed and headed for a long and overdue talk with his father and mother.

Monday morning, the ranch foreman galloped to the house with bad news. "Rustlers struck again last night in the south pasture. Made off with fifty prime steers, one of our best bulls, and about ten horses. Two of the boys are dead and one's wounded. I'll round up some hands and we'll track 'em down. Raid was early last night so they have a good start on us. It'll probably take a few days to catch 'em and bring back the stock."

Ben was angered and dismayed. "That'll leave us too short of men here. Pick three hands who are good with rifles, Buck, and I'll ride with you. Tell the boys to guard Nan and the house while we're gone. Son, I have to go."

Stone read Ben's reluctance to miss a minute of his visit and imminent departure, but his father's decision was the only one he could make. Stone knew chasing the bandits was perilous and he didn't want to risk losing Ben to an ambush. "I'm coming with you. When a rustler goes to killing, he's dangerous and tricky. You might need my help and guns."

Ben smiled. "Thanks, Son. You're better at dealing with criminals than we are. Let's ready supplies and move out in ten minutes."

Stone realized this episode would delay his trip, and perhaps that was intentional. Surely the trouble here could be cleared up in less than a week. It would take him about thirteen days to cross the Texas panhandle and northeast corner of New Mexico Territory to reach Colorado City. He should be finished here and on the trail shortly before Ginny reached her destination.

Be there and be ready to face me, woman, with the truth for once.

* * *

Forts Riley, Harker, and Hays and numerous other relay and home stations were left behind as Ginny's stage rumbled across the vast Kansas plains. They journeyed on the Smoky Hill Road that ran beside a river by the same name from Fort Riley into Colorado. The combination of occasional low, rolling hills, long stretches of flat terrain, scant trees except near waterlines, outcrops of rocks, and the seemingly endless span of grass became monotonous and nerve-wearing to several passengers. But not so to Ginny, who had never viewed anything like the landscape before her gaze.

She saw countless buffalo, deer, antelope, and foxes. She noticed a few Indians at a distance and was relieved they didn't attack the coach. Hills became more frequent as they neared the border. Afterward, she watched the Big Sandy River for twenty-five miles as it snaked along beside them in the arid region. She enjoyed the beauty of countless wildflowers, plants with blades that resembled mini yuccas, waving tall grass, several varieties of sagebrush, and amaranth that eventually became tumbleweeds. The openness in all directions amazed her.

Nights had been cool in this region for mid-June, making her thankful for her long sleeves and shawl. Days were often windy, with some gusts swaying the stage and stirring up choking dust on the dirt road.

They crossed the Rush, Horse, and Pond Rivers and passed a prairie dog town where she saw many furry creatures scampering about or standing tall and alert on mounds. The Rocky Mountains appeared on the horizon. Colorado City would be their last stop of the day, and Ginny could hardly eat her scant lunch as she stared at the awesome sight.

A passenger told her that the first gold strike—made by men from her home state of Georgia—was on Cherry Creek not far from Colorado City. In '58 the shout had been: "Pike's Peak or bust." The man gave a wry grin as he related that many had "gone bust."

During the last leg of the journey, Ginny watched snow-capped Pike's Peak grow in size as the stage neared its base where her destination awaited her. Her gaze picked out lofty ranges of towering slopes, sharp and rugged mountains, exposed rocks and lofty summits, and upturned foothills. Passes, valleys, canyons, and sandstone hogbacks filled her line of vision, their coverings and splotches of white telling her that winters in the high country were long, rough, and demanding. She couldn't imagine why her father had fallen in love with this wild area and remained here after the war.

The closer she rode to the city, the larger and taller those peaks and ridges became. Verdant foothills seemed covered in emerald fuzz of evergreens and hardwoods of late spring. Soil in shades of red ranging from vivid to dull, and rocks dotted the landscape. Nearing sunset, the tallest range and summit were like a pearly-pink ridge that drifted up into a startlingly blue sky. Ginny found the azure, green, white, and red colorings a striking contrast. She watched clouds and fog slowly lower themselves like cozy blankets over the jutting and chilly terrain.

Over the next rise, Colorado City sprang into view, nestled on relatively flat land at the base of the uplifted terrain. Apprehensions flooded her. She was afraid she wouldn't be able to locate her father, afraid she wouldn't be able to find a proper job before Bennett Chapman's money was spent, and afraid she'd never see Stone again. She hadn't expected Colorado City to be so large and settled. She relaxed as she realized it wouldn't be a small and rough and filthy town.

Yet as the stage entered the outskirts, Ginny realized she might have made part of that assumption too soon. She saw tents, shacks, lean-tos, and log cabins with animals and clutter around them that were interspersed with nice homes and businesses of many sizes and kinds. Freight wagons were backed up to stores either to unload or having unloaded their wares. Men were moving goods—picks, shovels, wheelbarrows—inside their stores for the night to prevent them from being stolen.

It was active and noisy this time of evening as work ended and recreation began. She heard laughter, shouts, muffled talk, and a contrasting blend of music from dance halls, brothels, and saloons. A mixture of smells filled the air, most from the preparation of food at eating establishments, some merely marked Grub or Eats. She saw ill-kempt men in shabby garments strolling the streets, others loitering at night places that appeared elegant and expensive, drunks lying against wooden structures, and scantily clad females enticing customers to spend their money at these locations. People milled everywhere she looked. This was a town of mixed inhabitants, a town of the rich and poor and the in-between, of the famous and infamous and the nobodys. She had learned those facts from several of her fellow passengers.

After the coach halted, the driver told Ginny, "You wait tilst I'm finished here, Miz Avery, and I'll see you to a nice boardin' house. You don't want any of that trash takin' charge of you and yore possessions." He made his remarks scornfully as he nodded to shabby men hawking business from newcomers. "They'll git you outta sight and rob you clean. You'll have to be careful here. Never go out after dark 'less yore with an escort who's well armed and good with his guns. No minin' town is safe fur a lady. Some of them men have lost everythin' they came with and will do anythin' to git another grubstake. A few of 'em have struck pay dirt and lost it faster 'an they dug it out. Gold fever kin be a dangerous sickness."

Ginny was fatigued, dusty, and sore. She was eager to be on her way but wisely waited for the kind driver to escort her. The man borrowed a wagon from the coach company, loaded her belongings, and took her to Hattie Sue Pearl's Boarding House. After introductions were made, the stocky female with graying hair in a loose bun led Ginny inside and to her new "home" of two small rooms—sleeping and sitting—and showed her where the bathing closet and privy were located.

Suppertime had passed, but Hattie warmed leftovers for her. The two women sat at the kitchen table, chatting. Ginny related the terrible conditions in the South since the war ended to Mrs. Pearl. "I'm an orphan," she began her fabricated reason for coming to the town. "I lost my home and family, everything,

366

during the war. I tried to work and make a new life there, but it's impossible until things change. I read about Colorado and decided to move here. It might sound impulsive and rash but I had to get away to make a fresh start. With all the mining and progress here, surely there are good jobs available for a strong and dependable woman. Who knows, I might find a proper husband."

The older woman grinned. "Please call me Hattie." They exchanged smiles before she said, "I think you're a brave and smart girl. I came from Mississippi three years ago and I'm earning good money. My husband and son were killed in that awful war and I lost everything, too, except for gold and jewels I kept hidden from them thieving Yanks. I used them to build this place and to invest in one of the hotels down the street. We got us plenty of unmarried men who have enough looks and gold to make a woman's heart flutter. I have my eye on a couple of prospects myself. I'm sure you'll have no trouble finding you a rich young man to snare."

"First, I need to find a job. My resources won't last very long. I lost everything to a Yankee carpetbagger. A friend loaned me traveling money. I was fortunate the driver brought me here to you. I've heard the hotels and most lodgings charge a small fortune for room and board."

"They do 'cause they can get it. Men who can't afford niceties live in awful conditions, some bedding down in alleys and begging for grub. When miners or prospectors come to town to rest and sport, they pay what you ask 'cause they think they'll find more gold the next day. After spending scary months down in somebody else's mines or scratching for nuggets on creeks and rivers, they're desperate for company and good food and a good loving, if you know what I mean." Hattie's eyes twinkled with mischief. "I know of a job that'll last a week at Mr. Trevers cat and book store. His wife needs a rest something fierce, been sickly. He mentioned it to me just today."

"Why cats and books?" Ginny inquired about the odd mixture.

Hattie chuckled. "All kinds of men in these parts, Anna. They need books to en'ertain and relax them after work in town or shoveling dirt all day, and cats made great pets and mousers. Camps and shafts are overrun with rats and mice, so they ain't hard to feed and tend. I've seen wagons bring as many as a thousand on one load and sell 'em faster than fleas multeeply on a dog. I'll take you to meet John in the morning. Mary Jane will be happier to see you than a bull in a pasture of eager cows. Them miners and cats keep 'er busy and she's in sore need of rest."

"That sounds wonderful, Hattie. I love both books and cats."

"Like I said, it'll only last a week. Unless John makes a bigger profit with a beauty like you working there," she jested. "It'll be a start, give you time to learn your way around and meet folks here. A beautiful and genteel lady will be in big demand. Don't let nobody hire you cheap and work you hard; too many jobs around here for that. You could earn a fortune if you like singing and dancing and making merry with men. We got more than our share of them kinds of places. Some men squander their whole earnings in one night in some of them holes."

From Hattie's look and tone, Ginny realized she wasn't serious. "I'm not interested in working there, quick and easy fortune or not," she clarified.

"Good girl. Just testing you," Hattie teased with a grin. "A real lady."

Ginny liked the friendly woman in her mid-forties who kept a clean lodging, was an excellent cook, and seemed kind and trustworthy.

"The water's hot if you're ready to wash off that coat of dust."

"Thank you, Hattie, and I'm more than ready. I haven't had a proper bath in ages."

* * *

"You're to feed and water the cats every day, Miss Avery," John Trevers said, "and make sure their pens are clean. I don't want none getting sick and dying on me; they're too valuable. When the men come in to check the books, make sure they wash their hands first. Talk to them and you'll know what to show them." They discussed the stock for a while, then John grinned and said, "Sounds like you know your books and writers. Good. I can use you from today until Saturday night. I'll pay you sixty dollars for the week's work and one extra for every sale you make. Does that suit you?"

Ginny smiled, as the salary he offered was a generous one. She concluded the high pay and his wife's need of rest must mean business was good and that she was in for a busy and hectic week. "Perfect, Mr. Trevers. I promise to work hard, be on time, and do a good job for you, sir."

The man thanked Hattie before the genial boardinghouse keeper left. He showed Ginny where everything was located and let her begin her chores before the store opened in twenty minutes.

As she worked, Ginny thought about her father. She couldn't ask around about him and tip off his enemy. Hopefully if he was in town, he'd see her and contact her. If not, she had a cunning plan in mind.

She also thought about Stone Chapman. She wondered if he had returned home and discovered the truth about her second deceit. Would he be glad she was out of his life or would he come after her? She loved him and missed him so much. She prayed he would understand and forgive her for duping him again, and would arrive soon. She could use his help and protection. Steve was a skilled agent and might be able to trace and find her father faster than she could, alone and inexperienced. It had been eighteen days since she'd last seen him, and she had an emotional and physical ache for him. She could close her eyes and envision him in detail, imagine his gentle touch and blazing kisses. Yet it was more than his handsome looks and virile prowess that drew her to him. He was the man with whom she wanted to share her life.

Mr. Trevers unlocked the front door for customers to enter and command her full attention with purchases and questions about felines and books.

Tuesday, as she was about to leave Trevers's Cats & Books to deliver two animals to a customer to be used for mousers in his restaurant, Ginny met Frank Kinnon, the man mentioned in her father's letters as a possible enemy of his. She listened to and observed him with interest.

John introduced them and told her, "Frank owns the bank and assay office next door, among his many businesses around town, and a thriving ranch ten miles away. Frank is rich, and powerful, Miss Avery, so be wary of him," the friend teased. "Oh, yes, Frank's also a bachelor."

Ginny watched the two men shake hands and chuckle. According to her father's missives, Frank Kinnon was also evil, selfish, and greedy, and perhaps a murderer of Matt's partner, Clayton Cassidy.

"I see John is keeping his new helper busy. Don't let him overwork you as he did his poor wife."

Ginny smiled at the pleasant and polite man in his late thirties. He appeared very distinguished in his expensive suit and with the silver streaks at his temples. "So far, Mr. Trevers has been a perfect boss."

"See, Frank, I'm not a slaver like Mary Jane says," John jested.

As the two men chatted, Ginny pretended to check the latches on the two cages to stall for more time to observe Frank. He was nice-looking, almost handsome. His dark hair was cut and combed neatly. His blue eyes sparkled with vitality, amusement, and secretiveness, and with desire when they touched on her. She wasn't surprised when he invited her to join him for dinner the next night, but the offer filled her with apprehension.

"O'Rourke's is a fine restaurant, Miss Avery. I'm sure you'll enjoy the excellent food and atmosphere. Please accept. I'll be a perfect gentleman."

She couldn't comprehend why she hesitated since she needed to get close to him in order to cull clues. "I don't know, Mr. Kinnon; we're strangers."

John provided help for his eager friend. "You'll be safe with Frank, Miss Avery. You can trust him to honor his word. I'm sure you two will become good friends. He might even be able to help you find another job next week."

Ginny made certain she behaved as a proper lady and didn't appear smitten by the valuable suitor, as that was how the man was behaving. "If you say it's all right, Mr. Trevers, I'll accept." She turned to Frank. "I'm staying at Hattie Sue Pearl's Boarding House. I'll require time to freshen up and change after work. You can call for me at seven-thirty."

"Perfect, Miss Avery, see you tomorrow night."

Ginny hoped she didn't blush or fidget beneath his fiery blue eyes. "I'll return soon, Mr. Trevers," she told her boss as she lifted the two cages and headed toward the door. She left the men talking. Before she was halfway down the street, Frank Kinnon hurried to overtake her and pulled the cages from her hands.

"Let me help you with these."

Ginny forced a warm smile. "You needn't bother, sir, I can manage them. I only have another block to go. I'm sure you're busy."

"Not too busy to assist and protect a beautiful lady. We have many rough men here, and I wouldn't want you to get a bad opinion of our town if some of them approached you. In a place like this, we have few ladies, but not for long. The whole state of Colorado is growing fast. Gold, silver, furs, and ranching make it enticing. Besides, I need the exercise."

Ginny eyed his powerful physique from the corner of her eye and knew it was an excuse to spend more time with her. She should be glad she'd seized his interest, but he made her ner-

371

vous nevertheless. He made her think of a starving man with a juicy treat before him. She decided not to play the coquettish southern belle to ensnare him tighter as that could be hazardous. She wasn't convinced she could carry out her ruse to let him romance her while she beguiled information from him.

They strolled past the many businesses, banks, offices of attorneys and doctors, many clothing and mercantile stores, and three saloons with gambling. Across the street she had seen a meat market, smithy, Brown's Hay & Feed, two freight companies, the Leavenworth & Pike's Peak Express Company with mail delivery, and Farrell's Drugs. Farther down, she noticed more businesses and more hotels and lodgings, restaurants, a church, and, oddly, many brothels and dancehalls. They reached her destination, delivered the cats, accepted payment, and returned to the store. Ginny smiled and thanked him, as his warning had been correct; if he hadn't been with her, gawking men might have approached her.

"My pleasure, Anna. I look forward to our dinner tomorrow night."

"Good-bye, and thank you for the escort, Mr. Kinnon."

"It's Frank, Anna. Please."

"Good-bye, Frank." Ginny watched the grinning man enter the building next door. She went to the store's back room to eat the lunch Hattie had packed for her, her mind drifting to what she knew and what she needed to learn.

Her father had written her that the only man who knew about his silver strike was the one who had assayed the rich ore: Frank Kinnon. He had related, "If his tests are accurate, the future mine will bring in great wealth and fame." Lincoln's Homestead Act of '62 had opened up this area to settlement: anyone could claim up to one hundred sixty acres of land. Mathew Marston had filed his claim in Denver at the Colorado General Land Office under the name of V. A. Marston for Virginia Anne Marston, not in this town to prevent Kinnon or others from knowing where it was located. Her father and Clay had found "a rich vein, one most prospectors would have missed even if standing atop it," its bluish-gray and bluish-black "rocks" deceptive to the ignorant and inexperienced. He had told her that gold was easier to find and collect, but not so with silver, which was embedded with other minerals and had to be separated. It required knowledge, work, equipment, and skill. It was almost mandatory to have investors because silver mining was expensive, took many workers to dig and to smelt, and others for hauling and guarding shipments.

Another assayer had been with Frank Kinnon that day and had prevented the man from lying to her father. Frank had been forced to reveal that the ore sample contained a high percentage of pure silver and little refining would be required. It was estimated that "each ton of ore will yield one thousand dollars in gold, four thousand in silver, and additional money in lead and quartz." Matt had kept his find a secret until he could work out the details for mining it because news of a strike would lure countless men into his area, men after the gold, men who would overlook or ignore the silver, men who would create problems. He had registered his land claim after he and Clay had pretended to lead spies to the right location and after Clayton Cassidy and another prospector had been killed and burned in a cabin. Matt didn't know if anyone—especially the villain and his cohorts—knew he wasn't the second man slain that day. Her father was supposed to leave the area to seek those needed investors and protectors, but she didn't know if he had made it out alive.

His letter had warned of claim-jumpers, widespread thievery, lynchings, murders, corrupt or incompetent politicians and assayers and claims' officials or surveyors, and the overworked special agents who tried to uphold the laws and capture criminals. The El Paso Claims Club had run Colorado City in '58 and had meted out justice and punishment to wrongdoers; they still had powerful members, including Frank Kinnon.

But the wealth available here was too tempting for some men to worry about how they collected it. Fur trade was bountiful in the mountains, and warm clothes were expensive. Farmers nearby raised much-needed food and charged exorbitant prices, as did freighters who brought in goods. Shops charged outrageous prices for supplies and equipment. It was relatively safe from Indians who had been defeated in '65; only a few attacks troubled settlers on rare occasions. It was the greedy white man who threatened those innocent and law-abiding fellow white men in this territory.

Ginny understood why her father couldn't expose his find and why he couldn't accuse Kinnon of murder. She grasped why he needed investors and why he had to remain "dead" until he found them for protection. But what, she wondered, was taking him so long and where was he now? If Stone were here, she would have asked him to guide her to the cabin where her father might be hiding out until his plans were finalized.

But one precaution she needed to take now was to be prepared to flee in the event Kinnon discovered her identity and motive for coming to Colorado. Without arousing suspicion, she must buy a horse, supplies, and rifle, and keep them stored in her room at Hattie's.

Saturday night, Ginny was having her third dinner of the week with Frank Kinnon. They had spent most of the day sightseeing at the Manitou Cliff Dwellings and enjoyed a picnic at the springs nearby. Tomorrow he was showing her the Garden of the Gods; they would share another meal in that ancient setting. She hadn't feared being with him away from town, as several armed men tagged along as guards against daring villains. She had agreed to the outings because she needed to learn her way around in case disaster struck and she was compelled to flee.

Obviously Frank had let everyone in town know he had "staked his claim" on her because no other men had dared to approach her. The Trevers were pleased by her "conquest" and urged her to continue it, as Frank would "surely propose marriage as soon as he thinks it's proper." In one way, she was glad he had prevented any competition for her as it allowed her to concentrate on her target. In another way, it alarmed her to have him too enamored of her. She was glad he was being cautious and leisurely in his pursuit. She could imagine how cruel a wicked man like him would be if he learned the truth about her. Before that day came, she must either find her father or find a way to prove Frank was a criminal.

"You look lovely tonight, Anna. I'm so happy you came to our town."

Ginny tried to appear poised but was unsettled by his ravenous gaze feasting on her. She hadn't allowed anything personal to occur between them, but she was sure he would attempt to kiss her soon and would eventually propose marriage. She hadn't decided yet how to handle those incidents. But if her ruse became perilous or if his chase became too swift and demanding and she couldn't slow things down between them, she was prepared for her escape. If only Stone would come to help her, she mused in brief panic, but she couldn't depend on that happening. "Thank you for the compliment, Frank; you're such a kind and polite gentleman. So far, things are going fine for me. I finished my last day with Mr. Trevers, so I'll be seeking another job Monday. Do you know of anyone who needs help?"

"That's my surprise for tonight: I do, if you'd like to go to work for me. The woman who did my records and letters at the assay office eloped with a miner sweetheart who struck it rich this week. Can you begin Monday? That is, if you think I'll make a good boss."

Ginny couldn't believe her good fortune—a way to get inside his files and view his records to check out her father's accusations. With luck, there was enlightening and damaging evidence in his office that she could use against him. "That sounds wonderful, Frank. Thank you, and I accept."

He chuckled. "You didn't even ask about salary and hours," he teased.

"I'm certain you'll be fair with me. Won't you?" she asked, and smiled.

"Of course I will. I'll make it such a good offer and such excellent working conditions that you won't ever search for a replacement position."

Ginny was relieved their meal arrived; it compelled him to release her hand that he had grasped and was stroking with his thumb as he stared into her eyes. She was grateful he wasn't rushing her, and she did all she could think of to make certain he continued his sluggish pace. Yet Frank Kinnon was clearly a virile man who went after what he desired; she wasn't sure how long she could stall him if he pressed for a commitment. For the present, behaving as a lady and acting skittish seemed to work in her favor.

"This is delicious," she murmured of the tender roast beef.

"It should be; I raised it on my ranch. You'll have to come out and visit one day. It's beautiful. I promise you'll love it."

"Perhaps, one day," she replied in a cordial tone. "It's too soon to come calling on a handsome bachelor. I'm sure you understand."

"Of course, Anna, but one day soon will come quickly."

"Perhaps," she said again, then flashed him a demure smile. For once, she was glad she was prone to blushing, as it aided her pretense, though wine and her apprehensions were really the cause, not feelings for the evil man. She realized she didn't feel guilty over duping him, as he deserved it.

"I would never do or say anything to upset you or to embarrass you, but I see I have done so."

"I'm certain you wouldn't, Frank. You're a fine gentleman. I'm happy we became acquainted so quickly as Colorado is a wild and dangerous place. You make me feel safe here. I treasure our friendship."

"She's a state of boom towns and ghost towns, a place where fortunes can be made and lost in the same day. I wouldn't allow anyone or anything to harm you, Anna. Whatever you need or want, just ask me."

"You're much too generous and kind, but thank you."

"When the right time comes, I want to be very generous with you."

As if she misunderstood him, she responded, "You said you would pay me a fair salary, so I believe you."

"That isn't what I meant."

"I know." Her point made, she changed the subject. "Have many big strikes been made near here? There's so much I don't know about mining. Which is better to find, gold or silver? You will let me watch you assay one time and teach me all I need to know to be a good employee?"

"I'm a rich and powerful man who's accustomed to getting what he wants, so forgive me for racing after the most beautiful and desirable woman in town. I don't mean to appear pushy."

Ginny lowered her lashes and smiled as he hadn't answered her questions. "Those are advantages, Frank, not flaws or weaknesses, so don't apologize for having them. I'm sure you realize you make me a little nervous. We've only known each other for less than a week. You must be patient with me."

"You don't know how refreshing it is to meet a lady like you out here. But I promise to behave myself and to control my eagerness to win you. Now, to answer your questions. We've had many big strikes in Colorado since '58 but most of them have been in other towns and up in the high country. Most of those have been in gold, but there's plenty of silver in there somewhere and lucky the man who strikes it. I've assayed ore that would make a prospector's eyes bulge. I'll teach you all you want to know. If you find assaying enjoyable, you can become my assistant. The process is simple but requires training and a good eye, especially with silver. Sometimes its tricky to detect by sight alone. I have several books on it you might find interesting. I'll loan them to you. After you read them, ask me any questions you want. Within a week, you'll probably catch gold or silver fever."

Ginny didn't want to appear suspiciously intrigued. "I can't see myself grubbing in the dirt or living as I've heard those miners and prospectors do."

Frank chuckled and nodded his head. "You're right. Dreams of riches craze them, Anna. It's much easier and cleaner to live off of their fantasies here in comfort and safety. In those camps, men *exist*, they don't live or enjoy life. They're plagued by poverty, illnesses, accidents, fights and bad tempers, loneliness, attacks by thieves or claim-jumpers, depression, disappointment. Hazardous weather condition, poor food or starvation, and freezing hands from mountain streams wear them down. Gold fever takes its toll on them."

As their desserts arrived, she knew the time remaining for questions was getting short. "How do prospecting and mining work? Can they dig anywhere?"

"Yes and no. A man can stake a claim and work it or he can skip from site to site, and if he finds gold or silver can stake a claim there on the spot. Men work alone or in groups. Often they form companies, sometimes doing their own work and sometimes hiring men to do it for them. If a strike is big, a company is best for protection and results. Sharing a lot of wealth is better than eking out a little alone. That's especially true of silver; it's hard and expensive to mine."

Ginny noticed how many times he mentioned silver and wondered if that was a clue. She smiled innocently and asked, "Why silver?" She listened as Frank told her the same things her father had in his letter. His mood and expression exposed his greed for the shiny metals. "That's fascinating, Frank. Have you ever considered investing in a claim or mine?"

"I have invested in two and both should be paying off soon. Don't tell anybody, but I have an advantage being an assayer. Sometimes men bring in samples, that they have no idea the worth of. I get paid a nice fee for steering them to investors and for advising ignorant prospectors they need them. It's true, so nobody is hurt and I make an added profit."

She saw him sipping too often from his wine glass and hoped its potent effect would loosen his evil tongue. With cunning and

378

desperation, she evoked, "It's good to put people who need each other in touch. Have you ever found something in an assay that a prospector or miner missed? I'm sure they would pay plenty for such information."

"Rarely."

Ginny caught a hint in his voice that said he wasn't being honest. "Perhaps one day you will find something special and become famous for being behind the biggest strike in this state."

"If that happens, I hope I'm involved as an investor."

"Or an owner. If a man doesn't realize what he has and offers to sell it to you, why shouldn't you purchase it? Fortunes are made on others' ignorance and greed . . . My goodness, that must sound terrible. I didn't mean to cheat someone. I just meant, if . . . Oh, my, how to explain myself?"

Frank chuckled. "No need, Anna. I understand."

Ginny was positive he didn't and prayed he misunderstood and misjudged her. "I'm glad because sometimes simple words can sound so cold and cruel and deceitful. Someone mentioned salting to me. What does that mean?"

"It's when a claim or mine is worthless or used up and the man tosses out nuggets to fool a buyer. That can get the seller killed or lynched fast."

Wide-eyed, she murmured, "I imagine so, if he isn't long gone by the time a mistake is discovered. Wouldn't a buyer bring samples to someone like you to be tested before he makes his purchase?"

"Usually not. Greed, Anna, the dream of striking it big, makes him foolish. He thinks he's making a good deal when he's being cheated."

"Don't such men deserve each other?" she asked.

"I guess so. You haven't told me why you came here."

Ginny was prepared for that question and fabricated, "I hate to tell you, Frank, but you deserve the truth." As if reluctant, she related the tale she had told Hattie and others. "Most of that is true, but there's more. I trust you, so I'll be honest with you. Besides, someone could arrive any day to expose me and get me into trouble." She noticed how that caught his interest. "My parents are dead and I did lose everything from the war. But my father, Charles Avery, was connected with the Ku Klux Klan." In case he checked on her, as a man in his position had the money and means to do so, her false tale should be foolproof. She related what had happened on the wagontrain, except for Stone's part in it. "I had to get away from the South before I was accused and arrested for being involved with his doings. I wasn't, Frank, but I doubt I could convince the authorities. I thought this was far enough away to be safe, to make a fresh start. Am I awful for not telling you sooner? You must be terribly disappointed with me."

"Of course not. It must have been awful for you. I'm glad you came here. Don't worry about anyone or anything harming you here."

Ginny knew she had intrigued and ensnared him. "Thank you, Frank. Now it's late so I should be getting home."

"You'll be at work Monday morning at eight?"

"Yes, I promise. You won't be sorry for hiring me."

"I'm certain I won't."

At the boardinghouse, Ginny bid him good night and allowed him to kiss her cheek. She walked to her rooms dreading what tomorrow's activity and Monday's challenge would bring. She realized it might have been too early to begin her ruse, but that couldn't be helped now. *Stone, my love, where are you? I need you.*

CHAPTER 17

Frank let Ginny into the bank and locked the door behind her after speaking to several customers who were waiting outside to do business with him. He smiled and asked if she was ready to begin the new job.

"Nervous, but ready," she responded, then forced a return smile. This was her perfect opportunity to search for clues and to win his confidence, so she told herself to be alert. She mustn't become distracted or reckless for an instant, something "Steve Carr" often had scolded her for doing during her training. She quickly dismissed her love from mind and observed her surroundings.

Four clerks stood behind a long U-shaped counter getting ready to open for business in twenty minutes. Frank whispered for her to notice that the workers had either no pockets or stitched-down ones in their trousers to prevent hiding places if they became tempted to steal a nugget or coin. The counter and floors were highly polished wood, but, as Frank whispered to her again, there were no chairs or sitting areas supplied to entice customers to remain inside the large room longer than necessary. He said she would grasp why when the bank became crowded and noisy soon.

In every corner there was a guard armed with a rifle at the ready to discourage or to defeat robberies. Most propped their buttocks on stools to keep from becoming overly fatigued or cramped during a long day of standing. She saw all the guards and clerks eye her for a moment. No doubt, she concluded, they also knew their boss had a "claim" on her.

Ginny looked at a large sign on one wall: The Frank Kinnon Bank. A clock was mounted on the opposite one. In the elbow of the waist-high counter was a shed-type case with scales for weighing gold dust, flakes, and nuggets, Frank said.

"It's glassed on the customer's side to keep wind from scattering gold dust on the scales when the door is opened and closed. It also lets customers witness the handling of their property to prevent any problems. Want a peek inside the safe before it's locked?"

"Yes. I've never been inside one before."

Frank guided her around the counter and to the large metal "closet." While blocking everyone's view, his deft fingers twirled the combination dial on the heavy door. With brute strength, he pushed the door aside and motioned her into the small, dark area that held numerous shelves from floor to ceiling. Using a lamp, Frank adjusted it to give her a good view of the contents: bills, coins, pouches of gold in three forms, ingots of silver and gold, and samples of ore on trays.

"What do those mean?" she asked, pointing to names on some bags.

"Men either sell me their gold and silver or they store it here for a fee. Whenever they need some, they have the clerks weigh out the amount they want. They sign a paper inside the pouch telling when and how much they withdrew and how much is left. Storing it here keeps them from carrying around large amounts and risking being robbed. It also keeps some men from being tempted or tricked into spending it all in one night after they get drunk and lose their wits at the gambling tables."

Ginny tried to read the names in a hurry to see if her father's or Clay's was among them and stalled for more time by saying, "That sounds very intelligent to me. What happens to a man's gold if he dies?"

"If I hear about a misfortune, I date his pouch and hold it for one year for family or partners to claim. If no one does, it becomes mine. Those eight on that shelf are patiently waiting to jump into my pocket."

Ginny's heart fluttered as her gaze touched on her father's name on a fat pouch. She wished she could peek inside to see what the date was but dared not show her interest to the man nearby. She was worried about finding it on that gloomy shelf, but Mathew Marston had been reported dead. She didn't want to imagine that might be true or to think about Frank taking something that belonged to her if Matt was gone. "There's a fortune here. Have you ever been robbed?"

"No. I keep four guards on duty day and night. It's expensive, but it increases business because men know their earnings are safe with me."

"What if something happened to you? How would they open the safe?" How, she mused, could she get her hands on her father's property?

"I'm the only one here who knows the combination. If I died, the governor has the combination in his safe. It's about time to open, so let's get in the back where we work." As he locked the enormous safe, Frank told her, "The clerks keep the banking records, but I check them every night for errors. You won't have any tasks out here."

On the back wall was a door into another section, over which a sign read: Frank Kinnon, Assay Office. He led her into a hallway and closed the door. "Nobody comes back here unless invited or by appointment." He motioned to three doors as he explained, "That's my assay room, my office, and where you'll work. I make notes which you'll write up in a report form twice: one copy for me and one for the customer. They're kept in a file in my office and it's always locked when I'm out. You'll also copy letters for me because my script, as you'll soon discover, is terrible. You'll keep the office books: charges, payments, supplies, and so forth."

Ginny followed him into the "laboratory," a clean but cluttered room. She laughed, "I almost feel as if I'm in jail; every window and door has bars."

Frank chuckled. "A man can't be too careful when he's responsible for so much wealth. It would shock you to know how much money and precious metals are in that safe. If anything happened to them, the men around here would lynch me in a second. I have to protect my business and reputation."

"It appears you're doing a good job with both."

"Thank you, Anna. Please look around and ask all the questions you wish."

Ginny glanced at cabinets that held supplies used in his trade. There were several long work tables. One had lines of metal weights and a scale. Another held a small crusher, a vise and hammer for sizing samples, many wooden trays to hold them, flux and burners and crucibles for tests, tongs for lifting hot objects, thick jars of nitric acid, and paper with ink and pen for recording results. "How does this process work?" she asked after he explained the use of each item, though many were obvious or were marked.

As he removed his coat, rolled up his sleeves, and put on an apron to protect his clothes, he said, "Pull up that stool and I'll give you a lesson while I do this sample. Kelly's coming by later today for his answer."

Ginny realized he was absorbed by his task or he would have fetched the stool for her. She sat close to the table as Frank Kinnon worked and talked to observe this man her father mistrusted and feared.

"I use chemicals and heating techniques to determine how much precious metal or mineral is in a sample. Most are scattered throughout. Flux helps melt it into what's called a button. It separates into slag, which is tossed out, and a button of mostly lead and hopefully something valuable. The button is melted to get out the impurities and to leave a dore bead, usually gold or silver, or a combination of both. I weigh the bead and record the figure. Next comes nitric acid bath to remove any silver. This is one of the trickiest and most dangerous steps; acid can burn worse than any flame. I weigh the gold I recover and subtract that amount from the first figure to determine how much, if any, silver is there. Take a look: gold with no silver tracings. Nuggets men find in streams don't need assaying; their value is obvious and their payment is easy to determine by weight. Mining gold is different; if it's embedded in rock, it has to be freed by pick and smelting."

"Fascinating," she murmured.

"No tests are necessary if a prospector brings in fool's gold. A trained eye can spot pyrite instantly, but it's tricked many an innocent man. It's sometimes used to dupe ignorant buyers into thinking they're getting a valuable claim."

Ginny looked at the samples of pyrite and gold Frank showed her. "You said silver was harder and more expensive to mine. How is it done?"

"Ore has to be crushed, calcined, washed, smelted, and cast into bullion. Stop me if I confuse you. Calcine is to convert ore into calx by roasting it in a way that it's exposed to air and oxidizing. Silver is a pure metal, but it's embedded in or with other materials, such as gold, quartz, lead, or copper. Most prospectors overlook it because of its color; they discard gray or blackish or bluish rocks without realizing what they've found. It requires lots of men, work, equipment, and money to extract it. A company needs furnaces and vats for removing roasted ore, then laborers to cut and haul wood and feed fires. They need smelters and crushers, and diggers and haulers. They require a water supply and trained men to cast silver into bricks. It takes guards for the diggings, company, and transport, plus drivers and wagons and teams. Silver mining is big business, Anna."

That explanation helped her to grasp her father's problems better. "My goodness, it sounds like it. Is that why you didn't get involved in it?"

"I haven't found a promising silver mine to invest in, only gold."

"You said you have books I can study?"

"Yes, over there on that shelf. Take what you want."

"I think it would be best if I familiarize myself with all of this since I'll be working here and living in this area. You're smart and skilled and I'm very impressed. It's going to be interesting and fun working here with you."

"It's good to know your surroundings. If you have any questions or problems, come to me. I won't mind being interrupted by you."

"Thank you, Frank. Oh, my," she said, and feigned a look of dismay. "Shouldn't I call you Mr. Kinnon at work?"

"No need. We'll see few people back here."

"What do you want me to do first today? Do I have a routine to follow?"

Frank related her tasks and schedule, then showed her to her office. "If you need anything, call me. I'll be back here or out front."

Ginny sat down, smiled, and watched him leave. She read over the notes she was supposed to copy neatly into a ledger and glanced at the reports she was to write out afterward. It was going to be a busy day. Before she began her first task, she wondered if Frank had requested information about her from any sources back South. He hadn't mentioned the half-true, half-false story she had told him about herself last week. If he suspected her of wrongdoing with the Klan or of coming here to seek a rich husband, it didn't show or didn't matter to him.

At least, she realized, there wouldn't be a pregnancy complicating her life, as her monthly flow began this morning. Yet she wanted to have Stone's children and, every time he touched her, the last thing that came to mind was worry over getting pregnant. Probably she was lucky his seed wasn't growing inside her as he might be lost to her forever. Three weeks ago today she had left Dallas. If he had returned home as promised and been told the truth, there had been enough time for him to reach Colorado City, if he wanted to come after her. Perhaps he didn't and never would. She ordered herself not to think about Stone Chapman right now as it evoked too many doubts, fears, and pains.

Ginny closed her eyes and envisioned the bulging leather pouch in the safe with her father's name attached. She could use that money to search for Matt; rather, to pay a detective to ferret out the truth. She was trapped in a bind: she couldn't get answers without asking questions, but she couldn't ask questions without exposing herself.

Soon, she promised, she would find a way to get at the truth.

All of Thursday, Ginny knew something was afoot. Frank Kinnon smiled, whistled, grinned, and hummed continuously. He dropped in for little chats. He adored her from head to foot with his eyes. He invited her to join him tomorrow for "a special dinner."

Anxiety nibbled at her as she feared he was going to propose. Whatever would she do and say if he offered marriage? She couldn't marry him just to extract clues. If he was that serious, dealing with him might become difficult. She hadn't expected her target to fall in love with her. Desire her; perhaps and hopefully. Love her; that was trouble. Propose; that was incredible. He could be her father's mur— *No, Ginny, don't think such horrible thoughts. You need more time to glean clues but Frank might not allow either one. Better come up with an alternate plan.*

Shortly before quitting time, Ginny was putting away the letters and reports in Frank's office that she'd done while he finished work in the assay room. She noticed a file marked *MM*. She glanced into the hallway and heard the man humming, obviously still busy working. Quickly she snatched out the file and read two papers inside. The same notes and figures in her father's last letter were recorded there, with the conclusion: *high grade silver ore, 80 to 90 percent pure.* Mathew Marston's name wasn't listed nor was a location of the strike, but she was certain this file was about her father. It was dated last June, a year ago. Yet her father's pouch of gold or silver was still in the safe so a year, according to Frank's rule, hadn't passed since its deposit. Her father's last letter to her had been dated July of '66 after Clay's death and his departure to seek investors: almost a year had passed. Would such a task require that long? And why no word from him since then? Unless he feared the wrong person might be watching her and might get their hands on any enlightening missives . . .

Ginny heard Frank coming down the hall, and panicked a moment. Thinking fast, she tossed the two files and other papers to the floor. She muttered to herself, "Look what you've done, Anna." She knelt to retrieve them.

"What's wrong?" Frank asked from the doorway.

Ginny looked up and sent him a wry smile. "I was pulling out the Maples file and another one came along with it. I dropped everything trying to replace it without putting down the stack. I'm sorry, but nothing looks damaged. I'll have this mess straightened up shortly. Two pages don't have names, so I don't know where they go."

Frank came over and knelt to assist her. He took the two papers and slipped them into the file marked *MM*. He chuckled and said, "That's one claim I'd like to invest in, but nobody knows where it's located. It could be anywhere in the Rocky Mountains or even in another state."

"What do you mean, Frank? Why does it only have initials?"

Frank squatted and looked at her. "Sometimes prospectors and miners don't trust local assayers or want news of their findings to leak out prematurely, so they carry their samples a long distance to have them tested. In this case, I understand why. I don't know where that sample was taken from, but it's one of the richest grades of silver I've seen."

Ginny watched him stare at his hands, then ball his fists until his knuckles whitened, that bittersweet vision seemed to bring a greedy and frustrated look to his face. Frank stood and helped her to her feet. He stuffed the file back into place, right where the name Marston would go.

"If there's as much silver and gold embedded in the area as

the ore they brought me implies, it'll be one of the biggest and best strikes ever made. That's how I know nobody's found it; there has been no big headline in newspapers across the country and it's been a year. They would have been wealthy and famous men. It's worth millions, almost pure. Lot of gold, too. It came out easy, so little refining will be required. I'd surely like to invest in whoever's company finds this strike. It even tempts me to go searching for it myself."

"I don't understand, Frank. It's already been found. You've tested the sample. Do you know the men? Have you seen them in town?"

"I knew both of them, but they were murdered last summer, probably by common thieves. No claim was ever filed at the local land office by Mathew Marston and Clayton Cassidy. The location of the silver remains unknown to this day."

Ginny was relieved she was able to control any outward reaction to his disclosures. He was relaxed and he trusted her, yet she must make sure to sound only curious. "Surely someone else will find it one day. There are so many men working the mountains that it can't remain a secret forever."

"But remember what I told you—silver is often overlooked by ignorant and inexperienced men. Matt and Clay recognized it from working a mine."

"It's a shame they were killed; it could have meant plenty of jobs and more progress in Colorado. What happened?"

"Their bodies were found in a burned cabin. Undertaker said both were shot first. Their mules and gear outside were used to identify them."

"Perhaps whoever attacked them forced them to reveal where the strike was located before they were murdered."

"That couldn't have happened, Anna, or it'd be big news by now."

"What if this villain staked a land claim and he's biding his time before mining it until the time he won't fall under suspicion by the law?"

"I thought of that. I tried to help solve the crimes by checking to see who registered claims here. But there's been nothing suspicious to date."

Ginny didn't dare remind him he'd said the strike could be anywhere and ask him if he'd checked with other land offices, such as the one in Denver. "I suppose you're right: it may never be found or not for a long time; their killers, too. A crime like that must be too old to solve even for a detective."

"I actually hired one to see if he could backtrack on them, but it was futile. I even thought for a while that somebody else may have been in the cabin and one of them escaped. That couldn't be true because nobody's seen or heard from either man and Marston has a gold pouch in the safe that he wouldn't leave behind."

Ginny gave a sympathetic sigh. "What a shame, to die just before you become rich. Did they have families? Does anyone here try to reach kin following accidents and deaths?"

"Cassidy had no family. Marston has a daughter in England, but nobody knew how to reach her or even knew her name. And she could be married and have a different one by now. They stayed here after being Galvanized Yanks for years in the state. Seemed like good men to me."

"How awful for a person's father to be dead and not know it."

"I wish I could learn more about her. If Matt sent her any news or maps, I could handle a mining company for her. We'd both be rich."

Ginny feigned an interested look. "Did you try hard to locate her?"

"Yes, but without a name or town, it was impossible. I checked with the Army, but they didn't have any records revealing anything about her. If I could just come up with the right clues, I'd be first in line to take over the claim from a criminal I'd exposed."

"You said one of them might still be alive. Why would he disappear?"

"I can't imagine."

"Nor can I. It would be nice to own a mine of such value. This has given me an idea. You could start another business, Frank: let men register their identities and prospecting locations or claims with you; then, when or if something happened to them, their families could be notified about inheritances. They could carry papers telling whoever found them to contact you for a small reward for their help. You could charge a fee and I could handle the records."

"That might be an excellent idea. I'll think about it this weekend."

She turned and finished her filing. She didn't actually expect him to act on her idea; she had used it to help dupe him.

A clerk knocked on the door and said, "We're closed, sir. You ready to check up?"

"Coming in a moment. You go home and rest, Anna. And don't forget about our special dinner tomorrow night."

She smiled and assured him she wouldn't.

Ginny finished her bath and returned to her room. She had eaten with Hattie and two other boarders, as the others were out for the evening. She was ready to turn in for the night, because she was emotionally and physically fatigued from her labors and discoveries today. She dreaded facing Frank tomorrow as she suspected what he had in store for her later that night. She locked her sitting-area door and entered the other room. She barely suppressed a scream as her gaze noticed the man half lying on her bed with his booted feet on the floor.

Ginny gaped at him as questions filled her head and spilled forth, "Stone, how did you get in here? Did anyone see you? How did you find me? Surely you didn't ask around to locate me?"

He sat up, exhaled, and looked at her. Light-brown hair tumbled over her shoulders and drifted to her waist. Hazel eyes were wide with astonishment and suspense. Her lips had remained parted after their rush of words. One hand gripped the edges of a night robe to keep it closed; the other held bathing needs with a damp drying cloth thrown over her forearm. *Shu,* she was beautiful and tempting with little—yet in another way, a vast—distance between them. He finally managed to speak. "Hello, Ginny Marston."

She stared at him and tried to ascertain his mood. The fact he hadn't leapt upon her and attacked her with harsh words or blows told her he had himself under rigid control. Her gaze took in the image of irresistible manhood. He wasn't an illusion, this man she loved clad in all black and with a short beard as if in disguise. Yet, neither had he leapt from the bed and taken her into his arms as she'd hoped when they next met. It was hard not to rush to him. At last, he was here. "Your father told you everything?"

Stone scooted to the end of the bed and propped one elbow on the wooden footboard. He placed his unshaven chin on the backs of curled fingers and drilled his gaze into hers. Before he answered, he wondered why she remained frozen in the doorway instead of hurrying to his aching arms. "Him and your letter. So, I finally meet the real woman. You aren't Charles Avery's daughter and you aren't Bennett Chapman's daughter. You've had a lot of fathers along your route to here. Have you found yours?"

"No. I was told just today that he and his partner were murdered last year, but I know—I hope—that isn't true."

"What is true, Ginny?"

She walked to the bed and sat down near him. After he shifted to face her, she confessed everything to the man she loved and prayed he felt the same about her and believed her. "I know Father wasn't in that cabin, but I don't know where he is now or if the killer got to him later. If he's still alive, I can't understand why he hasn't contacted me. I'm sure Frank Kinnon's involved and I'm slowly gleaning clues from him."

"It sounds as if you're as good at deceptions and investigations as I am." He saw her wince as if he'd insulted her or struck her a physical blow. "Don't fret, I didn't ask about Virginia

392

Marston, because Father told me about your dangerous predicament. I arrived this morning and I've watched the bank most of the day after I saw you enter at lunch and not come out again. I followed you here and waited until it was safe to sneak inside. I would have come sooner but we had trouble with rustlers at the ranch." He explained his meaning. "You might be pleased to learn Father and I have made peace and my parents are getting married as soon as I return home."

I *return, not* we? "That's wonderful news. I'm happy for them and for you. Please congratulate them for me. How soon are you leaving?"

He was baffled by her reaction of sadness and anguish to a mention of departure that should delight her and her father if they wanted him out of the way. If only he knew what she knew about the matter tormenting him. He dreaded to ask out of fear she might lie to him again, even if only out of mistrust or caution. He must wait and see how much she revealed.

Both felt the strain within themselves and the other. Each wanted to reach out but waited for the other one to do it first.

"I haven't decided. What you did to me and my family was wrong, Ginny, but I understand your motives. I want to thank you for giving Father a little of Johanna and for halting your ruse before it lasted too long." He witnessed a look of surprise and relief; then, sadness dulled her eyes again.

"Is that all you came to tell me, that you won't seek revenge?"

"No, I wanted to tell you, for one thing, I'm glad you aren't Johanna."

When he didn't say more, she probed, "Why?"

"Because she and I, as you discovered, were blood kin. It knifed me badly to learn I had made love with my sister and knew I had to hurt her again."

Be bold and brave, Ginny, or you'll never extract the truth, whatever it might be. "Did you say those cruel and painful things to me that night only to discourage me, or did you truly mean them? Were you only trying to halt things between us because you thought our relationship was wrong and had no future, or were you trying to convince me of your genuine disinterest? Was it just physical attraction for you, Stone, nothing more? Do you still want to discard me now that you know I'm not your sister or Anna Avery? Did my two deceptions destroy all respect and affection you had for me? Did they destroy any hope or chance of us building a future together?"

Stone gazed at the daughter of the man who had murdered his best friend, a man he'd sworn to kill. That was an impending task she might or might not know about, one that would affect the "chance" she was questioning. Clay's message had told him that Matt was acting strange. "I don't think I kan trust him ennymore," he had written Stone. "He's balking on filing our klaim. He says we have to keep it a sekret. I've had krazy akseedents with only Matt around. He's been my friend and partner but I'm skared to trust him. If ennything happens to me, my share of the klaim is yours. Here's the map and paper saying so. You know I don't have no family and yore my best friend. You saved my life more than once. If Matt balks, force it out of him. It's worth a fortune, Stone. That's what the assayer told us. If you kan kome help me with him, pleze hurry."

Stone felt there must be valid reasons for Clay distrusting Matt after the two men had been together for years as Galvanized Yankees and prospectors. With Clay dead and the land in the Marston name, Matt believed he owned it all. He had learned that Matt had registered the claim in Denver under Ginny's initials. He knew the strike's location, so he didn't need Matt or Ginny to lead him there. It wasn't the wealth that he wanted; he wanted Clay's killer exposed and punished. This thing with Kinnon, he reasoned from experience, was a smoke-screen like Indians sometimes used to conceal or protect their retreats across prairieland. If Matt wasn't guilty, he would have gone to the law; he would have helped them find and punish the killer of his friend and partner. Yet, even if there was a slim possibility Matt was innocent, Matt'd let the murderer go free just to keep the strike for himself. Perhaps he was off searching for investors as Ginny had said and he'd show up one day and plead ignorance of Clay's death and his own alleged one. Those were points he'd investigate soon.

Had Matt mentioned Stone in his letters to Ginny? Was duping him her real reason for impersonating his sister? Did she know about his lethal quest and inheritance? Those questions plagued him. If he asked them, would she be honest? His father had told him how she had escaped Fort Smith and his reach; she was cunning and brave. She'd come here alone and was doing fine by herself. His mother had urged him to—

"Stone, why did you really come here? A letter could have said all you have." Ginny was worried over his lengthy silence and impenetrable stare. "Does it take this long to decide how you feel? Was what I did so terrible that you can't understand it or forgive me?"

The Special Agent was skilled at tracking, outwitting, and exposing criminals. He was experienced at confronting troubles head-on with speed and accuracy and without fear. Somehow those traits deserted him tonight in Ginny's presence. She looked innocent and vulnerable, honest and tormented. "A letter can't look you in the eye when it talks. But even face-to-face, you can't always tell if someone is being honest with you; we've both proven that."

"Except for the false claims I made about my identity, I was myself with you," Ginny assured him. "I don't think the same is true of Steve Carr and Stone Chapman; you two are much alike yet greatly different. You're the stranger in this room." She didn't stop to think it might be the short beard that made him look different, mysterious and almost intimidating. "Even if you can't forgive me and don't want a personal relationship with me now or ever, please let me hire you to help find my father." *I have to keep you here until you realize the truth. You love me and want me, you stubborn creature. I need time to prove it to you.*

"You want *me* to help you look for Mathew Marston? Why?" Ginny misunderstood why he stressed the "me." "You're a skilled tracker and agent. I don't know how or where to search for him. I know to work on Frank Kinnon, but he's getting too—It's just so hard and scary working alone on a dangerous and enamored man. Do you despise me too much to help me? I'll pay whatever I can." *Stay and work with me, Stone. Give us time together to get past this strain between us.*

Ignoring the evocative deception he had in mind, he admitted the truth. "I don't hate you, Ginny. I haven't stopped wanting you for a moment since the day we met in Georgia. Things have been crazy and it takes getting used to. I have to deal with all these changes and deceits. But they weren't all your fault. I did my share of lying and tricking and provoking you to do more than you wanted to do. At the ranch when I thought you were my sister, I was tormented and stunned. I had to turn you against me, and I had to leave there fast. I made love to you on the trail because I wanted you and needed you. You, Ginny, not just your body. *Shu,* woman, don't you realize how you get to me? I've never wanted or needed anything more than you, not even for my father to acknowledge me as his son. When I learned the truth about your two ruses, yes, I was angry. And I was disappointed, hurt, and confused. I'm sure you've felt the same way many times with me. I didn't come here to punish you or toss you aside. I came because you were mine and I want you to be mine again . . . Why are you crying?" he asked as he moved closer and brushed away the tears rolling down her cheeks.

"I was so afraid I'd lost you, more afraid than I've ever been in my life. I love you, Stone. I've tried not to press you because you're so . . ."

"Skittish as a horse near a branding iron?"

His broad smile warmed her very soul. It was enticing and devilish and tugged at the corners of his wide mouth until it parted his lips and exposed even, white teeth. His dark eyes glowed with emotions that matched her own. She was no longer tired or afraid; her senses were alive and alert. He was utterly arresting, and she was susceptible to his charms. "I'm so glad you're here. I want you so much. It's been too long since you've held me and kissed me. Lordy, how I've missed you. Can you forgive me?"

For almost anything. He pressed kisses to her brow, nose, and lips. As his mouth left hers, he murmured, "Surely you know you're the only woman for me." His bearded chin gingerly moved aside the robe so his tongue could taste the clean flesh of her shoulder and neck.

"You're the only man for me, Stone." Ginny's arms tightened around him as she sought surcease for a yearning deeper and stronger at that moment than her physical desire for him. Her heart was so full of love, joy, and relief that she feared it might burst. Her body soon blazed with fiery passion. She wanted all of him. She lacked the strength and wits to deny what they both craved, a union of bodies despite any consequences. She surrendered to his intoxicating kisses and stirring caresses.

Stone longed to reveal everything within his heart and mind, but he couldn't until he confronted Matt and held the entire truth within his grasp. His hold on her was too new and fragile to risk breaking with a stunning confession about their mutual target. Maybe she was right and there was another villain to blame for Clay's death. If so, they would unmask him together. If Matt was innocent, it would be rash to expose his speculations and create new problems between them.

As Ginny kissed and caressed him and changed his line of thought, it seemed to Stone as if she entreated his touch and response as proof of his feelings and claims, as a way of evoking reassurance from him. It was true, she was the only woman who could have reached him and saved him from the destructive ravages of the past. His hands peeled the robe off her body to reveal creamy skin that beckoned his lips and mouth. With expertise and enraptured by her, he stormed her bared flesh with deft hands and captivating lips as he explored her curvy regions and flat planes.

Ginny hugged him possessively because she believed he was

yielding his all to her. She unbuttoned his shirt and removed it, then trailed fingers over his iron-muscled body. She yearned to make tender and passionate love to him. Nature and her entire being demanded she respond to the urgent messages passing between and within them. She gave free rein to those emotions and unleashed every inhibition.

Stone was enthralled by her urgency and his own. His head seemed as if it was spinning in a whirlwind. He parted them to hurriedly remove his boots and pants, as his weapons and hat were hanging over a chair nearby. He turned back to her to find her naked and her hand extended in a sweet invitation. Her hazel eyes beckoned. His fingers buried in her hair as his hand pressed her head closer to his to seal their mouths in a breath-stealing kiss. His embrace tightened and he refused to release her for a long time. His needs and kisses became urgent and demanding but he tried not to rush and to be gentle. He groaned in rapidly mounting desire. "I said you were a dangerous distraction and irresistible temptation; I was right."

"So are you, my love." Though smoldering with hot desire, she was dreamily aware of each kiss and caress, each sensation. She felt his hunger for her in his touch, heard it in his tone, and read it in those dark eyes that enslaved her.

Stone realized her desire was as tangible and evocative as a physical caress. Weeks of starvation for her ignited his body to a flaming torch, fires that licked precariously at his resolve to take her with leisure. His molten body covered hers and shared its seething heat. He was almost afraid to caress and kiss her lest his control be vanquished and he succumb to its coaxing to take her with swiftness.

He leaned over and tantalized her taut breasts with his lips while his hands drifted downward to stimulate her womanly center with love and tenderness. When his mouth returned to hers, their kiss fused into a savage and feverish bond. Their need so great, he eased between her thighs and slid himself within her, then halted to master his wavering control. Never had he taken a woman who enticed his manhood to seek bliss the moment he entered her body. She ensnared him with a speed and ease that nearly hurled him beyond reason and willpower. She smelled fresh as spring air and was as hot as the sultriest summer day.

Ginny's hands traveled from Stone's sable hair to his bronzed torso. His body was beautiful, strong, and stimulating. She arched to meet his hips each time he withdrew and entered her again. Her body responded to his instinctively, but what instinct didn't supply, he did. She writhed as his lips, hands, and movements worked magic upon her. She tried to relax, to give him full mastery over the situation, and to abandon her will to his; she couldn't stay still, not with him assailing her wits and body. The sensations he created were wonderful and intense. She tingled. She flamed. She wanted every instant of this union.

Urged onward by his insistent desire, Stone increased his pace and deepened his kisses. She was holding nothing back from him and that filled him with happiness.

Ginny felt her body quiver with suspense. Only Stone could quench this thirst for appeasement. "I want you and need you, my love."

"And you shall have me." He carried them to the peak of pleasure where she stiffened a moment and moaned in ecstasy. Her grip on him tightened and she pressed herself closer to him. He swept her over the precipice and beyond . . .

Blissfully sated, they didn't break or release their hold on each other. They snuggled together as their bodies quieted and glowed in passion's aftermath. They felt peaceful, warm, and happy.

Ginny nestled her cheek to his chest. With eyes closed, she sighed dreamily. She felt his fingers wander through her mussed hair and over her damp flesh. She smiled when he placed light kisses over her face. She felt safe, tranquil, and fulfilled in his arms.

Stone relaxed. Beyond any doubt, he loved her. He had taken other females but never *made love* to them; he knew the difference now. Ginny was totally satisfying in all ways. That was the secret to happiness and contentment: love. He rolled to his side and gazed at her. "Tell me everything about you again. I want to know every detail about my Ginny Marston."

It was nearing midnight when she finished relating her history from birth to this moment. "The last thing to tell you about Frank Kinnon is that I think he's going to propose to me tomorrow night. How can I discourage or stall him without breaking my hold over him?"

Stone knew he had to stay out of Kinnon's sight and remain unshaven to conceal his presence from a man who could recognize and expose him. If she was right, Kinnon or someone else could be guilty rather than Matt. If that proved to be true, it would be wonderful because he wouldn't have to hurt Ginny or risk losing her. "I don't want him touching you or kissing you, woman. I feel jealousy firing in me already. You saw your father's pouch in the safe and those reports in the file. What else could you learn from him? He won't confess he murdered two men. If you ask questions, he'll get suspicious. It's time to quit that job and stop taking chances."

"If I quit or suddenly change my behavior, he *will* get suspicious."

"Change your behavior? Have you been enticing him?"

Ginny toyed with his beard. "Not exactly. It wasn't necessary."

"I can believe that. You stole my heart and eye the first time we met."

She nibbled on his hairy chin. "Good, and I'll never return them."

"Back to Kinnon. You go to work as usual tomorrow but don't do anything to arouse his curiosity. I'll figure out what to do about him while you're gone. You may need to see him for dinner, let him propose, then ask for time off from work to consider his offer. That'll give us the opportunity to think this out. I don't like it, but it might be the only path open to us for now."

"Sounds clever to me. I'm sure it will work . . . Where will you stay?" she abruptly changed the subject.

"Are you asking me to leave?" he jested, nipping at her lips.

"It would expose us if you're found here with me. Besides, this is dangerous. Babies can come from wild sport like this."

He cupped her face between his hands and locked their gazes. "Doesn't matter at this point, Ginny love, if you'll marry me soon."

Her eyes widened and her lips parted. "You're asking me to . . ."

Stone chuckled, then kissed her forehead. "You look shocked that I love you and want to marry you. I thought both were obvious by now."

"I am and I'm not," she said amidst hugs and kisses.

Stone chuckled again. "I take your reaction to mean yes."

"Yes, yes, yes," she murmured in a happy rush. "Those are the most beautiful words I've ever heard. I love you, Stone Chapman."

"I love you, too, Ginny. We have to make sure nothing comes between us again to separate us." The moment that caution left his lips he wanted to cringe in dread of what he must do.

Her fingers teased his dark beard. "What could possibly go wrong, my roguish lawman? We love each other and have been honest with each other."

"Set a wedding date fast while I'm being brave," he pretended to tease.

"We should wait until after we locate Father."

I need to rope you quick, woman. "Why? We can get hitched as soon as possible. I don't want any children of mine born like I was."

He seemed afraid of losing her, which touched her deeply. "You won't lose me, Stone, so don't worry about hurrying me to the preacher. I'm wearing your brand on my heart and body already. I want my father there."

"It doesn't bother you I'm a . . ."

"You aren't a bastard. Your father has claimed you. You have his name."

"That wasn't what I was going to say. Have you forgotten I'm part Indian, part Apache? Our children will carry Indian blood."

"I love you, Stone, every part of you. Nothing changes my feelings."

"You don't know much about me, woman."

"Then tell me everything, just like I told you."

"You know how I was born and what my father's denial did to me, and maybe some of that damage was my fault because I reacted so badly to the situation." He reminded her of how he'd been adopted and had discovered Ben was his father through overhearing a quarrel with Stella. "As far back as I can remember, I was told to call my mother Aunt Nan to keep people from gossiping about her, from calling her an Indian whore. Her name, Nandile, means Sunflower; she was an Apache chief's daughter."

"You're the grandson of a chief? What a marvelous thing to tell our children and grandchildren. Be proud of that heritage, Stone."

"Father was captured by her tribe to exchange for arms and supplies to fight the white man. But Ben proved himself a great warrior and friend, so they gave him his freedom. When he left their camp, he took her with him. She's been his lover for almost thirty years. Ben always said they couldn't marry because people hated and mistrusted Indians, especially the feared Apaches, so it might ruin him. I always said I didn't understand and called him a coward and weakling, but I suppose I see his point now. Love and desire can make people do crazy things; you've taught me that much. I loved you and wanted you, but I was too scared to tell you. Maybe the same was true with Father; he feared the repercussions. Since leaving home, I've witnessed the hostilities between the two sides. When you're the one involved in a nasty situation, you can be blind to reality."

"That's true, my love, but that's how we learn and grow.

We're all human, so we have flaws and weaknesses. Sometimes we think problems are bigger than they are, and sometimes we make them larger so we'll have an excuse to ignore them . . . How did you get your name? It's so unusual."

"Mother named me Stone Thrower after my grandfather when he was a child. Ben kept the first part of it when he adopted me at age ten. I loved and trusted him and I believed until recently that he had betrayed me; I believed he used my mother and misused Stella, bad as she was, and she was bad, Ginny. I stayed at the ranch for years trying to punish him, but it only hurt both of us. I ran away at sixteen to find myself. I spent time with my mother's people and was taught many warrior skills. But a half-breed didn't fit in there, and I didn't like raiding. I wandered into the white man's world and did odd jobs but didn't seem to fit anywhere. I was confronted by the problems he'd tried to explain to me and Mother." He related many of the troubles he'd had in his early years as a result of being part Indian.

"I even worked as a Texas Ranger for three years. But things got too hot with the Apaches and I couldn't bring myself to help kill my mother's people or push them onto some filthy and barren reservation. When the war started, I saw it as an escape from my problems, another chance to use and hone my skills. But I was captured by Union soldiers in April of '63. I shouldn't have joined the war; it wasn't part of my world. But I was looking for something, something I didn't understand, not until I met you, Ginny Marston." He kissed her, then smiled. "I was trying to save a man's life when I was taken prisoner. After months of torture and captivity, I was asked if I wanted to become a Galvanized Yankee and serve my sentence in the Army out West. In July, I was on my way to a new life."

Ginny brightened. "My father was, too. He was captured at Stones River at Murfreesboro in early '63. He served at forts in and near here. He stayed after the war and did prospecting. He didn't want to return to Green Oaks and intrude on his family's new life; they all believed he was long dead and that didn't seem fair. Where did you go? What did you do?"

"They guessed I was a half-breed, so they figured they could use me to help out with Indian problems. I worked as an interpreter, scout, guide, guard, and plenty of other things that I mentioned that night in camp. When the war ended, I did much the same things, but for pay then. I agreed to help the Yanks because I wanted to be free, to stay on the move, to learn all I could for survival, and to get away from such cruelties. Two years ago, I met Warren Turner from the Justice Department. He was impressed by some of my missions and asked me to become a Special Agent. The work is exciting and stimulating. I thrived on the danger, challenges, and victory. I craved and needed the importance and respect I received from my successes. I liked having white men forced to depend on a half-breed for their lives and safety, forced to follow one's orders. Warren and I became friends; he's my superior. I've sent him a letter of resignation. I plan to return to the ranch and live there, if that suits you, Ginny. You will be my wife soon. We'll inherit it one day."

"What about my father and the silver strike?"

Stone hoped wealth wasn't that important to her; he didn't think it was. "He can run it if he's still alive. If not, you can form a company to do it. You said you know where the strike is, and the land is registered in your name so nobody can steal it from you."

"There's one point that needs handling if Father's gone: his partner. If Clayton Cassidy has family somewhere, part of the strike is theirs. Father said he had no relatives, but I'd like to make sure of that."

That moved Stone deeply and convinced him she was being honest. "If they're distant, why would they deserve it? You'll need investors, but all of this can be discussed and decided another time. It's late and you need sleep, woman. I'll sneak out, bed down someplace, and see you tomorrow night after your evening with Kinnon."

"I dread that, but it might help us learn something."

"Just don't go too far to dupe him."

"I won't, so don't worry. If there's one thing I've learned since leaving England, it's how dangerous and dark midnight secrets can be."

Stone prayed his remaining secret wouldn't be long or damaging, and he would confess it soon. To do it now might evoke suspicions. She needed him and, if she learned the truth about him, she might turn against him and find herself in danger. It was possible Matt had her duped and was deserting and betraying her as he was doing to the rest of his family in Georgia. When she discovered the truth about her father, he needed to be at her side. "I love you, Ginny. Whatever happens, you have me."

She cuddled against him. "I love you, Stone Chapman. I can hardly wait for this to be over so we can begin our new life together in Texas."

"I'll work hard to make sure it's very soon."

"Nothing can ever come between us again," she murmured as she kissed him, unaware that terrible "nothing" would appear within hours.

CHAPTER 18

"What?" Ginny heard the shout come from Frank Kinnon's office next to hers. Muffled voices reached her ears then another shout of "Damnation!" She wondered what had evoked her boss's anger. Surely, she fretted, she hadn't been exposed. Her apprehension mounted as she strained to eavesdrop, but she couldn't make out what was being said. She saw a shabbily dressed prospector pass her room while counting gold coins in his dirty grasp. Her tension mounted as she waited to see if he came to confront her. Two guards passed her office and entered Frank's, to stay only a few minutes.

She went to check out the matter. "What's wrong, Frank? I heard shouting. Is there a problem? Can I help?"

"That damn Special Agent is back in town again! Joe saw him and he's asking sneaky questions around the miners' tents and in the saloons. If he keeps looking for Clay's killer, he'll find that strike before I do."

Ginny tensed in dread of Stone being the agent mentioned and rashly exposing her. Yet Frank had said *again* and *keeps looking* . . . The pacing and scowling banker seemed so unsettled by the news that he spouted off a rush of disclosures that soon amazed and distressed her.

"Maybe Clay told him where the silver is located before he died. I wouldn't be surprised if Chapman knows and he's come to see if anyone's working the area. Maybe he was in on the strike and the claim is registered to him. I never thought to investigate that possibility. Hell, he could have been a third partner in the diggings; they were all friends. I'd better go to the land office and check it out. I'll soon see if Chapman's been fooling me."

Ginny was stunned by the intimidating hints in his words. "Wait. What are you talking about, Frank? You're so upset that you're not making sense. Did someone cheat you?"

"It's about that Marston-Cassidy silver strike, the one I told you was worth a fortune. A lawman named Stone Chapman was their friend; he served with them in the Army during the war and they worked odd jobs together. He and Clay were real tight for years, best friends. Chapman was away on a mission when Matt and Clay were murdered, I think scouting for a supply train for Captain McDougall of Company B in Denver. When he returned and heard the news, he was like a wild man. He's been here twice looking for the killer. He left the last time in early March, and I was hoping he'd given up and wouldn't return. Now, he's back again to thwart me."

Friends: Matt, Clay and . . . Stone? Her love wasn't a stranger here? Left in March to accept another assignment: the Ku Klux Klan mission. *This* was the "next job" he had mentioned to her several times? Her father had never written to her about Stone Chapman, but Ginny didn't doubt the truth of what Frank Kinnon was telling her because, if he even suspected who she was, he would have taken her to his ranch to question and then beat the truth from her. He wasn't even observing her for a reaction, so her identity and goal were definitely unknown to him. It sounded as if her boss had checked out the agent in the past, no doubt for clues to the silver. When the irate man started talking again, she listened carefully.

"From the questions he asked last time, he had a wild idea Matt's still alive and he's the one who killed Clay to get everything. He's back nosing around for clues. From what Joe reported, Chapman still thinks Matt's alive and is the murderer. It's crazy; Matt wouldn't desert such a rich strike or fail to stake a claim on it. He must be dead. My detective couldn't find news of him anywhere and what man would lay low for a year when he has a fortune to dig out? I have men taking samples everywhere to see if I can find a match to the one Matt and Clay brought in. So far nothing. Chapman can complicate matters for me. I know he won't rest until Clay's killer is found and punished, probably by his guns, and he's damn good with them."

Ginny didn't want to believe what she was hearing but sensed it was accurate. Stone hadn't come to fetch or help her, only to entice her to lead him to her father so he could . . . Kill or arrest him? How could he know her father and think him capable of cold-blooded murder? If her traitorous lover wasn't up to no good, he would have shared this information with her last night. The moment Ben had exposed her name, destination, and goal, he had guessed who she was, and might have known from the start. To conceal her shock and anguish, Ginny faked anger and disappointment. "That's awful, Frank. You've done more work to find it than he has. It would be terrible for him to ride in and snatch it away. Do you think this Mathew Marston is still alive? Do you think he killed his partner?"

"No, or he would have shown up or been located by now. He must have been the second man in the cabin. Chapman can't have evidence otherwise. He told the authorities here he didn't have proof it wasn't Matt."

"You think this Stone Chapman knows where the silver is hidden? You think he may have been a third partner? Maybe he wants Mr. Marston imprisoned or slain so he can get full control of the strike."

"It's possible, Anna. I'm having him watched to see what I can learn. Joe's pointing him out to my two boys and they won't let him out of sight. Maybe, with luck, he'll lead them to the strike."

"That's good, Frank, and very smart. You said he's a lawman, a Special Agent. Perhaps he's only trying to solve a criminal case; he does have a personal interest in it. Perhaps he doesn't know where the claim is located. I hope not. You've dreamed of owning it for so long."

Frank grasped her hands in his and gazed into her eyes. "I hope it'll be ours, Anna. I want you to marry me. I love you."

Ginny feigned astonishment. "You're . . . proposing to me?" He smiled and nodded. "But we've only known each other for less than two weeks. This is so sudden and unexpected. I don't know what to say, other than I'm flattered and taken by complete surprise. You're the most sought-after bachelor in town. Why me, Frank? And why so soon?"

"Love doesn't work on a schedule, Anna. This caught me by surprise, too. Sure, I've wanted and searched for a proper wife, but I couldn't find one. Then you appeared in my life, the perfect woman for me. I can give you anything you want, with or without that strike. I own many businesses, a prosperous ranch, a big house here in town, and investments in other areas. I'm a leading citizen of Colorado City and the state. I'm rich and powerful. People like and respect me. I have friends in high places, so nobody from your past could ever harm you under my protection. We'll have a beautiful family and give them the best of everything. You'll be the belle of Colorado City, Miss Anna Avery, if you'll become my wife."

She pretended to ponder his proposal for a minute and to fidget in uncertainty. "This is such an important decision, Frank. I need time to think. You don't know how tempted I am to say yes this very moment, but that wouldn't be fair to either of us. I must make sure it's *you* I love, not all you can give to me. Let's cancel our dinner tonight and allow me time to make the right decision. I'll see you Sunday and give you my answer then. All right?" *That will give me time to escape both yours and Stone's clutches.*

"Take off now. It's only a few hours to quitting time. Rest and think hard, Anna. I love you and I won't take no for an answer. If you don't love me now, you will one day. There's nothing wrong with marrying me knowing that, and you won't be duping me if you expose your feelings."

"That doesn't seem fair to you, Frank."

"Having you is the most important thing. Whether you love me or not, you'll make me a good wife, the perfect companion and partner. Now I need to get to the land office before it closes for the day. If I don't find anything registered there, I'll telegraph the one in Denver. By Monday, I'll have an answer about a claim registered under the name of Chapman or Marston or Cassidy. I'll call for you Sunday evening at six. Say yes, Anna, and you'll never be sorry."

"Whatever happens, Frank, I'll never be sorry I met you. I've learned so much from you. I promise you'll have my answer by Sunday night."

Ginny had no choice except to allow Frank to embrace and kiss her. Needing to dupe him, she responded demurely. "Please don't come around to influence me to say yes. I have to do what's right for me, for us."

"Sunday night it is, Anna. I know you'll agree."

Ginny and Frank parted outside the bank. Without being obvious, she checked her surroundings several times to make certain she wasn't being followed by her traitorous lover or by Kinnon's men. By now, Stone should be concealed or trying to shake his tails. She knew he was skilled enough to realize he had shadows, so precaution should keep him away long enough for her to elude him. If she confronted him, he would deceive her again and she couldn't bear that, not today. If he loved her and trusted her, he would have confided this secret last night. Stone must have been shocked to learn her identity from his father, but his knowledge couldn't be kept a secret for long. Surely he was intelligent enough to realize the risk of damaging their relationship was greater from her discovering he'd deceived her again than from a brief misunderstanding and suspicions that could be explained as coincidences and destiny. He could have told her at least part of the truth about their entwined pasts and given his old friend the benefit of doubt.

She must find her father first to help prove his innocence. Besides, she couldn't risk Stone exposing her to Kinnon, as his reckless and inexplicable investigation could do at any moment. How strange and cruel that mischievous fate kept throwing them together and yanking them apart. Every time things looked sunny and peaceful, new conflicts and dark clouds appeared. Perhaps they were ill starred.

Hattie's Boarding House came into sight and she hoped Stone hadn't taken refuge in her rooms. When she reached them, she was relieved to find both empty. With haste, she changed into a shirt, pants, and boots. She packed a few garments in saddlebags, and loaded the cloth sack with supplies, and filled her canteen. She strapped her derringer near her calf, then concealed a knife she'd purchased in her boot. She belted a new holster around her waist and slid the pistol taken from Slim into it. The rifle was loaded and more cartridges for all three weapons were stuffed into pockets of her flannel jacket. Months ago Stone had told her to keep extras close at hand for emergencies. He had taught her plenty she would use now to escape him and to protect herself in the wilderness. She dreaded heading into the mountains alone where countless men were seeking their fortunes, but she had no choice. Because of his rash probings, by Monday, Frank would know about a claim seventy miles away in the name of V. A. Marston. She couldn't let Kinnon beat her to the cabin and capture her father in case Mathew Marston was hiding out there from both men. If Stone knew the cabin's location and followed her there, she would force the truth from him and would convince him he was pursuing the wrong man. With Kinnon and a Special Agent after him, her father wouldn't, couldn't, return to town. Matt wasn't safe here and neither was she anymore.

Stone knew he'd been recognized, despite his short beard and all his precautions. He'd tried to ask his questions about Marston and the fire last year as cunningly as possible, but one of the prospectors had gotten suspicious. Within the last hour, he'd picked up two shadows, men he'd seen with Frank Kinnon yesterday. That annoyed but didn't surprise him as the banker had been searching for the claim since last year. Since he'd done the assaying and the strikers were dead, it wasn't odd for him to seek the rich site. He'd checked out Kinnon the last time but found nothing suspicious about the man. As far as everyone knew, Kinnon was an honest and upstanding citizen who'd never had any accusations against him to sully his good name. Yet, if Matt was being stalked or framed, it was up to him to help his old friend prove it. And if trouble had befallen Matt, Ginny needed him to help and protect her from that same threat.

Stone sipped a whiskey in a saloon that would be filled with customers soon; a big and noisy crowd would make it easier for him to lose his trailers. While he waited, his keen mind worked on his problem. Matt was the missing piece to the puzzle and he must find him before he could put it all together. If only Matt had sent him a message for help or left an explanatory note in the cabin, he could have solved Clay's killing by now and Matt would be in the clear. If Ginny's father had thought he couldn't trust the law or the officials in these parts, Matt should have known he could trust him. The fact Matt was also hiding from him created doubts of the older man's innocence. Or maybe his own troubled past was causing him to think evil of the man.

As soon as it was dark, he'd sneak to Ginny's room to wait for her to return from her dinner with the banker—and that one had better not touch her! He'd confess everything to her and trust her to believe him. Maybe she didn't realize her father might have changed during their long separation; she hadn't seen Matt since she was thirteen. The man had endured a bitter war where killings and cruelties had become second nature for many. Imprisonment, a loss of his plantation and family, and hardships in the wilderness must have worked on him. Matt was allowing his other daughter and wife to believe he was dead but he'd kept in touch with Ginny until last summer. Didn't that mean Matt loved and wanted his oldest child? Yet didn't he realize that news of his enormous strike would spread all over the country and expose him to his discarded family? Perhaps Matt was seeking investors so the mine and company wouldn't bear his name; perhaps he'd be a silent partner to protect his holdings from claims by other kin.

As he finished his drink, Stone knew he would have to persuade Ginny that her father might be a criminal. Yet, during this next talk, he needed to be totally honest with her. With Kinnon on to him and perhaps his true target, it was time to get Ginny out of town to safety. Before dawn's light came, they needed to sneak away to the cabin ten miles north of Weston Pass. If Ginny refused to listen or trust him tonight, he would rope and gag her, then haul her there where he could convince her in private! *Matt Marston, you'd better be innocent for her sake! Don't force me to lose the woman I love because I have to arrest you and send you to prison.*

As she completed preparations for departure, Ginny agonized over the dark span between them. While snuggled in her bed at midnight, Stone had led her to believe everything was golden and a bright future loomed ahead. She had not reached him and changed him. An evil monster dwelled between them, one Stone refused to slay. Love had blinded her to the real man and to the staggering facts. He knew how confused she was about her father; yet he had kept secrets that could explain certain matters about the past. His hatred, bitterness, and desire for revenge were apparently more important to him than their love, *if* he loved her. Until he confessed all to her and truly changed, there was no hope for them. If it must end between them, she wanted it to happen before more damaging evidence against him surfaced. If she was mistaken, he would find her and convince her of it.

Ginny penned a note to Hattie, who was out with a man who was attempting to woo the older woman. She revealed that Frank had proposed and she was going to Denver for a few days to consider her answer. She asked the woman to take care of her possessions until she returned. She twirled and stuffed her hair beneath a wide floppy-brimmed hat with a pinch-creased crown that concealed part of her face. She donned the oversize jacket that hid her curvy figure. She had eaten cold fried chicken and biscuits while she worked to avoid a revealing campfire in the hills later and she had wrapped extra food in a clean cloth to save her time and work for tomorrow.

Ginny checked outside in all directions before she went to the barn and corral out back to saddle her horse. She attached her supplies and saddlebags, then mounted. From sightseeing trips last week with Frank, she knew which road she needed to take. It was Friday at five o'clock; the town was busy and noisy enough that she should go unnoticed in her disguise, and she was visibly well armed to discourage trouble. There were about three to four hours of daylight left to assist her escape, time to get miles away and concealed in the forest. She scanned her surroundings and, seeing no one, she left the boardinghouse corral to head for her destination, about four days' ride from town.

Stone had finally shaken both men and sneaked to the boardinghouse barn to hide in the hayloft until later. He'd heard someone below him and stayed still and quiet. When the person had gone outside after saddling a horse, he'd peeked through a crack and seen his Ginny sneaking off alone and obviously prepared for a long trip! Astonishment, dismay, and confusion had kept him from exposing himself to her or to anyone who might join her.

Stone reasoned that she knew where the cabin was located and must be heading there. But why leave without him or not even telling him? If he hadn't been concealed here, she would be long gone before he was wise to her ruse. She had been such a genteel lady when they'd first met, but she'd learned plenty of tricks and skills since that day months ago. Stone read panic in her behavior and posture, and he wondered about the cause for them. Perhaps Matt had gotten a message to her to join him somewhere in the foothills. Or maybe she had decided to look for her father at the cabin. That was rash and dangerous, and not including him was suspicious. He would shadow her to seek the truth but not reveal himself unless she got into trouble.

Shu, woman, you said you told me everything. Said you loved me and trusted me. Why are you sneaking off like this? Maybe you knew I was keeping something from you and that caused you to doubt me and bolt. Or maybe you're just choosing your father over me. Mercy, Ginny love, how can I help you, protect you, and win you if you keep running away from me?

Ginny avoided the two toll roads that snaked into the foothills, ways of getting wagons and supplies inland. As she rode northwestward, she glanced at Pike's Peak and was relieved she didn't have to head in that direction or scale the towering summit that was still capped with snow despite the fact it was almost July. Yet many sharp ridges, plateaus, valleys, meadows, canyons, and rugged terrain lay between her and the secluded cabin. The lofty range before her was intimidating and beautiful. The landscape's colors were almost startling in their vividness: the sky overhead was an intense blue; trees, grasses, and bushes were various shades of green; upturned hills and boulders of red sandstone blazed like fire beneath the sun; and snow atop peaks or trapped in crevices of grayish brown or crimson rock was a pristine white.

She passed near Manitou Springs where ancient cliff dwellers had lived, hundreds of years ago. She rode through the edge of the Garden of the Gods and was fascinated by the unusual formations in red-and-white sandstone, some reaching two to three hundred feet tall. She followed the map's instructions, which she had committed to memory, staying within sight of the northernmost toll road but out of view from any travelers or workers on it. She knew the road and the stream near it would be her markers for a long time.

Gradually the elevation increased but not fast enough to

create a hardship on the horse or herself. Her pace was slow, but the ride wasn't difficult, yet. Pines and scrubs clung tenaciously to rocky cliffsides, creating a lovely contrast of emerald and vermilion. She ventured between rugged hogbacks with verdant coverings of piñon, oaks, juniper, alder, and birch. She saw trees twisted and stripped by the forces of harsh nature and creeks of swift, clear water which she discovered was cold when she halted to rest near one and drank from it. It had been warm today, but she knew the air would cool fast when dusk arrived in the mountains that engulfed her. The light jacket already felt good, but Stone's embrace, she mused dreamily, would have been better.

Don't do this to yourself, Ginny. He's left behind for now. Until Father explains his part in their past, you can't trust him.

The long and lonely journey continued. She needed to put as many miles as possible between her and Colorado City before dark closed in around her. It was fortunate there were no strikes and prospectors in the area she was covering, for now anyway. She skirted a rocky cliff where a stream of icy water shot over the precipice with a loud roar and in a burst of white. During her ride, she saw and heard squirrels, rabbits, chipmunks, bison, and pronghorn. Once, she and a moose startled each other in a low marshy place near a nature-made pond.

When she reached the highest elevation since departure, Ginny paused to glance back at Colorado City in the flatland far below her. It looked as small and alone as she felt in the heights around her and the vast expanse of the land before her. *Continue or turn back?* she asked herself.

There was no choice; she was committed. Frank wouldn't know she was missing until Sunday evening and might be fooled until Monday by the message in her note to Hattie and the possessions left behind. He might believe she had panicked and traveled to Denver to put distance between them, and perhaps search for her there. She hoped so as that would give her more escape time. But even if she headed back this minute, she wouldn't reach town before Stone realized she was gone, if

416

he found a way to get to her room tonight. She couldn't imagine what he would do when he discovered she had vanished again.

Damn you for lying to me last night. Can I ever trust you again? Ginny forced him from mind after warning herself to stay alert.

The forest-covered Rampart Range to her right was steep and rugged, and she was glad she didn't have to cross it. She heard a wagon rumbling down a slope on the road and paused behind bushes to stay out of view. She reached the point where it veered southwest beyond Cascade Creek; that knowledge supplied her present location. She was glad she'd practiced drawing the map from memory and she could close her eyes and visualize it with clarity.

Dusk approached and told Ginny she must halt soon to camp. At least a near full moon was rising to prevent the woods from being pitch dark on her first night out alone. That and having eaten before her departure would enable her to skip lighting a fire whose flames could be sighted and odor smelled by the wrong person. She was compelled to guide her mount into a rushing stream to avoid rough and uneven terrain. As they walked in the chilly water, she strained her ears to catch any sound of prospectors panning or camping ahead. She prayed she would see danger before it struck, as her view was restricted by twists of the hilly banks. By the time the terrain allowed her to leave the water, she'd only encountered animals coming to drink and she'd spooked them. She passed Sand Gulch and saw a cabin on one hillside with smoke leaving its chimney to reveal it was occupied. She rode onward, the elevation steadily increasing but the evergreen pass aiding her chore.

Not far ahead she stopped for the night at Crystola Creek. She unsaddled the horse to let him drink and graze. If peril came while she was sleeping, surely he would make enough noise to awaken and alert her. She spread a borrowed blanket on pinestraw-covered ground and placed her weapons beside it.

In the near darkness, Ginny heard all kinds of sounds. Nocturnal birds called to each other. Animals moved about in the brush, a browsing deer actually coming close before he sniffed her presence and darted away. Frogs and crickets were abundant near the water. It was chilly as she nestled into the blanket for warmth. When breezes stirred foliage and limbs, her imagination fashioned them into scary threats. Her heart pounded and pulse raced. She trembled. A few times, her teeth chattered. It didn't help to try to convince herself she was being childish and cowardly. At last, exhaustion allowed her to sleep.

Stone crept close to her position, tossed a blanket over him, and slept nearby to guard her. He wanted to ease her fears but needed, if he could, to wait until she exposed her motive for running away.

On Saturday Ginny crossed the South Platte River and trekked through Wilkerson Pass in the lower mountain range. She was surrounded by trees of various types: a world of vivid green with smells she found refreshing and heady. Purple fringe, daisy, columbine, and monument plant gave certain areas beautiful splashes of color; so did the numerous butterflies and other insects working on them. She smiled as a pair of red foxes paused to watch her pass before returning to their playful rolls in the grass, and almost laughed aloud when a fat porcupine waddled across the trail and caused her mount to prance and whinny in fear of tangling with those sharp spines. She saw many large hares leaping for cover and wondered how one would taste roasted over a fire until crispy brown. Mule deer and elk grazed in meadows and only lifted their heads a moment to make certain she wasn't a threat to them. She listened to squirrels chattering in trees and noisily feasting on the seeds inside pinecones. It was an awe-inspiring territory that was lovely and peaceful for the time being.

For the past two nights Ginny had refused to fret over the three men in her life and allow such thoughts to distract her concentration. She didn't want to worry and suffer over her father's survival. She didn't want to fear over Frank's vengeful pursuit. She didn't want to agonize over Stone's possible betrayal and treachery.

But she could no longer keep the men from her thoughts. She scolded herself for not giving Stone a chance to explain before she acted on impulse from anguish and shock. It was probably foolish and dangerous to have ridden into this vast wilderness alone. Anything could happen to her. She could have an accident and be far from help. She could be attacked by a band of men like Bart's gang. She could encounter a perilous wild animal; already she had seen two large bears this morning. She could fall prey to a renegade Indian or a desperate prospector driven mad from defeat and solitude. She could miss a marker and get lost, as mileage was difficult to judge in the rugged terrain. No matter that Stone was misguided and mistaken about her father, she was certain he loved and wanted her and wouldn't harm her. It had been stupid to take off without speaking with him and bringing him along. He must be thinking horrible things about her.

She had warned him that Kinnon was dangerous, though Stone could take care of himself; if Kinnon believed he knew where the silver was located, he could try to beat the information out of him or even ambush and kill him. Stone could be in danger this instant. Probably the only reason Kinnon hadn't attacked Stone so far was because the villain knew he was a lawman whose murder would entice other agents to investigate and possibly unmask him. Kinnon had no way, she hoped, of knowing what Stone may have written in his official reports about him.

Without a doubt, the moment that telegram arrived from Denver with a claim listed under V. A. Marston, Kinnon would head for the same location she would reach on Tuesday. If Stone didn't arrive soon after she did and her father wasn't there, she must ride to the closest town for protection while she decided what step to take next.

She retrieved her attention as she saw a distant cliffside

honeycombed with tunnels. Sluices and flumes snaked their way down rocky walls to a place where workers waited to separate gold from gravel and sand. Men with rakes, picks, shovels, and wheelbarrows labored under the late-June sun or in the near darkness of shafts. She watched a while, then journeyed onward until she found a sheltered area near Wilkerson Pass and camped.

Monday, July first, Ginny left the dense forest for a time to travel across a plateau of scattered trees, scrubs, and rolling grassland. She used the fieldglasses and compass she had purchased in Colorado City to spy her markers and to provide the right direction. She continued to be successful in avoiding gold-seekers and fur trappers on creeks and streams. She skirted the area where she saw a grassy hillside dotted with shaft entrances, some disappearing inward and others downward. Many men were mining the obviously productive site. Tents, shacks, lean-tos, and dugouts were scattered nearby for shelter and sleeping. Wagons and teams waited to be filled with gathered ore to be taken to a smelter or a Sampling Works, as she saw no processing structure. At the latter, Kinnon had told her that ore was purchased, assayed on the spot, and the miner paid, with a deduction for smelting and transporting charges. She made certain to go unnoticed.

Before Ginny camped that night in a gulch, she checked the sky and air for signs of rain to prevent being trapped during a flash flood. Kinnon had told her how many men ignorant of this area were killed that way.

She had finished her chicken and biscuits Saturday night. Yesterday she had risked a fire long enough to cook johnnycakes, warm beans from a tin, and to brew coffee, but she had doused it the moment her meal was ready. She did the same tonight. Tomorrow, she would eat the leftover bread and dried beef. She had been fortunate to have a constant water supply along the way. She longed for a relaxing and muscle-soothing bath but couldn't risk being caught naked and unarmed by man or beast.

When she finished eating, she stretched out her sore body on the blanket. This time, she dreamed of Stone when she slept.

Tuesday she crossed another section of the South Platte River, a well-worn animal or Indian trail, and a creek with large boulders piled in a right-angle bend: all markers on her mental map, which told her she was still on the right path and nearing the cabin. Forest enclosed her again. Ridges of rippling hog-backs filled her line of vision and peaks towered in most directions. Weston Pass southward and Mount Lincoln northward stood out as two of the tallest, with the cabin she sought located halfway between the two majestic points that were guiding the remainder of her journey.

Shortly after midday, Ginny spied the rustic cabin perched on a large shelf of a steep hillside with a swift stream at its base. It looked unreachable on its lofty perch of sharp and slick rock. The relatively flat ledge and three cliffsides were strewn with trees to provide wood for winter fires and cooking. She wondered how her father and Clay had constructed the sturdy dwelling in such a difficult place. A ladder was raised to prevent entry to trespassers or attackers, but she knew how to lower it. The place appeared to be deserted for a long time. She watched for a while but heard and saw no one nearby.

Ginny rode to the stream and dismounted. "Father! Matt Marston! Are you here?" she yelled. "Is anybody inside? Father, it's Ginny!"

There was no response, which distressed her. She wondered if he was at the silver site but doubted it because there was no horse or mule nearby, or any tracks fresh or old. All she heard was the rushing of the stream and birds singing. She guided her horse across the cold water to a grass spot, then dropped his reins. She unloaded her supplies and possessions in case something endangered him and he abandoned her.

She stood below the ladder and gazed up at it. She didn't like how rickety the climbing device looked and wondered if it was too old for safe ascent. But if her father had left a message there for her, she must—

"Do you know how to lower the ladder and get inside?"

Startled, Ginny whirled, her eyes wide, her mouth agape, and her hand going to the butt of Slim's pistol. "Stone! How . . ." He looked so handsome and she was so happy to see him that she almost flung herself into his arms before reality returned with his too quick reply.

"I've been on your tail since you deserted me. You did a good job of leaving unseen and getting here safely. You're smarter and braver than I realized, woman. I've been guarding you day and night during the journey."

"Guarding me or letting me lead you to my father so you can kill him?"

"So, you did know the truth all along, just as I feared and suspected."

Stone's hazy answer tormented Ginny's heart and she was glad her father wasn't there to confront and challenge this beloved enemy.

CHAPTER 19

Ginny glared at him as she tried to conceal her anguish. "You're sadly mistaken, Mr. Special Agent. I didn't know about your lies and sinister plans until you riled Frank so badly Friday that he tattled on you."

Stone tensed in dread. "What did he tell you about me?"

"The truth, Mr. Traitorous Chapman."

Stone realized that this conversation wasn't going to be easy. "What is 'the truth' Ginny?"

"Why didn't you tell me you knew both my father and Clay? Why didn't you tell me you've been here many times, that on some of those visits you came searching for my father to kill him for something he didn't do? He would never murder anyone, especially not Clayton Cassidy." Before he could respond, she said, "We'd better prepare for an attack by Frank's men. He said he was having you followed so you probably led them straight here. They'll kill us both to get information. I was wrong about you. I thought we had been honest with each other. I told you everything about me and thought you'd done the same."

"Then why did you take off like that? You didn't even allow me to explain. You believed what Kinnon—a stranger and your target—said over what the man you claim to love and trust told you. And don't worry about Kinnon's men; I lost them

Friday afternoon before I sneaked to Hattie's barn to wait for you to get back from your romantic dinner with your boss."

To clear the oppressive air between them, Ginny knew she must be cooperative and honest and pray he would be, too. "I'll admit it was foolish and dangerous to take off like I did," she began her explanation, "but I was too hurt and angry and scared to think straight, and I was too far along on the trail to turn back when my head cleared. Besides, Frank telegraphed Denver to check on three names for land registration: Marston, Cassidy, and Chapman. He'll get a response Monday and I'll be exposed, thanks to your reckless nosing around. He thinks you might have been a third partner in the strike and that you filed the claim for yourself. He suspects you know where it is. Did you already know about this location?"

"Yes, because Clay left his half of the claim to me. He sent a map and will before his death. Besides, the location is listed in the Denver General Land Office."

She gaped at him. "You . . . own half of this claim?"

Her reaction told him she hadn't known that fact. "I was Clay's best friend, like his family. He has no other kin . . . You're saying you ran only because you'd be exposed Monday and because you thought I'd lied to you?"

Ginny noticed how he quickly changed the subject. "For those reasons and to save my father's life. Frank said you three were in the Army together, were friends. How can you believe Father could do such a thing?"

"Your father isn't the same man you left at thirteen, Ginny. He's ridden through hell a few times since then and it's obviously changed him. I suspected him because of Clay's last message to me." He repeated what the letter had said. "Clay didn't trust him anymore and I can't tell you why, other than those curious accidents and Matt's strange behavior. I do know Matt didn't file the claim until after Clay was dead, and he put it in your name. It seemed to me as if he disappeared for his own gain instead of helping the law find Clay's killer. He didn't even ask for my help in solving the crime. What was I supposed

424

to think, Ginny? And how could I confess such things to you right after we finally reconciled? I didn't want to lose you, at least no sooner than necessary. I wanted as much time with you as possible before I had to confess something that might tear us apart again. I was going to tell you everything when I saw you Friday night, but that didn't happen. You left before I had the chance." Stone grasped her by the forearms. "Don't you understand I was afraid of losing you because of who I am and what I must do? If Matt's guilty, I have to arrest him and see him punished. I owe it to Clay. But if he isn't to blame, I'll help clear him and protect him; I promise. What more can you expect of me? I've sworn to bring in the killer."

His words moved her. He had acted unwisely but from good motives, something she understood from her own foolish actions. "Believe me, Stone, it isn't my father."

"Wanting that to be true doesn't make it so. This is the third father to come between us. I hated to defeat Charles Avery because I knew it would hurt my Anna. I hated to desert Ben, but I knew staying home would hurt my Johanna more. Now I hate to chase Matt because it can hurt you, maybe destroy our future together. Please don't let that happen, Ginny. I love you and need you. Mercy, woman, why do you always put me in a bind?"

She wanted to fling herself into his arms and kiss him, but more needed to be said first. "Don't you think my father was also hurt, afraid, and confused? His partner and friend was murdered and somebody tried to kill him. He probably knows even you don't believe him and are chasing him. If a friend doubts his innocence, why should he think the law would believe him? He could be dead and buried somewhere."

Stone pulled her into his arms. "Don't cry, love. I'm sure he's alive. If we can only find him and learn the truth, things will be all right."

Ginny leaned back and looked into his eyes. "What if he can't prove he's innocent, Stone? What if Clay's killer is never found? Can he be arrested and imprisoned on suspicions alone?"

"No, Ginny, he can't. But he's made it look bad for himself, so he'll be investigated. Have you told me everything you know?"

"Yes. It's Frank Kinnon's wicked deed; I'm certain of it." She related how the man had behaved and what he'd said when he'd discovered Stone was back in town. "He wants this claim so badly, he's obsessed."

Stone stroked her flushed and dampened cheeks as he reasoned, "Why would he kill Matt and Clay before they revealed where it was? If he'd gotten the truth from them, he'd have the mine going by now. He wouldn't still be searching for clues or be riled by my return."

"I realize it doesn't make sense to kill the only sources of information for something you crave, but I'm sure there's an explanation. Maybe his men made a mistake in killing both partners. Maybe they didn't realize both men were in the shack when they fired on it and burned it. Maybe Frank thought he could get to me or to you." With reluctance she added, "Maybe it wasn't Frank. Maybe it was a common thief."

Stone felt he had to point out that couldn't have been the case. "Their animals and possessions weren't stolen," he explained. "And the two men inside were shot then burned beyond recognition for some reason I can't figure. But I suppose a spark from the fire or a lantern shattered during the shooting could have set off the blaze. Shacks of dry wood fire up fast and easy. It's possible the fire wasn't set on purpose, or maybe Matt could have done it afterward to dupe the killer into thinking him dead. They were identified by those belongings left outside. I figured somebody wanted to make certain the remains were believed to be those of Mathew Marston and Clayton Cassidy."

"You mean 'somebody,' as in my father?"

"Yes, Ginny, that's how it looked to me. I guessed Matt's things were left behind as proof he was there, but we both know he wasn't the second victim. I discovered that by the fact, he

426

registered the claim days after the incident. The minute I heard V. A. Marston, I knew who that was. Matt took off from the shack with nothing, went to Denver and registered the claim, then vanished. You said he wrote to you that he was searching for investors. His claim was safely staked, so why did he flee, Ginny? Where is he now? What's taking so long to announce the biggest strike this territory has known? With that assay report, he should have investors begging to be part of his new company. Why doesn't he seek help and protection from the law? What doesn't he contact me, his new partner? Why didn't he mention me to you or explain this suspicious mess to you?"

The speculations didn't sound good for Ginny's father. "I don't know," she admitted. "Maybe Clay didn't tell him he left his share to you. He must have been afraid for his life or he wouldn't have sent me the map and told me to wait for him in England. If something hasn't happened to him, he would have written again by now."

"Letters get lost or slowed down or stolen during robberies. You and Johanna left London in late February. Maybe you missed a letter from him."

"If so, Ben should have it by now. We asked for all mail to be forwarded to us at the ranch. I was to visit with her before I came here, before she died and everything went crazy. You would have loved her, Stone. She was wonderful, special. I miss her terribly. It wasn't fair for her to die so young. It wasn't fair for her to never reach home and make peace with your father." More tears spilled forth as bittersweet memories filled her head.

Stone cuddled her in his comforting arms, his hand stroking her back and hair. "That's how I felt about Clay, Ginny. A best friend is hard to lose and harder to replace. What happens to us if Matt . . . is guilty?"

She gave his question serious thought. "Don't worry, he isn't."

Stone couldn't help but envy the total faith she had in her father when she had lacked it in him. He told himself she'd had good reason to doubt him, and he didn't refute her.

Ginny saw his concerned reaction. She smiled and coaxed, "Don't worry. Whatever happens won't affect our relationship. Just don't be the one to arrest him. Do that much for me, for us. I love you, and I believe you did what you thought was right. We have a lot to learn about each other but we'll have plenty of time—our whole lives."

He almost held his breath as he entreated, "You mean that?"

She hugged and reassured him, "Yes, Stone. I love you and I'll marry you. We'll settle things here and return to Texas to live."

"When?"

His elation and excitement made her smile. "I don't know how long this will take. What do you think?"

He deliberated a few moments. "I don't know. I've investigated this several times before and found no clues to lead me to Matt or to the killer. Do you think if we form a company of our own, Matt will show himself?"

"If he hears about it, I suppose so. Wouldn't you think he'd keep his eyes and ears on this area no matter where he is?"

"I would think so. So you agree to my plan?"

"Yes, but I prefer to put the mining company in your name until my family in Georgia can be given the news if Father is alive. They think he was killed during the war. Hearing he lived and never contacted them would come as a shock. I'm also sure my stepmother and stepbrother will try to claim part of the earnings. I don't want to have anything to do with them. I told you how they cut me off when I was stranded in England."

"I'll handle any problems for you."

"Thank you." A whinny from her horse pulled her eyes in that direction but nothing appeared wrong and Stone didn't go to investigate. "Why don't we get inside? I'm starved and tired. We can talk more later."

"That's a good idea. I'll lasso the ladder and pull it down."

"No need." She walked to where bushes and vines grew along the rocks. Her fingers probed until she located a rope. "Yank on this."

Stone obeyed and the ladder released and lowered noisily to within a few feet of the ground. "Clever." He whistled for his horse and the well-trained animal came galloping forward from the woods.

"Father made one like this for me when I was a child. I had a small house in a big tree and this is how I reached it. I loved doing boy's things; that's why I needed to go off to school to learn to become a lady."

Ginny gathered her supplies and possessions while Stone unsaddled both horses and fetched his gear. He steadied the shaky ladder while she climbed to the top. She lowered the rope he had given to her to drape over her shoulder. He tied cloth sacks to it and she hauled them upward. The action was repeated until all the goods were on the wooden landing.

Stone scaled the squeaking rungs with caution and agility, his weight heavy on them. He pulled up the device and locked it in place, to tower above the cabin. "Now, we won't be disturbed or endangered. Chuune will guard your horse for us."

She glanced down at the reddish-brown sorrel with its light mane and tail. "What does his name mean? I presume it's Indian."

"It's Apache for *friend,* and he's surely been that for years."

"He's magnificent and smart and loyal."

"Like my new best friend: Miss Virginia Anne Marston."

Ginny smiled and hugged him. "You're my best *chuune,* too."

Thunder rumbled in the distance and Stone glanced that way. "Going to rain later. Let's get inside and check for any clues."

Ginny felt the threat of a powerful storm, but not from nature. It came from intense emotions building within her body at having the man she loved near.

Stone opened the door and pushed it ajar. With fingers grazing his pistol butts, his keen eyes scanned the interior. "It's safe."

The cabin was dim because the wooden shutters were closed, the walls were of thick logs, and their bodies blocked much of the sunshine. Her eyes adjusted and her gaze moved about the last home of her missing father.

"I'll open the windows for fresh air and light," he said, cognizant of what she must be experiencing.

While he did his task, Ginny carried in their belongings and closed the door. She glanced around once more, trying to envision a southern plantation gentleman in such barren and musty surroundings. It was a big change from Green Oaks and the luxury he had known there. The cabin was small, dusty, and smelly. Its only furnishings were two bunks, a table, two chairs, a stove, and one large cabinet containing dishes, cookware, and supplies. A few garments hung on pegs, looking pathetic in their rumpled and faded state. A pair of well-worn boots with crusted mud and snowy cobwebs rested on the floor near one bed. A deck of old poker cards were scattered on the eating table; more cobwebs displayed themselves there and on the two chairs to tell how long it had been since they'd been used or wiped. Rusty splotches on the stove said it too, hadn't been used in ages. Everything revealed a layer of thick dust and no fingerprints to indicate they'd been touched recently. A look of long abandonment brought sadness to Ginny's heart.

Her somber gaze locked with Stone's, who'd clearly come to the same conclusions. It seemed obvious, but she said, "He hasn't been here."

"That doesn't mean he isn't alive somewhere, love. Have faith."

Sensing nothing of her father in the meager room, she walked onto a rock porch out back that was covered by a shed-type roof and supported by two rough poles. There, she noticed rusting prospector equipment: picks and shovels and pans. Overhead were hooks for hanging garments to dry or for suspending meat to cure. She tried to imagine her genteel father living in this rustic setting and working under arduous conditions. He had not been much of an outdoorsman except for occasional hunting, but had become one to be a miner. His hands had been soft and little exposure to sun had not tanned

430

or wrinkled his face. She wondered how he would look when she saw him again after many ravages had worked on him.

Mathew Marston had lived and worked as a prosperous and refined southern gentleman. What she saw here told of a man who knew hard work and sacrifice, a man without wealth and comforts, a man without the amenities of civilization, almost without the bare essentials and necessities for survival. Fate in the guise of bitter and greedy war had taken so much from him and changed him, as Stone suggested. He had endured prison and many losses and hardships, so many denials and torments, according to Stone. He had lacked a devoted family during his dark hours to give him support. He had been compelled to accept and adjust to his losses alone. She hadn't noticed this shocking effect on him in his letters, but this harsh setting exposed it in vivid and heartrending detail. *Oh, Father, what has life done to you?* Tears eased down her cheeks, and Stone hurried to wrap his loving arms around her for solace. When her weeping was controlled, she told him what she had been thinking and feeling.

Stone had also been in deep thought about the past. He had called to mind days and nights with Clay and Matt. "It's like this for many men now, love; war does that. Being on the wrong or losing side makes it worse. A man's pride takes a beating; when that happens, either he gets stronger and tougher or he gives up. But Matt was a good and kind man. I'm sure I misjudged him. I wasn't in any frame of mind to be clear-headed; I allowed Clay's curious accusations to cloud my wits. Something must have happened after I saw them that last time to cause trouble between them."

Ginny stiffened and paled. She sealed her gaze with Stone's and asked, "What if Clay is the one still alive? What if he filed the claim? What if my father wrote that letter before he was killed and Clay mailed it to me?" Ginny shook her head. "That isn't right; it had news of Clay's murder in it."

Stone tensed, too. "Are you sure it was in your father's handwriting?"

She mused a moment. "Almost positive. But I didn't examine it closely. I had no reason to suspect it wasn't from him. If Clay wrote it, why send me a map? Why register the land in my name?"

"If Matt was in the shack, you'd be Clay's partner. And putting your name on the deed would conceal him as the survivor. He could be waiting for you to get worried and come looking for Matt. Maybe he didn't want to put bad news in a letter."

"We'll have to wait and see who shows up, or if anybody does."

"You're right. No need to waste energy on wild thoughts. I want to check out those woods, make sure nothing looks unusual there. I'll be back soon, love."

Ginny looked at the verdant trees. She noticed a stack of chopped wood that was rotting, the sharp cliffs that would guard their flank and sides, and a rapid waterfall shooting over one precipice. She walked to that lovely scene, silently complimenting her father for selecting an easily defensible site with wood and water sources. With adequate supplies, a person under siege from villain or weather could hold out here for a long time. Between two jutting rocks was a hunk of gradually dissolving soap that would have been gone by now if not for its protective shelter. It and a raggedy drying cloth lying over a limb implied the spot was used for bathing. As Stone joined her, she moved closer and stuck her fingers under the rush of water, then shrieked and jerked them away. "It's almost freezing! I need a bath desperately, but I'm going to start a fire and warm water first."

Stone locked his arms around her waist and smiled when she leaned back against him. "Sounds good to me, but I'm used to washing off in cold streams and icy creeks. I'll be done before the first bubble rises in your pot."

She turned in his embrace to find him grinning. "You aren't serious?" He nodded and chuckled. "You're going to stand under that arctic flow?"

"Yep, soon as I shuck these clothes." He unbuckled and put aside his weapons. He doffed his boots and clothing and stepped under the cascade of invigorating liquid to wet his body. When his hair and body were wet, he stepped from beneath the flow to tend his task. With his back to her, he worked the soap free of its prison and whistled as he lathered himself.

"Ouch!" she wailed. "How can you stand that? Just the spray and wind from it are chilling me."

Stone glanced over his shoulder and grinned. "It's not bad. You get used to it fast after the first shock. Livens you, woman, and cools you off. I need that about now or we won't get supper anytime soon."

Eat? her mind challenged as she stared at him and let his voice wash over her. *Who could be hungry for food at a time like this?* She couldn't think or do anything at this moment except gaze at the irresistible man before her. His darkly tanned body appealed to all her senses. His flesh was taut and smooth. Few scars were visible and none were detracting. His broad chest was hairless. He was lithe and sleek. His firm muscles rippled with each movement. Her gaze drifted over strong shoulders, powerful arms, narrow waist, firm buttocks, and long legs. Fiery desire attacked her. On impulse she yanked off her clothes and joined him, backing into the flow. She gasped in shock as the cold water dashed over her skin and created goosebumps and shivers. "You li-lied, St-Stone; it's li-like ice."

He chuckled in amusement. "Not for long, my brave filly; a good rubbing will warm you." Using his bandanna and sliver of soap, he moved her long hair aside and briskly washed her neck, back, and arms. Then he turned her and lathered her breasts, passing the cloth over them with tantalizing leisure. He sent her a mischievous grin and asked, "How do you like this bath, Mrs. Chapman, if you don't mind me practicing that name?"

"Since I've used so many with you, my love, please do. It sounds wonderful." She gave a dreamy sigh. *"This* feels wonderful, frozen and all. My hair's soaked, so I might as well scrub it, too. I can't get any colder."

"I'll do it," he volunteered eagerly. He washed and rinsed it twice as instructed by a laughing Ginny.

She turned and murmured, "Marvelous hands, kind sir; you can use them on me any time you wish. I'm so limp I feel as if I could melt."

"How does this please you, Mrs. Chapman?" he asked as his mouth covered hers in a searing kiss and their tongues danced playfully. He enjoyed the feel of her slippery hands on his face as she caressed it. "Or this?" Stone's deft hand continued its delightful task and grew bolder as the soapy cloth was worked downward past her ribs, waist, and hips.

Ginny trailed her fingers over his slick body, his actions staggering to her spinning head. Despite the temperature of the water and breeze over her flesh, she blazed inside and his skin felt warm to her touch. His mouth left hers and trekked down her throat to tease her sensitive breasts. She closed her eyes a moment and her head seemed to roll around on her neck like a slowly spinning toy top. She looked down as his tongue drew circles around her taut nipples. With smoldering eyes, she watched the intimate action, feeling no modesty. The beauty of their love flooded her soul. When his mouth returned to hers, she feasted upon it.

Stone rubbed his body against hers to increase her warmth and pleasure. His gaze roamed her face before his fingers caressed the silky skin there. One thumb moved over her parted lips and he felt her tremble. She glowed with radiance from love and desire. "You're so beautiful, Ginny. Do you realize how you get to me?" he asked, voice thick with emotion.

Her gaze took in his dripping sable hair, damp lashes encasing dark and sparkling eyes, and the clear drops running down his stubbled face. "I hope it's the same powerful way you affect me."

He quivered with yearning as her lips and tongue made love to his thumb, sending torrid messages to every part of his being.

His soul and loins throbbed to possess her fully. His breathing quickened. "You're the first woman who's stolen my heart. I haven't been able to get you off my mind since we met. It was hard understanding and accepting what you do to me. I was afraid if I ever weakened but couldn't win you I'd be tormented for life, and I'd had my share of suffering. I couldn't believe a woman like you—the most precious in the world—could want a half-breed bastard. I've almost lost you so many times, Ginny, that it scares me to think about them."

"You'll never lose me, my love, never. You're the only man I've ever wanted, or ever will. So many times I was terrified you didn't love me or would never admit it. I was afraid that I was too blinded by love to realize you didn't feel the same way. I couldn't bear to lose you, Stone Chapman."

"When I'm near you, Ginny, I want to kiss you, touch you, hold you. I want to hear you laugh and see you smile and watch everything you do. I want to talk with you and be with you. I want to protect you and make you happy. If I don't watch out, my flaming beauty, you'll totally consume me."

"How can fire consume fire, my love? You engulf me head to foot."

"*Shu*, it's strange hearing me say such words. I've never talked about my feelings before and tried to keep them bridled, but I want you to know them, all of them, all of *me*, Ginny. You're the most important thing that's ever happened to me. I never knew such feelings existed in me. But you make it easy for me to feel them and share them. You've been a terrible distraction, woman. You stole my attention and time and energy without even trying. My wits were so dulled I made mistakes in thinking. I'm sorry for tricking you in the past. I promise it won't happen again."

Those admissions sent potent charges through her. Yet he looked a little uncomfortable at being so open for the first time in his life. To help him get past the difficult moment, she smiled and quipped, "I didn't mean to be a distraction, Stone, only an irresistible attraction."

He nibbled at her lips, grasping her thoughtful ruse and appreciating it. "From here on, woman, I'm keeping a keen eye on you. If I don't, you'll be leading me around like a mustang on a rope and have me too tamed to keep my mind on other things when it's necessary."

"We certainly can't have that, now can we?" she teased. His touch and nearness assailed her head to foot. "I've missed you and wanted you so much, Stone." She placed her hands around his neck, drew down his head, and covered his mouth with hers. The moment she had craved—and feared lost—arrived in glorious splendor. She yearned to taste and share his tender and torrid passion. He was such a powerful force. When he kissed her, he stole her breath away. When he touched her, she lost her will to him. She became shameless with him, a wanton and greedy creature.

He groaned in desire and tightened his hold on her. He kissed each feature on her face as he murmured over and over that he loved her. His hand renewed its prior task and eased the soapy cloth between her thighs to bathe and stimulate the core of her womanhood.

Ginny felt as if the very essence of her being was under beautiful siege, and she willingly surrendered. Every inch of her was alive, aware, eager, aflame. Her secret place enticed, summoned, begged him to conquer it and enslave her. "You're driving me mad, Stone. I need you now."

Stone hurriedly rinsed the soap from their bodies, lifted her, and carried her into the cabin. He lay her on a bunk and took a position half atop her on the narrow space. His mouth and hands went to work to brand every part of her as his. He trembled with need as soft moans escaped her throat and she writhed from the flames he kindled. He wanted her so badly and quickly that he feared to enter her too soon and lose mastery over himself.

Ginny pulled him closer. "If you don't feed me now, I'm going to starve from hunger for you."

Stone obeyed her urgent command, each stroke and thrust

evoking another and another. He tried to take deep breaths and think of other things to help retain his control, but it soon became impossible. Ginny *made* it impossible by responding to him with such ardor that his mind couldn't think straight. When he halted a moment to recover himself, she continued to drive him wild. He cautioned in a husky voice, "Be still a minute, love. I'm barely restraining myself."

Entrapped in a swirling vortex of desire, she coaxed, "No need to wait, Stone. I'm more than ready for you."

That was all the invitation and encouragement he needed.

Ginny thrashed upon the bunk and kissed him with total abandon. Love's music wafted over her mind and body, rapidly increasing in pace and volume. As if the most magical violin in the world was playing, passion's strings struck the sweetest notes she had ever heard. Its stirring and romantic chords touched her very soul with harmony and pleasure. Faster and louder the strains flowed over her until a crescendo thundered in her ears. She clung to him in rapture.

Blood pounded through Stone's being like drums during an Apache victory dance. "I love you, Ginny Marston, I love you."

They kissed deeply and then, breathless and sated, they nestled together to share their contentment and joy. At last, they were one in mind, heart, and body, and a bright future awaited them.

Stone held her and kissed her with such tenderness, gentleness, and possessiveness that she almost cried with happiness. He belonged to her now of his own free will and admission.

As if reading those thoughts and sharing those conclusions, Stone murmured, "You're all mine, Ginny. We'll never be parted again. I promise, never another secret from you."

They rested and relaxed for a while, then Ginny's stomach growled as breakfast was far behind her. Stone smiled and said, "Suppertime's calling. Let's rinse off and dress. I'll make a fire in the stove and we'll cook together while you dry your hair before you get too chilled."

"If I freeze again, I know somebody who can heat me up in a delightful manner." She kissed him seductively.

"He will be more than willing to obey after supper and a rest."

"This is wonderful," Ginny murmured as she ate a hot meal and sipped coffee, snug in a blanket and cozy cabin with the man she loved.

"Yep, it surely is, woman. I can get used to this kind of living. I know the perfect spot on the ranch to build our house."

"Don't you think we should ask your father's permission first?"

"He'll agree. He'll be happy to have his son and new daughter settle down there. And he'll be after us to give him grandchildren quick. So will Mother. I told her how I feel about you and she spoke in your favor."

That news pleased Ginny. "If we keep practicing, I'll be with child before we say 'I do.'"

"Not if we get married in Denver. Why not do that? Why wait any longer?"

Her pulse raced with anticipation. "Are you sure you're ready to give up the trail for a demanding wife, confining home, and noisy children?"

"Sounds more than appealing to me, woman."

"My goodness, you have changed, my once-skittish guide," she teased, slipping a morsel of bread into his mouth.

Stone captured her fingers and licked them clean. His dark eyes glittered with strong emotion. "*You* changed me, Ginny. Thanks. You made me show my best side around you. I didn't even realize I *had* one until you pulled it out of me. If anybody had told me in March I would be getting married in July, I'd have thought him loco."

"I can say the same thing. I never expected to meet anyone like you. Steve Carr swept me off my feet and Stone Chapman kept me there."

"We're perfect for each other, Ginny," he said in a serious tone.

"Yes, my love, we are. Fate must have believed the same thing because she kept throwing us together. Isn't it wild how coincidences work sometimes? First the wagontrain, then the ranch, and now here."

"Amazing. My guiding spirit is showing me favor this year."

"You'll have to tell me all about your mother's people one day."

"Soon they'll be gone. White men will wipe them out or imprison them on confining reservations that will slay their spirits and bodies."

"I'm sorry, Stone; that must be hard for you and your mother."

"It's the way of life, Ginny, for the stronger to survive. The whites have more people and better weapons for the battle to possess all."

"And more greed. Maybe things will change and peace will come."

He shook his head and lowered his cup. "Never."

"That's what you said not long ago about yourself changing. And look at me, a pampered southern belle making it through the wilderness alone because of all I learned from a tough scout. Change is possible. *Anything* is possible; we're proof of that."

Stone grinned and nodded. "You're right, woman."

They ate in silence for a few minutes, then Ginny asked, "What will we do next about settling matters here?"

"Let's rest tomorrow and leave for Denver on Thursday. I'll telegraph Father to see if a letter from Matt came for you. While we wait for his answer, we'll get married and set our mining plan into motion. A lot of big companies are in that area. We won't have trouble finding investors and someone to run it for us if we have to leave for home."

"Perfect. We'll be safe there, too, from Frank. Maybe Father will . . ."

"Many signs indicate Matt hasn't been here in a long time.

I'll look around tomorrow to see if anyone else has been nosing around the claim. Nobody can get to you up here while I'm gone for a few hours."

"I would scrub this filthy place while you're out, but we'll be leaving the next day so no need to waste energy better spent on other things."

"You're right again, woman. Yep, I lassoed me a smart filly."

"I'll get the dishes done and the beds freshened. Too bad they're nailed to the walls and can't be pulled close together; and they're so narrow."

"That wouldn't be smart anyway. If Matt returned, it would be hard to explain that to a protective father." He chuckled, then suggested, "I'll do the dishes and you get us ready to turn in. We'll have to shut the windows soon; storm's almost atop us. Not much oil in the lantern to keep it burning much longer. I guess we'll have to sit in the dark until we go to sleep." He chuckled again and winked at her.

Ginny adored seeing him so relaxed and happy. "Sit, indeed," she quipped. "I lie down to rest—and to do other things."

"Don't put me in a fire like a branding iron, woman," he warned, "or I'll be all over you with my mark."

Ginny looked at her arms and legs, then peeked down the blanket covering her naked body. "You mean you missed some places earlier? I was certain every inch of me had a tiny *S. C.* on it. Of course, I could be wrong. You'll have plenty of time to examine me and correct any oversights."

"With a temptation like that, I'd better do my chore fast or it'll have to wait until morning. Get to work, woman."

They shared laughter and exchanged smiles, then got busy.

Twenty minutes later, a storm broke overhead. Stone closed the shutters to keep out the slanting rain and latched them against the wind yanking them open. He bolted both doors, though he doubted anyone could get to the cabin, especially with the hidden pull rope curled on the landing and the ladder

440

out of reach. To make certain no one could lasso it and lower it, he had tied it securely in the raised position.

"We'd better put out the lantern or we won't have any oil left for tomorrow night. You ready to turn in?"

Ginny grinned. "Yes, sir. I removed the musty bedding and put ours down. Which one do you want, right or left?"

"To start with, the one you're in."

Ginny loosened and dropped the blanket around her to her feet. She sat down. "We'll try this one tonight and the other one tomorrow night."

Stone smiled as he removed his pants. He walked to her and placed the lantern on the floor. He doused it and joined his love for the next hour . . .

Ginny stirred and stretched like a contented feline. She realized what had awakened her: the smell of food and coffee. She sat up and her loving gaze found her future husband working at the stove. "Good morning," she greeted him.

Stone turned, smiled, and responded, "And a beautiful morning it is, but not as beautiful as you are. Breakfast is almost ready."

The shutters and doors were open. The storm had ceased and bright sunshine flooded the cabin. She heard birds singing and the waterfall and stream gushing from their recent refills. A fire crackled in the stove and food cooked upon it. "How did you do all this without awakening me?"

"You were exhausted from lack of sleep on the trail. You got plenty of exercise yesterday and a relaxing bath. A hot meal filled your belly, and I was quiet as a mouse stealing corn from a crib."

"You're marvelous, Stone Chapman. Most men would have pushed the woman out of bed to do these chores. Thank you."

"That would be silly and selfish when I can do them just as well. I'm used to tending myself and you needed your rest. But if you take a nap while I'm gone, you can stay up later tonight."

"Yes, sir," she responded amidst laughter, securing the blanket around her. She washed her face and hands in a basin that was bent in several places. She pushed saddening thoughts from her mind of her father doing the same thing. She brushed and braided her hair, then asked how she could help.

"Pour the coffee and take a seat, ma'am."

Stone served her biscuits, fried ham that was cured to perfection, and red-eye gravy. He took the chair across from her.

Ginny leaned forward, closed her eyes, and inhaled the delectable odors rising from her plate and cup. "Paradise, my love."

Stone ate while he observed her savoring every bite as if it were the best food she had ever put in her mouth. *Shu*, how he loved watching her, being with her, talking with her, and doing things to make her happy. She appreciated and warmed to the smallest kindness from him. He realized it wasn't the size of a deed or gift that made it special; it was the love and thoughtfulness behind it. He was impressed that for a woman who had possessed so much in her life, it didn't require wealth or pampering to satisfy Ginny. Without a doubt, they could be content anywhere together.

As she sipped the last of her coffee, she asked, "What are you thinking about?"

"Daydreams . . ." he murmured. "I never put any stock or hope in them until you came along, Ginny. You fill my head with plans for us. Do you know how much I love you and how proud I am to have you? You make every part of me feel alive."

She rose, rounded the table, and leaned over to hug and kiss him. Stone pulled her down into his lap. His fingers roamed her face with a light touch and snailish pace. She nestled her head against his bare chest and listened to the pounding of his heart.

Her eyes widened. "You shaved."

Stone laughed with amusement. "About time if I don't want to scratch this pretty face again."

She stroked his jawline and added, "Or cover this handsome one."

They kissed and caressed until passions blazed and had to be cooled with a heady bout on the bunk.

Both were bathed and dressed and saying good-bye for a while. Ginny raised the ladder after Stone reached the ground and secured it as he'd shown her. She watched him check the cliffside to make certain there was no way anyone could get to her during his absence.

"Stay out of sight, woman, until I call your name. Don't answer anybody else. There are dangerous and desperate men in this territory. They'll pull any kind of trick to get up there. Even if they say they're wounded or starving or whatever, don't come out or help. Understand?"

"Yes, sir. Be careful and come back soon."

"I'll do both," he mounted his sorrel, then, vanished into the trees.

Ginny closed the front door and looked around the cabin. The campfire had been put out to prevent smoke from alerting anyone to her presence. Yet if someone came close, her horse would expose her. If she didn't respond, he could be stolen. At least she could fire her rifle and frighten away a thief.

You heard him: he said don't show yourself or talk. Obey, woman. Woman, that was his motive, she decided; he didn't want anybody to know a female was here by herself. Men alone for months could become just as hungry and greedy for a woman as they could for gold. She remembered how Bart and his gang had lusted for her and what they'd planned for her. Stone was right: She must stay hidden no matter what she saw or heard.

It was late afternoon when he returned. She hugged him and kissed him the moment his boots touched the landing. "I'm so glad you're safe."

"If this is the welcome I'll get after a short separation, imagine what it would be like if I were gone for a week!"

Ginny poked him in the stomach. "I'd take a brush broom to your backside, Mr. Chapman, if you deserted me for that long."

He threw back his head and laughed. "I can feel it. Ouch. I'll confess now that it'll be necessary to leave you once a year when we return to the ranch. Ever hear of cattle drives? They take several months."

She had read about them in dime novels. "Yes, but I'll go with you."

He kissed the tip of her nose. "You can't bring babies and children along like on a wagontrain. It's too dusty and dangerous."

"That's a sneaky trick to get time away from your wife."

"Maybe Father will leave me in charge of the ranch until he's too old and feeble to make such a long and hard trip."

"Is that another sneaky way of enticing me to give in to letting you go?"

"Of course not," he vowed with a broad grin.

"We'll see if you tire of me and start joining the boys for diversions."

"Where do you get ideas like that, woman? I'm your man."

"In England, many men have mistresses and lovers. In America, too."

"Not Stone Chapman. One woman is enough for him: you, Ginny."

She blushed. "I suppose I sound silly and jealous. I just love you so much and winning you was so hard. I don't want to lose you for any reason."

He cupped her face and locked their gazes. "I promise you'll have me forever, woman. I love you. Besides, no other female would want a man like me. I'm too stubborn and tough. Look what a time you've had with me."

"Any woman would give a fortune to have you. And I'm glad you were too blind to realize that truth before we met. If you asked me to walk away from this strike to have you, I would."

444

Stone knew she was telling the truth and it touched him deeply. "I wouldn't ask you to give up what's rightly yours."

"And half yours," she reminded.

"The claim wasn't filed while Clay was alive and it's in your name. He's not here to dispute it. By law, it belongs solely to you if Matt's . . ."

"That doesn't matter to me. Clay was a partner and he willed his share to you. Now, either you and my father are partners or *we* are."

"Do you realize what some women would do with what you own? I don't think you understand how much it's worth."

"Frank said millions over time. Money is wonderful, Stone, especially when you don't have any. But wealth doesn't make one happy. My family had plenty of money and prestige, but it didn't keep us from losing everything. Love and friends are more important. I would give up this claim if I could bring my Johanna and your Clay back to life and have my father returned."

"I believe you, Ginny, so would I. We'll have everything we need at the ranch and we can work for anything else we desire."

She brightened. "We could help your mother's tribe. A fortune could buy a large cattle spread where they could live in peace and pride. It can buy clothes and food and a school. We don't have to turn them into whites, but we *can* help them adjust to the strange world engulfing them."

Love surged through him. "You're amazing, woman, always thinking of others, like you did with your friends on the wagon-train. It could work."

"Then we'll do it."

"What if your father's still alive? The strike would be his, not yours."

"But half will be yours, remember?"

"Not if Matt refuses to acknowledge Clay's partnership and will."

"If he wants to keep his daughter, he won't contest your claim."

"You would do that for me, for my people?"

"Yes, Stone. When I marry you, we become as one. I owe you even more loyalty than I would my father. The same is true for you: a husband, the Bible says, cleaves to his wife, not his parents. It's cruel, damaging, and wrong to side with parents against your mate. I hope you agree."

"Yes, my beautiful and precious love, I do with all my heart."

"Now, tell me what you found out there."

"No signs of anyone nosing around. Even if ore was found, nobody can stake a claim or start a mine; that's what's needed to remove the silver."

"Did you find the second map Father mentioned to me?"

"Nothing to even hint one had been there. Must have changed his mind about drawing out the locations of the veins. It would have been a dead giveaway if it had been found. He must have figured if the property fell into your hands, all you had to do was hire a skilled miner to find them. Smart action."

"Yes. Now what about putting a little food in our stomachs for energy?"

He grinned. "Just what I need about now: nourishment and you."

Thursday morning, they were ready to leave for Denver. The shutters and doors were closed and the cabin was straightened. Stone lifted their supplies, lingering to say, "It's only seventy miles, but it'll be slow traveling. It's high mountains and rugged passes all the way. We'll be heading into heavy prospecting and mining country, so we'll have to stay alert."

"No fooling around on the trail?" she hinted with a grin.

"That's right, woman, but we'll be there soon. Denver has good food and hotels with soft beds. We can do those things we missed in Vicksburg. We can—" Stone pressed his fingers to her lips before she could question his action. "Somebody's out there," he whispered, on full alert.

She heard Chuune neigh in warning, then a bone-chilling shout.

"Come on down, Mr. Chapman, Miss Marston. If you don't, we'll starve you out or burn you out if you force my hand. We can camp here for as long as it takes. There's no escape. Be smart and don't rile me further."

Ginny panicked. "My heavens, Stone, it's Frank Kinnon! This soon?"

CHAPTER 20

"We'll bluff our way past them, love. Once we're in the forest, we can lose them. Trust me and obey." Stone explained his daring plan in a rush.

"Come out, you two, or we'll start firing!" Kinnon shouted again.

Stone pulled Ginny into his arms and fused their lips as if saying a bittersweet farewell. Frightened for their lives, she clung to him and kissed him with feverish desire, stormed by a mixture of emotions. She wished there was time for more words and another union of bodies. She didn't want to break their holds on each other. She didn't want to challenge impending danger. She didn't want to lose him forever. When he murmured his love, hugged her tightly, and meshed their mouths again, she trembled and prayed it wouldn't be the last kiss they ever shared.

"You're provoking me to attack, Chapman!" Frank shouted.

She realized Stone hated to separate and endanger them as much as she hated for him to do it. The tender look in his dark eyes made her heart beat faster. "I love you so much. We have to survive this."

"We will, my love. Be strong and brave. We have to begin our ruse."

Stone opened the door and yelled, "Hold your fire, Kinnon, until you see what I've got to bargain with. Attack and your fiancée will be the first one to die." He shoved Ginny into sight with faked roughness, a pistol pointed at her head, and her hands appearing to be bound behind her back.

"Help me, Frank!" Ginny shrieked. "He kidnapped me Friday night and said he would kill me if you don't do as he says. Don't let him hurt me."

The banker ordered his men to be calm, but to stay alert.

"Better listen to her, Kinnon, or your future bride is dead."

"You can't fool me, Chapman. I know who she is."

"So do I: your woman, the one you plan to marry. If you love her, you'll save her hide by following my orders. I'll trade her to you for a confession that you killed Clay Cassidy and Matt Marston."

"Are you crazy? I know this land is in her name. She's Marston's daughter, isn't she? You two came to town to trick me. You disappeared together because you knew I was on to you. I received some interesting news from Denver on Saturday. Told us where to come to find you two."

"You're a fool, Kinnon. Virginia Marston Blake is in London. She doesn't know the strike is filed in her name, and I didn't plan to tell her either about that or her father's death until I had his killer behind bars. I trailed you to the telegraph office Friday, so I knew you wouldn't be fooled much longer. Course you got here sooner than I expected."

Stone was at the ready to return gunfire and to yank his love inside if the desperate ruse failed. His keen eyes took in the attackers' number, positions, and arms; and he mentally plotted how to respond to an assault. "I was about to leave you a note on the ladder with my offer, then hide her in the woods. I did some checking in town and learned you'd found yourself this pretty thing to wed. Everybody knows you've staked your claim on her and dared any man to come near her. You even talked with a jeweler about furnishing gold to make her a wedding band. That sounded like mighty serious intentions to me. I gambled you'd do about anything to save her skin and get her back. We both know you murdered Matt and Clay. Give me a confession and she'll live."

Ginny clutched a loaded pistol in her hidden grasp as she entreated, "Please, Frank, help me. He's crazy! He means it. He thinks you killed those two men. I told him he was wrong, but he doesn't believe me. Do something to convince him he's made a terrible mistake."

"You lied to me and duped me, woman!" Frank accused. "You're in on this scheme to entrap me! You're Matt's daughter, aren't you?"

Ginny feigned astonishment, terror, and distress. "No, I didn't, I'm not; I swear. I can prove I'm Anna Avery; telegraph my aunt in Savannah. I'm not that Miss Marston. I'd never heard of Mathew Marston or the silver until you mentioned them to me. I'm not part of your quarrel with this lawman. You can't let him harm me, and he'll do it. I'm so afraid. Please help me."

"I can't trust you, woman."

Ginny noticed doubt in the man's expression. She pressed the tiny advantage. "You said you loved me and wanted to marry me. Now you won't do anything to save my life. This silver strike you both mentioned means more to you than I do. To think I was going to say yes to your proposal. You're as wicked and mean as he is." She glared at Stone and challenged, "A lawman can't do something like this. Let me go, you beast!" She pretended to try to jerk free of the grasp of his arm across her chest.

Stone struggled with her a moment and visually tightened it. "Not so fast, woman. Be still and shut up or I'll give you a blow on that lovely face. Better make a deal fast, Kinnon, she's annoying me."

"There's nothing to work out, Chapman. You can't escape."

"If I die, so does she." As Stone stroked her flushed cheek with the weapon's cold barrel and she flinched, he said in a defiant and cocky tone, "Mighty young and pretty to have her face and body smashed on those rocks down there. If you want her back unmarred and alive, better do as I say."

Ginny screamed and thrashed as if in panic. "You can't do this! Frank, please, do something, anything. You have lots of armed men. Force him to release me." She began to cry, relieved she could summon the fake tears.

"Shut up, woman!" Stone ordered. "I can't think with you bawling like a calf who's lost its mother. You picked yourself a sorry man, so accept the truth. What's it to be, Kinnon, a shootout or a trade?"

"The only thing I'll trade is your life for hers."

Stone sent forth sarcastic chuckles. "That's not the deal I want. As long as I have her, you won't attack and risk her taking a stray bullet."

"You can't remain up there long, Chapman. Supplies run out. I bet you only have enough for a few weeks. I can send for more and outwait you."

"If I run out of food, Kinnon, I'll have to feast on something else. I'll have me a taste or two of your sweet thing." Stone nuzzled his head against hers. "Yep, if you don't cooperate, might as well enjoy myself before I die."

Ginny wriggled in his grasp and jerked her head away from his. "You animal! You wouldn't dare touch me! I'll kill you first!"

"That'll be a little hard, Miss Avery, all tied up and at my mercy. I'll probably give you more pleasure than a stuffy old banker could."

"Leave her be, Chapman, or you're a dead man! We'll compromise. I'll give you half of this strike in exchange for her. It's worth millions. Touch her and I'll have you sliced into little pieces and fed to buzzards."

Stone comprehended that he had infuriated his target and that Frank was no longer positive she was Virginia Marston. "You ain't in no position to make that compromise, Kinnon. Matt's daughter in England owns half of this land. Clay left me the other half before you did him in."

451

"He *what?* You knew all along where this claim was located?"

"That's how I knew where to come. I guessed you'd be along soon. You just messed up my schedule a mite. It's the confession or nothing."

"If you think I'm confessing to murders I didn't commit, you're crazy. I'm not going to prison for something I didn't do. Sure, I want this claim, but I didn't kill Matt and Clay to get it. You think I'm fool enough to shoot the only two men who knew where the silver is?"

"Then who did kill them?" Stone scoffed.

"If you've been doing any clever investigating, lawman, you'd know I've been trying to learn that same thing. At first, I guessed it was a claim-jumper. When time passed and nobody started a mine the size this one would be, I decided I was wrong. It must have been bandits, or maybe they shot each other in a dispute."

"You expect me to buy that load of empty barrels? Do better, Kinnon. Put something valuable and tempting in them. I already own half of this claim, so that isn't an acceptable trade. What I want is Clay's killer. If one of your men exceeded his orders, turn him over to me and we'll be settled."

"If you harm her, you can't get away, and the law won't look kindly on a Special Agent for kidnapping and abusing an innocent lady, and certainly not on murdering one. You wouldn't dare harm her. You're bluffing."

"Sorry, love," Stone whispered as the hand over her chest snaked to her hair, seized a handful, and yanked her head backward.

Ginny screamed in surprise and pain. "Stop it! You're hurting me! Frank, do something!" She wiggled her shoulders and head to break free as she pleaded with her captor to halt his torment and release her. She was relieved that during her shock she hadn't exposed the weapon behind her.

"You'll pay sorely for hurting her! I'll rip you apart with bare hands!"

Stone eased his grip on the light-brown mane as he chuckled

452

and taunted, "You'll have to capture me first, and that ain't likely to happen. I think we'll go inside, Kinnon, while you give your choice some thought. You have two hours to make a decision. Take any longer than that and I'll be overly tempted to sample your sweetie's treats." Stone backed her into the cabin and closed the door as Frank shouted another warning.

"You're dead, Chapman, if you touch her!"

Stone holstered his pistol and guided Ginny to the floor. "Let's stay down in case they start shooting. These thick walls are impenetrable but these shutters and front door aren't. We'll let him stew a while and get worried about what I'm doing to you in here. At least we've got him baffled about who you are. He's mighty hungry for you, my love, so he won't act rashly." He looked into her eyes. "Sorry about pulling your hair." His fingers massaged her tender scalp. "There was no way to warn you of what was coming. You were quick-witted to keep your pistol hidden. I'm proud of you." He closed his mouth over hers and kissed her deeply.

Ginny responded as if her survival depended on his nourishing nectar. When their lips parted, she gazed at him. "Will we get out of this alive? Do you believe he'll let us leave when you demand to use me as escape cover?"

"I think so, but I'm not sure. That silver has him crazed. He wants it and you, my love. If it comes to taking one or the other, I just don't know which he'll choose. He's already rich, but he's greedy. He should think he stands a better chance of getting you away from me if we're on the ground."

"I pray your cunning ruse will work. You think he believed my act?"

"I hope so. You did a good job out there of confusing him about your identity." He trailed his fingertips over her silky skin and smiled. "If I weren't retiring soon, we'd make a good pair of agents."

Ginny knew he was attempting to calm and distract her from their peril. She ruffled his sable hair and teased her fingers over his strong features. "If this is similar to your regular missions, no thanks. One day you'll have to tell me about your past adventures. From the ones I shared with you, you've certainly led a dangerous and exciting life." She had to be persuaded of imminent success. "What now?"

Stone shifted to lie on his back and warmed when she cuddled against him. "We wait for two hours and try to force his hand."

Ginny's fingers toyed with the buttons on his shirt, then her palm flattened on his chest. She felt the steady beating of his heart beneath her hand. Despite the perils outside, she wanted him this very moment. She wondered if it was crazy to be thinking of such wanton things in the face of death. She decided, it was normal to desire the one you loved, to want to end one's existence locked together as closely as possible. "Are you sure there's no other way out of here?"

"Not unless you're a goat or a ram or a puma. If we tried to scale those cliffs behind us, they'd see us and circle around before we reached the other side, which we couldn't, since they're too steep and slick." Yet Stone knew if it came to the last minute of hope, he'd try that—*anything*—to save her. He didn't want to die but he'd faced that possibility many times; he didn't fear it, not if it meant Ginny would survive. If he did have to sacrifice his life for hers, he prayed she was carrying their child so she'd have something of him to comfort her and to compel her to stay brave and strong.

"There's no place to hide in here or on the shelf," Ginny murmured. "Why would Father build in an area where he could be trapped?"

"It's a good place for defense against enemies and wild animals. Besides, love, this cabin is sitting atop part of the very thing Kinnon craves."

She stared at him. "You mean we're sitting on a silver vein?"

"Yep, a rich one, high grade, almost pure. Plenty of it, too."

"That's very clever of them. Who would think to prospect under a cabin? What if we sign over the land in exchange for our freedom?"

"He wouldn't let us go, not once he learned we are the real owners."

"Why did you tell him Clay left you his half?"

"To get his attention off you as full owner and to let him know not to go shooting at either of us too impulsively."

"But he could decide I'm V. A. Marston and that he can get the claim in his greedy hands by slaying you, partner, and holding me prisoner. If he killed both of us, what would happen to ownership of this land? Could he stake it?"

"Nope, and I'm sure he realizes that. Our families would inherit our shares, so he has to take them from us with legal signatures. No matter how rough it gets, love, never—I mean *never*, woman—admit to him you're Ginny Marston. You'll have to keep him duped until you can escape him."

She grasped the meaning behind his alarming words: if he was murdered. "We live or we die together, Stone Chapman. I'm not going to him."

He rolled half atop her, cupped her face, and imprisoned her gaze. "Listen to me, Ginny. It's crazy and wrong for both of us to die, if it goes that far." He shifted to caress her abdomen as he said, "You could be carrying our child so you might have his life to think of, too. You also have to think of what losing both of us will do to our families. I've ridden a hard and fast trail, woman, and stared death in the face lots of times and it never troubled me. Then I found you and changed. More than anything, I want to live and be with you. If it's too late to snatch more time from the Great Spirit's hands, though, let me die like a man, die knowing you and perhaps our baby are safe. Do whatever you must to survive for all of us. Swear to me you will. You also have to do this for my mother and father."

"I can't. I love you and need you. I can't live without you."

"You can and you must, woman. If you really love me, live for me."

She wanted to protest but knew he wouldn't argue the matter. When he pressed for her promise, she gave it with reluctance and in a strained voice. "Perhaps he'll relent to your demand," she sighed. "If you were alone, could you get out of this?"

"What do you mean? Surrender to him in exchange for my release?"

"No. If I pretended to overpower you and got down the ladder, could you escape without me to worry about?"

"No way, woman, would I turn you over to that devil while I'm alive."

"But if you're free and we're both alive, you can rescue me. This standoff won't last long, Stone. We need a backup plan. I won't lose you."

"If we have to, we'll stay up here until they get tired and careless. We have enough supplies for two weeks if we're careful. I won't do anything rash. I'll try picking them off one at a time with my rifle."

"After you shoot the first one, they'll take cover. He won't give up, Stone, no matter how long it takes to starve us out and win. I wouldn't be safe with him because I couldn't dupe him for long if he tried to touch me. And I'd never be able to escape because he's sure to mistrust me for a while and have me guarded. If he lets us leave with only your promise to release me down the trail, I'll be shocked. We must stay up here until our supplies are gone. Maybe help will come before they're depleted."

"That isn't likely to happen, Ginny love; there aren't enough men to defeat Kinnon and his gang. They'd kill anybody who tried to rescue us, or anyone who witnessed what's going on here. It's us against them."

"At least we'll have two more precious weeks together. Longer if we don't eat much to extend our supplies. We have water. They can't get up here to attack or disturb us. If Frank balks, why risk death sooner than necessary?"

"The longer we're alone where anything could be happening between us, the less Kinnon's gonna want you back and the madder he'll get. A crazed man is unpredictable. But you're right about not being safe with him. I can't allow him to capture you."

"Then we are trapped, and trying to outwait him won't make a difference. If Frank rejects your bluff, we're doomed, my love."

Stone knew he had to give her comfort and hope, so he made up a deception to possibly use. "I can leap off the cliff onto Chuune's back and gallop off. At least half of them will chase me. Kinnon will figure you're tied up and I'm going for help. I'll either ambush my pursuers or elude them in the forest, then sneak back to disable the others."

"That's a wild chance, Stone. You could be killed."

"Might be our only one if he's determined to outwait us, or decides you aren't Anna Avery, or if he's willing to sacrifice whoever you are for the strike." He smiled and caressed her cheek tenderly. "Don't worry, Ginny love, I've jumped off higher roofs and boulders than that cliff out there. Landed in my saddle every time." He chuckled. "Chuune knows that whistle. It'll work fine."

"They'll see you, Stone, and shoot at you at close range."

He kissed the tip of her nose. "Not if I do it after dark."

"There's a full moon. They'll see you and come running."

"It'll happen too fast for them to react. I'll take them by surprise. Once I'm on the ground, I can pick them off like I did Bart and his men."

"Bart and his gang weren't expecting your attack. Frank knows you're skilled and determined to get him. He'll be on alert for cunning tricks. There are too many of them and only one of you."

"I've fought more men alone than he has out there. But I need an advantage. I don't have one up here, and not while you're in danger. We may have no choice. Please trust me and do what I say when the time comes."

Ginny didn't want her love to risk his life on such a hazardous ploy, but she knew Stone Chapman had the prowess to carry out his daring idea. "I do trust you and I will obey. But

457

if they start firing at you, I'm going to give you cover with my rifle. I'm a good shot because I had a good teacher. I don't care if it tells him I'm on your side. I'll pin them down while you get yourself concealed." She was relieved when he grinned and didn't argue. To get away from the distressing subject a moment, she asked, "Do you think there's any truth to his claim he didn't do the shootings and burning?"

"Nope. I think you and Matt are right; he's the target I want."

Ginny smiled and hugged him. "Thank you for believing us."

They began sharing kisses and caresses until their deadline arrived.

A rider approached the anxious banker's location in the edge of the dense forest. He dismounted, glanced at the band of men, and asked in a polite tone, "Frank Kinnon, what are you doing on my claim?"

"So, you *are* alive, just as Chapman suspected. He wants to find you and kill you. Looks like I saved your life by getting to him first. I have the sorry bastard pinned down in your cabin. He'll surrender soon."

"Stone Chapman? He's up there?"

"That's right, Matt, with your daughter. Isn't that a surprise?"

"With my daughter? That's impossible. Ginny lives in England. Even if she came to America, she doesn't know where this claim is located."

"She didn't have to know; Chapman brought her here."

"Stone and Ginny don't know each other. I've never mentioned him to her. He's a lawman, Kinnon. This is crazy. What did he do to provoke you?"

"A few weeks ago, a beautiful woman came to town. She went to work for me and we got real close. I was going to marry her until I found out she was your daughter and the strike's filed in her name: V. A. Marston. She and Chapman took off for this cabin Friday when they realized I had caught on to their scheme. We trailed them and have them trapped up there."

"She's an imposter. They're lying. Ginny hasn't had time to get here since her last letter, which said nothing about a trip to Colorado. She's to stay there until I send her and Robert the money to join me. Something's amiss. What 'scheme' are you talking about? How does my land figure into it? And it *is* in my name: Virgil Aaron Mathew Marston. I was named after Mama's three brothers who were killed in the last war with England. That clerk must have left off the *M* in V. A. M. Marston. It's on my deed."

"Maybe Virginia talked her husband into letting her come search for you or persuaded him to bring her. Haven't seen him, though."

"Robert would never allow such foolishness and Ginny's an obedient wife. The woman up there isn't my daughter; she can't be. If she thinks she can impersonate Ginny to take over my claim, she's wrong. If Stone's in on her lies, he's wrong, too. I'll tell them so right now. But why are you—"

"What does your daughter look like?"

"Flaming red hair and blue eyes, about five feet three inches tall, slim. Why? What's going on? Nobody's stealing my claim, not even a past friend and his female cohort. Whatever scheme he has in mind, it won't work. I'm alive and this land is mine. But it isn't like Stone Chapman to work with another agent, and he's never shown any real interest in a woman. Are you sure she came here willingly? Stone's one to use any trick to accomplish his missions. He hates defeat. Maybe he planned to force her to pretend to be my Ginny to entice me out of the cabin if he found me here. I know he thinks I killed his best friend, but he's wrong and I'll tell him so. Why don't you explain what's happening here before I go talk to him?"

"Chapman said he kidnapped my fiancée to use her to force me to sign a confession that I killed you and Clay. When I found out about the claim registration on Saturday, I surmised she was your daughter and that her behavior with me was a trick to help him expose me. Obviously it isn't."

"Why would Stone think you were involved? That's crazy."

"That's what I told him, but he doesn't believe me. Where have you been? Why did you disappear after Clay's death? And why have you come back now?"

Mathew Marston related clever answers to those questions.

"Your timing is a little suspicious. First she comes, then Chapman, then you: all within a few weeks of each other. Mighty strange to me."

"Not if Stone's been tracking me and knew I was about to return. If he's got it in his head that I killed Clay, or you did, I'll have to convince him otherwise. Let me talk to him and get this matter cleared up."

"I can't let you join him, Marston. We have him outnumbered."

"Then keep my weapons down here."

"He probably has extra ones you can use to help him."

"Then I'll speak to him from the ground. I don't have to go up there. I need to set him straight on some matters. I don't want him terrifying an innocent young woman on such foolish notions about you or me."

"You think you can talk him into coming out and giving up the girl?"

"I'll try my best. I don't want her harmed and I want him to stop chasing me. I have work to do, a mine to get going."

"If he's dead, he can't trouble you again."

"I don't want him killed or injured. He was my friend for a long time. Clay lied to him about me. Things will be fine when he hears the truth. Besides, you can't gun down a lawman without terrible repercussions."

"He's stubborn and he might not believe you. We'll have to trick him to flush him from the cabin. I don't want Anna harmed."

"Who is Anna?"

"Anna Avery, my fiancée, the woman he's holding captive."

"I thought you just said she's Stone's cohort and impersonating Ginny."

"That was a trick to see if you and Stone are working together."

"We aren't. What I can't understand is why he's trying to force a confession out of you when he thinks I killed Clay. It could be he thinks we did it together and he's after both of us. We'll do it your way. But no shooting. I don't want his agent friends coming after me."

The two men walked into the clearing before the stream. "Chapman! Chapman, I have a new deal for you!" Frank shouted.

"What now? Time isn't up yet," Ginny fretted and held Stone tightly.

"Don't worry, love, I won't let him get you. Stay down while I see what he wants. He's in a quandary; he doesn't know if you're lying."

"Use me for cover again," she urged.

"No, you've taken enough risks already."

"Yes, Stone. Until he's sure I'm tricking him, he won't shoot me."

Stone cracked open the door and shouted, "What is it, Kinnon? I'm busy getting to know your woman. I can see why you wanted her so badly. I would, too, if she wasn't so enchanted by a varmint like you."

"You bastard! Accept my bargain or your friend's dead! He showed up in the nick of time to save your hide. We all thought he was dead, but here he is, my prisoner. Let Anna go and you can have your friend in exchange. We'll ride out and forget everything. All I want is her. That's my offer."

"Friend?" Ginny murmured. "What friend? Clay?" she hinted.

"I'll have to take a peek."

Ginny grabbed his arm and restrained him as she said, "No. He'll shoot you the minute you show yourself. It's a trick. He

461

probably has rifles aimed on the door. I would look, but I don't know Clayton Cassidy."

"You're lying, Kinnon," Stone yelled, "and I won't fall for any tricks! I guess you don't want your woman back. Too bad for her."

"It's me, Stone, Matt Marston. I just returned. What's going on here? What are you doing up there? Why did you take his fiancée hostage?"

An astonished Stone looked at a pale-faced Ginny.

"Father . . . That beast has my father prisoner! What shall we do?"

Stone was worried about the suspicious timing of Matt's return.

"We can't let Frank torture and kill him. We have to do something."

"It's been years and you've probably changed. Will he recognize you?"

Ginny nodded and replied in dismay, "Yes, I look like my mother. He'll be so stunned to see me here and in danger, I'll be exposed. My heavens, Stone, he has all of us captive now. We'll never escape. He'll torture us until we sign over this claim; then he'll kill us anyway."

"I won't let that happen, Ginny. If Matt can't get a look at you, he can't expose you. We'll still call our bluff and ride out of here. I'll hide you in a safe place and return to rescue your father. You have to do as I say."

"But—"

"No buts, Ginny. Didn't I teach you the importance of obedience during your training in Georgia? Remember how I tricked and captured Bart's gang? I'm experienced and skilled at this kind of ruse. But I can't let you be around to distract me and endanger all of us. You have to trust me."

"If you cover my head, Frank will be suspicious. You need a shield."

"I have an idea . . ." Stone prepared her for initiating it, then shouted, "Coming out, Kinnon, but she's first. Better relax those trigger fingers."

Ginny was guided through the door, a wide bandanna secured over her mouth and nose. Her hair was pulled back and stuffed beneath the floppy-brimmed hat. At that distance and with her face partially concealed, the couple hoped their disguising ruse would work. She ordered herself not to do anything to arouse suspicion as her gaze sought her father below. Matt was standing with Frank Kinnon; he was smiling and appeared to be relaxed.

Stone grinned. "Hope you don't mind that I gagged her, Kinnon. Got tired of her chatter and crying. Matt, my treacherous old friend, what brings you back after so long? I was finally convinced you were dead, but my first thought was accurate after all. Your timing is mighty strange. I was about to trade Kinnon's sweetheart for a confession he murdered you and Clay." The Special Agent's tone altered to one of coldness and accusation. "Where have you been, you sorry snake? What happened at that cabin last year? Were you and Kinnon working together all this time? Have you been hiding in the woods until he needed to use his ace? It won't work, old friend. You'd shoot me in the back the moment it was turned."

"You're wrong, Stone," Matt argued. "About me and about Kinnon. He wasn't the one who attacked me and Clay; it was a gang of claim-jumpers after Pete's diggings, not after us or ours. Why would I kill him? He saved our lives that time at Perry's Ford when we were captured by those redskins. He walked into their camp and used himself as bait to get us free. He was my friend, my partner. Remember what we said that day: nobody could take us when we had friends to help. I'm here to help you get out of this mess. Trust me like we trusted Clay that night."

Stone prayed he wasn't wrong about thinking Matt was sending him masked clues and that he was reading them right. If that was true, everything would be fine. There was no way to relate his hopeful assumption to Ginny, so he had to continue his act of suspicion. "You expect me to believe that mush and give up my advantage? If you didn't kill Clay or have him killed, why hide from me for a year?"

"I wanted to send for you, Stone, but I didn't know what you were thinking. I was scared you'd shoot before asking questions. Clay said he'd written to you to come after me if anything happened to him, and it did, but not by my hand or order. I don't know why he became so mixed up in the head. He had a few curious accidents and accused me of being behind them. I wasn't, Stone; you must believe that. I would never harm Clay. I ran because I was afraid people would think I'd murdered him; you can't blame me, not after the way he was talking and acting before he died."

"Why'd you come back now? Your timing is mighty coincidental."

Matt rubbed his thighs as he explained, "I was laid up for months in Virginia City with two broken legs and a busted shoulder; almost died twice. Two varmints attacked me and robbed me clean, pushed me off a cliffside and left me for dead. Some miners found me and carried me to town. I can thank Dr. Lynch for patching me up and saving my life. He was almost sure my walking days were over, but I was determined to prove him wrong. It took months to get on my feet again. Legs still hurt if I ride or stand too much. I had to work a long time to earn enough money to pay Andrew because I always take care of my bills. Doc Lynch let me stay at his home and he took good care of me, so I owed him. I also had to earn enough money to buy a horse, saddle, and supplies to get back to my claim. I didn't want to write Virginia for any money and worry her into coming here to check on me. This territory is too wild and dangerous for a refined and gentle lady. I'd told her in my last letter it would be a long time before I wrote again, so I knew not hearing from me wouldn't overly concern her. By now, I hoped the trouble and danger were over for me here. I decided that once I got the mine going, I'd have enough money and power to clear myself and catch the guilty parties."

"You're him or the man beside you is, or both of you are to blame."

"Stone, Stone, don't be fooled by Clay's crazy accusations. Kinnon is the one who assayed the ore sample for us. He asked about investing in the mine. I liked him and was impressed with him. Before we could talk, Clay and I were attacked and I had to get out of sight. I decided to ask Kinnon to become one of my partners. I'll need a good banker, one close by, a well-known and respected man who can protect me against unjust charges for murder. Please come down and let's get this nasty misunderstanding straightened out. You don't want to keep frightening that innocent young lady. You can't blame Kinnon for being riled by your treatment of her. After we settle things here, we'll catch Clay's killers."

Stone gave a derisive laugh. "You think Kinnon's gonna let me live if I turn over his girl? No way, Matt. He won't let you live, either, past partner or promise of future partner. He wants that silver too badly."

"Matt's right," Frank argued. "I was only riled because you stole my woman and tried to accuse me of murder. I'll be satisfied to be an investor."

Stone laughed once more. "Yeah? What about your earlier threats?"

"I told you, you riled me by kidnapping and abusing my Anna."

"When you got here, you didn't even believe she *was* your Anna. You thought she was Matt's daughter, my cohort. You were going to attack both of us. Trust you to let me ride away unharmed and alive? Do you think I'm loco? You'd sacrifice your own mother to get your hands on that silver."

"I know she isn't Virginia Marston Blake. Matt's daughter has red hair and blue eyes. It was only a bluff to get you to release her. I know the woman with you is Anna Avery. I love her and plan to marry her. I'm sorry, Anna dear, for scaring you while I was trying to persuade him to let you go."

Ginny struggled in Stone's hold to let the man know she'd

heard him. Yet she was confused by the lies everyone was telling.

"Listen to him, Stone," Matt urged, "he's speaking the truth. He didn't attack us. He didn't kill Clay. I didn't murder Clay. This can all be worked out if you come down and discuss it. You're a lawman, remember? We'll answer your questions. Surely you realize we wouldn't dare harm you and provoke other agents to come after us. We'll put up a reward for Clay's killers. We'll hire skilled detectives to locate and arrest them. I want myself cleared, and Kinnon wants to get out from under suspicion. Don't forget half of this strike is yours. You can't profit from Clay's love and generosity if you kill us. Let's all shake hands and work out a deal to get our mine going."

"Let me think about your offer for a minute," Stone replied.

"I'll forgive you and forget about this, Chapman, if you stop it before it goes any further. I can understand how your grief over the death of your best friend could cloud your wits. But isn't it better to become friends and partners rather than shooting each other? You know you don't want to harm Anna and get into trouble with the law you're supposed to uphold. You've investigated me long enough to know I'm a man of my word. I promise, no revenge."

"You'll be getting just what you want, Kinnon: the girl and the silver. I guess I will, too: the silver and Clay's killers when we catch them. Matt will, too: the silver and exoneration. I suppose it's a good bargain for all of us. No shots have been fired at each other, so maybe . . ."

"Do it, Stone, come down and talk," Matt coaxed. "Do it while I'm in a position to help you two. If you stay up there, everything could go wrong."

"How will we get down?" Ginny whispered through the bandanna. "They'll shoot you as soon as your shield is missing. He's making Father say those things, so don't believe them. At least force Frank to send his men out of firing range but keep them in sight to watch for tricks."

466

Stone realized that was an excellent idea. He gritted out without moving his lips, "Don't worry. Matt's on to him."

"What?" she asked, her eyes wide with confusion and fear.

"What's your answer, Chapman?" Frank shouted. "You're stalling."

"We're coming down. No tricks, Kinnon. I'm tying her wrist and mine to the same rope. If you shoot me and I fall, so will she. Keep your word and nobody will get hurt." While her body blocked the men's view, Stone pretended to cut her bonds free but was actually taking the pistol from her hands and sliding it into his belt. He pulled the knife from his boot, cut a strip of rope, and secured it around his wrist first and then hers. "Duck behind a tree when I give the word," he whispered.

"But—"

"Don't worry; it's all right."

"Come on down before I get nervous and impatient, Chapman. You've frightened and mishandled my fiancée long enough. Hurry."

"I want your men to holster their weapons and move to that clearing over yonder while we talk," Stone yelled. He motioned to one a distance away, right where he wanted the gang. He quelled his grin.

"Us lay down our arms while you keep yours?" Frank replied.

"If you're duping me, Kinnon, I'll have time to defend myself. You're armed, so hold your pistol on me if you like. Then if you're trying to pull something, we'll shoot each other. That's only fair since I'm outnumbered."

"How do I know you won't shoot me anyway?" Frank asked.

"Because your boys would get me before I could escape. I'm good, Kinnon, but not that good so I can take down ten men before they killed me. You get Anna as soon as I'm convinced we can make a deal."

Frank smiled. "Agreed, Chapman. Boys, put up those pistols and walk over there. I'll signal you if there's trouble."

After the gang obeyed and only Kinnon was close enough to

be a threat to their safety, Stone headed down the ladder first and Ginny followed a few rungs above him, their wrists linked by the rope. The aging ladder groaned and protested, but Stone knew it would hold up long enough to get down.

As his boots touched the ground, he helped Ginny make the final descent. With an uncocked Colt to her back and her walking before him, they approached the men. Ginny worried over her father recognizing her and wondered why he had said she had red hair and blue eyes, and why he hadn't reacted when Frank called her Virginia Blake. It was difficult to be near him and to look at him as if he were a stranger; he made it easier for her when he didn't take notice of her. Apparently his mind was elsewhere. She didn't have time to study his physical changes while listening to the crucial talk.

"Well, speak up and convince me," Stone coaxed.

"Untie and ungag Anna first. Let her come over here with me."

"Give up my cover?" Stone teased.

"You don't need her anymore, partner. I gave my word. I'll keep it. Besides, you're armed, so she's still in danger. I won't risk her life by trying anything reckless with you."

Stone eyed the man closely and knew he was lying. He smiled and said, "All right, partner. No need to create more ill feelings."

Stone freed a nervous Ginny. *No,* she wanted to shout. *Don't let Father see me! He'll expose us from shock!* She lowered her head as the bandanna was removed so the hat would conceal most of her face.

"Come here, Anna, you're safe now, my love."

Ginny hurried to stand beside Frank with her back to her father. The villain smiled at her and put an arm around her waist. To play her part, she returned the smile and cuddled against him for a moment, hating to do so. She noticed he kept a cocked pistol in his other hand, aimed at Stone's broad chest. She was glad when Frank removed his repulsive arm, but she kept her back to her father and dared not sneak a peek at him.

468

"No need for this now," Stone said. "You're blocking me as a target for your men. But I warn you, Kinnon, if you use that pistol, I can clear leather and fire on you before I hit the dirt."

Ginny panicked when Stone holstered his Colt and Frank didn't. To make matters worse, her father had no gun. "I have to sit down, Frank, my legs are wobbly and I feel weak all over. This has been a terrifying and exhausting experience for me. You should be punished, you insufferable beast," she said to Stone.

"Sorry, Miss Avery, but I thought it was a necessary action. It's obvious I was mistaken. I apologize."

"That doesn't excuse your vile behavior, does it, Frank? He should be horsewhipped for abducting me."

"Relax, my dear," the banker said, "this will be over soon."

Ginny sat on the ground behind Frank. With relief, she decided her father hadn't recognized her voice. She couldn't grasp why Stone hadn't used her distracting act to get the upper hand. With caution she worked the derringer free and eased it into her jacket pocket, fingers locked around it, with one on the trigger. Before leaving the cabin, Stone had ordered her not to do anything until he gave a signal: *Duck*.

The youngest man hinted, "I'm not hearing anything from you two."

"It's like I told you, Stone," Matt said, "we didn't have anything to do with Clay's murder. We'll ride back to town together and meet with a lawyer to get our plans into motion. We'll be partners in the Ginny M. Mine."

"I don't think so," Frank announced, brandishing his pistol.

"What do you mean?" Matt asked, taking a few steps backward.

"That will give me two partners too many."

"Hold on, Kinnon; you can't be in on the mine unless me and Stone let you join us. We each own half."

"If Chapman's dead, you own it all. If you sign it over to me, I own it."

"We aren't killing Stone! And I'd never sell my half."

Ginny couldn't believe Stone made no attempt to draw his weapons, as only Frank was armed and nearby. Why didn't he get the drop on the villain and use him as a hostage? He just stood there watching and listening.

"I have heirs, Kinnon," Stone said, "so my share wouldn't go to Matt."

"It will if you sign it over to him, and you will, Chapman."

"Why would I do that?"

Frank explained with a wicked grin, "To save his life. I'll kill him, slowly and painfully, if you don't cooperate."

"This was a trick," Stone accused. "You two are working together."

"No, Stone, you're terribly mistaken," Matt argued.

The lawman eyed his old friend. "Tell me, Matt, how hard will he beat you to convince me you aren't his partner in crime?"

Frank did the answering. "He isn't my partner, Chapman. This is the first time I've seen him since he disappeared last year. If I have to, I'll kill both of you and force the claim from your daughter. Now that I know who and where she is, I'll take it from her."

"You go near my daughter and I'll kill you!" Matt warned.

"How will you do that, Matt, when you'll both be bulging out some buzzards' bellies? I'm going to enjoy finishing you off, Chapman. You made a big mistake taking my woman."

Ginny felt she had to get close enough to take action soon. She stood and asked, "What are you doing, Frank? It sounds as if . . ."

"He's trying to double cross us," Stone finished for her with a scowl. "Let the snake talk, Miss Avery; I'd like to know the truth before I die."

Ginny couldn't understand why Stone didn't give the signal, as he had seen her pocket her small weapon. "Don't you call my Frank names."

"It's all right, my sweet," the banker said. "I have tough skin."

Matt looked at his daughter, "I'm sorry you have to witness such a crime, Miss Avery. Your fiancé had us both fooled. If I were you, I wouldn't marry a low-down skunk like him."

Before she could halt herself, Ginny half turned and looked at Matt. At her slip, her pulse raced and her heart pounded. Yet, he said nothing!

"Let me handle this, Anna. These are bad men and they deserve to die. Soon we'll be rich beyond your dreams. Matt promised me a share of the mine, then backed out on me. I have a right to it. I promise to make you forget this incident. You'll be happy with me."

Ginny knew her father must have recognized her as he was staring into her face, a reflection of her mother's, the woman he had loved beyond measure. Something, she decided, was going on that she didn't grasp. Her father and lover were trying to keep from exposing her. It seemed as if they were working together to try to extract an admission of guilt from Frank Kinnon. But if that were true, Stone would have told her; he had promised no more secrets between them. "I don't agree with what you're doing, Frank, but I'll trust you to do what's best for us," Ginny said. "I don't want you going to prison for a mistake you made last summer. I love you and want to marry you. Just don't . . . deal with them with me watching."

"Why don't you join my men over there until I'm finished here?"

Stone couldn't allow that to happen. "Why not stay and watch him kill us?" he sneered. "I should have known you'd be just like him. You two deserve each other. She's as greedy as you are, Kinnon. I'd be careful she doesn't learn from your example and double cross you one day."

"She's perfect for me: beautiful, refined, a real lady. She deserves to be dressed in silks and satins, to travel the world, to have people bow down to her like a queen. I can give her all of that."

To help keep her with them, Matt scoffed, "With our silver.

If you're going to kill us anyway, why should we turn over our claim?"

"To be given a quick and easy death and to keep me away from Ginny."

"You did kill Clay like Stone said, didn't you, Kinnon," Matt accused. "And you tried to murder me that same day last summer?"

"That action was a little premature. The boys thought you'd led them to the right claim. I told them to get rid of you two as soon as they had the location of it. I was furious when you two 'died' with your secret intact. Even when Chapman kept asking questions about you and searching for you, I believed you were dead. This time, you will be. The giveaway was in registering the claim after you were supposedly dead. Very clever to do it in Denver where I wouldn't think to look. The date told me you hadn't died in the attack. That's probably what tipped off Chapman you were still alive. If he hadn't come nosing around again, I wouldn't have found out the truth. It's amusing you two are old friends who didn't trust each other."

Suddenly Frank burst into raucous laughter. "What am I thinking? I don't need either of you to sign your shares over to me. The strike is registered in the name of V. A. Marston; she will be the sole owner when you two are dead. Cassidy's name isn't on file, so he can't leave Chapman half of something he never owned. I won't have any trouble getting the land from Matt's daughter. I'll bring her here from England, tell her I have her father prisoner, get her to sign everything over to me to save his life, then . . . You catch my drift. It will be as easy as taking a toy from a small child."

Ginny panicked when the ruthless villain moved his pistol closer to Stone's body. "No, Frank, it won't," she refuted, jabbing her derringer into his side. "Do anything I don't like and I'll shoot; the bullet will enter your kidney and you'll bleed to death, a slow and painful death. Ask Stone and he'll tell you what an expert I am with firearms. Let's not alert your men. Holster your pistol and keep smiling."

"What are you doing, Anna? I have it all figured out. We'll be rich."

"I'll be rich, Frank, but *you'll* be in prison for murder. Put up your pistol, now. Don't drop it, just holster it," she warned.

The banker gaped at her in disbelief. "You're going to kill them and pin it on me? Use my plan to get everything for yourself?"

"Of course not. You're going to prison for murdering Clayton Cassidy."

"Are you a Special Agent working with Chapman?"

"No. The gun, Frank, put it away. I don't want your boys to attack. You could get shot by accident. I want you to go on trial and be punished."

"Are you Clay's kin? Or his woman?"

"Neither. If you don't disarm yourself instantly, I'm going to shoot."

"Then why are you helping these men and doing this to me?"

When Frank shoved the weapon into its holster, Ginny relaxed. Now she could tell him the shocking news. "I'm saving them because one is my father and the other is the man I love and am going to marry." When Frank glared at her, she said, "Keep quiet or you'll be trapped in the middle of a shootout with your men."

"You're . . . you're Virginia Marston Blake, Matt's daughter? But you're already married. Matt and Stone said so, to Robert Blake."

"No, and I've never been married, but Stone and I are to wed soon."

Frank paled and gritted his teeth aloud. "You bitch, you tricked me."

"That's right, with my love's help. Stone, if you'll take over here, I can speak with my father; it's been years since we've seen each other. Then we'll have to figure out how to get away from Frank's men."

"That won't be necessary, Ginny, my friends have them in

473

custody. Stone and I were enjoying your arrest so much that we allowed you to finish it. Take over, Stone, it seems my daughter has a few things to tell me."

In that moment of distraction for everyone, Frank growled like a wild animal, grabbed Ginny's wrist, twisted the derringer around, and fired it as he shouted, "No man will have you if I can't!"

CHAPTER 21

A bullet whizzed through Ginny's jacket and past her side without wounding her. She didn't even notice the scream that escaped her lips. Stone leapt on the enraged man, wrestled him to the ground, and pinned him there. Soldiers rushed forward from concealment and took control of Frank.

The lanky officer in charge said, "You're under arrest for the murder of Clayton Cassidy and the attempted murders of these three people."

"It's a lie! A trick! I'm innocent!"

The officer told the wild-eyed and shaking banker, "We heard it all, Mr. Kinnon, so save your breath for the trial."

Soldiers bound and led a mumbling Frank away to join his captured men. The defeated villain kept glancing back at the woman who had betrayed him, the woman he loved and had tried to murder.

"Stone, you remember Captain Andrew Lynch, don't you?" Matt said.

The Special Agent and the man in blue shook hands and exchanged smiles. "I surely do remember who gave us orders every day for years after we reached Fort Wise. How have you been, Andy?"

"Fine, Stone, a little saddlesore. Didn't get to rest in Denver before Matt hauled me here to help him. Seems we arrived at the perfect time."

"You certainly did. Sneaked up and took them without firing a shot. You still have your cunning skills," Stone complimented, then glanced at his love. "Ginny, this was our commanding officer when we were released from that Union prison and sent west as Galvanized Yankees. He taught us plenty and kept most of the recruits alive with his skills and courage. Andy, Miss Virginia Anne Marston, Matt's daughter and soon to be my wife."

Andrew and Ginny shook hands and smiled. "A pleasure and an honor, sir. Thank you for the rescue."

"Congratulations," Andy responded. "Never thought to see the day when a woman, especially a fine lady, would snare this renegade. I hope you'll be very happy. Does this mean you'll be retiring?"

Stone wondered if Matt was shocked by this news and would be disappointed with his daughter's choice. "Yep. I've done my last mission. Gonna give ranching a try. My father has a large spread in Texas. He's been trying to lure me home for years to join him."

"And she changed your roaming ways?" Andy jested.

"Yep, she surely did. I'm lucky we met."

Matt wanted to know every detail about how that event had occurred, but he would probe it later in private. "You're a grown woman, Ginny, a *beautiful* woman like your mother. Lordy, how I've missed you, girl."

Ginny went to her father and hugged him. For a few minutes they remained in a loving and comforting embrace while they experienced the joy of being together again. Their hearts were full of love and their minds filled with relief. They leaned back to study each other with moist eyes.

"You look wonderful, Father," she said, though he had lost weight, half his brown hair had grayed, tiny wrinkles etched his tanned face, and he needed a shave from many days' growth of wiry whiskers. "I was so worried about you when you didn't write again."

Matt stroked her mussed hair, hugged her once more, and

disclosed that he had written two more times, in October and in late February.

"I didn't receive either letter, Father, nothing since last July. The first one must have gotten lost and the second one would have arrived after I left London that month. I came by wagon-train and stagecoach. I've been in Colorado City since the middle of last month. It's so good to see you."

Matt stroked his thick mustache as he grinned and said, "You and Stone took me by surprise being at my cabin and with your little ruse up there. We rode Kinnon's tail almost the whole way here but didn't expect to find you two present. We overheard your talk and carried on with our trap."

"How did you know to come here today?" Stone asked.

"I was in Denver finalizing plans with my investors when Kinnon telegraphed the land office for information. It alerted us to his renewed interest and to possible trouble. I told the others he was the man who had assayed the ore sample and gotten all sparkly-eyed; then it was no time hardly before Clay was murdered. I suggested I hurry back to see what was going on with him because I was certain he'd had Clay killed. I'd already seen Andy when he arrived, so I explained matters to him and talked him into helping me settle this problem. When Kinnon left town with his men Sunday morning, we followed him. I decided the best place to trick him into confessing was at the very site he craved and in what he thought was privacy. Andy agreed. Kinnon fell right into the pit we dug for him."

"Thank goodness you came, Father. We were running out of ideas fast. Stone was talking about sacrificing his life to save mine."

Matt smiled at her and placed one arm around her shoulder. He looked at his old friend. "Thank you, Stone, for protecting her."

Stone's dark eyes visually caressed Ginny's face, and his gaze softened and glowed. "She would have given her life for me, too. She's the bravest and smartest woman I've ever met. You should be very proud of her; I am."

"You won't believe all the things he's taught me, Father, or the adventures we've shared. We'll tell you about them later."

Matt felt the powerful and tender bond between them and noticed the way they looked at each other: they were undeniably in love. "When Kinnon called out for Miss Marston to show herself, my heart almost stopped. Then Stone came outside with you as his captive and saying you were Kinnon's fiancée. You were begging for help from the man I was trying to snare for murder. I was totally shocked and confused. I didn't know if Stone was truly using you to outwit Kinnon or if you two had somehow connected and were attempting to entrap him yourselves."

Matt looked at the man who loved his daughter. "You were mighty rough with her, Stone, but I was certain you wouldn't really harm her. You took a big gamble using her for cover to dupe Kinnon. I'm glad you gave him that deadline so we'd have time to outmaneuver him."

"I'm still dazed by seeing you, Father, and discovering this cunning hoax. Don't blame Stone for our dangerous deception; we were hopeful our ruse would succeed. I've been letting Frank court me for weeks—as Anna Avery—so we were almost positive we could fool him. At least confuse him long enough to escape. We didn't have any choice."

Matt sent her a smile of understanding and acceptance. "I gave Kinnon a false description of you because I had to keep him believing the woman with Stone was Anna Avery. I pretended to believe he was innocent of that trouble last summer. For a scary minute, Kinnon hinted that the three of us were working as a team. He suggested killing Stone, but I told him I'd clear your head. He's the one who came up with the idea how to entice you outside so I could talk you down."

"I almost fainted, Father, when I heard your voice and name. I lost all hope of us getting away from that evil man."

"I'm sorry I frightened you, Ginny, but I had to get you two to come down. I knew you wouldn't be in much peril, not with soldiers hidden in the woods and ready to defend us. I was sure

Kinnon would get cocky and chatty and unmask himself. It was a risk, I admit, but I had to take it to clear up this matter. He confessed, thank goodness. I was only worried Stone wouldn't understand and cooperate."

"You were cunning with your words, Matt. I caught your clues about Perry's Ford, Andrew Lynch, Virginia Blake, and the deceitful description of Ginny. At least, I *hoped* I was reading your hints right."

"I was praying you'd catch them and trust me, Stone. I was certain you'd remember you were the one who saved me and Clay from those Indians and how you'd done it with hidden soldiers. I hoped using the same name you had for her would tip you off that I'd been eavesdropping."

"You did a good job, Matt, Andy. So did your daughter. It was Ginny's idea to send Kinnon's men upstream out of firing range. I wanted to let her know not to worry, but I couldn't risk Kinnon seeing us whisper."

"I had no clue it was a trap, even though Stone mumbled for me not to worry," Ginny said. "I was afraid you'd be so shocked to see me, Father, that our deception would be exposed. When Stone holstered his pistol and made no attempt to attack Frank, I was petrified."

"I guessed that Matt had been lurking nearby from the start when he used the name Blake." Stone looked at the observant Captain Lynch. "I'm glad Kinnon exposed himself before witnesses, Andy; the law may have thought I had selfish reasons to let Matt go and to use Kinnon as a scapegoat. I'm sorry, Ginny, but I couldn't alert you to what was going on."

"I tried to keep my head down and my back to you, Father, to conceal my identity. I finally realized something was afoot when I turned before thinking and you didn't react to me. At first, I thought maybe it was to protect me, but then I sensed it was something more. I thought Stone wasn't attacking because he was afraid of endangering me. I shouldn't have let down my guard after Frank holstered his weapon. Stone will tell you I have a bad habit of being distracted at the worst times. He's tried to cure me of it, but I have occasional relapses." She wiggled her finger in the bullethole in her jacket. "We're lucky none of us got shot."

"We sure are, Miss Marston," Andy agreed. "It's good to see my past troops haven't lost their skills or forgotten their training. Stone, Matt, and Clay were three of my best soldiers. We shared good and bad times."

"That's the most you've said since we arrived, Andy," Matt teased. "He's still not much of a talker, is he, Stone? 'Course we haven't given him a chance to get many words in."

"Papa always said a boy couldn't hear and learn when he was running his mouth like a racing horse, so I guess it became habit to be quiet. Except when I'm giving orders, then I can out shout the loudest of men or women. Times like those, my men wished I'd stayed quiet."

Everyone laughed at Andy's amusing grin and tone.

"It's good to see you again, Andy," Stone repeated his earlier words.

"I've missed you riding with me, Stone," the officer responded. "I always knew I could depend on you more than anybody to obey without thinking about any peril involved. No matter what happened, I knew you would never take off and leave any of us in danger. Some of the boys I've had since you left would desert their own mothers to save their hides. My duty is up next month. I'll have to find me something like ranching to do. And find me a pretty lady to marry like you have. You're lucky."

"More than lucky," Stone amended. "She's perfect in every way."

Ginny felt a flush race over her body as he complimented her. Not only had he learned to express his feelings to her but he no longer concealed them from others as if they were something to be ashamed of. She read love, pride, and happiness in his expression. She had her father and future husband with her, and all were safe. She felt alive and aglow and bubbling with energy and anticipation. "You're biased, Mr. Chapman. Besides, I'm the fortunate one. If not for you, I'd be in terrible trouble by now. You're right about him, Captain Lynch, he's the bravest and most dependable man I've ever met."

"When did you two meet?" Andy asked. "How? Where?"

"On Sunday morning, March the twenty-fourth in Savannah, Georgia," Ginny answered with a radiant smile. The officer had earlier referred to Stone as being a Special Agent, so she didn't think it too revealing to explain that he was on a mission and was posing as the guide and leader for the wagontrain she was taking west. "Are you the one who taught him to be such a tough and demanding teacher?" she laughed and asked. "He worked us women every day as if he was drilling soldiers until we almost collapsed each night. But it was worth every pain and irritation. By the time he finished our lessons, we could do anything the men could do, and sometimes better. We owe our lives, safety, and success to him."

"That was a lucky coincidence, you two meeting like that so far away."

"More than luck, Captain Lynch, *destiny*. Stone's sister and I were best friends during our years at boarding school in London. We were heading for the Chapman ranch after we docked in Savannah. Since we met, our lives have been entwined. Haven't they, Stone?"

He chuckled and concurred. "The strange part is, I was working as Steve Carr and she was traveling as Anna Avery; we didn't know for a while we had two connections: her father and my sister."

Andy was intrigued. "Why under a false name, Miss Marston? Didn't Stone's sister burst his cover?"

Ginny related her connection with Johanna and her subsequent ruse. When she had finished, she was aware her father hadn't asked any questions or made comments. Stone hadn't stopped any disclosures yet, so she assumed all she'd said so far was all right with him; in fact, he was smiling and nodding agreement. But the next part of the story was too personal to tell someone who was a stranger to her, so she laughed and raced beyond it to all that had happened after and how she finally connected with Stone in Texas and wound up here in search of her father.

"That is quite an adventure, Miss Marston."

"Please call me Ginny."

"If you'll call me Andy."

No one spoke for a few minutes as Ginny pondered if she'd talked too freely before telling her father such important things.

"What happened here last summer, Matt?" Stone finally asked in reluctance. "Between you and Clay, I mean."

"I'll explain everything later, Stone. Andy wants to eat, then head for Denver. He has to be back by Monday night. He can make it by using Kenosha Pass and getting started soon. If you don't object, I'll offer Andy the job of heading up our mine and transport guards, if he's interested in being a boss, choosing his own men, and making a good salary."

"A great idea, Matt. What about it, Andy? Need time to think on it?"

"Nope, sounds good. I'll give it a try. Thanks."

The men shook hands on the deal. "I'll contact you from town later," Matt said. "We'll spend the night here and discuss a few family and business matters. It appears I have a lot to learn about my daughter and partner."

Ginny saw her father glance back and forth between her and Stone and knew one topic that intrigued him was the extent of their relationship. She wondered if it was obvious how far it had gone. Would he be angry with her and Stone? Would he, she fretted, object to their marriage?

By two o'clock and with about seven hours of daylight left, the soldiers and prisoners were on their way to Denver. The three left behind for the night were relieved to have privacy. Ginny, Stone, and Matt sat near a campfire and sipped coffee. It seemed as if each of them was waiting for another one to begin their long-anticipated conversation.

"Well, Matt," Stone prompted, "you ready to talk about Clay?"

"You realize now that I didn't kill him. I understand why you'd suspect me and I don't blame you. I know how bad it looked. After we made our strike here, we took a sample of the ore to Frank Kinnon. We'd met him a few times when we were in town and we both liked him, thought he was trustworthy. But I saw how Kinnon eyed the ore. He told us the truth about it being high grade and almost pure and what the mine would be worth. He asked to become an investor and we told him we'd think about it. I could see his palms itching and his eyes burning to have a stake in our diggings." Matt leaned forward on the rock seat as he recalled that time.

"I was worried because I knew we were being watched and followed. I tried to explain the dangers to Clay, tried to convince him we needed to file our claim in Denver and to be careful. He couldn't seem to grasp or accept what I was saying. It was as if he'd also become blinded by the idea of wealth. I'd never seen Clay act like that before. He changed after Kinnon told us the value of our strike. After being poor all his life and living hand-to-mouth as we did while prospecting, I guess I can understand how such news could affect him like that. I told him we needed investors we could trust, but he wanted to file in Colorado City, bring Kinnon in on the deal, and start mining immediately. I convinced him to pan and dig here and there for two weeks to get enough gold for supplies and to dupe anybody trailing us. But he got impatient and downright nasty with me on a few occasions."

Matt looked sad as he reflected on the deterioration of the friendship and Clay's baffling mental state. "When we'd meet up with other men, I'd almost have to gag him to keep him from boasting about being rich. He wanted to go into town, reveal the news so he could get credit or a loan, and use the money to live it up with women and gambling. He was almost uncontrollable, Stone. He had several curious accidents and started looking at me strangely. His girth strap came loose and his tent caught fire and some other things. He finally accused me of trying to get rid of him, said I had chosen this location and found the silver and wanted it all to myself. That wasn't true; I'd never felt that way. I didn't have to be greedy; there's enough silver here to make us rich a hundred times. I was worried, and I was unconvinced he wasn't behind those episodes to force my hand. He wanted to announce the strike to everyone that very week. I tried to tell him how dangerous and unwise that would be. Every time a big one is revealed, prospectors flood the area. I said we had to keep quiet until we worked out the details of our company. I suggested filing it in Ginny's name to protect us. Clay refused and got angry."

Matt sipped coffee to wet his throat. "We stopped by Pete's new shack until I could be sure we'd lost our shadows. While I was in the woods relieving myself, I heard gunshots. I stayed where I was for a while because I didn't have a weapon with me. When I sneaked back later, Clay and Pete were dead. I knew it wasn't a thief because our horses and belongings hadn't been taken. In a way, I'm to blame for Pete being killed. I shouldn't have led Kinnon's men to his location. They must have thought it was ours and that they were getting rid of us. I knew when the bodies were found, the culprit would realize he'd missed me. I burned the cabin to conceal my escape."

Matt waited for Stone to object to that action, but he didn't. Nor did Stone protest or refute what he was hearing about their deceased mutual friend. "I disguised myself, took Pete's mule and gear, left my belongings, and sneaked into town. I found out that Kinnon filed on the land Pete had been prospecting. I heard that me and Clay were declared dead, so I let everyone continue to think that. I hurried to Denver and registered this claim in the name of V. A. Marston, then sent Ginny a map and a warning. You received them?"

After she nodded, Matt explained, "I didn't file in Colorado City because some surveyors and officials were close friends of Kinnon's. I was afraid if I showed myself, Kinnon would sic his friends on me and frame me for Clay's murder because I had

484

a damn good motive for getting rid of him. I decided, if I stayed 'dead,' the killers might be caught by a smart lawman like you, Stone. I didn't want any shadow of doubt cast on me. There was no hurry to mine the silver; it wasn't going anywhere and the claim was safe. I knew Clay had written to you. I hoped you'd come and investigate and find evidence to clear me. I also realized that if I announced the strike, the killer might never be found because there'd be no reason to expose himself. I reasoned that when I got everything set, I would use myself to entrap the murderer as I did today."

Matt looked at Ginny, then at Stone. "Do you understand that I couldn't allow myself to be charged with murder and that I needed time to find somebody I could trust to help me unmask a rich and respected man like Frank Kinnon?" They both nodded. "I decided it was best to head for other parts—Montana, Arizona, Nevada, and California—to study silver mining and to locate investors, men who would have the power and wealth to protect me and help me. I'm not a coward, Stone, but I knew how bad it looked for me. I knew how much Kinnon wanted my claim. I realized there were corrupt officials who could be bribed to frame me. I had no proof against him, and who would take my word over his?"

"You can stop worrying now, Father; it's over and we're all safe."

"I think you did the right thing, Matt, and I believe you."

"Thanks, Stone; that means a lot to me."

"Are you all right, Father? Why didn't you send for me sooner?"

"What I said about my broken legs and busted shoulder was the truth. The only place I visited was Virginia City. That trouble kept me there for almost a year. I couldn't decide when to return and see how things stood here. I didn't know how or where to reach you, Stone. And I didn't want to worry Ginny with such bad news. I wrote her in October that everything was going fine, but that letter must have been lost or stolen during a stage robbery. I sent you money in February to sail for

America this month. I told you to take the train to St. Louis and telegraph me from there so I could come for you. I concluded my problems would be settled by the time you got here in August."

"You should have told me the truth, Father. You were hurt and in trouble and you needed me."

"I was afraid you'd come here and I'd be too injured to protect you. This is wild and dangerous territory, girl. Men can get crazy or desperate. Tell me, Stone, what did Clay write to you?"

The younger man related what had been in their friend's last message to him. "I'm sorry for doubting you, Matt, but it did look suspicious to me."

"I understand. In your place, I'd have thought and done the same thing. I didn't know Clay had given you his share of the claim, but that's not a problem. Now that I know I have a partner, I'll have to work out a new agreement with the investors I've chosen. They're awaiting news in Denver. I'll telegraph them from town in a few days. Dr. Wilton Clancy, the man who saved my life in Virginia City, is one of them. I hope you don't mind that I've put things into motion without conferring with you first."

"Of course not. Whatever you do is fine with me. I plan to be a rancher in Texas with my father. I've asked Ginny to marry me and she's agreed. We'll be living there, but you're welcome to visit anytime. Do you have any objections to me joining your family?"

From the time they had spent together today, Matt could read the changes in Stone Chapman, which were clearly results of meeting and loving his Ginny. He had always believed the young man had plenty of good traits and strong emotions inside him but was fearful to expose them. It was obvious Ginny had brought the best in Stone to the surface and the man had dealt with his bitter past, whatever that was, as he hadn't talked much about it to him. Matt saw her reach for her sweetheart's hand and squeeze it, then smile. "From the way my daughter looks at you and speaks about you, I doubt it would make a difference if I did. But don't worry, Stone, I think you'll make Ginny a perfect husband and me a fine son-in-law. I can see that you've resolved and discarded any troubles tormenting you. This is the most I've seen you smile since we met years ago. The hardness in your eyes is gone. The chip's off your shoulder. You were always your own worst enemy, Son, but I'm convinced you've made peace with yourself."

Stone's thick voice exposed his feelings. "Thank you, Matt. You won't be sorry you've entrusted her to me. I love her very much and she's been the best thing that's happened to me. I was riding a self-destructive trail until I met her, but she changed that for me."

Ginny smiled at Stone and her father but didn't speak because she wanted them to get closer and thought any words might disrupt the special moment.

Matt sighed and told them, "I hate to lose her so soon after our reunion. This news does come as a big surprise, but I'm happy with your decision. I think you two have a bright future ahead. Now, I want to hear more about you two meeting and getting here." His inquisitive gaze focused on his daughter. "What's this about traveling with a stranger who was dangerous and evil? You should know better, Virginia Marston! What did they teach you all those years in that fancy boarding school?"

"Charles Avery wasn't a totally evil man, Father. He was a tormented and misguided one. We liked each other, and I was never in any peril from him. Besides, he couldn't harm me with Stone and so many people around on the wagontrain. I don't know if you've heard about what's happening in the South since the war ended. I couldn't believe what I saw after docking there. The South is like a captive to the North; they rule it with an iron hand. Many people lost everything because of the war. Husbands, fathers, sons, and brothers were killed. Women, children, elderly parents, and orphans must fend for themselves. There was so much wanton destruction, more than was necessary to win a war. It left people without homes and ways to support themselves. Horrible things are taking place and Southerners are still suffering terribly."

She caught a breath before going on. "The North has many secret and dangerous organizations, like the Loyal League. They claim their purpose is to help ex-slaves learn to become citizens, but they also arm, train, and coax resentful ex-slaves to attack vulnerable whites. None of the instigators or villains are ever punished or halted. I can grasp why men like Mr. Avery would become bitter and desperate, but that does not justify what they're doing to equally innocent blacks and whites. Wicked men on both sides must be stopped, Father, by our government."

When Matt didn't interrupt, she continued. "Some men in the South have formed a secret group whose purpose, they claim, is to fight terrorism and injustices and to protect their lives, families, and homes. It's called the Invisible Empire, the Ku Klux Klan. They dress in flowing robes and hoods to conceal their identities from victims and witnesses. Mr. Avery was a member of the most notorious Den." She related the deceased man's personal motives about becoming involved with the nefarious group, the Red Magnolias.

"Mr. Avery's Den wanted money for arms and ammunition for their battles and to locate and murder officers whose orders almost destroyed the South, like Sherman who crushed Georgia. They got the payment for those plans through robberies in the North and in foreign countries, including England—mostly valuable, untraceable gems. Mr. Avery was chosen to deliver the payment to a man in Missouri who was going to fill their order. The Justice Department assigned Stone to unmask the carrier and stop them. It was a dangerous mission; several agents had been murdered while gathering information, so he pretended to be Steve Carr, our guide for the wagontrain. But things went wrong in Vicksburg." She explained all that had transpired until their arrival in Fort Smith.

"Lordy, girl, you could have been killed many times! You shouldn't have taken such risks, Ginny."

"Thanks to everything Stone taught me, Father, I did fine."

"I can see that you did. I'm proud of you, Ginny. Stone, too. But what happened to his sister? Why did you continue to pretend to be Anna?"

Ginny looked at her love as if to ask how much to reveal.

Stone smiled and replied, "Tell him the truth about me and her."

Ginny talked about the close friendship with the girl who had been like a sister to her and the relationship and repercussions of Ben's love for the Apache woman. "They had a son together: Stone." She saw Mathew Marston glance at the other man for a moment. She continued the story of the fragmented Chapman family, Stella's death, then her misadventures as Anna Avery and why she had used that identity on the wagontrain.

She decided not to confess her Johanna deception with the Chapmans and would ask Ben not to mention it to her father when they met. Nor would she tell him about the many misunderstandings and love affair with Stone since their meeting. "I hid out from the authorities while visiting Johanna's father. I had left Steve Carr a message telling him where to find me. I knew, if he felt the same way I did, he would come after me when his mission was completed."

Ginny knew that Stone would catch the deletions and deceits in her story, would understand, and agree with her motive. She continued to relate the events leading up to the present one that had halted their departure to Denver. She told him the rest of the plan they'd had in mind and finished with a point important for her father to know. "Nandile is still Mr. Chapman's housekeeper. They love each other and plan to marry soon. She's a kind, beautiful, and wonderful lady, Father. You'll like her. You'll like Mr. Chapman, too. He's a good man. In many ways, he reminds me of you."

"I'm a Chapman by birth and adoption," Stone affirmed, telling Matt his father had only recently acknowledged him. "I didn't know I was Bennett's son until I was ten and overheard him and Stella quarreling before she took off with my half sister.

We had problems over the years because I resented how I was born and because he refused to marry my mother, but we love each other and we've made peace," he explained. "Does it bother you that I was born a half-breed bastard? Do you think that makes me unworthy of Ginny?"

"No, Son, and it helps me understand what drove you. I'm sure you endured a hard life and plenty of troubles. During our Army years, I saw both sides of the Indian dispute, so I grasp your father's dilemma. I'm glad he's found the courage and strength to marry the woman he loves. Besides, I can't speak badly of him for marrying Stella. After I lost Ginny's mother, I married a woman I didn't love for all the wrong reasons. I wouldn't be surprised to learn she and Stella are a lot alike—greedy and selfish women who snare men while they're vulnerable. My second wife took up with a Yankee carpetbagger after I was reported dead. I have another daughter, six years old, who I've only seen once, near the time she was born before I was called away to war. Amanda doesn't know me; she probably thinks that Yankee who stole Green Oaks is her father. I went back after the war to let them know I was alive. Clay went with me. You were up in Dakota on a long mission. Remember? Everything was lost. She was married and expecting his child. I didn't show myself. We returned west and started prospecting."

Matt stared unseeingly into the forest. "I still haven't written to my wife and baby. I decided it was best for all of us if I remained dead to them. It didn't seem fair to Amanda to disrupt her life, and going back couldn't change anything for me with the plantation and my lost family. Soon, though, I'll have to contact Cleniece. I'll need a good lawyer to handle our divorce, or whatever one does under such mixed-up circumstances."

"You should do it quickly, Father, before you announce the strike. Once that greedy woman hears how rich you are, she'll swear she's still married to you and leave her Yankee mate. Even if she loves her new husband—though I doubt she can love anyone—her son will persuade her. You remember how he is. I told you how they abandoned me after you were reported dead. I was ordered never to come home again. Get the divorce first to prevent problems with her. If she doesn't want to tell Amanda about you, you can still send money for her support."

"From what Ginny's told me about them, Matt, she could be right," Stone added. "A strike this size will be news all over the country. She's bound to hear about it."

"I agree and I'll handle the matter immediately."

Ginny wanted to ask how Stone, Matt, and Clay had met and what things they'd done together. She decided those questions should wait until another time when all their torments and losses were less painful. She concluded they had been placed in the same Army unit after they had arrived in the West. His motives for becoming a Galvanized Yankee were probably the ones her love had mentioned that night on the wagontrain trail.

"We'll head for town in the morning and put our plans into motion," Matt said. "I'm sure you two want to leave for Texas next week. If you can hold off for a month until August third, I can finish here and make it to the ranch in time to give away my daughter to a fine man I'll be proud and pleased to call son."

"That sounds like a fine date for a wedding to me, Matt, and I'm sure my parents will agree to that date for theirs. What do you think, Ginny?"

"Waiting only one more day is too long, but I agree."

They talked, laughed, and planned until it was time to cook and eat.

"Before we begin chores, I'm taking a bath in that freezing water," Ginny said with a playful grin. "I'm not heading off on a four day ride in this sweaty condition. Why don't you two chat about old times until I return?"

Matt chuckled and said, "I see you located my chilly shower."

"I saw the soap and drying cloth and stuck my fingers under

the flow. If you can suffer through something like that, I can, too. I guarantee I won't take long. Ignore any screams you might hear."

The men chuckled, then watched her scale the rickety ladder.

"She's very special and precious," Stone murmured as if to himself.

"She certainly is, Son. She favors her mother. Lordy, I miss that woman. You never get over losing a love like that; nobody can replace it."

"As Ginny hinted, I was too stubborn for a while to recognize and accept what she could give to me. I had a hard time believing she could love and want a man like me or that I could give her what she deserves. I do love her with all my heart, Matt, and I'll take good care of her. I can't imagine losing her as you lost your wife."

"You two will be fine, Son," the older man said with confidence. "I'm glad you were here today so we could make peace. It's time for new beginnings. I look forward to having a happy and close family again."

"So do I, Matt, for the first time."

The two men looked at each other, smiled, and changed the subject.

Supper and chores were completed. Matt and Ginny lay on the two bunks. Stone rested on the floor in his sleeping roll. The cabin was quiet except for the sounds of breathing and dark except for the slanting light from a full moon. Through the windows came a cool breeze, the rushing sound of the stream below, and combined noises of nocturnal creatures and insects.

Ginny enjoyed the tranquility of the moment. It was July Fourth, Independence Day. They were free and safe and content. A bright future awaited all of them. Problems and perils were things of the past. Surely no more dark clouds would appear to hover over and threaten them.

CHAPTER 22

Ginny, Stone, and Matt arrived in Colorado City near dusk on Monday without any problems befalling them on the trail. They reached Hattie Sue Pearl's boardinghouse and astonished the woman with their story about Kinnon being arrested for the murder of Clayton Cassidy. Nothing was mentioned about the silver strike, but they told her they had all worked together to set a trap for Frank and it had succeeded. The woman was delighted to meet Stone and Matt and fascinated by the exciting tale.

Following the delicious meal she prepared for them, Stone and Ginny took a stroll while Matt and Hattie talked and laughed over a cup of coffee.

At the corral, Stone gazed at her and noticed how moonlight flowed like silky water over her. It brought out the golden tones in her hair and skin as if to announce her value. "You're so beautiful," he murmured. "I can't even glance at you without wanting you. How do you have such power over me?" He pulled her into his arms and kissed her. He quivered with desire. His lips roamed her face, sampling every inch of its satiny texture. His hand moved her long tresses aside so he could taste her neck and nuzzle her ear. His playful nips caused her to tremble and giggle. "Ginny love, you're driving me wild and I can't have you tonight. A month seems like forever."

Her fingertips trekked over his face as she replied, "It's

twenty-six days, my love, and it does sound like forever. How shall we manage until then? We haven't been alone for days. With our separate trips staring us in the face, we won't even see each other for two weeks. Why can't we travel together? I have a horse, too. Father could rent one instead of using mine and selling him before he leaves. Besides, we've been on the trail in private before. Why must I go by stage? I'm dying for you."

Stone's fingers stroked her curls and caressed her face. They moved over her lips, and both trembled with mounting desire. "I know, love, but we can't sneak off together from Matt. And there's no way me and Chuune could keep pace with a near runaway stage. We'll head south and swing over to Dallas and reach there about the same time you do. Then, woman, I won't ever let you out of my sight again. For now, we'll have to be satisfied with stolen kisses and hugs. At least we're together."

"For one more day, and for the rest of our lives after we reach Texas. Two weeks without even seeing you . . ." She rested her head against his chest and listened to the steady drumming of his heart. "It would be easier if I didn't know what it was like to have you completely. I never want to be separated from you again."

"You know I can't sell Chuune or leave him behind," he said, gazing fondly at the sorrel.

"I know. Who would have thought I'd become jealous of a horse?"

They shared laughter, then remained there for an hour, holding each other and sharing kisses and talking of their future.

Ginny's body felt light and her head dreamy. His lips were sweet and stirring each time they captured hers. His fingers drifted up and down her back, an action more stimulating than soothing. Her arms encircled his body as her mouth fastened with greed to his.

When their passions threatened to kindle too high, Stone suggested they go inside before they lost their heads. With reluctance, she agreed, and Ginny went to her rooms to cool her blazing body and to long for the day her lover would be at her side.

On Tuesday, the investors in the future Ginny M. Mine arrived to discuss business with Matt in private. Captain Andrew Lynch had met with them and reported the successful trap and Matt's impending trip to Colorado City. They were not upset about learning there was a previously unknown partner in the company and seemed pleased to meet Stone Chapman. They decided to keep the news concealed for as long as possible.

Afterward, Stone telegraphed his parents to relate their victory and their imminent departure for Texas tomorrow. With a stroke of luck, he met an ex-soldier who was heading home to Texas and hired him to deliver Chuune to the ranch. He knew the sorrel understood when he whispered in the stallion's ear to go with the other man.

It was at the evening meal that the two young lovers noticed how taken Matt and Hattie seemed to be with each other.

When they strolled again after supper, Stone and Ginny held hands as they kept looking at each other, smiling and halting every few minutes to kiss and embrace. Aware of the peril of becoming too aroused, they made certain to control their heady desire, also aware it wouldn't be for long.

Stone grinned and hinted, "I have a big surprise for you, woman."

"What? Tell me."

"I'm coming with you on the stage tomorrow." He explained the details.

Thursday morning, July eleventh, Ginny and Stone left by stage for the Chapman ranch. Matt remained behind to conclude his business in time to leave by the following Friday to join them. The journey through Kansas, Missouri, Arkansas, and Oklahoma Territory to reach Texas didn't seem as long and as monotonous to Ginny as the trip in the opposite direction had, since she and Stone were pressed together in a coach for fourteen days and too cognizant of their physical contact during every mile. Also, two of the stops were made in towns with cozy, romantic, and private hotels . . .

Ginny sighed dreamily in Stone's arms. "This is wonderful."

He lifted his head and gazed down at her with an expression of mischief and passion. His eyes slipped over her tousled hair. "That's what you said in Fort Smith," he teased as his tongue traced patterns down her throat and across her collarbone to her breasts.

Ginny's hazel eyes sparkled with the memory. "You took me for a ride down a new trail, my lusty guide, and gave me another adventure I hadn't known existed. Perhaps I should interrogate you, Mister Lawman, about where you acquired such knowledge and skills."

"Don't be jealous; I've never used them on a woman before. You're just so delicious and I was so hungry that I couldn't resist tasting you from head to foot." His tongue flicked over her breasts and made her quiver. His mouth captured one peak and tantalized it before doing the same to the other one. His hands caressed her warm and supple body, fondling each curve and mound and plane they encountered. He savored his potent effect on her. He shifted to lie half atop her so his lips could explore hers. He tried to go slowly, but it was hard to control his ache for her.

Ginny responded with unbridled need as he claimed her. No matter how many times they joined, she never had enough of him and it took only a touch or look to intoxicate her. He sent her senses spinning. Her hands roamed his muscled back and shoulders. They played in thick hair as shiny black as a raven's wing beneath the sun. Her flesh quivered and pleaded from his burning kisses and searing caresses. There wasn't an inch of her that wasn't sensitive to his ardent attack. Wild and wonderful emotions assailed her. She always wanted to travel love's journey in leisure with him but his actions evoked her to race faster and faster toward victory. As his fingers roved down her stomach to seek out the hidden place that heightened her desires, she moaned and writhed.

Ginny clung to his sinewy frame, surrendering her all to him in a near-wild frenzy. All doubts and worries left behind, she let him guide her where he willed. He was strong, yet his touch was as gentle and light as sunshine playing over flowers. She was like a slender limb being blown to and fro by a powerful wind that shook her to her core. "I love you so much, Stone Chapman."

"I love you, Ginny," he replied in an emotion-thickened voice.

Ginny rolled him to his back and almost leapt upon him. She dropped kisses as light as feathers on his face, then confined his head between her hands to ravish his mouth with hers. Her lips went from feature to feature as they traced each one. She wandered down his neck and over his hairless chest. She smiled and blazed as he moaned and squirmed as he'd made her do at their last stop. Her exploring hand trekked down his torso and claimed the prize it sought.

Stone trembled and moaned at the stimulating action as her lips and hands played over his body. He wanted to let her continue with her blissful torment, but he also wanted to seize her and make swift love to her. "Mercy, woman, you have me boiling like a pot of coffee on hot coals."

Ginny laughed and teased, "Like you perk me every time you take me? This is far more sporting when I participate." She returned to work on him.

Soon, Stone was compelled to flip her to her back so he could take them to the golden summit.

Together they gathered priceless nuggets of glittering splendor. They wanted nothing less than total love, commitment, and appeasement. Their mouths meshed to prevent joyful outcries of pleasure achieved. They kissed and caressed as their sated bodies cooled and relaxed.

Stone turned to his side and drew her into the curve of his body. She snuggled against him, using his arm as a pillow. Her fingers roamed the tawny terrain of his chest. Both were amazed and awed by how simple contact or a mere look could enflame their passions to such soaring heights. They loved and felt loved. They took and they gave and they shared. No doubts troubled their dreamy thoughts; no uncertainties teased their hearts. They were separate beings, yet one in spirit and goal.

"You're mine, Ginny Marston, forever."

"Yes, my love, forever."

Bennett and Nandile awaited the beaming couple when the coach halted in Dallas on the twenty-third. They let the cloud of dust go by and their loved ones get out before they rushed forward for hugs and kisses.

"Heavens be praised, Son, it's good to have you home again. Ginny, I'm happy you roped this boy and convinced him to settle down. You did what nobody else could, not even Stone himself: you gave me back my son."

"He was difficult to catch, sir, but I tired him out and lassoed him."

"I'm sure my son didn't put up too much of a battle," Nan jested as she stood there smiling with Stone's arm around her shoulder. Yes, she told herself, this was destiny; this was Stone Thrower's rightful Life-Circle. Just as Bennett Chapman, she added with immense joy, was hers.

Stone laughed. "How could I get away when I had all of you pushing us together? I never stood a chance of escaping three ropes."

Ginny relaxed when she saw that neither Ben nor Nandile held any resentment toward her for her deception. It warmed her heart to see him and his family so happy. It had been a long and tough battle to get close, but they had won it together. In the heavy southern drawl she had lost while living in London, she purred, "Stone Chapman, are you accusing me of using my wiles unfairly and charging them of assisting me?"

His other arm pulled Ginny close and embraced her as he

chuckled. He dropped a kiss on her forehead and smiled at her. "You needed all the help you could get, woman, and thank goodness you received it. I would have stormed my way into Colorado City if my parents hadn't talked sense into me. They beat down my pride and forced me to see the truth."

"Let's get your things and go home, Son. We have a lot to share."

On the way to the ranch, they chatted about the younger couple's adventures and about the double wedding to take place soon.

"What about round-up and the cattle drive, Father?"

"Don't worry, Son, I wouldn't pull us away from our new brides that soon. Buck can handle them this year."

Nandile grinned and told Ginny, "Our men have changed, my new daughter, when their work comes second to love. I'm too dazed to think."

"Now, Mother," Stone teased, "you're the one who ordered me to go fetch this girl and bring her back. I'm only being an obedient child."

"You're no longer Stone Thrower. You have become a strong and proud man, a smart one, too. The Great Spirit has smiled on both of us."

"Yes, *Shima*, He has." It was good to finally call her his mother.

The following day was spent in making plans for the double wedding in eleven days. Friends were written and ranch hands delivered the invitations to them, including those to Ginny's four friends from the wagontrain who had settled in or near Dallas. She was eager to see them again and looked forward to swapping tales. She explained her ruse about being Johanna Chapman as necessary to protect her from vengeful attacks by friends of Charles Avery or Bart. She lightly glossed over her real identity and motives.

While she was writing, Ginny penned a letter to Charles

Avery's sister Martha in Savannah to give the woman comfort and enlightenment about her brother's loss. She knew that Negroes and Indians must be accepted one day or terrible times were ahead for all three clashing cultures.

As they worked, she enjoyed Nandile's company and realized—as did Sunflower—they got along very well. She listened with enthusiam as the woman told her many things about her beloved fiancé. Ginny wanted to hear more about the Apache people, especially her tribe. She wanted to relate the plans she and Stone had mentioned at the cabin but thought it wise to wait until she was certain they could carry them out for her band. She learned that Nandile's parents were deceased and her tribe was far away. Yet, they contacted Nan occasionally to relate their whereabouts.

Meanwhile, Stone and Ben went to study the site where the ex-lawman wanted to build his new home. It was located atop a rolling hill with verdant trees scattered about and a stream-fed pond nearby. One could see for miles from up there and the view was lovely. It seemed as if the green landscape fused with the azure heaven in all directions. Birds sang and a variety of wildflowers abounded in colorful splendor.

"I wanted to check this with you, Father, and get your permission before I show it to Ginny. It's close to you and Mother but still private for us, about a mile from the house. If there's an emergency, a bell could be heard at that distance. And there's plenty of water and grass. It's perfect, isn't it?"

Ben eyed the setting, thought of their reason for being there, and sent Stone a broad smile. "Yes, Son, it is. We'll start immediately, as soon as you and Ginny decide what kind of a house you want."

"We haven't talked about that." Stone laughed. "Big enough for us and children but plenty of space so they don't get underfoot at the wrong time."

Ben chuckled. "Grandchildren . . . A new chance to do things right this time. I didn't with you and Johanna. I'm sorry, Stone, and I'll do anything to make it up to you."

"You have, Father, by acknowledging me and accepting Ginny. If we have any control over it, there'll be lots of tiny Chapmans running around soon."

"Your mother and I will be overjoyed. I love you, Son, and I'm glad you're home for good. Thank God you've forgiven me for hurting you."

"I love you, too, Father. I never stopped, hard as I tried. After I met Ginny and learned what love was about and saw how I resisted the truth, I came to understand what you'd endured because of those same things. I behaved just like I always accused you of doing. I was selfish, denying my feelings, avoiding responsibilities, punishing and hurting myself and others, and being too blind to see my mistakes. I was more like you than I realized. It's a good thing we both changed and softened or we'd have lost the most important people in our lives. It's over now. We have peace."

Later, Ginny and Stone visited Johanna's new grave. The body had been sent by train to Vicksburg, then brought the rest of the way by wagon, as had the possessions that had been left in Savannah with Martha Avery.

Ginny knelt and lay flowers where the headstone would be placed soon. "I wish she were alive and here to share everyone's happiness."

Stone bent and clasped her hand in his. "I'm sure the Great Spirit is allowing her to do so where she is. She'll always live in our memories, my love. She's a special part of each of us."

"You're right, Stone. Good-bye, Johanna, my sister."

"Good-bye, Johanna, *shi-k'is 'ikee naaghan*," he murmured, too.

As Ginny looked at the mound, she knew the Chapmans loved, believed, and accepted her. And they would have done so even if her father's last letter hadn't been forwarded from school to the ranch to prove she had intended to come here in the beginning not to impersonate Johanna but to visit as her friend. If she and Stone ever had a daughter, her name was ready.

By the time they reached the house, the ex-soldier was reining in with Chuune in tow. The two seemed happy to be reunited. As always, it amazed Ginny that the animal was so smart, seemed almost human.

Mathew Marston arrived on August first. He was beaming, and spoke often of Hattie Pearl. Two of the investors, mining experts, had been left in charge of ordering equipment and finalizing preparations. "So far no news has leaked out. I hope we can keep it that way until that lawyer I hired straightens out the legal entanglements of my marriage. I'm sure Cleniece will be shocked to learn she has two husbands. Hopefully she'll also want things unraveled fast. I'll decide later if I should keep out of Amanda's life. That depends on what Cleniece tells me."

"What's best for Amanda is what you must do, Father, hard as it might be."

Matthew nodded, then told Ginny that he had recovered the pouch of gold he had on deposit in Kinnon's safe, and that the authorities seized control of the bank until its fate is decided.

Saturday, friends gathered in the Chapman house to observe and to help celebrate the marriages of Stone to Ginny and Bennett to Nandile. They stood before the minister as he began the joint ceremony. "Friends and loved ones, we are gathered in this loving home today to join these two couples in the holy bonds of wedlock. Our Father in Heaven and all of you are here to witness this happy occasion. Who gives these fine women into marriage?"

Stone said, "I do," as he placed his mother's hand in his father's, then kissed her cheek. The three exchanged heartfelt smiles.

"I do," said Matt, then placed his daughter's hand in that of his old friend and partner. He kissed Ginny's cheek and shook Stone's other hand. He stepped back to stand with the other guests, beaming with pride. He wished his beloved wife—her mother—could be with them today. Or Hattie. Matt's heart thudded with excitement as thoughts of the woman far away came to his mind. He felt his loins stirring with desire. It had been a long time since he had experienced such potent feelings.

The clergyman said stirring words, read appropriate scriptures from the Bible, then asked them to exchange their vows. For a while, none of the four was aware of their guests. The older couple went first. Ben faced Nandile as their words were spoken from deep within their hearts. For them, this day was a glorious victory following a thirty-year conflict.

Stone gave Ginny's hand a gentle squeeze as he watched his parents speak their vows. He realized they were as much in love as they had been when they met so long ago, a powerful love that had given him birth, one that had never dulled over the years and never would. Nandile wore a pale-blue dress that enhanced her dark-brown eyes, tawny skin, and silky black hair that flowed down her back like a tranquil river. Stone thought she was beautiful and radiant. He glanced at Ginny, who was clad in a soft yellow dress that brought out the sunny highlights of tresses that tumbled down her back in waves and curls. His breath caught in his throat and tightened his chest. She was his forever.

Ginny noticed how handsome the two grooms looked in their dark suits, white shirts, and polished boots. She trembled in elation and anticipation of this special moment they were sharing and of what would follow soon.

"Do you, Stone Chapman, take this woman, Virginia Anne Marston, to be your lawfully wedded wife, to love, honor, and cherish her in sickness and in health, in good times and in bad, for richer and for poorer, until death do you part?"

Stone gazed into her hazel eyes as he replied, "I do, with all my heart and all I possess." *Shu,* she looked so exquisite! He quivered with desire. Thank the Good Spirit he had found her and won her.

"Do you, Virginia Anne Marston, take this man, Stone Chapman, to be your lawfully wedded husband, to love, honor, and cherish him in sickness and in health, in good times and in bad, for richer and for poorer, until death do you part?"

Ginny's softened gaze remained fused with Stone's engulfing brown one. "I do," she said, then added the same stirring words he had, "with all my heart and all I possess." No words or emotions had ever been truer, more meaningful, or sweeter to her.

"The ring," the minister prompted Stone, who seemed lost for a time in the wonder of his love. He lifted it from the young man's palm. "A circle without an end, as true love and marriage should be. Slide it on her finger, and repeat after me: With this ring, I thee wed until death."

Stone slipped the gold band in place, kept his fingers on it, looked into her eyes and said, "With this ring, I thee wed until death."

Ginny clasped his hands and repeated after the minister, "This ring I accept as a bond of our wedlock until death."

Ben and Nandile looked at each other and smiled. They were ecstatic by what they witnessed and shared with their son. They had come full circle like the ring on Sunflower's finger: the three were together again as a close family. The young woman joining their lives today was responsible for their joy. They would all be grateful to her forever.

The clergyman had each of the four place their left hand on his Bible, one atop the other, then covered them with his own. "By the authority granted to me by our Heavenly Father and the great state of Texas, I pronounce you man and wife," he said to Ben and Nan. He looked at Stone and Ginny. "I pronounce you man and wife. What God hath joined together, let no man put asunder. Gentlemen, you may kiss your brides."

At last, Ben and Nan thought, they didn't have to conceal their love. At last, they could hold hands, embrace, and reveal their feelings in public without fear of exposing their forbidden love. If anyone scorned them, so be it. They deserved this moment, each other, and the sunny future beckoning them onward. They hugged and kissed.

Ginny and Stone wished they could mesh their mouths longer, but this wasn't the time and place. Later, it would be . . . They listened as the preacher spoke his final words and said a prayer to end the bonding ceremony.

He turned the newlyweds to face their guests. Standing between them and with an arm around the shoulder of each, he said, "Friends, I present to you Mr. and Mrs. Bennett Chapman." He moved to do the same with Ginny and Stone. "I also present to you Mr. and Mrs. Stone Chapman. May both of your unions be long and happy. God bless you all. Amen."

The witnesses cheered and congratulated the glowing couples. A merry party ensued. Ginny chatted with her friends, who were excited and intrigued by her many adventures, though they weren't told about Stone's secret mission to foil the Red Magnolias. The incident was disguised as a jewel theft that he was assigned to solve and that he couldn't act until the gang was exposed. Ruby, Mary, Lucy, and Ellie whispered mirthful and romantic advice to the blushing bride.

Food and drink were abundant. Stone and Ginny danced, laughed, fed each other treats, and had fun with friends. Others watched and joined in on the activities. Even Lucy with her gimp ankle moved around the dance area with her husband. Everybody's fresh beginning seemed to be working out, evidenced by the cheerful smiles, elated moods, and genial behaviors of all.

Ginny danced with her father several times, and they chatted about Hattie again. She suspected there might be another wedding soon, in Colorado. She shared Matt's happiness at finding new love and believed Hattie to be a good choice. Yet she didn't press him about a decision and acknowledgment of his feelings. She wanted him to enjoy the heady mystery and stimulating chase of a special experience, his second one.

When she took a break to refresh herself, Ginny thought about the doll lying on her bed in the house. She wished her mother could share this day with her. Perhaps, as with Johanna, both women were observing her happiness.

Stone whirled Ginny around and around as his gaze refused to leave hers. The August heat almost went unnoticed, as their minds were filled with other thoughts of what awaited them later. They were eager to be alone to consummate their vows with fiery passion.

At seven, the guests realized it was time to head to their homes before dark overtook them on the road; and it was time to leave the two pairs of newlyweds in romantic seclusion. Congratulations and best wishes were offered a final time. Farewells were exchanged and plans for future gatherings were made. At last, all friends and ranch hands were gone.

Ben glanced at his son, winked, and flexed his sturdy body. "I don't know about you two, but Nan and I are exhausted from so much activity at our ages. We're turning in. Cleanup can wait until morning."

Stone sent his father a smile of gratitude. "So are we. Young or not, we're tired, too. Ready to call it a day, Mrs. Chapman?"

Ginny glowed as she replied, "Yes, my husband."

Ben looked at Nan. "You ready to call it a day, Mrs. Chapman?"

Nan grinned at Ginny and used her same words, "Yes, my husband."

Embraces and kisses were shared before they parted for the night.

Later in their bedroom, Ginny revealed, "Something was supposed to happen the day we arrived here, my love, but it didn't, and hasn't, yet."

A beguiling grin flickered over his face and settled in his dark eyes. "What was that, woman? What did I forget?"

Ginny unbuttoned his shirt, peeled it off his shoulders, and snuggled against his chest. Her fingertips made tiny circles

506

there. "You didn't remember not to get me pregnant before we stood before a minister."

Stone captured her face and lifted it to look into her compelling eyes. "Are you sure, Ginny love?"

She raised on her tiptoes to kiss him before admitting, "No, but my monthly visit has never been late before. If it's true, it happened at Hattie's or the cabin or on the way here, so I'm not far along, a month or less."

"That's wonderful news, my love. A baby . . . Our baby . . . If it's true, Ginny Chapman, we'll have our new home finished just in time for his birth—or hers. A father . . . Me, Stone Chapman, a father . . ."

Ginny saw how his dark eyes glowed with joy and pride. She knew he would make an excellent parent. He would shower their children with love, protection, and attention. He would make certain they were happy and would never suffer as he had. He was free of his bitter and imprisoning past, and he belonged to her. Never again would another midnight secret come between them.

Stone scooped her into his arms and carried her to the bed. He lay half across her body as a playful grin danced in his eyes. "Wait until Warren Turner hears about this news. He'll be as stunned as he was about my retirement. If Washington weren't so far, he'd have come to the wedding. This isn't another one of your daring deceptions to make me stay home to watch you grow with our child, is it, my clever filly?"

"No, Mr. Suspicious Chapman. If I ever tricked you again, you'd send that tough and demanding scout, Steve Carr, to abduct me and punish me. We have so much to be thankful for, Stone. We're going to be so happy."

"Yes, my love, we are. What shall we do now?" he teased.

"I bet with a little cunning and investigating, my ex-Special Agent, you could find a clue to lead you in the right direction to solve your current mission. With your skills and prowess, your job shouldn't be hard."

Stone nuzzled her face with his and murmured in a voice

made husky with love and desire, "This is one job I'll gladly scout for."

Virginia Marston Chapman grinned and enticed, "Then let's ride, my love, toward paradise together," and they did.

AUTHOR'S NOTE

If you would like a current Janelle Taylor newsletter, complete booklist, and bookmark, send a long self-addressed, stamped envelope to:

Janelle Taylor Newsletter
P.O. Box 211646
Martinez, Georgia 30917-1646

Until we meet again on the pages of my next novel, I wish you fun reading, great romance, and an exciting fantasy or two of your own.

CATCH A RISING STAR!

ROBIN ST. THOMAS

FORTUNE'S SISTERS   (2616, $3.95)
It was Pia's destiny to be a Hollywood star. She had complete
self-confidence, breathtaking beauty, and the help of her domi-
neering mother. But her younger sister Jeanne began to steal the
spotlight meant for Pia, diverting attention away from the ruth-
lessly ambitious star. When her mother Mathilde started to return
the advances of dashing director Wes Guest, Pia's jealousy surfaced. Her passion for Guest and desire to be the brightest star in
Hollywood pitted Pia against her own family — sister against sister, mother against daughter. Pia was determined to be the only
survivor in the arenas of love and fame. But neither Mathilde nor
Jeanne would surrender without a fight. . . .

LOVER'S MASQUERADE   (2886, $4.50)
New Orleans. A city of secrets, shrouded in mystery and magic.
A city where dreams become obsessions and memories once again
become reality. A city where even one trip, like a stop on Claudia
Gage's book promotion tour, can lead to a perilous fall. For New
Orleans is also the home of Armand Dantine, who knows the secrets that Claudia would conceal and the past she cannot remember. And he will stop at nothing to make her love him, and will
not let her go again . . .

SENSATION   (3228, $4.95)
They'd dreamed of stardom, and their dreams came true. Now
they had fame and the power that comes with it. In Hollywood,
in New York, and around the world, the names of Aurora Styles,
Rachel Allenby, and Pia Decameron commanded immediate attention — and lust and envy as well. They were stars, idols on ped-
estals. And there was always someone waiting in the wings to
bring them crashing down . . .

*Available wherever paperbacks are sold, or order direct from the
Publisher. Send cover price plus 50¢ per copy for mailing and
handling to Zebra Books, Dept. 4181, 475 Park Avenue South,
New York, N.Y. 10016. Residents of New York and Tennessee
must include sales tax. DO NOT SEND CASH. For a free Zebra/
Pinnacle catalog please write to the above address.*